MENACE

Stories by

MARK ANTHONY

CRYSTAL LACEY WINSLOW

ERICK S. GRAY

J.M. BENJAMIN

AL SAADIQ BANKS

with a foreword by

SHANNON HOLMES

This is a work of fiction. All of the characters, organizations, and events portrayed in this novel are either products of the author's imagination or are used fictitiously.

 For information, address Melodrama Publishing, P.O. Box 522, Bellport, NY 11713.

www.melodramapublishing.com

Library of Congress Control Number: 2008940451
ISBN-13: 978-1934157169
ISBN-10: 1934157163
First Edition: March 2009
10 9 8 7 6 5 4 3 2 1

Previously published as: *Menace II Society*

MEAN STREETS

BY

SHANNON HOLMES

FOREWORD

For many people, the street life is a fad, a trend, a phase, a culture craze that everyone from Hollywood, to sneaker companies, to music moguls, wishes to exploit for financial gain. In boardrooms across America, marketing executives are thinking up new ways to appear more street so they can tap into that urban market. The street is what's poppin' right now. Don't take my word for it; look at some of their advertisement campaigns. Now almost every major urban fashion line has a street team, plastering the hood with stickers and posters, hawking their product to the masses.

The street life is portrayed in the print media (novels and magazines) and in music videos as the "cool" or the "in" thing. Like a gangsta, thug, drug dealer, or ho is something little kids in the hood should aspire to be. Unfortunately for our people, many of our kids grow up in single-parent homes, unsupervised while watching these movies and videos; thus, they can't tell the difference between fact and fiction, fantasy and real life. They can't tell the difference between O-Dog (the character from *Menace II Society*) and Larenz Tate, the actor.

From the outside looking in, it looks like it's all gravy. That is, till the undercurrent of the street life comes knocking on your door. Suddenly, nobody wants to be down anymore. When the hood shooters roll through the block and do what they do, where ya ride-or-die niggas at, then?

Yo, fuck real talk; this is real life. My life and your life. Those who have played the street and those who are in so deep, they can't get out. Sad to say, for some of us it's the only life we know.

Street people are members of that not-so-secret society that lies just underneath that nine-to-five society. These are the people that are coming in the house when you're leaving for work. The kind of people who party while you sleep. The street is that uncontrollable element, that walk of life or way of life that most law-abiding people are either too naïve to see or (for whatever reasons) choose to ignore. But whatever the case, let me be the first to tell you it's there, alive and well, and it ain't nuttin' nice.

I, Shannon Holmes, am a direct product of the street life. I feel that I am more than qualified to write about it. I got time in, running the streets and playing the game. Matter of fact, I spent so much time in prison, I decided to take a time-out. I'm not glamorizing my lifestyle, but hey, it is what it is.

I could remember a time when I didn't want to be Shannon Holmes. When I had open court cases in three different states. When I was on the run from the authorities, facing time in the double digits. Nowadays I hear other authors say, some jokingly, "I want Shannon Holmes' money." Meaning, they want a six-figure book deal. And I ain't mad at them. But on the real, they don't want go through what I went through. Being on the front line, slinging crack in a hood that ain't even yours. Where every day your life was on the line, just 'cause of where you're from. They don't want to see the shootings, the murders, and the jailhouse stabbings. They see where I'm at now in the literary world, at the top of the food chain, but not where I've been in the streets.

By the grace of God, I'm still here today to tell you that the end does not justify the means. If I became a millionaire tomorrow, I still couldn't buy back all the time I've spent in prison. That's fuzzy math to me, because it don't add up.

The crazy thing about my life or my current status is this: some of the same things I write about are some of the same crimes I've committed. And now my knowledge of the streets are feeding my family. That's poetic justice.

I'm out! I leave you as I came: in peace.

Welcome to the streets!

ANIYAH'S LOVE

BY

ERICK S. GRAY

ONE

A blissful moan echoed throughout the three-bedroom apartment in Brooklyn that was fully furnished with the best money could buy. Sprawling plush carpeting from wall to wall enriched the room, while a luxurious, supple, and rich dark brown sofa set lit up the room with importance. A high-end entertainment center with a 60-inch plasma screen mounted high on the wall showed the latest rap video, which was muted. Ample speakers extended from corner to corner of the room, and a stylish golden ceiling fan hung above.

The moan continued, coming from the last bedroom down the hallway. The door was shut, but the passionate cries of a young woman roared out like a small being in need.

"Aaahhh . . . shit, fuck me!" Aniyah cried out with a profound craze.

Aniyah was butt naked on her swanky, soft bed. She clutched the bedpost tightly with her face downward in the pillow, knees sinking into the mattress. Her ass was in an arch, and her face twisted in exasperated thrill. Twilight seized her naked hips, spreading her legs wider and thrusting more of his nine inches into her.

The bedpost rattled as Twilight thrust into Aniyah fervently. He was sweating profusely and trying to brew up a good nut to let loose in her. Aniyah held tightly onto the bed railing, feeling that it would give her some kind of stability from the hard fuck she was enduring. She bit down on her bottom lip, grunting and moaning, with Twilight's erection feeling like it was rooted deep into her stomach.

The stereo system in the bedroom played Jay-Z's newest track to a low, with Aniyah's passionate cries drowning out the hardcore lyrics.

She screamed out, "Fuck me!" panting loudly like she just ran the marathon.

And Twilight did just that.

The bedroom was dimmed, illuminated only by the Azure display light coming from the stereo and the open bedroom window. The apartment stood four floors up in the notorious housing projects on Dumont Avenue.

Twilight reached under Aniyah and cupped her breast strongly and gripped around her leg with the other hand, pulling that ass back against him with might. Aniyah closed her eyes and enjoyed every minute of the dick being pushed into her.

Her cell phone suddenly began to ring on the nightstand near the bed. But she ignored it. She had no time to be interrupted from the beautiful ambiance Twilight was putting her in. Twilight hesitated with his sexual onslaught when he heard her phone ring, thinking that she might want to answer it. But Aniyah turned to face him with an irate expression as he slowed his rhythm into her.

"Don't stop, baby . . . keep fuckin' me," Aniyah cried out with desperation like an addict.

Twilight grabbed Aniyah by her hips and swiftly flipped her over onto her backside, with her sizable tits flopping around loosely. She chuckled like a schoolgirl, staring up at Twilight with pleading eyes that said, "Shit, nigga . . . put that mutha-fuckin' dick in me."

Twilight smiled. He leaned his six-three physique in near Aniyah's welcoming body with her legs spread widely waiting for his re-entry into her. Aniyah had the body of a video vixen, thick and curvy in the right places, with long, gleaming, bronze legs that could make the most thuggish man quiver when they wrapped around him. Her long, sensuous black hair was in disarray from Twilight pulling and grabbing and her twisting and turning abruptly, and her pants and moans were pleasing to hear from any man's ears. To be with Aniyah, some said it was the closest thing to being with Beyoncé.

Twilight neared the pussy with a hungry gaze displayed across his smooth brown face. He slowly sank between Aniyah's hospitable thighs and opened up her pussy with nine thick inches of dick for her to play with. Aniyah wrapped her legs around him and leisurely dragged her manicured nails down Twilight's sweaty back as he grinded like a machine between her warm, smooth thighs.

In an exasperated tone, Aniyah cried out, "Oh shit . . . I'm coming. Fuck me!"

She was sinking into the mattress with her hair spread wildly about behind her, nibbling on and panting into Twilight's ear like a winded athlete. Suddenly her cell phone rang loudly again, vibrating against the wooden nightstand. It was annoying Aniyah.

But once again, she ignored the call and told the nigga who was beating up her pussy not to stop. She was soon gonna get hers.

Five minutes later, her cell phone went off a third time and Aniyah cursed loudly at the menacing thing that wouldn't stop ringing and wouldn't allow her to get her groove on without any interruptions. She was ready to reach over, snatch up her phone, and toss it out the window or into another room. She didn't think once that maybe the phone call was urgent.

It was bad enough that she was fuckin' Twilight—who wasn't her man, but the enemy of her current boyfriend, Ozzie. Ozzie and Twilight had an ongoing beef between each other for years, and sometimes it became deadly between their crews. Before Ozzie, Twilight was in Aniyah's life since they were young and she loved him deeply, but on Aniyah's twenty-first birthday, Twilight caught a state charge and had to do five years upstate for drugs and attempted murder. So Ozzie soon appeared into Aniyah's life with his magnetic charm and thuggish demeanor, and Aniyah shortly fell in love. But she never forgot about Twilight being her first love.

Aniyah gave birth to Ozzie's son soon after and Twilight felt crushed and betrayed while he was rotting away in Attica. He knew about Ozzie, and they always had their differences on the block back in the day. But Twilight felt that their beef had become extremely personal, when Ozzie fucked his bitch and taunted his name on the streets. So Twilight put the green light on Ozzie and Aniyah at first, wanting them both dead—but he soon had a change of heart for Aniyah, and kept the green light just on Ozzie. Twilight was coming home within a year and wanted his boo back in his life without there being any problems—and Ozzie was a problem.

A week after Twilight authorized the green light, two goons shot up Ozzie's truck on Rockaway Avenue in Brooklyn with him and his three-year-old son inside. The gunmen let off a barrage of shots from their Uzi's and riddled Ozzie's burgundy Yukon with gunfire, making the truck look like Swiss cheese. After the gunfire and the smoke cleared, Ozzie survived, but was critically injured. His son, Damien, didn't. He was shot once in the head and once in his chest.

Aniyah was devastated with the news and almost went crazy. She went to visit Ozzie in the hospital almost daily to help him recover while suffering the loss of their first son. When Ozzie was back in service, he suspected who planned the hit against him and wanted Twilight dead. He kept the information a secret from Aniyah, knowing that one: she wouldn't believe him because of Twilight being her first love, and two: she was already in pain from so much that had gone on in her life. Ozzie wanted Aniyah to be at peace for once. And besides, he knew once Twilight was out his way, there would be nothing to worry about—he would have the streets on lock, along with Aniyah's heart. Ozzie set up an inside hit on Twilight one month after the attempt on his life. He green-lighted to have Twilight killed while still on the inside.

Six months before his release, Twilight was chillin' on the third tier in front of his cell when he was confronted by a group of young Bloods. He recognized a few faces, and knew by the way that they approached him—with scowls across their faces and in a threatening number—something was up. So he prepared himself for anything and stealthily removed the shank he had hidden on him into his hand and concealed it behind his back. Twilight stood tall, carried a deadpan gaze, and waited for the head nigga to step to him.

"What's good, nigga?" Twilight asked in a stern tone, with his eyes focused intensely on the one in charge.

The leader of the pack glared at Twilight, unfazed by his severe street reputation, and replied in a raspy tone, "You killin' babies now, nigga."

Twilight was upset that the nigga brought up his mistake in the hit he had ordered seven months ago. Twilight was crushed to hear about the boy being killed, even though it was Ozzie's child. Twilight followed a golden rule: you don't kill kids or the elderly, and if he had known that Ozzie would have his son with him when the killers approached, he would have called off the hit till another time. But the deed was done, and Twilight knew that he would have to live with that boy's death on his mind for the rest of his life.

But Twilight didn't like the fact that some nigga was reminding him about the mistake he had made, and that disturbed him even more. Twilight clenched the shank he had in his hand tightly and replied with, "Nigga, fuck you! Don't judge me, muthafucka, cuz I live wit' the death of that child on my mind every fuckin' day."

The man turned to glance at his homies and then steadied his look on Twilight with his face twisted up in anger. Twilight took a glance at the small, sharp blade the main Blood gang member carried in his grip and knew that death was coming for someone today. The main Blood didn't care about Ozzie's son being killed; he was being paid for a hit, and it didn't matter what Twilight said to them or how apologetic he sounded. The nigga had to die and be gutted like a fish. Ozzie's orders from the outside.

Twilight braced himself for the attack. He was outnumbered six to one and knew his chances of survival looked very bleak. But he knew that he wasn't going to die alone. The guards were nowhere around and Twilight knew that Ozzie had the influence to pay off the guards to look the other way and not be around on a certain tier at a certain time of day. It was a well thought out hit.

Suddenly, the main Blood lunged forward with the blade aimed at Twilight's stomach. Twilight hastily jumped back, directing the blade from his person. In one swift movement, Twilight swung the shank he carried from behind his back and quickly thrust it into the man's neck, striking an artery, causing blood to gush out like a fountain. The man's eyes went black, his body stiffened, and he dropped dead where he stood with the shank still stuck in his neck.

His goons took action immediately and they all came at Twilight with their own personal weapons for kill. Twilight tried to protect himself and fight them all off, but they continued to come at him like a swarm. In the blink of an eye, Twilight was getting hit in every direction—blades and sharp metal tools jabbed into him like his skin was paper thin. He jerked and stumbled, but still tried to stand tall and fight. He grabbed one of his attackers and held on to him strongly and was ready to break his fuckin' neck. He could feel his warm blood seeping through his skin, staining him everywhere. He felt his life draining from him slowly and could feel the pain from the stabbings ripping him open like a Christmas gift. He felt himself being pushed over the tier and rapidly grabbed some unlucky nigga to fall over with him. When they went over, Twilight braced himself for the fall. He landed on his side, cushioned next to the second victim, who landed first on his neck and helped Twilight embrace the fall better. Twilight had survived the fall, but he didn't know if he would survive his injuries.

He spent weeks in ICU, in critical condition. Word got out about the attempt on Twilight's life and his crew knew that there would be hell to pay and much blood to spill. Their number-one suspect was Ozzie, and a war was inevitable.

When Ozzie found out that Twilight had survived the attack, he cursed loudly and started tossing shit. And then out of the blue he chuckled and smiled, sayin' to himself, This persistent muthafucka, and that they both were two peas in the pod. They both had survived the vicious attacks they set for one another, and both were still alive. Ozzie had to give Twilight credit; he was a tough muthafucka, like himself. But he knew the flood gates had opened and now Twilight would be coming at him more intensely. Ozzie would be doing the same.

After the bloody incident with Twilight and the Bloods, the prison was on lockdown for two months. Twilight spent six weeks in ICU and then spent the remainder of his time recovering from his injuries in the prison hospital with one thing on his mind—revenge.

Twilight was soon released and was welcomed heavily by his old Brooklyn crew, who had sworn revenge on Ozzie for the attempt on Twilight's life. Twilight had revenge on his mind also, but his heart and mind were weighed down greatly with thoughts of Aniyah, and he was dying to see her again. But he knew Ozzie was trying to have her on lockdown from fear of their reunion. Twilight would be relentless in getting the woman he had loved since the fourth grade, and he knew that Ozzie would do anything to try and end his life and keep them apart.

The streets of Brooklyn would be painted red with blood, and while both crews would think that they were warring at each other over drugs, territory, and revenge—in both men's hearts, they knew the war reached deeper than that. It was truly over love.

Aniyah had Twilight pressed down on his back as she straddled him tightly and felt his erection pushing deep into her. Her body trembled slightly with every thrust Twilight forced into her, and the spicy passion that filled the room was soon to make Aniyah's body befall limp. She pressed down on his chest, digging her nails into his skin and fucking him like a stallion. She gyrated her hips back and forth rapidly, causing Twilight to grip her moist hips, throw his head back against the pillows, and his eyes roll to the back of his head because the pussy was feeling so good.

"Shit, baby . . . Shit!" he cried out.

"I missed you, baby," Aniyah replied faintly, feeling the dick slide in and out of her repeatedly.

Twilight reached up and cupped her tits and moaned, wanting the blissful feeling to last forever. He had killed for her and knew one day, she would be his again. He felt that their love for each other was just too strong for any nigga to come in between.

Aniyah loved every inch of Twilight, and had missed him so much. She remembered when he'd first come home a month ago. He was looking so buffed and cut up in his wife-beater and boot cut jeans, his stylish braids reaching shoulder length. She heard he had finally come home and she'd heard about his near death experience with the Bloods while locked down. Aniyah suspected that Ozzie had something to do with the unpleasant incident, but she didn't confront him about it. She was just happy that Twilight was still alive.

It took them almost two weeks to see each other. Aniyah was willing to chance Ozzie finding out and probably killing her, just for that lustful romance with her first love.

The two met discreetly at his place one late night while Ozzie was on the block getting his money right. Their first experience reunited was a memorable one. Twilight and Aniyah fucked each other's brains out for hours and then nestled comfortably in each other arms and reminisced about the good and bad times they'd had together.

Twilight wanted Aniyah to leave Ozzie, but Ozzie had been taking care of her since Twilight's incarceration years ago. He'd showered her with money and gifts and she once had his baby. And even though Aniyah's love for Twilight ran strong, she felt more secure with Ozzie in a way. Ozzie was making his money hand over fist, and had Aniyah living in a lavish three-bedroom apartment in the projects. She was aware of Twilight's situation also. He'd just come home into a little something and was working his way up on the streets, but he didn't have the influence that Ozzie had in Brooklyn. But knowing Twilight, he was nothing to play with and was a definite threat to Ozzie and his organization.

Aniyah felt herself about to come, as she swayed her hips back and forth like a machine against Twilight's thick physique, loving how the dick pushed deeply into her. She then heard her cell phone ring a fourth time. She sighed, wanting to curse someone out.

Twilight looked up at her and said, "Yo, just fuckin' answer the phone."

She sighed again and climbed off the dick and reached for her phone on the nightstand. She looked at the missed call and saw that it was Jazz, her best friend, calling so many times. Aniyah knew something had to be up, because Jazz knew Aniyah was spending some quality time with Twilight and definitely wouldn't be calling unless it was an emergency. Jazz knew everything about Aniyah and vice versa. They'd been friends since the second grade, and Jazz was the one true friend Aniyah trusted with her life.

Aniyah showed a concerned look that caught Twilight's attention. He looked back and asked, "What's wrong?"

"I don't know yet," Aniyah replied, fumbling with the phone.

The cell-phone went off again in Aniyah's hand and she quickly answered, knowing that it was Jazz calling.

"What's up?" Aniyah answered.

"Yo, why the fuck you ain't pickin' up? Where the fuck are you?" Jazz barked.

"You know I'm still with Twilight . . . why, what's wrong?" she asked.

"Yo, Ozzie got a crew of niggas on their way to the crib right now. He knows you got Twilight up in there wit' you. I tried to call you before, but, bitch, you wasn't pickin' up. You need to get that nigga outta there," Jazz spat in one breath.

"What? How the fuck he found out!"

"I don't know, but yo, they on their way now, and them niggas is strapped heavily. They want Twilight's ass bad," Jazz continued.

The sudden troubled look that Aniyah carried on her face now caught the attention of Twilight. He propped himself upright against the bedpost and focused his attention on Aniyah and whoever she was talking to over the phone.

Aniyah hung up the call and looked over at Twilight with a worried stare and exclaimed, "Yo, get dressed. Get dressed, now!"

"What the fuck is up?" Twilight questioned.

"Ozzie got niggas coming over here right now to come see you."

TWO

Twilight needed to hear no more. He rushed out of bed, collected his clothing, and reached for the guns he had laid out on the dresser—two .9mm Berettas, fully loaded with the hollow tips.

Aniyah donned her white Terry cloth robe and then heard a loud knocking at her front door.

"Shit!" she exclaimed.

Twilight knew it was death banging on the door for him. But he kept his composure, cocked back both his guns, and was ready to kill anything that came his way. Aniyah looked edgy. She stared at Twilight at a loss.

"Go answer the door. I'll just go out the fire escape. You'll be good. You know I love you," he said with a slight smile.

Aniyah nodded and went to the door cautiously. The loud knock at her apartment door bothered her. She knew it wouldn't be pleasant. She just hoped Twilight slid out the bedroom window onto the fire escape like he said he would.

The banging continued and she heard from the other side of the door, "Yo, open the fuckin' door before we break this shit down!"

"Hold the fuck up. I'm comin', damn it!" Aniyah shouted.

Aniyah moved closer to the door and glanced out the small peephole. She could see a small crowd of niggas gathered outside her apartment door. Her heart began to beat fierce and her mind filled with worries and concerns. She tried to remain calm and handle the situation without there being any bloodshed in her place.

"Yo, bitch, open the fuckin' door!" she heard one of Ozzie's goons yell out.

Aniyah slowly turned the locks to the left, and before she could open the door herself, she felt it being pushed back forcefully, almost knocking her down. Niggas began pouring into her apartment like they were police and shit. Their guns were visible and their demeanor was far from friendly.

Aniyah quickly counted about five of them. They glared at her and then demanded, "Where the fuck is that nigga?!"

"He ain't here," Aniyah spat back with anger.

"Fuck he is . . . don't lie to us, bitch. I'll fuck you up, not caring that you are Ozzie's bitch," one replied harshly.

Two rushed toward the main bedroom, while the other three goons went into the kitchen and the other two bedrooms. Aniyah's heart began to beat frantically with her eyes glued to the main bedroom praying that Twilight was far gone.

"Y'all need to get the fuck out my house!" she screamed.

But they paid her no mind and began searching through her place like animals. The door to the main bedroom was pushed open widely and the first goon walked in with his .380 in hand and was ready to kill a nigga—but unexpectedly he felt the cold tip of a .9mm quickly pushed against his temple and the last words he would hear were, "Fuck you and Ozzie."

Blam!

His brains and blood splattered all over the bedroom wall from the hollow tip round exploding in his head and the nigga dropped in a crumpled heap against Twilight's feet. The second goon was shocked to see his comrade fall before him, and before he could react, Twilight emerged from behind the bedroom door with his two nines trained at his victim. He quickly squeezed off multiple rounds into Ozzie's second goon, pushing him back down the hall in a hail of gunfire that opened up the nigga's chest like air conditioning—breezy. He fell back in a bloody mass, twisted with shots. And then the chaos ensued.

Aniyah screamed out fearfully and wanted to run to her man to protect him, as the remaining three goons came running out hastily, guns firing erratically into the main bedroom down the hallway. Their faces twisted up in rage from seeing two of theirs already shot up and dead.

"Shoot that muthafucka! Shoot that muthafucka dead!" one yelled, opening up his .45 like a soldier at war.

Bullets riddled the door and the walls of the narrow hallway, and shots echoed out from the apartment, which startled a few neighbors. Soon hysterical fingers would be dialing for the assistance from 911.

But the killers who were after Twilight weren't remotely worried about police arriving. They had their orders, and they were planning on executing them to the fullest. But by the time the remaining three rushed into the apartment, Twilight was descending down the fire escape fast and was ready to jump from the second floor. But the killers were persistent and numerous. Gunshots lit up the night—ricocheting off steel fire escapes and barely missing their target. Twilight quickly turned around and returned gunfire, forcing the goons to retreat back into the window and regroup. When they emerged, Twilight had jumped and was almost cleared from their danger.

"Fuck!" one of the goons shouted, watching Twilight flee from them, disappearing into the night.

Aniyah came storming into the bedroom, her face stained with tears, fearing that she was going to witness the worse. But there was no body, and that meant her lover had escaped harm. But she knew that her life was now in jeopardy and she would have to face Ozzie with the truth—that she was still deeply in love with Twilight.

THREE

Ozzie stood silently over his baby boy's grave in a Canarsie cemetery. He gazed at Damien's headstone with a deadpan look. A single tear shed from his eye, with his soul feeling empty, his heart crushed like ice. Ozzie missed his son dearly. The tone of the atmosphere in the cemetery seemed to correspond with his mood. The air felt still around him, the sky graying and gloomy above, the sun nowhere to be found, with a small breeze disturbing the leaves in the trees that towered over his son's peaceful grave.

Ozzie was dressed in baggy denim jeans, a crisp white button-down under a denim jacket, and was sporting a pair of fresh beige Timberlands. He stood five-eight, his short cut hair spinning in waves, and his darkish, even, smooth skin looking like bronze. He was short somewhat, but a bit stocky underneath the clothing, and his vicious reputation in the streets carried farther than any man's reach.

He continued to stand in front of his son's grave with his hand clasped in front of him and thought about the three short years he had spent with Damien. He wondered how he could have prevented the tragedy from happening.

It was nearing the anniversary of his son's death and he still didn't feel vindicated. The shooters responsible for his son's loss were tortured, butchered, and then killed, their dismembered bodies stuffed into black garbage bags and tossed into the East River. But the man who ordered the hit was still alive and still pursuing the one woman he loved. Ozzie vowed to have him destroyed by any means possible.

As Ozzie stood erect staring down at his son's grave, he heard foot steps approaching from behind. He slowly reached for the .380 that was tucked and concealed in front of him. Being very cautious Ozzie then turned, only to see his right-hand man, Dink, approaching with the same unsmiling stare that Ozzie carried.

Dink stood next to Ozzie, giving his respect. He was a bit taller than his partner in crime and sported growing dark dreads, but he wore almost the same urban wear as Ozzie—baggy denim jeans, a blue and white button-down under a dark jacket, and Timberlands. He had been by Ozzie's side for as long as they both could remember.

Ozzie stayed focused on his son's grave and stated in a grim pitch to Dink, "Muthafucka took my son from me, Dink. Tell me that nigga is toe-tagged and in a fuckin' box, rottin' in hell right now."

Dink bothered not to turn and face Ozzie, but looked at Damien's grave with a somber look of guilt and then said, "We missed our shot."

Ozzie stood there silent, looking somewhat unruffled by the news. He heard what Dink had said and was highly upset, but didn't show it.

"What happened?" he asked coolly.

"He took out Mason and Monroe, and then escaped out the window onto the fire escape," Dink said.

"So you mean to tell me that five of our guys couldn't take out that nigga on a fourth-floor apartment, with one way out, while he was fuckin' my bitch? The nigga ain't Superman, Dink!" Ozzie exclaimed.

"I know . . . I'm gonna handle it, Ozzie," Dink replied.

"I want him dead yesterday, you hear me Dink? The nigga ain't got nine lives . . . fuck his shit up."

"Definitely," Dink responded, hanging his head. "I will."

Ozzie stepped closer to his son's grave. Their discussion was put on hold for a minute for some more silent mourning. Dink stood behind Ozzie looking impassive, his deadly .40 cal holstered underneath his jacket and his cold, vicious eyes looking black like a moonless night.

"You know what it feels like to have your child die in your arms, Dink?" Ozzie asked rhetorically.

Dink remained silent.

"Being shot up in that truck and then watching my son fight for his life, it turned me into sumthin'," Ozzie continued. "I just don't give a fuck anymore. All I know is Twilight killed my son and is fuckin' my woman. He's a disrespectful muthafucka! And now here you come wit' the news that he killed two of my men in the apartment I'm paying for, after fuckin' my bitch. Dink, I want this nigga gone. I want Twilight to suffer. Find something he loves and destroy it."

Dink stepped closer to Ozzie. "What about Aniyah?"

Ozzie turned to face Dink with a baffled stare. "What about her?"

"Look, no disrespect, Ozzie, but it seems Twilight loves her a lot, and me personally, I feel that it's a slap in your face for her to be fuckin' the nigga in your crib after everything you done did for her."

"What you gettin' at, Dink?"

"Do I gotta make it any clearer to you, Ozzie? Kill two birds wit' one stone."

"That's the mother of my son, nigga!"

"Was," Dink corrected. "Look, I don't know what kind of hold Aniyah has over you, but don't slip, my nigga. The only way to get at Twilight is obviously through her. You already see he's willing to risk his life just to see her . . . that was her first love. You, my nigga, you don't have any bond to her anymore. Your son is dead. No disrespect, my dude. But to keep her around, that's only your ego talking. I've known you since grade school, Ozzie, and this ain't you, my nigga. Any other bitch, we woulda been put in the ground for less than what this bitch done put you through."

Ozzie was hearing Dink, but he wasn't listening. He loved Aniyah and he had his reason why she was still alive. But Dink was right about him somewhat—it was his ego talking. He couldn't bear the fact that there was a possibility that Aniyah loved Twilight more than him. And he felt killing her was just too easy. There were other ways for Aniyah to pay for her betrayal against him.

"Where's Aniyah now?" Ozzie asked.

"She's at the apartment," Dink answered.

"Bring that bitch to me. We need to talk."

Dink nodded and walked away. Ozzie remained by his son's grave for another half-hour. He cherished the alone time he had; it gave him time to think. He did ponder on what Dink had told him, but he wasn't ready to take it there yet with Aniyah. He was willing to give her another chance to redeem herself. Ozzie had a strong love for Aniyah that ached throughout him and it pained him to know that Twilight was a threat to their relationship and also a threat to him in the streets. Twilight had survived two brutal attacks and his name was becoming a legend in Brooklyn—so Ozzie had to stop that shit indefinitely.

"I love you, Damien," Ozzie tenderly proclaimed.

He wiped the tears from his eyes and walked away. Ozzie knew that by summer's end, one would fall victim to the sword and then there would be only one vying for Aniyah's love.

FOUR

"Yo, why the fuck do you keep risking your life for that bitch?" Twilight's older brother Knocky asked with an annoyed tone.

"She ain't a bitch, Knocky . . . watch your fuckin' mouth about her," Twilight warned.

"Whateva, nigga. All I'm sayin' . . . you know we at war wit' Ozzie. You know the nigga is gonna have soldiers on shorty constantly now, knowing that you're home. Nigga, be smart for once. Stop thinkin' wit' your fuckin' dick."

"Nigga, I can handle myself, you hear? I just needed to see her anyway," Twilight said.

"Nigga, you ready to die for some pussy that ain't even yours right now?"

"I'll die for anything that I love," Twilight returned.

"Then you're a bigger fool than I thought."

"She was taken from me once, Knocky. I ain't gonna let it happen again, and if Ozzie steps to a nigga like me again, I'm gonna smoke that nigga, and I ain't gonna miss a second fuckin' time," Twilight exclaimed with a murderous look.

Knocky walked up to his younger brother with a concerned gaze. They locked eyes and Knocky knew he couldn't control Twilight, but could only advise his wild baby brother, who was tearing up the streets. When he had heard the news about the shootout that his brother was in with Ozzie's goons, Knocky almost lost his mind and was ready to wild out on Twilight for being so stupid and then hunt down Ozzie himself. But he wanted to beat the shit out of his brother for being so reckless with his ways. He almost lost his little brother once while Twilight was locked down, and Knocky didn't want any more tragic losses in his family.

The brothers lost their father to mob violence when Twilight was only three years old. He was shot twice in the head in a drug deal gone bad in Harlem. They lost their oldest cousin to a drive-by shooting in Bed-Stuy five years ago. They lost their mother to crack/cocaine when the brothers were in their late teens. Police found her naked body, beaten and raped in a Bronx alley on one of the coldest days of the year, sprawled out in the cold snow. Their uncle Mitch was on death row for a triple homicide he committed seven years earlier. Dealing with the drugs, the streets, and the war with Ozzie, Twilight and Knocky had lost a lot of good homies to gun violence over the years, and gradually, it had begun to take a toll on Knocky. Knocky was reaching forty in three years, and he had seen enough shit in his lifetime to make him rethink the violent life he and his brother had lived on the streets.

Twilight was the only family Knocky had left. He wanted Twilight to chill and keep a low profile, but Twilight was a firecracker with a short fuse. Between pussy and his temper, the two things Knocky feared most were his brother catching his third strike and spending life in prison, or being carried by six to his homegoing.

"Listen, Twilight, you need to really chill from Aniyah, fall back on that . . . at least until this war with Ozzie is done with. Think for a minute, nigga. Wit' Ozzie finally gone, that's gon' leave the streets wide open, and leave his bitch the same. You just a fool to keep chasin' sumthin' that's poison, nigga," Knocky advised.

"Fuck you talkin' 'bout, Knocky? I've known Aniyah since the fourth grade," he spat.

"People change, my nigga. She ain't the same woman she used to be back in the days. You was locked up for a long time, and a lot done happened over the years," Knocky tried to explain.

Twilight remained hardheaded though. "Nigga, you do your thang, and I'm gonna keep doin' mines. You hear? Ozzie and me, we gonna finish this shit . . . and Aniyah, I know she still loves a nigga. I see it in her eyes."

"Man, Twilight, you gonna jump off bad chasin' that bitch," Knocky warned.

"Nigga, I said watch your fuckin' mouth. Big brother or not, I'll lay you the fuck out," Twilight shouted.

Knocky just stood still and gave off a smirk, like Whatever, nigga. He shook his head at his brother's ignorance and foolishness. He wanted to grab Twilight by the collar and just beat some sense into him.

"Yo, we done here, Knocky. I'm out, nigga. I got things to take care of." Twilight walked from the room.

Knocky stood still, gazing at his brother's back as he left their conversation at a cliffhanger. He wanted to tell his brother the truth, but didn't know how he would react. There were things Twilight needed to know before he jumped into the fire chasing some pussy, but Knocky didn't know how to tell him. Knocky was one of the hardest gangsters in Brooklyn, but when it came to telling his younger brother that he was also fucking Aniyah and she might be a month pregnant with his baby—he would bitch up and keep the news mute from Twilight.

But now seeing that Twilight was risking his life to see Aniyah, Knocky knew that the truth had to be told soon—or else his baby brother would die for a bitch who wouldn't even be worth it.

"Why didn't you tell the nigga, Knocky?" Jay-T asked, as he emerged from a back room. He'd pretty much heard the whole conversation.

Knocky turned to look at his right-hand man. "I will, Jay."

"You frontin' on the nigga, Knocky. He's your little brother, so you need to tell that nigga that his boo is a straight scalawag that you knocked up on a humble. Sooner or later, he's gonna hear about it in the streets, and then he's gonna hate you more," Jay-T stated.

Knocky remained quiet, thinking about the situation he'd put himself in. At first, Aniyah came to him for comfort and advice, when Ozzie would be on his disrespect shit from fuckin' other bitches, including some of her close friends, to putting his hands on her when he became angry. So Aniyah, knowing Knocky through his brother from back in the days, would go running to Knocky with her problems. They would talk, and Knocky would try and advise Aniyah. She would listen and take in his advice sometimes, even though she loved Twilight and missed him and was in a relationship with Ozzie, who was supporting her with the finer things that money could buy. With Knocky, he was like a father figure to her and she cherished and loved every moment that they spent together. It came to the point that Aniyah would be looking forward to talking to Knocky and spending some time with him, even if it was on the down low.

Then the night came when the two became really close. She had snuck off to his place in Queens—a cozy, two-bedroom, well furnished apartment in Rochdale that could make any woman feel at home. The two had wine and good conversation. It was clear that they were both attracted to each other. But Knocky tried to play the reserved position, knowing it was his younger brother's girl or ex-girl who was getting his dick hard. However, with Aniyah clad adequately in tight-fitting jeans that highlighted her thick hips and a pink tube top that was screaming to be pulled down to show her tits, it was hard for Knocky to fight off the temptation.

She began nestling close to him and saying things in his ear about how good he looked, and how she loved his swag. Then she went on to curse ever getting with Ozzie and say she needed a man like Knocky in her life. Then came the nibbling at his ear and the touching of his thigh. Curiosity and temptation got the best of Knocky and he soon returned the favor. With one passionate moment leading to the next, Aniyah's jeans came sliding off, followed by her panties. Her tube top was pulled down and her thick dark nipples ended up in Knocky's mouth.

Knocky slid into Aniyah's glorious inside without thinking about any protection and enjoyed the blissful moment they shared on the cushy living room couch. He came, she moaned, they panted and sweated simultaneously and then afterwards, each promised the other that it was a mistake, and it would be their first and last night together intimately. But a week later, they found themselves at round two—Knocky fucked Aniyah's brains out, doggy-style in the back of his pimped-out Denali—her legs sprawled out across his backseat.

The affair went on for months. Aniyah couldn't get enough of the dick and Knocky couldn't get enough of the pussy. In fact, he was seeing why his younger brother was tripping over the pussy—she had that gushy, wet, tight, creamy coochie that could put a nigga in convulsions after a good nut. It was doing wonders for Knocky, having him thinking some crazy shit like, I'm lovin' this young bitch.

But in the end, Knocky knew that their affair couldn't continue. First, she was Ozzie's bitch and the brothers were warring with Ozzie. Second, she was Twilight's main squeeze before any nigga came along to tap that ass before she turned out to be damaged goods.

But the bombshell was on Knocky when Aniyah informed him of her pregnancy three weeks before Twilight was coming home, claiming that the baby was his. He was furious and knew he fucked up, and that there was a strong possibility that she was carrying his child, because they were fuckin' crazy like rabbits, and not once did Knocky think of strapping up to protect himself.

Jay-T was the only one who knew about Knocky's dilemma, unless the stupid bitch decided to open up her mouth and tell someone. But with Aniyah refusing to get an abortion and Twilight risking his life for the bitch, Knocky knew something had to be done quickly before shit really hit the fan.

Twilight jumped into his pearl-colored Benz, which was a coming-home gift from Knocky, and sped off. He had nowhere to go in particular, but just felt like driving. The night was young, with the temperature warm and the city being his playground. He was leaned back in his seat, blasting some T.I., and styling in his black and white Air Force Ones, MEK jeans, and his well-built physique in a black tank top that had all his tattoos showing. A long diamond Cuban link chain hung from around his neck, with the matching bracelet and 14-carat diamond pinky ring and diamond studded earrings in both ears. Twilight was lit up like the sun and was proud of every piece of jewelry he sported. It showed he was about money and his business, and he loved to flaunt his riches.

He sped down Rockaway Avenue and wanted to chill in the city, with three stacks in his pocket. It was money he was ready to blow on drinking and pussy. Twilight thought about Aniyah and wanted to risk seeing her again, but his brother's words of warning kept creeping into his head. He was almost ready not to give a fuck and call Aniyah on her cell phone again and set up another rendezvous with her—just thinking about that pussy was making his dick hard. He had fucked hundreds of bitches, but had loved Aniyah since day one.

As Twilight made his way down Rockaway Avenue, heading toward the Jackie Robison Parkway, his celly went off and he quickly answered. "Yo, who this?"

"Nigga, what the fuck you mean, who this?" his boy Tempo said. "Nigga, your moms ain't ever taught you how to answer the phone?"

"Nah, because I was always too busy on top of yours learning other new things," Twilight joked.

"Nigga, you lucky you my nigga and you just came home," Tempo replied lightheartedly. "Where you at anyway?"

"On my way to the city, tryin' to spend some money and get my drink on, maybe take a bitch home for the night."

"Nigga, fuck the city. Come meet me at the Executive," Tempo suggested.

"What's goin' on there?"

"Me, Locks, Joe, and Trish got sumthin' nice set up for the night. Nigga, you know how we do," Tempo explained.

"Oh word? Say no more, I'm there, my nigga." Twilight hung up.

He busted a fast U-turn and sped back the opposite way, going toward the hood. He was ready to chill, get tipsy, smoke some piff, and feel up on some booty. Twilight wanted to get his mind off Ozzie and get into some new pussy for the night. He cranked up T.I.'s "ASAP," making the bass rattle in his car, and raced to his location with a feeling of hype and security, knowing Brooklyn was his town and no nigga could touch him or fuck with his gangsta or swag.

Aniyah studied her naked stomach in the mirror and wondered what she would look like pregnant a second time. She posed from left to right, and then turned and tried to imagine the feeling of being with child once again. She wasn't nervous and didn't believe in abortions, but there was much concern about who the child's father was. She stared at her lovely image in the bathroom mirror, and even though she was such a beautiful, striking woman, she felt so ugly on the inside. She felt that her reputation or image would soon be tarnished—it was inevitable.

Ozzie had been her lover for several years now, and she loved him somewhat, but was far from being in love with him. At first, Ozzie was just a rebound for her when Twilight became incarcerated—but soon came the gifts, the dick, the money, and her lavish lifestyle, and she'd grown to love him over the years. But she knew the baby she carried was not his.

Aniyah thought about her affair with Knocky and knew he was a strong possibility, and the guilt of fuckin' Twilight's brother did bother her to some extent—but she was lonely and Knocky was comfort and companionship. Then there was a second possibility that another nigga she was fuckin' could be a strong candidate. Over the years, enduring Ozzie's infidelity and abuse toward her, the tragic loss of her first child, and Twilight being in jail for years made Aniyah run into the arms of other men who gave her passion and comfort. She didn't want to take in the fact that she'd become a ho, so she tried to justify her promiscuous actions by accusing others of wronging her for her happiness.

Yes, Ozzie took very good care of her with the money he earned from the streets, but Aniyah always felt that there was something missing in her life. She lost her mother at an early age to drugs, and her father didn't want anything to do with his daughter. So she was forced to move from Queens to live with foster parents in Brooklyn. She met Twilight soon after.

She loved Twilight a lot, but knew that she'd changed over the years—and that wholesome, ride-or-die chick, hold-a-nigga-down, faithful style of bitch she used to be died within her the day her son was killed and the day Ozzie raped her in front of his crew just to prove a point.

Aniyah heard keys rattling outside her door and knew it was Ozzie coming to see her. She knew it was only a matter of time before he came to check her about the incident with Twilight. Ozzie paid the rent to her place and paid for every lavish piece of furniture, clothing, jewelry, and shoes she had. He had other cribs scattered throughout the city and only came to Aniyah's place when he wanted some pussy or had a beef with her. He came and went whenever pleased and dared her to have any nigga staying in the apartment he was paying for.

But Ozzie had some good ways about him also—if she had any problems with anyone, he would handle it. If she needed money for anything, he had it. She treated herself to spas, trips, dinners and shows. Ozzie couldn't come close to Twilight when they fucked, but he pleased Aniyah in his own way, and the way he would eat her pussy when he was in the mood would have Aniyah squirming in bed like a fish out of water.

Aniyah stood in the center of the living room clad in her white Terry cloth robe and watched Ozzie walk into her home with Dink coming in behind him like the loyal right hand he was. She locked eyes with Ozzie and stood there looking disciplined. Ozzie carried an expressionless gaze and calmly walked up to Aniyah, and then slapped the shit out of her with a hard, open hand, causing Aniyah to stumble backwards and almost fall over the glass coffee table.

"Bitch, are you fuckin' crazy?" Ozzie barked, his face changing to anger.

Aniyah clutched the side of her face with a vexed stare toward Ozzie. Ozzie approached closer and turned over the coffee table, shattering the glass. He continued his vent. "You fuckin' this nigga in my crib? You got the nerve to fuck that nigga on the same bed my son was conceived on. Are you fuckin' serious bitch?"

Aniyah stumbled back, fearing he might strike her again. Ozzie was heavy handed and his blows really hurt her at times. Ozzie came closer to Aniyah while Dink witnessed the ordeal silently.

Ozzie quickly grabbed Aniyah by her robe and pushed her against the wall with force, and then removed his .45 from his waistband and pushed the tip of steel to her temple and threatened, "Tell me why I shouldn't kill your trifling ass right now."

Dink stared on, wanting for his boy to pull the trigger and finish the bitch. He felt that Aniyah was a handful and had caused enough trouble over the years. He never trusted her and forever warned Ozzie to get rid of her.

Aniyah stared at Ozzie with tears of hurt and pain streaming down her face. She readied herself for what was to come, having Ozzie's strong hold on her. She saw the rage Ozzie had in his eyes and knew that with love and emotions mixed, a nigga was capable of anything. And she didn't want to die tonight. Her heart raced and she trembled slightly in his violent hold feeling the gun against her skull.

"I'm pregnant with your child again," Aniyah blurted out.

Ozzie was shocked by the sudden news. He wanted another child from her. He removed the gun from her head and looked at her closely, trying to see if there was some truth to her words. He thought maybe the bitch was lying to live. He wanted to kill her and knew he couldn't come across soft in front of his crew. He loved her strongly and her actions and betrayal would bring out the beast in him.

"Bitch, you lying to live," he challenged with a hard gaze.

"I just found out that I'm six weeks. It's your baby, Ozzie. I can show you the results if you want," she stated.

Ozzie dropped his aggressive hold on her, moved his gun down to his side, and stared at Aniyah. He didn't know if he should smile or wild the fuck out.

"Aniyah, you serious? You're pregnant again? With my baby?" She nodded and asked with a wayward smile, "You happy, baby?"

She lied to save her life. But the way Dink stared at her, she knew he didn't trust her, and with everyone came dark secrets that, if told, could kill.

Ozzie glanced over at Dink, his deadly temper seeming to fade out for a moment. He then focused on his boo, and the thought of her being with Twilight made him want to go into that rage again. He hated the nigga with a strong passion.

"We gonna be a family again," Ozzie said.

Aniyah looked at Ozzie with some ease and said, "Yes."

"But how, wit' that nigga Twilight around and you letting this nigga fuck you every chance he gets?"

Then Ozzie raised the gun to Aniyah's head again and exclaimed, "How the fuck do I even know it's my baby?"

Aniyah was shocked to be staring down the barrel of his .45. Her heart raced and she explained, "Can you please think? I'm six weeks pregnant. Twilight's only been home for a month. It's yours, baby . . . believe me."

The lie sounded convincing enough for Ozzie to lower the gun from her head and rethink everything. Ozzie had his image to uphold, and he was finding himself torn between his love for Aniyah and Dink in his ear about Aniyah's disrespect toward him and how he needed to do away with her finally. But his one problem was Twilight; he was like a thorn in Ozzie's side.

"We gonna talk," Ozzie said to her.

Dink's cell phone rang, interrupting their conversation. Dink quickly answered and the information he received on the other end made a minor smile appear on his face. He hung up and looked over at Ozzie.

"What?" Ozzie asked.

"He onsite, " Dink stated.

Knowing what Dink meant, he smiled, then turned to Aniyah and said, "I have eyes all over this fuckin' city lookin' for that faggot. We gonna end this triangle once and for all. And then I'll deal wit' you later"

With that said, Ozzie and Dink walked out of her apartment to handle some overdue business, leaving Aniyah to ponder what was going on. She sighed somewhat, thanking God that Ozzie believed her lie about the baby. She was subtle with her affairs, but knowing Ozzie he always was suspicious of someone or something, and she didn't fully trust what was going on.

SIX

Twilight parked his Benz nearby and hurried to the club entrance. He strolled up to the door with a walk that said P.I.M.P., and he was ready to have a good time with his peoples. Club Executive was a popular club in Brooklyn with some of the finest ladies and the most paid ballers around that loved to pop bottles and flaunt their cash, and Twilight loved being among the elite doing his thang.

The busy street was lined from corner to corner with high-end cars and trucks, and the line to get in almost stretched a block long. The crowd was out tonight, and the ladies were clad in their sexiest attire and the fellows were eager to get some of that prime attention from the best the club had to offer.

Twilight bypassed the long line and went straight for the front entrance, having those waiting on line curious about his status at the club. Twilight was met by two beefy bouncers dressed in black standing behind the velvet rope. One looked at Twilight, holding the VIP list in his hand and knowing Twilight's face from around the way.

He nodded and said, "You home, huh?"

"A month now, baby," Twilight responded with a smile.

"Good to see you again," the bouncer stated.

"I'm good, right?" Twilight asked.

The bouncer nodded. He didn't have to look at the list to know Twilight was already VIP. The man detached the velvet rope that separated them and stepped aside, allowing Twilight to enter. Twilight gave him dap and a nod and walked in.

He moved past the small crowd gathered in the entrance hall, who were willing to pay their twenty-five for entry, and walked down the short flight of steps that led down to the large dance floor, which was teeming with revelers jamming to some Nina Sky and Rick Ross. Twilight was definitely feeling the aura and was ready to grab up some big booty cutie and start jamming like everyone else.

He moved through the crowd smoothly, catching stares and eyes from a few ladies who peeped him on the low, liking what they saw. Twilight was headed to the back, near VIP where he knew his niggas would be at, popping bottles and flirting with the ladies.

"There go my nigga right there!" Tempo shouted when he spotted Twilight emerging from the crowd.

Tempo stood up with a bottle of Moet clutched in his hand and some piff dangling from his lips. He was nestled comfortably in the VIP section next to his niggas and a few scantily clad ladies who adored the attention.

Tempo, excited to give his nigga Twilight some urban love, tried to move his way out from the cushy seat he was in—being in the middle of everyone.

"Move, bitch," Tempo said, shoving some lady's long, gleaming legs from his direction.

"Get out the way," his boy Trish joked.

The young lady looked over at Trish, not amused. Trish just shrugged it off, not giving a fuck how she felt about the comment. Tempo finally removed himself from the seating and walked up to Twilight with open arms. They gave each other a brotherly hug and dap.

"What's good, my nigga?" Twilight greeted.

"Nigga, it's finally good to have your ass home," Tempo exclaimed.

Tempo had just gotten back in town a few days ago; he had just completed a run to North Carolina for Knocky. When he came back into New York, he knew he had to see his nigga, Twilight—the nigga did five years. They'd been friends since the fifth grade and were like brothers and unbreakable.

Twilight greeted everyone with love—Trish, Lock, and Joe—and then took a seat among his friends in VIP, where more bottles of champagne were ordered and the piff was being sparked up.

The old Brooklyn crew partied, drank, smoked, and reminisced about the good times they had. Twilight wasted no time pulling a young whorish girl onto his lap and talking something naughty into her ear. She smiled and chuckled and allowed Twilight to slide his hand up her skirt to play with something nice. She was immediately attracted to him and craved his attention ever since he'd walked in.

"What's your name, beautiful?" he asked, rubbing her inner thighs soothingly.

"Ashley," she said with a flirtatious stare and a giggle.

"Word, Ashley . . . you know I just came home, right, and I'm tryin' to get into some things."

"Things like what?" she teased, smiling still.

"What you think, ma? I like what I'm seeing . . . you smelling and lookin' all nice, feeling fine and shit sitting on my lap. You feel that?" Twilight joked.

Ashley shifted her position on Twilight's lap a tad, feeling his erection poking into her ass cheek. She didn't mind, though, feeling how thick his manhood was through the jeans.

"What's that you stickin' me with, a gun or sumthin'?" she asked playfully. "It better not be loaded."

Twilight just showed off a mischievous smile and knew he had to get up in that pussy tonight.

"My nigga . . . do your thang," Tempo shouted out.

Twilight gave his man the head nod and was ready to retreat somewhere private with Ashley so he could show her what he was really working with. His hand brushed against her pussy and when he touched that bare pussy, seeing she had no panties on, he knew it was time for him to be ghost.

"Yo, let me holla at you in private somewhere. We need to talk fo' real," Twilight said, giving off that sexual insinuation.

Ashley nodded, knowing what time it was. She picked herself up off his lap, pulled down her skirt, and they made their way out of the area. Tempo stood up and called out to Twilight. Twilight turned, eager to fuck his prize catch for the night, but took a moment to holla at his man.

"What's good, my nigga?" he asked.

"Yo, real talk . . . I need to pull your coat to sumthin' when you bounce back from that, ayyite?"

Twilight nodded. "Ayyite, my nigga. We gonna talk."

"It's important business that you need to hear," Tempo added.

"No doubt."

Twilight was eager to get at that pussy and gave Tempo dap and moved on, following behind Ashley. Tempo watched his best friend trail off toward the bathrooms down the hall and smiled.

"Crazy-ass Twilight," he said to no one in particular.

Twilight and Ashley disappeared into the men's bathroom and rushed into one of stalls to get it popping. Twilight locked the door and quickly went to work on Ashley, pulling her skirt up and panties down. He then unzipped his jeans, whipped out his nine-inch dick and curved the bitch over the toilet and thrust something lovely into her creamy snatch.

SEVEN

Three black Kawasaki Ninja bikes roared toward the club, catching the eyes of those waiting on line for entrance to the Executive. The bikes were sleek black, but very loud and appealing, piercing the night with the sounds of power and tires burning against asphalt. The men on the bikes looked menacing, clad in all black leather from head to toe, dark helmets disguising their faces.

The bikes roared toward the back alleyway near the club, and the men parked their bikes and stepped off. They were not there to party, but had a purpose to carry out. The ninjas were slightly hidden from street view and so were the riders. All three men opened up their jackets and pulled out micro Uzi submachine guns. They were ready to spread death and chaos for a large fee, and they had their objectives in mind and weren't there to miss. With the weapons of death cocked and ready for murder, the men looked at each other and nodded, knowing what to do.

One pulled out a cell phone and speed-dialed a number.

"We're ready and in play," he spoke.

He then hung up. They kept their sleek, dark Icon Domain motorcycle helmets on to conceal their identity, but knew once they were in the club all attention would be on them and hell was going to break loose. So the hit had to be quick, before their target got wind of anything.

Soon a side door to the club opened and they were let into the club discreetly, with their weapons in hand. The thunderous music from huge speakers plastered all over and the club blared into their ears; hearing T.I. with Jay-Z, Kanye, and Lil' Wayne spitting "Swagger Like Us."

The three hitmen followed their connect through the club, and looked unfazed by the music, the crowd, the ladies, and everything else that surrounded them. They moved through the mob of revelers like programmed androids focused on one thing—their kill. They definitely stood out among the group, in their helmets and the Uzi's down at their side and almost looking impossible to tell apart because of the large mix of people among them.

They approached upon the VIP section to see a group of men living it up with the finest of women, downing Moët and Cristal and getting high off weed. They spotted Tempo and everyone else and knew what was to come next. Tempo laughed and clowned around with a voluptuous lady friend who was sitting on his lap when he suddenly looked ahead and noticed what wasn't right—two towering dudes in all black, wearing dark helmets and aiming for him. His eyes widened with fear and he pushed the chick off his lap, trying to move for cover fast.

Abruptly, a spurt of loud gunfire erupted in the club, quickly causing panic and chaos. The short bursts from the Uzis tore into the men and women sitting in VIP viciously, shredding through everyone like they were paper. Blood and flesh was splattered everywhere as the gunfire continued on, bringing death to six in the ill-fated group. The screams and shots drowned out the club music, and hordes of panicking clubgoers rushed for the exit, bathrooms, or any cover they frantically searched for.

Tempo had lain low, and when the gunfire seized for a moment as the two men reloaded, he sprinted from his covered position and ran for the nearest exit. But his escape was short-lived when he was stopped in his tracks by the third veiled gunmen who loomed from the shadows in the back. He had his Uzi trained on Tempo closely. Tempo gazed at death with his eyes wide with fear. He stepped back slowly with his arms out-stretched in a surrender stance and said submissively, "Yo, c'mon now . . . it ain't gotta be like this.

Whoever's paying you, I'll triple that shit, fo' real."

His pleads fell on deaf ears. The gunmen quickly opened fire on Tempo, pushing him back intensely and shredding him to pieces at close range with the Uzi. Dozens of hot rounds ate Tempo's chest up and had him sprawled out in a bloody mess across the large table.

The three men walked up to the collection of dead bodies piled over each other with death written across their mugs and examined the bodies, searching for one particular one in the mix. But so far, they were coming up empty—no Twilight among the carnage.

EIGHT

Twilight was in the stall busting Ashley's pussy wide open in the doggy-style position, when suddenly hordes of people came crazily running into the men's room.

"They shooting, they shooting!" someone screamed out.

The bathroom became cramped with frightened men and women and the loud gunfire could still be heard. Twilight and Ashley quickly made themselves decent and Twilight rushed from the stall into the crowd, worried about his peoples, especially Tempo. He pushed his way through the crowd, yelling out, "Move, move! Get the fuck out the way!"

He removed the .380 he had concealed and rushed out into the hallway with his gun cocked and ready. He ran down the hall and came upon the carnage. The shooters were already gone. The first body he saw was Tempo's bloody, contorted corpse sprawled out across the table. He lowered his head somberly and mumbled, "Not my nigga."

Twilight gripped his gun tightly and was ready to let off shots, not giving a fuck. He held back his tears and knew he couldn't hang around the crime scene too long. He was still on parole and there wasn't shit he could do for his peoples but get revenge. Ashley soon appeared behind him and screamed in horror, witnessing her girlfriends shot the fuck up and looking like bloody rag dolls.

The club was clear, and security rushed into the room to survey the damage done. Twilight grabbed Ashley by her hand and said, "C'mon, we gotta go."

Ashley was reluctant to leave, because one of the dead was her cousin Sue. But Twilight pulled her from the room and they exited out onto the Brooklyn street, where there were crowds of people looking horrified and shaken as they waited for police to show up.

Twilight hurried to his Benz and peeled off, knowing he'd escaped death a third time. But he was going to make it really ugly in Brooklyn, especially for anyone connected to Ozzie. He sped toward Atlantic Avenue, shedding tears for his friend Tempo, whom he'd known for over fifteen years. He picked up his celly and dialed up his brother.

"Twilight, what's good?" Knocky asked.

"They bodied my nigga, yo," Twilight blurted out.

"What the fuck you talkin' about, Twilight?"

"Ozzie's goons just ran up in the club and bodied Tempo and my niggas," Twilight exclaimed. "This shit ends tonight, Knocky. You hear me? I'm gonna murk this nigga and take my bitch back."

"Twilight, chill the fuck out and don't do anything stupid. Come see me now, nigga," Knocky suggested.

"Fuck that, Knocky. I'm gonna see this nigga right now," he exclaimed, speeding toward Atlantic.

Twilight was never one to talk. So he hung up on his brother. He was on a death wish and was determined to kill all around Ozzie and knew that tonight he would be either in a box or in a cell. There was no turning back.

NINE

Ozzie was occupied with business in a downtown Manhattan bar with an important client of his. They were in a private room by the bar having drinks and talking about money when Ozzie looked up at the mounted television behind the bar and saw the words BREAKING NEWS flash across the screen. He recognized the Executive and thought to himself that Twilight had finally gotten his.

"Yo, turn that up," Ozzie instructed the bartender.

The bartender picked up the remote and raised the volume so Ozzie could hear better. Ozzie's full attention was on the news, as his client wondered what was going on. The newscaster went on to explain about the fatal shooting that happened inside the popular Executive just a few short hours ago. The anchorwoman stood outside the club, which had police, homicide detectives, and CSU teeming all over for information and evidence on the deadly shooting. The anchorwoman gave some details of what had transpired.

"It is confirmed that six people were fatally shot, as three masked gunmen in dark motorcycle helmets just walked into this night club called the Executive behind me, and opened fire on the group as they sat in VIP. The names of the victims unknown. Police are withholding that information from us, with a full investigation underway. But once again, six people were shot and killed at the Executive night club. We will get back to you with more information to this story."

Ozzie clutched his drink and never diverted his attention from the TV.

"Something wrong?" Mr. Lea asked.

"Nah, everything's good," Ozzie said.

Dink came walking into the room. He had just gotten off his cell phone with some information and had some urgent news to tell Ozzie. Ozzie waved him over and Dink walked up to the men with a stone cold look on his face.

"What's up?" Ozzie asked.

Dink sighed and said to him, "He ain't dead."

"You mean he's shot up and survived the hit?" Ozzie questioned.

Dink shook his head. "He wasn't among the bodies."

Ozzie knew that couldn't be possible. His main eyewitness had spotted Twilight come into the club and watched closely as Twilight partied and drank with friends. So the eyewitness made the sudden phone call to Ozzie. Ozzie was on it quick and gotten the Fallout Brothers to do the hit immediately. They were ruthless, vicious killers and didn't give a fuck where or how they got the job done, as long as it was done. How they could miss the nigga had Ozzie puzzled.

Ozzie became furious. He abruptly threw his glass across the bar, and it shattered against the Johnny Walker and E&J bottles.

"Why is this muthafucka so hard to kill?" he screamed out. "He ain't got a fuckin' 'S' on his chest and he ain't got fuckin' nine lives. Damn it!"

Dink and Mr. Lea remained quiet and watched Ozzie go off. He picked up the Moët bottle off the countertop and tossed it across the room, having it shatter against the wall. Ozzie knew now that Twilight was a definite time bomb ready to go off. They'd killed Tempo, his childhood friend, and he was now more of a threat than before.

Ozzie turned to Dink, and said, "Tell our peoples to tool up and watch their backs, cuz now the nigga is definitely comin' for us."

Dink nodded and walked away.

Mr. Lea looked at Ozzie and asked, "Shall we continue our talk on a later day?"

"Nah, I'm good . . . this nigga ain't gonna stop me from gettin' that paper, just sit the fuck down," Ozzie stated.

TEN

Aniyah sat in her living room, worried about the sudden events happening around her. She'd just heard about the shooting at the Executive and knew it definitely revolved around Ozzie and Twilight. The news said six were dead, and her conscience was eating away at her heavily. Even though she had nothing to do with the deaths directly, indirectly Aniyah felt responsible. Because of her, two influential and violent men were at war with each other, and innocent lives were being lost.

Because of Ozzie's involvement in the street life, her son was killed, and she had her speculations about what had happened that day. Twilight was jailed on her twenty-first birthday and she was pregnant by a much-known hustler who she wanted to keep a secret until the time was right. Her life of glamour and riches were weighing down on her heavily. Aniyah would ask herself, Is it worth it?—the money, the notoriety, and so on.

Aniyah sat on the plush couch, soothing the bruises Ozzie had left on her face and neck. One thing she gave Twilight credit for was that he never had to hit her when he became angry. He was a beast in everything else, but never succumbed to domestic abuse like Ozzie.

But Twilight had other vicious demons that plagued him, and Aniyah knew that even though Twilight didn't strike her when angry, she kept in mind that he was still a malicious and hardened criminal who could wind up back in jail at any given time, and she wanted something different in her life. But she still loved Twilight; it was just the times were becoming different for her. She rubbed her belly and thought about her unborn child and thought about Damien and his murder. She feared losing another child to violence because of the men she had in her life or surrounded herself with and knew she couldn't make the same mistakes again.

There was a knock at her door and Aniyah stood up, tied her robe together, and walked toward the door leisurely. She was in no rush. She wasn't expecting company and wondered who it could be. The knocking continued and Aniyah looked through the peephole only to see her best friend Jazz waiting impatiently out in the hallway.

"Aniyah, hurry up and open the door. I ain't got all day out here," Jazz beefed.

Aniyah quickly unlocked her door and welcomed Jazz into her place with open arms. They hugged each other strongly and were happy to see one another.

"Damn, gurl. You okay?" Jazz asked.

Aniyah nodded meekly, but wasn't sure herself. Jazz noticed the bruises on her face and exclaimed, "Yo, that nigga put his fuckin' hands on you again?"

"I'm good, Jazz," Aniyah replied, turning her face away from Jazz.

"Nah, fuck that nigga, Aniyah. Why you keep letting him do you like that?" Jazz yapped.

"Just let it be."

Jazz sucked her teeth and didn't want to let it be. Aniyah had been her homegirl since grade school, and she wanted to be there to protect her girl from any harm. Jazz was straight-up hood—a ride-or-die chick ready to pop off for her peoples she had love for. She stood five-eight, and was a cutie with the seriously big booty. She wore long cornrows stretching down to her back and had eyes like an angel, but her smile was like the devil. Her thick, curvy figure was wrapped in smooth, dark skin, and a small scar from a rival's razor lined her right cheek, further evidence of her wild ways.

Jazz and Aniyah had been in many fights and battles together in the hood, and to Aniyah, Jazz was like the sister she never had. They always had each other's back and both would give the shirt off their backs if needed. Jazz never liked Ozzie and she thought Twilight was too wild a nigga to fuck with her girl, Aniyah. But she tolerated both men because of Aniyah. But if Jazz had her way, she would step to them both with her blade and her loaded .22 and do with them both. But Jazz held back her wild ghetto side and played the sideline for her friend.

Jazz embraced Aniyah and wanted to hold and console her friend for the night. Jazz was there when Damien got killed. She was there for Aniyah the day Twilight got sentenced. She was there during her pregnancy, the abuse, the cheating, the fights, and so much more, and Aniyah couldn't ask for a better friend.

"What you gonna do when this baby comes?" Jazz asked.

Aniyah shrugged. "I don't know."

"You should know. You don't need that nigga around this kid. You don't need to have this child around any of the bullshit that you had Damien around. You hear me, girl?"

Aniyah let go of a few tears, reflecting on the past for a short moment. She moved on, but still missed her son deeply. The pain was never really gone for her, and time was taking too long to heal.

"Look, Aniyah, you know I'm here for you always, you know this right?" Jazz said, taking a seat next to Aniyah on the couch. "This war between Ozzie and Twilight is only gonna get worse . . . these niggas is fighting over pussy, not love. You think they love you? It's their fuckin' pride their warring over."

Aniyah looked at Jazz, but was silent. She's been pondering the relationships she had with both men. Even though she loved Twilight more, she was very aware of his violent ways and hardcore demeanor.

"I know you're used to living nice in this crib, but you need better, girl. You don't need this shit, Aniyah. It ain't worth it," Jazz continued.

She pulled Aniyah close to her in a warm embrace and let Aniyah's tears run onto her chest. Jazz consoled her friend with the warmest heart and most compassionate reaction.

"Them muthafuckas ain't no good for us, Aniyah. They took away my godson because of the foolishness between the two of them . . . don't let them destroy this child growing in you also. You hear me, Aniyah?"

Aniyah kept herself embraced in Jazz's arms, her tears flowing against Jazz's tight shirt, with her heart worried and pained from the wrong she'd suffered over the years. But what Aniyah didn't know was that Jazz had a strong deep-rooted affection for Aniyah since their senior year in high school. It was a forbidden desire that Jazz felt for her close friend. She hated to see Aniyah mistreated by the men, and knew she was the only one in Aniyah's life who could love her best. They knew things about each other that they didn't dare tell anyone else, and the way Aniyah felt in her arms, Jazz wanted to hold her friend forever and forget about everything else.

Jazz ran her hand through Aniyah's dark, flowing hair and sighed heavily. She wanted to tell Aniyah how she really felt about her, that she wanted to be more than friends with her—she wanted to become her lover. Jazz craved for Aniyah's soft touch against her. She loved the way Aniyah's meaty thighs looked in a skirt, and how her thick hips and ass formed in a pair of tight-fitted jeans. She loved the way Aniyah's long, sensuous hair flowed down her back, and how her smooth, brownish skin was wrapped around her full, curvy figure so perfectly, like God took His time gift wrapping her perfectly for life. Jazz was in love and wanted to express her love toward Aniyah, but felt she was too vulnerable right now. But then she thought, If not now, then when?

Jazz slightly pushed Aniyah from her embrace. She had her eyes fixated on Aniyah's tearstained face and her beauty. Jazz took a deep breath and she was ready to express all that she felt toward her friend since senior year.

Aniyah noticed the eccentric look Jazz was giving her and asked, "What's wrong?"

"We need to talk," Jazz replied mildly.

"About what?"

Jazz reached over and took Aniyah's hands into hers and held them gently. She focused her attention on Aniyah and then said to her, "Aniyah, on the real, I've been in love with you since high school."

Aniyah was taken aback with wide eyes. "Excuse me?"

"I know this is kinda fucked up to hear, especially now with what's happening . . . but I really wanna be with you . . . intimately and physically. I think about us a lot. I know it's strange to hear . . . but those two niggas that's fighting over you, they don't know you like I know you, Aniyah. I love you, and I wanna be there for you till the end," Jazz proclaimed strongly.

Aniyah was stunned—lost for words. Jazz still held her hands in hers, but she didn't have a straightforward reaction. Aniyah loved and always thought of Jazz as a friend, but never thought about them becoming a couple. But then Aniyah started to think about the men in her life and wondered if being with a woman could be any worse. And for Aniyah, Jazz did have a valid point; they'd known each other since the second grade and pretty much knew everything about each other.

Jazz knew that Aniyah was contemplating the idea by the look she gave off, and she didn't want to rush Aniyah into anything, only give her a little bit of reassurance. Jazz continued to hold onto Aniyah's hand and gently pulled her close. Aniyah didn't resist, and they both leaned toward the other. Soon their lips were pressed closely and that curiosity about being with the same sex was met as they passionately kissed, their tongues entwining and the love between them ensuing even stronger.

For both women, that was just the easy part. The hard part was Ozzie and Twilight and the confrontation that was about to come their way at full throttle. But Jazz had a plan on how to handle the situation.

ELEVEN

Knocky and Jay-T rode around the dark streets of Brooklyn aimlessly in search for Twilight. Both men were armed heavily, and Knocky kept a keen eye out for his little brother. They drove out to every spot they figured Twilight might be, including a few strips clubs, a few of Ozzie's well known spots, and some Brooklyn corners. But they had no luck; Twilight was still in the wind. He wasn't surfacing up anywhere, and Knocky was becoming worried. He was hitting up all his connects on the streets frantically, asking about Twilight, but no one had seen him in hours. The streets were buzzing with the news about the hit that'd happened at the Executive, and the streets knew that it was only a matter of time before retaliation was a must and it wouldn't be minimum.

"I told this nigga to let the bitch be and stay low for a minute, that he just came home and things done changed. But this nigga is so fuckin' hardheaded and don't wanna fuckin' listen to nobody," Knocky barked.

"Don't worry, Knocky, we'll find him. He ain't got that many places to go. He's only been home for a month," Jay-T assured him.

The polished green Yukon moved down Linden Blvd with dawn soon to break the skies. The streets were tense, and the traffic was sparse, which made it easier for Knocky and Jay-T to move around.

Knocky's eyes were becoming heavy. He'd been up all night, and sleep was gnawing at him like a hungry predator. But he was relentless in finding Twilight before any more bodies fell in Brooklyn or before the cops picked him up. Knocky knew that Twilight was riding dirty and was in a bad temper mood, not giving a fuck. And when Twilight was in that state of mind, it was only a matter of time before evil happened.

"Yo, Knock, you need to go home and get some sleep. I got this, my nigga. I'll keep lookin' around for him," Jay-T suggested.

"Nah, not till I find this nigga. I ain't gonna rest, cuz this nigga got my nerves on edge right now," Knocky replied.

Jay-T shrugged and kept on driving.

Knocky checked his cell phone again and dialed a few numbers, hoping there was some good news about his brother's whereabouts. But it was the same thing; he wasn't popping up around anywhere, and that worried Knocky even more.

He turned to Jay-T and stated, "I swear, Jay, I wish we both never jumped in bed wit' that bitch. Look at all this shit she done put me and my brother through. Niggas out here warring over some pussy. Yo, the game ain't never been this fucked up, ya heard? I swear, if that bitch wasn't pregnant, I'd put a bullet in her my damn self. Bitch is trouble, fo' real."

"I coulda told you that, my nigga. But first, we need to find Twilight and worry about that other shit later," Jay-T said.

Knocky nodded. He wanted out of the game. It was becoming more trouble than it was worth, and with him reaching forty, he just wanted to own a few businesses and live like a civilian. But with Twilight coming home and stirring up so much shit on the streets, Knocky hated to have the dumb thought in his head, but he wished that the system kept Twilight inside for a bit longer, 'cause the nigga was far from rehabilitated and now his wild actions were cutting into business.

"I swear, Jay-T, if I find my brother before anyone else, I might just kill him myself for fuckin' putting me through this bullshit," Knocky said.

Jay-T just shook his head and kept on driving. The sun was fully out and Brooklyn was lit up like a lamp, but the streets were far from bright and the venomous intensity between Twilight and Ozzie was thickening with every minute.

TWELVE

It'd been hours since the violent nightclub shooting that left six dead and eight wounded. The cops had shut down the block and majority of Brownsville and Bed-Stuy looking for suspects, witnesses, or anything that would break the case wide open. But no one knew anything that could help the police with the case. The gunmen were well masked, and it happened so quickly that everyone was just trying not to get shot up and was running for cover.

Twilight took refuge at Megan's crib, an old jump-off that he had in Jamaica, Queens. She was willing to have Twilight stay at her crib for the night and get his mind right. His firepower needed to be deadlier. He only had the .380 on him, because the twin nines he had before had two bodies on them, and he needed something that would lay the block down viciously.

He called up his old gun connect from Long Island named Monroe and wanted the guy to link up with him in Queens. Twilight had three stacks to spend on some heavy artillery and was about to give Monroe every last dime of it. He had a strong hunger for revenge, and his emotions and temper were running high. He had a taste for blood.

It was late evening the next day, and Twilight waited patiently for Monroe to show up with the artillery up for sale. He sat on the living room couch with Megan's five-year-old son on his lap. Twilight was watching cartoons with him and it was helping him relax a bit before the murders he planned on committing tonight.

Megan came out the kitchen draped in a long white T-shirt and stared at Twilight socializing with her son with a smile. Megan had been in love with Twilight since the day he cocked her legs back in the back seat of his H2 a year before his incarceration, and her pussy was still throbbing from that morning, when Twilight busted her coochie wide open.

"The food's ready," Megan said.

"That's what's up, luv," Twilight replied.

Twilight picked up the little boy in his arms, having him laughing and giggling, and trotted off with him into the kitchen. Megan wished Twilight was her man, but knew he was a hardcore gangsta who was far from settling down, and she knew about Aniyah. So she played secondhand and got what she could from him—sex, money, etc.

Twilight looked at the time and it was nearing seven in the evening. Megan knew something had gone down, because usually he would come by for some pussy, get his nut, and be gone within an hour or two. But now he was spending a lot more time with her and her son than usual. But she didn't want to ask any questions; she just enjoyed the time she had and wished it came more often.

By seven-thirty, Twilight's gun connect called to inform him that he was getting off the Belt Parkway and would be at the house within ten minutes. Twilight threw on his shirt and Yankees fitted, and when the silver Benz pulled up in the driveway to the one story ranched home off of Merrick Boulevard, Twilight stood out front to meet Monroe.

Dusk was settling over the hood once more, and Twilight carried a collected look about him. Monroe stepped out of the Benz clad in a white and gray tracksuit, with a gray fitted and fresh Addias. He was a pretty boy Italian with rich olive skin, sleek greasy black hair, and he had a hoodlum look about him. He was the young son of a slain member from the Gambino crime family and didn't trek too far from his father's gangster ways.

Monroe and Twilight met each other when they were both locked up in a juvenile detention center at thirteen. They became good friends, and over the years they both became very resourceful and useful to one another. Monroe always came through for Twilight when he needed guns.

"My nigga . . . it's finally good to see you home again," Monroe greeted with a smile and embraced Twilight with a hug and dap.

"Same here, my dude," Twilight greeted back.

Monroe gazed at his longtime friend for a minute, taking in the reality that it'd been five years since he seen Twilight.

"You look good, Twilight," Monroe complimented.

"You know, when you're locked down, you gotta stay sharp, keep on your wits, and get your lift on. It's been a long time though, nigga. What's good wit' you? I'm glad to see you ain't changed the number on me."

"Nah, can't . . . I get a lot of business wit' that number. Besides what the fuck you gonna do without me. Nigga, you know I'm the light to your black ass," Monroe joked.

"Yeah, you came through for a nigga a few times," Twilight replied.

"A few." Monroe smiled, and playfully threw some punches at Twilight.

"But yo," Monroe continued, "I've been hearing about you through the grapevine, yo . . . heard you almost came out in a box while locked down. And I'm hearing this shit about you and Ozzie. Don't tell you still warring with this dude over Aniyah. I thought you been done with her, yo."

"Man, this shit got even more personal," Twilight explained.

"Talk to me."

"They killed Tempo last night."

Monroe's heart sank to the pit of his stomach. "What? You shitting me, yo."

"They gunned my nigga and his crew down in cold blood in a crowded club, Monroe. You know that shit can't go untouched," Twilight proclaimed.

"Damn, not Tempo. He was a cool-ass dude, fo' real."

"But you know, I'm home now, so I need some heat that's gonna lay the fuckin' block down like fuckin' dominoes falling."

Monroe looked at his friend for a moment. He knew Twilight all too well. He was familiar with the temper and the murders, and he knew Twilight was planning on going into retaliation full force, holding nothing back.

"You home a month now, Twilight. I know Knocky's been telling you to lay low and chill. I'm wit' you on this and you know I got much love for you, but as a friend—"

"Fuck that shit, Monroe," Twilight chided. "I ain't in the mood to talk or be lectured like I'm some off-brand nigga. I called you for a fuckin' reason, my dude, not to stand here and reminisce like we on Sesame Street, nigga. You know what I need from you, and I ain't cheap wit' it."

Twilight reached into his pocket and pulled out the wad of hundreds and fifties he had on him and tossed the cash to Monroe. Monroe quickly caught the cash and looked at it. He then looked at Twilight and said, "I don't feel too good about this one, Twilight. It ain't about the money—"

"Nigga I don't give a fuck how you feel, I want my fuckin' guns, Monroe. I called you here for business, nuthin' personal wit' you, but either you do or you don't. Either way, niggas is gettin' handled tonight. Now, I rather give you the bread and we be cool about it, or I'll just go somewhere else and handle my business."

Monroe sighed and then gestured him over by the trunk. Twilight followed.

Monroe popped the trunk to his Benz and revealed to Twilight the merchandise he had for sale. Twilight whistled loudly, loving what he was seeing. "That's what I'm talkin' about."

Twilight didn't want any handguns from Monroe. He just eyed the heavy submachine guns. He picked up the MP9 submachine gun and loved how it gripped in his hands.

"Yeah, I like this shit. I can definitely lay down a few niggas wit' some shit like this in my hands." He then turned to his friend and asked, "How much you ready to give this up for anyway?"

"That's forty-five hundred right there . . . but you peoples, so what I got in my hands from you, we good," Monroe said.

Twilight nodded and was ready to go to war with the deadly gun. Monroe closed his trunk and then said, "Twilight, you know I don't feel too good about this."

"Well, I do," Twilight replied frankly.

Twilight concealed the deadly weapon in the back of his Benz and was now ready to bounce back into Brooklyn. Monroe hesitated in leaving Twilight's side. Both men stood in the driveway for a short moment and then Monroe said, "You be safe. I know Tempo was peoples to us, but we ain't kids anymore, yo. Tempo was into some shit like we all was, and you know in this game, tomorrow ain't ever promised to us. Shit done changed for you and me, Twilight."

"It ain't never changed for me and what I'm about," Twilight replied.

Monroe looked at Twilight like it would be the last time they would ever see each other. It felt like Monroe knew what the future was for his friend, and it saddened him. Monroe had seen enough murders, money, and grief that he wanted out from the streets, knowing how it snatched his father's life away so violently. So he was working on change for himself and told himself that this would be his last gun deal ever. He was saddened that his friend Twilight, after doing five years, didn't have that same desire to change and didn't want something better for himself.

Monroe gave Twilight dap and embraced him in a strong hug. "Be safe, my nigga. I'm gonna miss you, and I don't wanna be hearing about you on the ten o'clock news," he said.

"I move in violence and in silence, nigga," Twilight replied, somewhat in humor. "But on the real, thanks, and it was good seeing you, my dude."

"Same here, yo."

Megan couldn't help but to be nosey. She'd watched the whole transaction take place from behind the curtains in her living room window. She was worried about Twilight, but knew she couldn't talk him out of doing shit. He was hardcore and hardheaded down to the bone and could be so naïve at times. She was passive about his business and prayed that one day she wouldn't regret it.

Monroe then backed out the driveway and slowly drove off. Twilight rushed into the house where Megan stood next to a chair holding her sleeping son. Twilight didn't have any time for a formal goodbye. He just wanted to get his shit and leave.

Megan watched him grab his bag and saw that he was willing to leave without acknowledging her one bit. She became hurt and upset. When Twilight had his hand on the doorknob, she quickly placed her son on the couch and then exclaimed, "You just gonna leave without saying bye?"

"I got business to take care of," Twilight replied impolitely, not even turning to face her.

"You know what, nigga . . . you've been gone for five years. I've been playing the secondhand bitch to Aniyah since the day I met your ass. I'm always giving you my time and my body, and you come to me wanting a place to chill and stay, and I did that for you and gave you some pussy, and now you just gonna bounce like that—no fuckin' kiss, no goodbye like I don't even fuckin' exist. Nigga is you serious?" Megan barked, as she began to shed a few tears.

Twilight turned to look at her and retorted with, "Bitch, you knew what the fuck I was about when we met. So don't act like this life I live is brand new to you. It is what it is."

He then walked out her life without saying anything else to her. Megan was hurt and enraged when she saw the door slam behind him. She snatched up a glass pitcher from the table and hurled it at the door, smashing it to pieces.

"FUCK YOU!" was all she could scream out before dropping to her knees and crying in full tears. She felt played and used and knew that she would never see the man she loved so strongly again.

THIRTEEN

Aniyah's passionate cries echoed throughout the room like a calling as she clutched the bedroom sheets to her sweaty, sensitive breasts with her chest heaving up and down. Her body felt like it was about to explode. The pleasure felt unnatural for her in her mind, but it felt so good everywhere else. Her soft moans were in a rhythm with her eyes closed and her legs wrapped around something so nice that had her inner thighs quivering.

Jazz had that pussy in her mouth like a pair of vice grips—licking and sucking on everything from Aniyah's sweet clit to her moist walls. She was hidden underneath the covers, with Aniyah's legs wrapped around her, and her pelvis moving up and down from the almost unbearable sexual position.

"Oh shit . . . Oh shit . . . damn it . . . shit," Aniyah cried out.

Jazz wanted to please her fully and didn't hold back any skills. She knew what a woman wanted in bed and used it on Aniyah. She ate that pussy out slow, soft, and caring and then rough and fast like a beast, pushing fingers into Aniyah and tasting in between her thighs like it was candy. Aniyah continued to quiver and gyrate her hips against Jazz and felt herself about to come.

"Shit! Oh shit! I'm gonna fuckin' come!" she exclaimed, thrusting her hips and back upwards and clutching the bed sheets for dear life.

Jazz didn't let up or show any mercy when eating that pussy. She thrust her tongue into Aniyah's sweet inside and circled that shit all around the pussy. Jazz cocked Aniyah's legs back even more and then went in on her asshole just for fun. Fifteen minutes later, Aniyah's body went rigid, and she let out a howl like a beast was present in the room. She then bit down on her bottom lip, feeling her body about to explode abruptly. Her legs couldn't stop from shaking.

Jazz allowed Aniyah to come in her mouth, and when all her juices were released, Jazz cleaned it up with her tongue and then loomed from out the cover and rested against Aniyah's naked frame.

Aniyah looked spent as she exhaled faintly and looked to be in a zone, thinking, Ain't no nigga never ate my pussy out that good. Jazz smiled and neared her face toward Aniyah and gave her a loving kiss.

"You liked that, baby?" Jazz asked.

"Hells yeah," Aniyah responded with an entrenched smile.

Jazz grabbed Aniyah up in her arms lovingly and stated. "I love you so much, boo."

The feeling was going to take some time for Aniyah to get used to. Jazz was still her best friend and they had just crossed into foreign territory with each other. But Jazz felt really comfortable and knew it was meant to be this way for them. She held Aniyah in her arms, as they were nestled together like lovers. Aniyah turned to face Jazz and asked, "How long you've been a lesbian?"

"Since high school," she answered.

"But you had boyfriends."

"And? Niggas don't mean shit to me, Aniyah. I'm better off without them, and so are you. I mean, you've seen how fucked up and twisted my life was when I had that nigga Marcus around. I almost went bankrupt fuckin' wit' his ass. And let's not get into Keith and L-Dog; them niggas were a fuckin' joke. But when I'm wit' a woman, I just get this different feeling . . . like I'm just me and complete.

"See, you need to think, Aniyah. What the fuck you really got goin' on wit' Ozzie and Twilight? You don't need them niggas around, or any other muthafucka. Niggas is just selfish and stupid sometimes."

Aniyah lay in Jazz's arms, listening. She had to admit that she felt comfortable being so close and intimate with her friend. Her body did the talking, but her mind wanted to do the walking.

"I'm just scared, Jazz. I mean, this is new for me, you understand? I've been with Ozzie for a long time, and I loved Twilight since forever. What if this don't work out? What if they find out about us?"

Jazz gave off a serious gaze and said to Aniyah, "Look, baby, I love you so much, and I promise you ain't no nigga gonna hurt you or that child while I'm around. You hear me? I'm gonna keep it real wit' you. I got a plan and believe me, we gonna be good. I don't care whose baby that is you're carrying, all I know is only you and me will be the one raising that child, cuz anyone else, is just poison, as far as I'm concerned. This ain't gonna be Damien all over again. You trust me?"

Aniyah nodded.

Jazz smiled and said, "That's all I need to know, baby."

FOURTEEN

Twilight made it back to Brooklyn around ten that night. He was clad in all black with the MP9 resting in the backseat. He had gotten the call about Ozzie's people—especially his younger brother Jones P. Twilight had the lowdown on the family, where they be hanging out at mostly and was ready to have their mama buy that black dress for a closed casket funeral. An eye for an eye, Twilight thought.

He moved his Benz slowly through the streets of Brooklyn, making sure he didn't catch any suspicion from the police and get pulled over. The way Twilight felt, if police were to fuck with him tonight, he was ready to bang out with them too.

His cell phone kept ringing constantly, and it was mostly Knocky, or Aniyah calling, and he didn't feel like talking to either one of them at the moment. Twilight wanted to stay focused on his mission and was ready to kill everything in sight. When he came near the intersection of Rockaway Avenue and Riverdale Avenue, Twilight saw the corner liquor store that Jones P owned. It was a family business. He slowly passed the spot where there were half a dozen young men lingering out front. They all noticed the polished Benz ride by slowly, but it was hard to see in the car because of the dark tints.

Twilight nodded with a cunning smirk and kept it moving. He wanted to catch all those niggas out front slipping. He even peeped Jones P hanging with his crew, with a fifth of Hennessy in his hand, and he knew what time it was.

Twilight continued down Rockaway Avenue casually and made a right on Livonia Avenue and circled around the block and parked his ride on Riverdale, just a few feet from the liquor store. It was dark out, and two of the street lights above were broken, which worked to Twilight's advantage. He stepped out of his ride with the MP9 gripped in his hand. He wanted the hit to be swift and accurate. The bodega on Riverdale Avenue was already closed for the night, so the crowd on the block was sparse. He moved in close to the graffiti scrawled wall of the store, trying to be incognito. He heard the crowd in front of the Buy Rite liquor store carrying on, as they gambled and got their drink on. They weren't paying their surroundings no never mind.

As Twilight neared the corner, he thought about what they did to Tempo. He didn't know the perpetrators that actually carried out the hit, but Twilight figured that killing Jones P and his peoples would do for now, until the true trigger men's identities were revealed.

The traffic on the street was at a minimum and Twilight crept toward the corner like a trained soldier in war, gripping the deadly piece of steel close to him and keeping a keen eye out for any surprises he may encounter. He inched near the corner and the chatter from the group could be clearly heard. Now or never, Twilight said to himself.

"Roll them dice, nigga. Watch me break them pockets and send you home to your bitch broke. You can't break this bank, nigga," Twilight heard someone shout.

"Nigga, you ain't fuckin' Vegas," someone replied jokingly.

The men were heavily involved in the dice game, circled around a cluster of tens and twenties spread against the weathering pavement. Jones P had the dice in his hand, and he raised his fist in the air, shaking the dice, trying to win over the pot of cash. He took a quick swig from the fifth of Hennessy he clenched and launched the dice from his grip against the wall of his store. It came up trip sixes, and Jones P won the pot of five hundred dollars.

"Yeah, niggas, pay the fuck up. Y'all niggas give me my fuckin' money . . . told y'all niggas I'm breaking bank today," Jones P hollered.

He went to collect his cash, but something caught his immediate attention from the corner of his eye. He turned slightly to see Twilight quickly emerge from around the corner dressed in all black and what looked like a small machine gun clutched in his hands. He became wide eye and the other group of men suddenly looked horrified.

"Oh shit!" someone screamed out.

The crowd tried to scatter rapidly—scrambling about hastily, but a loud burst of gunfire quickly mowed three niggas down to the pavement. Twilight moved in for the kill. Jones P was hit and stumbled, but he didn't fall. He and a friend tried to escape through a neighboring alleyway. The sixth man ran into the street, looking like he had the speed of The Flash. He never looked back to see if he was being chased.

Twilight rushed after his attended target and followed them into the alleyway. He trained the MP9 at the niggas' open backs as they tried to run from death, and he squeezed off shots into them from a short distance, having a few hot rounds eat into the two men's backside. Jones P and his friend dropped into some debris. Twilight continued on. He noticed Jones P was still alive—barely. He was crawling on his knees and stomach, covered in blood and dirt. He had nowhere to go, and was whimpering like some injured bitch. His breathing was sparse and his legs were crippled.

"Yeah, nigga . . . tell Ozzie what's good now, huh. I told the nigga don't fuck wit' me," Twilight taunted.

Jones P bothered not to look up, but looked away from his attacker and felt his life slipping away from him leisurely. Twilight stood over the man with his gun aimed for the back of his head.

"Fuck you and your brother," Twilight cursed and then squeezed off rounds into the back of Jones P head, making his skull look like some smashed piece of watermelon.

Twilight's heart raced against his chest and he became excited seeing how the gun tore viciously into his victims so easily. He peered down at the bodies for a moment, but not feeling he'd avenged Tempo's death yet or truly hit Ozzie where it hurt. But he was determined to do so very soon.

Twilight took off running back to his ride knowing that the loud gunfire had awakened and disturbed plenty of folks around the way, and he already heard the police sirens blaring from a distance.

Twilight jumped in his ride and sped off knowing that he sent a clear cut message to Ozzie saying, "I'm coming for you next, nigga!"

FIFTEEN

Knocky was in his crib trying to get some rest when he got the news. Jay-T came walking in with a concerned look.

"What, nigga? What you gotta tell me?" Knocky asked, knowing the news had to involve his brother.

"They found Ozzie's brother Jones P and his crew shot the hell up in front of his liquor store on Rockaway Avenue. It's ugly . . . they sayin' the nigga's brains is leaking out of his head and word on the streets is that they seen your brother's car in the area right before it happened," Jay-T informed him.

Knocky didn't look too happy about the news. Twilight just made the streets hot like fire, and now with the club shooting and Jones P and his crew being gunned down twenty-four hours later, it wouldn't be long till either the feds got involved or the state came crashing down on everyone with a shit load of charges because of the violence that was happening.

"Fuck me . . . fuck!" Knocky shouted.

He kicked over a chair and tossed the phone across the room. He was clearly upset with what was happening in his hood and even more upset that Twilight was the center of it all. Money on the blocks was slowing up, niggas were dying, cops were putting pressure on hustlers for information, and the streets were pointing at Twilight and Knocky behind the reasoning.

"It's gonna get ugly, Knocky, either wit' the police or wit' Ozzie wanting to come at us now for Jones P's murder. I'm not tryin' to be in your ear wit' the wrong thang or about the wrong man, but we gotta do sumthin, or it's gonna get bad on us," Jay-T said.

"Sumthin' like what, nigga?" Knocky glared at his right-hand.

"Look, I know he's your little brother, but he fucked up, my dude. And between you and me, if it was anybody else causing this much heat on us, they would have been gone. Now I know you're feeling guilty about fuckin' his bitch and probably knocking her up, but it's way past that now. We talkin' about war. We talkin' the feds up in our shit for the murders. We talkin' about twenty-five to life if that nigga flips and starts talking to the wrong sources. He's outta control, Knocky. Everything that goin' on links back to him, and he links back to us," Jay-T stated.

Knocky stood still and quiet. It was making him sick to his stomach to even consider the idea of killing his younger brother. He had his attention turned from Jay-T and stared out his living room window, gazing out at the concrete jungle of Brooklyn, where it laid home to so many gangsters, hustlers, killers and so much money. He stood four stories up in a newly lavish apartment complex in Do or Die, Bed-Stuy and felt a strong smoldering pain in his heart. He looked out into Brooklyn and feared that this dreadful day would come with the decision of what to do with his brother. He knew his choices were few, and Knocky would rather kill Twilight himself, than to see him suffer in his enemies' hands or rot away in prison for the rest of his natural life.

Knocky let fall a few tears from his glossy eyes, as his interest was still focused out the window, studying Brooklyn with a profound gaze. He let out an eerie chuckle and then said with his face still at the window, "And to think, all this shit started over a fuckin' piece of pussy. A fuckin' bitch is gonna be the end of all of us one day."

Jay-T shrugged nonchalantly.

Knocky wiped the tears from his face and turned to face Jay-T. He quickly regained his composure and said, "Just bring him to me first. I'll deal wit' it."

Jay-T nodded and walked away, leaving Knocky to ponder about his choice.

SIXTEEN

It'd been hours since Twilight did the hit on Jones P and his goons. He knew Brooklyn would be hot and flooded with police, so he wanted to lay low, rethink his tactic, and finish up Ozzie once and for all. In the span of a little over twenty-four hours, the hood had collected eleven bodies.

Twilight had been home a little over a month now, and once again he had the streets on fire and his name was buzzing throughout the hood. Some were praising his gangsta and some were upset that he was bringing too much heat on them and they wanted to see the nigga disappear for good.

The cops and his P.O. got wind of some information from a snitch and were now in search for Twilight, who was their main lead or suspect to three vicious homicides in the past week alone. The word was out: Twilight was a wanted man.

Twilight had a small apartment out in Queens that only Knocky and Aniyah knew about. He kept it a secret because of times like this—when he trusted no one and Brooklyn was too hot for him to step foot in. So he finally decided to take his brother's advice and lay low—but it was a little too late for that.

Twilight drove his cream colored Benz into a narrow and dark driveway adjacent to his one-bedroom apartment. He had the MP9 concealed in the trunk, but had his .380 stuffed into his waistband for protection. When Twilight stepped out of the car, the motion lights quickly came on, flooding the darkened area with brightness around him to keep anyone from creeping up on him.

Twilight felt comfortable when he approached the door. He kept his gun near his reach and dug into his pockets for his keys. Twilight was cautious, but felt a little comfortable. He just wanted to relax, watch some television, order some Chinese food, and get his mind off the drama he'd created in Brooklyn.

Twilight was three steps away from his door when he heard some movement nearby. He turned, reaching for his gun at the same time, but then suddenly felt the side of his neck explode. He jerked and stumbled back, clutching his neck and saw that his hand was coated with blood. His eyes became wide with panic. He was shot, but didn't see any gunman. Twilight fell against the wall to his place, needing some support, trying to keep himself from falling and tried to reach for his gun again. But a second shot tore into him, ripping through his side. He dropped to the pavement on his back, squirming in pain. The shooting was silent, which meant the gunman had a silencer at the end of his weapon.

Twilight was barely still alive and breathing. He felt paralyzed against the cold pavement and knew his end was coming near. He always knew that one day he would die by the gun because of his violent ways. Twilight clutched his neck tightly, trying to stop the bleeding, but he felt his life being drained from him so slowly. It was becoming hard for him to speak. He was able to keep his eyes open and witnessed his assailant appear from the shadows.

"Fuck me," Twilight mumbled, surprised to see who'd loomed from the dark.

The assailant stood over Twilight's wounded body and aimed the gun at his head. All Twilight could do was accept his fate. He was going to die tonight. He looked up at the barrel of a .9mm with the silencer and chuckled in a ghostly way. His attitude said "Fuck you" to the shooter.

The shooter said no words, just stared down at Twilight with a look of disgust and gripped the gun tightly. It was ironic to see such a vicious killer from Brooklyn looking so helpless. But now was not a time for compassion. Twilight was wicked and ugly and his judgment needed to come.

Poot! Poot! Poot! Poot!

The shooter put four rounds into Twilight's face at close range, contorting his handsome features into a bloody disaster. The roadway was covered in a crimson stain, and the night air felt still. The shooter walked away casually like he was taking a walk in the park.

One of Brooklyn's notorious gangstas and killers was no more—nothing but a memory and street talk for those that knew him or heard off about his reputation. His violent reign had finally come to an end.

SEVENTEEN

Knocky soon got news about his brother's murder and he was called down to the morgue to identify his brother's body. When he heard, it felt like a delusion to him—hearing his brother was shot six times, four shots to the face. Knocky couldn't help but to cry over the tragedy, even though he knew it was inevitable. But the problem was that Jay-T or any other niggas in the crew didn't carry out the hit; it came from someone else and it pained Knocky that Twilight was killed in such a vicious way.

Jay-T drove Knocky down to the morgue where his brother lay dead. Both men followed the pathologist down the long, grim corridor into a disturbing, still, chilled room. A covered body lay against a long creepy piece of table that symbolized death. Knocky walked into the room first, followed by Jay-T.

The pathologist stood near the covered body and stared at Knocky, waiting for the signal. Knocky nodded slightly and the man removed the sheet from the body, showing the identity of the dead. It was a gruesome sight to see, his face was contorted in such a damaging way, that it would have to take a miracle to reconstruct his human features. Twilight's right eye was shot out; a bullet was embedded into his jaw, shattering teeth and bones. Another bullet was rooted into his forehead. His skin looked warped and was caked with dried blood. The face looked inhuman, but even through the ugliness of the body; Knocky knew that it was Twilight. He shed a few tears and confirmed it was his younger brother. The pathologist quickly covered the body and Knocky left the room with an empty spirit and a crushed soul.

"You good, nigga?" Jay-T asked.

But no, Knocky wasn't good. The game had taken away so much from him that he didn't have the strength to carry on any longer. Seeing his little brother shot up and dead like that changed something in him. He didn't know what to think. Knocky, whose real name was Jonathan Tyler, was the last generation of the Tyler name. The majority of his family had been wiped out by either drugs or violence. And both brothers didn't have any kids.

"Knocky, you good, right?" Jay-T asked again.

"Nigga, no. How you think I fuckin' feel? My brother is lying dead in a fuckin' morgue shot the fuck up and I feel responsible for that. I can't do this shit anymore, Jay. It ain't in me anymore."

"It was goin' to happen anyway," Jay-T said.

"Not like that. They fucked him up bad, probably gonna have to give my brother a closed casket funeral."

Jay-T sighed.

But Knocky was just fucked up period. He was nearing forty soon, and it dawned on him that he had no more family left and he had nothing to show for himself in the game—nothing but misery, death, and problems.

Knocky had over two hundred thousand stashed away secretly and said to himself, No more. His heart wasn't into the streets any longer, and his mind was telling him to get out now. But he regretted that he couldn't save his brother and that he and Twilight didn't have any children, cuz Knocky did love kids, but he didn't want any while he was in the life.

But then for some strange reason, his thoughts were on Aniyah and he remembered that she was pregnant, and possibly by him. And in some strange way, he had this overcoming feeling to become a different man, and wanting to become a father, because he was no longer an older brother. He had this longing for a change and something different.

When the two were outside and approaching the truck, Knocky turned to Jay-T and said, "I'm out."

"Out what?" Jay-T questioned.

"I'm out this fuckin' game. It ain't for me anymore. I got enough money saved and this shit ain't me anymore."

Jay-T thought his friend was talking crazy, but when he saw the seriousness in Knocky's face, he knew there was some truth behind his words.

"You serious, nigga?"

"I never been so serious about anything in my life," he replied. "You can have it all, Jay . . . my connect, the corners, everything. I just don't give a fuck anymore."

Hearing that made Jay-T smile. Knocky didn't want revenge for Twilight's murder. He just wanted some peace in his life now, and to be happy. He just wanted to disappear for a very long time. He walked away, leaving Jay-T standing by the truck with the keys in his hand.

"Knocky, you don't wanna ride back?" Jay-T called out, staring at Knocky's backside.

Knocky ignored him and kept it moving. He just wanted to be alone.

"Knocky . . . yo, Knocky," Jay-T kept on calling.

But his shouts were falling on deaf ears. Knocky was in his own world and wanted to grieve for his brother in private.

EIGHTEEN

Ozzie was elated when he heard the news about Twilight's murder. He looked at his right-hand man, Dink and stated, "See? I told you the muthafucka wasn't Superman."

But his celebration was short lived anyway because of Jones P's death and it fucked him up, learning how Twilight killed his brother—machine gun style like in Al Capone's era. Ozzie realized that there weren't any winners in this war, just causalities. He lost his son, his older brother, his peoples, and possibly he would lose Aniyah too—cuz he was going to kill the bitch.

He got an anonymous phone call from someone proclaiming that Aniyah was a traitor and a snitch and that she was talking to police and was behind Jones P's death. The caller was saying that Aniyah gave up lots of information to Twilight and helped him out with the murders. And it was making sense to Ozzie, because how else would Twilight attain such personal information about him?

Ozzie was fuming and was ready to put a bullet in Aniyah, but her death was definitely inevitable when the caller also informed that it wasn't his baby Aniyah was carrying. Ozzie's heart sank and his face became tightened with rage, especially when Knocky's name came up about being the possible father.

The only thing on Ozzie's mind was, I'm gonna kill this bitch slow.

When he relayed the information to Dink, all Dink had to say was, "I told you never to trust that bitch."

They raced to Aniyah's crib and Ozzie kicked in the door, and stormed into the apartment with a pistol in his hand.

"Aniyah! Where the fuck you at?" he screamed out.

He rushed through the house, kicked open the bathroom door and found Aniyah in the bathroom wrapped in a towel. She screamed. Ozzie rushed up to her and brought the pistol across her head, pushing her back aggressively and then grabbed her by the hair and dragged her into the center of the living room.

Aniyah was naked. The towel came off as Ozzie dragged her down the hallway by her hair. He stood over the trembling and crying Aniyah, and had the gun pointed at her head.

"You a trifling-ass bitch. You know how much I lost cuz of your mouth and stupidity! And you lied to me, bitch. Who the fuck baby is that in you?" Ozzie exclaimed. "Stand your fuckin' ass up."

Dink just played his position as usual, watching Ozzie abuse his bitch and knew it would be the last show they would put on, because Ozzie was going to kill her. Aniyah was in tears and knew there was no talking her way out of the situation this time. She stood up slowly; her eyes were glossy and her face a bit bloody from the hard blow.

"You gonna kill me now because you think I betrayed you?" she spat back. "Nigga, you're just so fuckin' naïve at time. I'm not the one you should be worried about."

Ozzie was taken aback by her rawness and the statement.

"What the fuck you talkin' about, bitch?" he asked.

"Yeah, it ain't your baby and I'm glad it ain't. But you need to be watchin' niggas in your camp more closely than trying to keep tabs on me all the fuckin' time," Aniyah chided.

"Bitch, don't play games wit' me," Ozzie exclaimed, pointing the pistol at her head.

"Games, huh nigga? Dink is the one playin' games wit' you," she admitted.

Ozzie's expression changed to sudden bewilderment. "Fuck you talkin' about?" he asked through clenched teeth.

Dink's face became tense, as he glared at Aniyah, wanting the bitch to keep her stupid mouth shut. But Aniyah was ready to let the cat out the bag.

"Tell him, Dink, who also could be the father of this baby . . . tell him how every time Ozzie had his back turned handling business, you was up in my pussy lovin' it for a minute. Tell Ozzie how I used to suck your dick and you would come begging me for more. Tell him how you were in love with me, and wanted me to love you back, huh . . . but how you hated my love for Twilight and Ozzie and if I was to give the word, you was ready to kill him for me. Tell Ozzie how much shit you used to talk about him and how he was a stupid muthafucka, and you was the one that did the work and had his name buzzing in the streets," Aniyah confessed with a smirk.

Ozzie's grip around the pistol tightened so hard that he was ready to break the gun in half. He didn't face Dink, but looked beyond Aniyah, zoning out somewhere else. But in a chilling tone he asked, "What the fuck is she talkin' about, Dink?"

"The bitch lying to live," Dink said causally.

"Really, nigga? You think I'm lying," Aniyah replied. "You're a snake, Dink, and it's time Ozzie knows the truth about you. Why you think he wants me dead so badly, fearing that I'll talk and let the truth be known when my baby is born and DNA don't lie, nigga. I don't give a fuck about both of y'all niggas anymore."

Ozzie felt betrayed and angry. He turned to Dink and said, "You were ready to stab me in the fuckin' back, nigga . . . over some pussy. You were my nigga, Dink. I loved you like a brother and this is how you do me? Over this bitch?"

Ozzie was on the verge of killing Dink. He had the gun in his hand and a deadly fire of hatred burning within him. Aniyah stood quiet and knew that only one would leave the apartment alive, she just wondered which one. Dink and Ozzie glared at each other intensely.

"You just became weak, nigga. You ain't the same in this game. You let this bitch run over you cuz you thought she loved you and Twilight made a bitch outta you. Nigga, you know what? Fuck you," Dink exclaimed.

Dink suddenly had a .45 pointed at Ozzie and before Ozzie could react, a loud shot was fired into his head and he dropped dead beside Aniyah's feet. Aniyah stepped back wide eyed.

Dink then pointed the gun at her head and said, "You just couldn't keep your fuckin' mouth shut, you dumb bitch. But it was never love between us."

Aniyah stared frightfully down the barrel of his gun, waiting for something to happen. A loud shot went off, but Aniyah wasn't the one shot. The side of Dink's head exploded and he dropped dead not too far from Ozzie's body. Aniyah turned and saw Jazz holding the smoking gun in her hand.

"Fuck them both," Jazz cried out.

She went up to Aniyah, consoling her boo. "You okay, baby?"

Aniyah nodded.

"Go get dressed. We gettin' the fuck outta this city for good. I told you that you wouldn't have to worry about these niggas anymore. I took care of everything," Jazz said.

Aniyah ran into the bedroom to pack, while Jazz looked down at the bodies. She was a sneaky and bad bitch, laying out the traps and knowing niggas would fall for the bait. She took out Twilight knowing he would always be a threat to her relationship with Aniyah and knowing he was the one behind Damien being killed. So he had to go. And she was the one who called Ozzie with the information about Aniyah, knowing he would become so ticked and pissed off he would come running to the apartment upset and as always wanting to beat on her. It was only a matter of time before both men would fall.

Jazz looked down at the bodies and said, "Niggas is so fuckin' predictable, especially over some pussy."

She was waiting for Twilight and Ozzie to kill each other, but they couldn't even do that right. So she stepped in and took them all out.

Twenty minutes later, Aniyah was packed and ready to leave town with Jazz. They hugged and kissed each other. Jazz had her car parked outside the building and was ready to disappear with her boo. Both girls rushed outside, planning to call 911 when they were far away from the apartment.

Jazz threw Aniyah's bags in the trunk and Aniyah jumped in on the passenger side. She definitely wanted a change, especially after all the bloodshed and abuse she endured. She asked no questions where they were going, but just wanted to go. She thought about Twilight, and still had love for him, but Jazz was something different and refreshing—especially with a baby on the way.

Jazz was smiling when she walked toward the driver's side, and Aniyah was pleased too. But that pleasing feeling was short-lived when unexpectedly the back of Jazz's head exploded brutally and she fell slumped against the car with her blood and brains all over the hood and windshield. Aniyah screamed out frantically. She was in shock by the sudden murder of her friend/lover and the dreams of happiness she'd allowed herself to believe in.

Suddenly the passenger door flew open and Knocky approached Aniyah with a wild distraught look and shouted, "Where the fuck you goin' carrying my baby!"

SNAKE EYES

BY

MARK ANTHONY

ONE

BROOKLYN, NEW YORK 2:00 AM

When me and my girl crossed the Brooklyn Bridge and maneuvered toward the club, which was located on Flatbush Avenue, the scene we saw as we drove closer to the club was absolutely bananas! There were people and cars everywhere. The line to get inside the club stretched about a block-and-a-half long. And there was just this buzz of excitement that filled the air, and it let you know that other than where we were at, there was no other place to be in New York City.

I had been on the run for more than a year. And more specifically, I had been hiding out in Philly with my new girl for the past six months. Although Philly was about a two-hour drive from Brooklyn, New York, word about a club called the Brooklyn Café had spread all over the East Coast, and news about the club had reached Philly.

Word on the street was that the Brooklyn Café had it going on! It was part strip club on one level and a hip-hop/reggae club on the other level.

But what made me risk my freedom and travel to New York to see firsthand what Brooklyn Café was all about was the fact that I had heard that my mans and 'em, Squeeze and Show, actually owned Brooklyn Café. I desperately wanted to get back to New York to link up with Squeeze and Show, but knew I had the feds and the NYPD looking for me, so I had to be careful.

My girl, who I had met in Philly, was a Puerto Rican chick who had a body like J-Lo and an attitude like Eve. Her name was Marissa, and she also wanted to come with me to New York to see what all the hype was about concerning Brooklyn Café.

We let the valet park Marissa's silver 745 BMW, and the two of us headed straight to the front of the line and searched for the VIP entrance. There was no way in hell that we was gonna wait on that long-ass line!

"Who y'all wit'?" the bouncer asked us as he put his forearm against my chest and grabbed Marissa by the arm to prevent us from walking inside the club.

"Yo, my man! Are you fucking crazy or what? Don't be putting your hands on my girl like that!"

"Calm down, money. I just wanna know who y'all wit'! I just can't let y'all walk up in here like that. Are y'all on the guest list?"

As I purposely tried to disrespect the bouncer and walk by him, I replied, "Come on, man! We ain't on no list! I own this muthafuckin' club!"

The bouncer was not going for it and he wasn't gonna be easily intimidated by me. He stood at about six-foot-five and looked as if he weighed about 300 pounds. He was wearing one of those tight, black, fitted shiny shirts that showed off his chest and his arms.

"Yo, money, you about to get knocked on your ass right in front of your girl, so I suggest you back da fuck up right now!" the bouncer said as he came right up on my chest.

Coming from inside the club I could hear Fat Joe's smash hit song, "Lean Back," playing in the background.

I lifted my shirt and exposed the handgun that I had in my waistband and I replied, "And yo' big ass is about to get *leaned back* if you don't let me up inside this club!"

I immediately got the bouncer's respect. It was more than just the steel that I had flashed. I got his respect because he knew that the person holding the steel had the balls to use it and wouldn't hesitate to lay his big ass out on the concrete.

Just as the bouncer stepped away from me and as I was about to pull out my gun and blast him, Show happened to be stepping outside of the club's entrance.

Another bouncer had come to the first bouncer's aid. People standing around waiting to get inside the club could tell that something ugly was about to go down.

"Promise?" Show asked with a questioning look on his face.

"What up, nigga!" I yelled as I quickly forgot about the bouncers and gave Show one of the biggest ghetto hugs that I had ever given anyone in my life. As the two of us embraced each other in the most loud and rowdy way, we almost lost our balance and fell to the ground.

"Yo, I ain't know if you was dead or what! Where the hell you been at?"

At that point the bouncer stepped up and asked, "Yo, Show, is dude cool wit' you?"

"Yeah, no doubt! This is my muthafuckin' man right here!"

The bouncer came up to me and attempted to give me a pound as he stated, "Yo, pardon me, I was just doing my job. I . . ."

As Show asked was everything a'ight, I didn't even acknowledge the bouncer. I simply took Marissa by the hand and followed Show into the packed club.

"Yeah, everything is cool, that wasn't nothing," I replied as I began to introduce Marissa to Show.

"Lean Back" was still blasting in the background and people were literally losing their minds on the dance floor doing the Rockaway dance.

I shouted over the song, "Marissa, this is my man Show! He's the one that I had been telling you about! Show, this is my girl Marissa. I'm staying with her out in Philly!"

"Oh word! A'ight, a'ight, yeah, nice to meet you!" Show shouted back as he also scoped out Marissa's body. Marissa was wearing some open-toed high heeled shoes, a miniskirt, and a backless top, and she had tattoos in all the right places.

Marissa began grabbing on me, trying to get me to dance, but I wasn't in the mood for dancing. How could I wanna dance after just being reunited with my peoples, who I hadn't seen in over a year? And now there I was, finally chillin' with them? Right on cue with the song, I recited the lyrics to Marissa: "Niggas don't dance we just pull up our pants, and do the Rockaway, now lean back . . . lean back . . ."

Show led us to the bar, where he got us some drinks, and then he took us to the crowded VIP area, where I immediately saw Squeeze posted up with two broads.

I used to sport braids and I would never have much facial hair, but since I had been on the run, I decided to keep my head bald and to grow out my mustache and goatee.

I wasn't sure if Squeeze immediately recognized me when he saw me, but I had certainly recognized him.

"What up, baby pa?" I said as I looked at Squeeze and attempted to get a pound and a hug from him, all the while interrupting the conversation he had going on with the two broads.

Squeeze paused and looked at me. I couldn't tell what was going on in his mind because I knew that he had to know who I was. After all, I had been his man for years.

"It's Promise!" I replied to Squeeze's blank look.

Squeeze finally snapped out of whatever zone he was in.

"Ohhh shit! Yo, excuse me, ladies. My muthafuckin' nigga Promise! Where the fuck you been at, dog?"

"I been hiding out, nigga. *Jake* is looking for me, kid!"

While lifting his drink to his mouth and purposely showing off his iced-out watch, Squeeze took a sip of his drink and replied, "Yeah, I kinda figured you was on the run. I mean, the news had you on TV like every night for a couple of weeks."

Squeeze then took me to the side so that we were out of earshot from everyone else and asked, "Dog, I been wanting to ask you, what da fuck was you thinking when you popped that cop? And then on top of that, you tossed the gun in the sewer while somebody was watching your every move?"

Actually, I had never known that someone had seen me toss the gun in the sewer. I had just figured that it was good police work that had led them to the murder weapon so quickly.

"Squeeze, on the real, I don't even wanna talk about that right now. I just gotta get my hands on some paper and get my situation correct. The muthafuckin' state got my daughter and the whole nine! And yo, remember that chick Audrey that I was fuckin' wit'?"

"The schoolteacher?"

"Yeah, her . . . well, she got bagged! She doing fed time because of a nigga."

"Get da fuck outta here!" Squeeze replied.

"Word is bond! We was robbing banks down in Virginia, Bonnie and Clyde style, and the feds rolled on us and she got caught out there. But I bounced on them cats and made it to Baltimore. I was hiding out there and hustling out there for a minute. Then I met my girl Marissa, and I been chillin' wit' her for the past six months. Yeah, she's been holding me down. Her man is locked up, but he stashed some paper before he went up, and we been eating off that."

Squeeze shook his head. He took another drink from his cup and looked at me with the cockiest look imaginable. He stuck a toothpick in his mouth and twirled it around and shook his head again while he smiled. "Dog, see, you in the predicament that you in 'cause you started to lose that hunger! You kna'imean?"

The music was blasting inside the club and I could barely hear what Squeeze was saying. Marissa spoke into my ear and she told me that she was gonna head down to the dance floor. I instructed her to meet me in the strip club area in about fifteen or twenty minutes.

I replied to Squeeze because I didn't know where he was coming from. "Whatchu talkin' about, kid?"

"Come on, man! You know exactly what I'm talking about. You started getting soft on niggas! You started losing that thirst for the streets. And that's why right after Pooh got killed, when me and Show started coming up and we got this club and we took over the Tompkins Houses, it didn't even phase me that you wasn't around to trick off on all the cake that we been getting."

I looked at Squeeze and before I could comment he replied, "Yo, dude, I'm just keepin' it real wit' you. I mean, a lotta cats, if they ain't see you in a year, and y'all had been running together back in the days, they would look at you and tell you '*it's all love*' and invite you right back into the mix to get this cake together. But I'm sayin,' you know me, dude! And you know how I gets down. We boyz and all, but I'm just sayin' . . ."

As I stood there and listened to Squeeze spit and sound arrogant like he was the man, I couldn't help but get heated. I knew how to cut to the chase and get right to the heart of what Squeeze was getting at.

Although I was heated, I managed to drum up a fake smile, but as I began to speak, Squeeze cut me off and continued feeling himself.

"I mean, look at tonight for example. You come up in *my* spot wit' your bad-ass Puerto Rican chick, talkin' about how she's been holding you down wit' *her man's money*? I mean, come on, kid! Even if you are on the run, nigga, you gotta get out there and get yours!"

I looked at Squeeze and the only thing that I could say was, "What da' fuck?"

"Promise, you my man, but I'm just sayin', I gotta tell you what you need to hear. And straight up on the real, you gotta decide what you want! Is it leeching off these hoes? Is it your daughter? Or is it this paper?" Squeeze stated while pulling out a knot of hundred-dollar bills.

I was heated! But I had to remain on the humble, because I wasn't in no position to come at Squeeze in any other way. See, one thing about niggas is that if you let them talk long enough, eventually whatever is in their heart will come out of their mouth. And from what Squeeze was spittin' at me, he was basically saying that the fact that we had been boyz for years, that didn't mean shit. And the fact that we had done countless stick-ups together, that too didn't mean shit.

Money definitely changes niggas. And wit' Squeeze, he was making it clear to me that he didn't give a damn about me and my situation. The only thing that he cared about was his money.

Back in the days, if a cat had to go up north and do a bid, he could always count on his homeboyz for holding down his spot for him until he did his time. And in my case, it definitely should have been the same way. I had been on the run for a year, not because I wanted to be, but because of the cards that I had been dealt.

Matter of fact, it was Squeeze who had called me and told me that Pooh had been shot and that him and Show were ready to ride on Nine and his crew. I guess that my only mistake was trying to be a real nigga and be there for my crew. Yeah, and look where that got my ass? It left me assed out! If I'da stayed my ass home wit' Audrey that night, then I never would have been in the position to shoot the cop. And I never would have had to rob banks and all of that nonsense! But it was a'ight, though. Squeeze was helping me to see niggas for their true colors. I knew just how to play the game.

"Squeeze, I feel you, man!" I said as I gave him a pound. "You right. I gotta decide what it is that I want and just go after it. I had been thinking that and that's the main reason that I came back to Brooklyn tonight. I mean, I was like, fuck it! Fuck the feds and fuck the police! I knew that I had to link back up wit' y'all and just get busy, and I'm ready for whatever."

I was just attempting to tell Squeeze what he wanted to hear, but he wasn't buying it. I could sense that he wasn't.

"So what exactly are you sayin'?" Squeeze asked.

"What I'm sayin' is I need to get this paper! My niggas is holding figgaz, I been laying low and outta the game and I'm ready to do what I gotta do."

Squeeze attempted to play me as he sarcastically responded, "So in other words, you need some money and instead of just asking me to hit you off wit' some dough, you gonna stand here and front like you still gangsta!" Squeeze began to laugh as he shouted, "Oh my gawd! Niggas is funny! Word is bond!"

Again, I held my position and remained humble as Squeeze continued to play me.

Trying to switch gears I replied, "Yo, take me to see the strippers in the strip club. Introduce your boy to some pussy!"

Squeeze smiled as he put his drink down and led me to the strip club. As we walked I shouted, "Yo, gimme your cell number so I can program it into my phone!"

I know that Squeeze heard me but he ignored me and kept walking.

I pulled out my cell phone and began programming Squeeze's info into the cell phone.

"Yo, Squeeze, what's your number, kid?"

"My cell?"

"Yeah."

"Let me give it to you in a few days 'cause too many people got this number and I'm about to switch it up."

"Oh, a'ight," I replied.

As we made it to the strip club area, I could see Marissa chillin' wit' Show. And before we reached where they were standing, I attempted to get some more info from Squeeze.

"So, Squeeze, how much are y'all niggas holding? What exactly are y'all sittin' on?"

"What da fuck? You working with the feds or what?" Squeeze asked me as he patted me down, acting as if he was checking for a wire. He tried to play like he was joking, but I knew what time it was.

"Son, it ain't like last year, kid. We holding some major paper. But I'll bring you up to speed. Just chill and have a good time tonight."

Marissa was mad cool and she didn't trip about all of the guys losing their minds over the thick strippers that were in the joint. In fact, she even paid for a lap dance for me.

Show was definitely feeling Marissa's style, and just from the vibe that he had been giving off, I could tell that he was still really my man. Or at least it seemed that way. He had given me his home and his cell number and told me that he had bought a crib out in the Canarsie section of Brooklyn.

From the looks of everything, I could clearly see how Show could afford the cribs in that area. The club had to be making money hand over fist, and I knew that Show and Squeeze were getting other kinds of money, but I just didn't know all the ins and outs.

From the cocky way Squeeze had been acting all night long, it wasn't long before I was ready to bounce. I just couldn't take the way he was feeling himself. And I also had the real uneasy feeling that there were plainclothes cops all over the place inside the club. All of my instincts were telling me to get the hell out of the club, so that was exactly what I did.

Marissa wanted to stay and enjoy herself, but I explained to her why we had to bounce and she clearly understood. Before we left, Show handed me $500 dollars and he hugged me and said, "Bring yo' ass back to New York and let's get this money, nigga!"

"No question, kid! I'ma holla at you tomorrow."

Squeeze pretended to be wishing me the best as I prepared to leave, but I could see right through his phony ass.

"Yo, Show, that nigga Promise is working wit' the feds. Tell him not to bring his ass 'round here no more!" Squeeze stated as he began laughing and stretched out his hand to me for a pound.

"My nigga!" Squeeze stated as he grabbed my hand and pulled me close to him. In my ear he stated, "You still my dog fo' life. Just let me know what you wanna do."

"No doubt," I replied as I walked out of the club with Marissa. Squeeze walked out with us and waited for the valet to bring us Marissa's car.

As we waited for our car, I couldn't help but have that paranoid feeling that undercovers were everywhere and that people knew my face and knew what I was wanted for. It's a constantly-looking-over-your-shoulder feeling that's hard to describe, and only cats who've been on the run can relate to that feeling. Not to mention that only a month ago the TV show *America's Most Wanted* had done a segment on me, so I was really paranoid everywhere I went.

Fortunately, Marissa and I made it on to the New Jersey Turnpike south, and I was able to breathe a little as I felt somewhat safe.

As we drove, Marissa asked, "What's up wit' your boy Squeeze?"

"What?" I asked.

"Homeboy is on some other shit! I don't know what it is, but he ain't really real."

"You peeped that too, right?"

"Yeah, the nigga just come across like *he the man*. Like his shit don't stink. I don't know about that dude. You should just chill out here in Philly wit' me and try to get something going wit' these Philly cats. 'Cause that nigga Squeeze, he come across like a snake-type nigga."

Marissa was right on the money and she had only been around Squeeze for a short time. But see, the thing that was motivating me to get back to NY and to try and make some dough out there was the fact that my daughter Ashley was in New York. I couldn't confirm anything, but I had this sick feeling that she was being bounced around foster homes, and that was driving me insane.

My plan was to get to New York, get my hands on some real long money, find out where Ashley was staying so I could straight-up kidnap her and bounce for good out of New York and never return.

So if putting up with Squeeze and his phony ass was gonna get me the things I wanted and get me in touch with my daughter in the shortest amount of time possible, then I was willing to put up with whatever it was that I had to put up with. But at the same time, if that nigga tried to snake me or play me, I wouldn't hesitate to go to war wit' his ass.

TWO

The next day, when I was in Philly, I made numerous attempts to contact Show. I called his crib and I called his cell phone and each time, his phone would just ring out to voicemail. I left the nigga like seven messages and he never called me back, not once.

My head was really spinning, trying to figure out what was up with Show. Maybe Squeeze had started filling his head with some garbage about not messin' wit' me. I didn't know.

As Marissa walked around her house in a red thong and a matching red bra, she reminded me so much of Audrey in terms of the advice she would give me.

"You see this tattoo?" Marissa asked, referring to the tattoo of a pair of yellow and black snake eyes that was on her lower back.

"Yeah." I couldn't help but also stare at Marissa's big Puerto Rican booty.

"I put that tattoo there because cats always wanna get at me because of my body. And they always wanna 'hit it from the back,' and they are always happy as long as they're getting what they want. And see, it's all good when they getting what they want, but I know that even the niggas that I let hit this, as soon as they feel they don't need *it* anymore, those are the *exact* niggas that will snake my ass the fastest. They'll snake me faster than my biggest enemy simply because they feel like they know me better than any of my enemies."

"So? I still don't get the whole reason behind you tattooing the snake eyes on you," I replied.

"Well it's basically like this. Nobody knows a snake better than a snake. And nobody knows how to get back at a snake better than a snake. So niggas might get close to me and then later on try to get over on me and snake me, but it's like my snake-eyes tattoo is letting niggas know that I can be a snake too, and if they try to snake me, I'll come right back at them and snake they ass right back!"

After that long, drawn-out explanation of her tattoo, I sarcastically asked Marissa, "So is there a point to why the hell you brought that up?"

Marissa playfully punched me as she said, "Yeah there's a point to what I'm getting at. What I'm trying to say is that your boy Squeeze is gonna try to snake you, so you better be prepared to strike back and snake his ass, too."

"Yeah, I know that. You right. I don't trust that nigga no more. Especially the way his ass was coming across all sheisty."

Later that night, after Marissa and I had had sex, she fell asleep but I stayed up and watched music videos. It had to be about four o'clock in the morning when I heard some noise outside that sounded like an army of footsteps.

The only light that was on inside the house was the light that was coming from the television in Marissa's room. I immediately turned off the TV, went downstairs and ducked and crawled to the living room window and peeked from behind the burgundy vertical blinds.

"Oh shit!" I said to myself. "Muthafucka!"

Marissa's front yard was crawling with cops who were more than likely about to raid her house in an attempt to capture my ass.

I darted back upstairs to Marissa's second-floor bedroom and violently shook her as I yelled, "Marissa, get the fuck up! Five-O is rolling on me right now!"

Thank God Marissa immediately woke up and she was somewhat in a daze, but she came to her senses very quickly.

As I grabbed my .9 mm handgun, my heart was pounding ten thousand beats a minute. “Hurry up and run downstairs to the door and try to stall them for, like, a minute!” I instructed Marissa.

Marissa quickly grabbed her robe and did exactly as I’d instructed.

I paced back and forth as I quickly weighed my options. Fortunately for me, I had prepared for this situation many times. I had my escape route planned well in advance if the cops ever tried exactly what they were currently trying.

My escape route was out the second-floor window of the bedroom, which was right next to Marissa’s bedroom. The reason being was that right underneath that bedroom window was sort of like a two-foot ledge that I would be able to stand on and launch myself off of and into the neighbor’s yard. That was all assuming that I would be able to clear the neighbor’s ten–foot-high fence in the process.

My belief was that although Marissa’s yard might be filled with cops, the neighbor’s yard was not. And if I were able to make it into the neighbor’s yard with the big fence, then I would be able to buy myself about thirty seconds to a minute of lead time to get away on foot from the pigs.

I stood at the top of Marissa’s steps and gripped the gun and listened to what was going on. I didn’t wanna just open up the window and jump out until I absolutely had to.

Marissa opened the front door but she kept the metal screen door locked, which separated her from the police. Based on what the police were shouting, Marissa must have surprised the cops.

“Can I help you?” Marissa asked.

“Philadelphia police! Open the door right now!”

“Is there a problem?”

I could hear the sound of metal clanging, it sounded as if the cops were trying to pry open the front door.

“You know why we’re here! This is your last warning! Step away from the door!”

As Marissa asked the cops if they had a search warrant, I knew that the cops were not there simply to question people; they were coming in the house and there was no two ways about it!

With the vertical blinds closed and all of the lights off in the house, I darted to the escape window and I made sure not to create much movement at the window.

I attempted to open the escape window, and that was when I realized that I had fucked up big time. Not once had I ever practiced opening the window. The unlocked window was stuck, and it was not budging! I began to panic as I heard all kinds of noise and commotion coming from downstairs.

"Get the fuck outta my house!" I heard Marissa yell.

At that point I knew that the cops were inside the crib.

"Goddamn!" I yelled to myself. I was beyond shook and didn't know what to do or where to go.

"Go!" I heard the cops yell. Then seconds later I heard them yell, "Clear!"

I knew that they were checking room by room, and I ran from the window and hid in a closet that was in the same room.

I could hear mad footsteps and mad noise. I felt like I was in a horror movie, running from Jason or Freddy. My heart was beating so fast I thought the cops could hear it.

I gripped my gun with both hands and hid behind the clothes that were hanging up in the closet. My legs and feet were fully exposed, so if the cops were to open the door I would immediately be busted.

"Clear!" The cops shouted from another room. They were definitely on the second floor of the two-story house.

I looked down and I could see light from a flashlight creeping underneath the closet door. I knew the cops were now in the same room as I was.

"What the fuck? What the fuck? What the fuck?" I cursed to myself.

I didn't know if I should just let them open the door and hope that they wouldn't see me, but I knew that that was a long shot, and the odds would be against me. I also wanted to just bust out of the closet and run, but that would have been an even longer shot.

For some strange reason I remember thinking about my daughter Ashley. And at that point something told me to grab the doorknob. And that is exactly what I did. I took my left hand from off the gun and grabbed hold of the doorknob.

As soon as I grabbed the knob I could feel it slowly being twisted.

I knew that playtime was over and there was no time left to figure out what I was gonna do. I immediately put both of my hands back on the gun and stood off to an angle so that I was not right in front of the door. Although I was nervous as hell, I made sure not to make any noise.

Before I knew what was what, the door violently swung open.

I began screaming, "Muthafucka!" At the same time, I rapidly fired three shots.

"Gun!" one of the cops yelled.

I knew that one of the cops had gotten hit, and I couldn't tell if the other cops were shooting back at me or what. Maybe it was my shots ricocheting off their protective shields that some of the cops were carrying.

My shots had definitely caught the cops off guard, and I had a split second to capitalize on them having been surprised. As I yelled, I continued firing shots and I bolted from the closet. When I was about three feet from the escape window I closed my eyes and dove headfirst out the window, breaking the glass and everything.

THREE

"Ahhhhhh!" I yelled as glass shattered and numerous shots rang out from what sounded like every direction. The advantage that I had was that the cops didn't want to get hit by their own friendly fire, so they had to hold back somewhat as they fired at me. And the craziness and boldness of me jumping out of the window was my other advantage.

It was pitch black outside and I hoped and prayed like hell that I would clear the neighbor's fence before I hit the ground. The move was mad risky on my part because I couldn't see where I was going and I could have literally killed myself. But I had no other options and I had to do what I had to do.

In a matter of seconds, I came crashing down, face- and body-first, into the neighbor's garbage cans. The crashing sound was tremendous! Glass rained down on top of me. The wind had been completely knocked out of me, and all kinds of pain shot through my body. I was going off adrenaline as I quickly made it to my feet. I stumbled a bit and tried to gather myself.

Shots were being fired at me from what sounded like shotguns as well as handguns. I didn't wanna waste any time shooting back at the cops, but the truth was it wouldn't have mattered because I had dropped my gun when I jumped out of the window and it was too dark to look for it, not to mention, I didn't have the time to look for it.

I got my wits together and I immediately hauled ass, jumping over neighboring fences. I could tell that the cops would soon be right on my tail as I heard all kinds of commotion, yelling, tire screeching, and numerous police sirens.

Somehow I made it into an alley and came across an abandoned car that looked as if it had been stripped for its parts. The tires and everything were missing as the car sat only on its four axles. The abandoned car was extremely close to the ground and it didn't look as if a human being could fit underneath it.

That was my only hiding spot and chance of escape. I knew that and I had to act quickly. I dropped to my stomach and forced myself to squeeze underneath the car. I scraped so much of my flesh in the process, but that was my least worry. I squirmed and squirmed, as I wanted to make sure that all of my body was fully underneath the abandoned car. I could barely breathe due to the weight of the car pressing down on me, which barely left any room for my lungs to contract and expand. Since I was hyperventilating due to nervousness, I was in a very tough predicament.

It was a hot and humid summer night, and I was sweating my balls off!

Suddenly I heard footsteps.

I could only look one way because there was absolutely no room for my head to fully turn. I tried to force myself not to breathe, but I was out of breath from running, and the pressure of the car on top of me forced me to breathe real heavily. I was afraid that the cops might hear that.

"I know that black bastard is out here somewhere," one of the cops said.

My heart continued to pound into the pavement. I saw at least six sets of feet, and I knew that there had to be more cops than that, but I just couldn't see them all.

Then things just got really quiet. And I saw the six sets of feet briskly walking off.

"Just chill right here, Promise," I told myself as I wondered whether the cops had seen me and whether they were just frontin' like they were walking away, in order to bait me out of my hiding spot.

I didn't know. But I did know that it didn't make any sense to take a chance on coming out of my hiding spot, so I just lay face down on the ground and tried to calm down.

Then I saw more feet.

"Goddamn!" I thought.

"Who got hit?" one cop asked another.

"Schwartz got hit, and so did the bitch! She took one in the neck and Schwartz got hit on the wrist."

"Anybody else?"

"That's all we got so far, but it could be more. I bet you that bitch fucked up the raid! This job ain't meant for no woman!"

From what I could make out, the cops had to be talking about their co-workers, who I'd shot.

"No way! We can't just blame it on her because she's a woman. It's that motherfucking criminal bastard! Can you believe the balls on that cocksucker? I tell you what, if I see his ass out here, I'm blasting him! I don't give a shit if he's armed or not. Shit, call Al Sharpton, call Jesse Jackson, I don't care. I'll shoot that bastard in the back of his head if I see him!"

"I'm with you on that. And I didn't see anything when the district attorney questions me on it."

See? That was exactly why I didn't care about bussin' down a cop! It's like they got they own little gang or something. I couldn't believe how they were talking.

As I continued to lie on the ground, the entire area around me became bright as daylight. The sound of a helicopter hovered above and it must have been shining its searchlight down on the ground.

"Just relax. They don't know where you at," I told myself.

I lay on that ground for hours. The sun had come up and I was still on the ground underneath the abandoned car. It had to have been at least five hours since I'd made it underneath the car and cops were still mulling around, checking for me and checking for clues.

I had been smoking weed and drinking Hennessy all night long up until the cops had showed up at Marissa's. But I had never made it to the goddamn bathroom and I had to shit and piss like a muthafucka!

There was still no way that I was gonna take a chance and come from underneath that car, and I literally couldn't hold it no more. So right there on the ground, I straight pissed in my pants. All that Hennessy was coming out of me by the gallon!

My stomach and my legs and my crotch got warm as hell from the hot piss, but I had to do what I had to do. I just was hoping that the piss wouldn't start to roll from underneath the car. But I felt confident that my clothes would absorb it all.

Pissing had solved one of my problems, but I still had to take a shit in the worst way! I was ready to shit in my pants just to get some relief, but I couldn't take the chance on the smell possibly giving me away. So I clinched up my butt cheeks and held on for as long as I could.

As I lay there, scraped up, swimming in my own piss and in pain, I got more vexed by the minute. "That nigga Squeeze had to tip off the cops!" I convinced myself.

I was coming to that conclusion because I just found it too much of a coincidence that right after I had visited the Brooklyn Café, and Squeeze was acting all shady, that's when the cops show up. Come on! Any nigga wit' common sense could put that together and know what was up.

But the thing I couldn't figure out was why would the nigga do me so dirty? I had been his man for life! And I always had the nigga's back, no matter what.

Maybe him and Show was seeing some major figures and he didn't wanna split none of it wit' me? But if that was the case, cool. I would have been like, whateva. But I'm sayin', if the nigga ratted me out, then he is beyond foul! Niggas don't do they mans and 'nem like that! Word!

More hours passed by and I was still face down on the ground, smelling like piss. I had endured an entire day underneath the car, a day of intense summer heat and humidity. A number of times I felt like I was gonna pass out from the heat.

Nighttime rolled back around, and that shit that I had to take from earlier in the day, well, it managed to creep back up on me. Soon it would be a total of twenty-four hours since I'd been underneath the car, but my freedom was at stake so I still wasn't confident that I should come out from underneath the car. Yet I still had to shit!

I couldn't hold it anymore. So right there I shitted on myself. And since I don't know how to shit without pissing, I also pissed on myself again. This had to be the absolute lowest point in my life, bar none!

As I lay there in my own shit, I further convinced myself that Squeeze had ratted me out. And what pissed me off was that I wouldn't have been on the run and dealing with all that I was dealing wit' if the muthafuckin' rat bastard Squeeze hadn't called me and begged my ass to ride with them when they were rolling on Nine and his crew that night.

I vowed to myself that if I made it up out of this present situation without getting bagged, I was gonna go all out and get back at Squeeze and his punk ass! Even if I had to murk him, I was willing to do it.

I was certain that he had gotten Marissa's license plate or something when he walked us out of the club that night. That had to be how the cops rolled on me. How else would they have known where I was resting at?

About two more hours passed by and I just couldn't take it anymore. If the cops were still staking out the area that I was in, then I would just have to take the loss. But I was ready to come out.

There was no easy way for me to get from underneath the car. In fact, it seemed like it was harder for me to get out than it had been for me to originally get under it. Fortunately, I finally did manage to free myself.

As I stood up and brushed myself off, I remember feeling very lightheaded and mad nervous. My wrists, arms, and chin were scraped up from the concrete, and I smelled worse than a street bum in Times Square. Dogs were barking and I wanted to get out of that location as soon as possible so I could take off my pants and get out of my underwear, which had been violated with feces.

So that I wouldn't leave any evidence lying around, I decided to keep on my underwear and just troop it. My pants were sagging real low; not because I was trying to be stylish, they were sagging because of the crap that was in my underwear! I couldn't walk as fast as I wanted so I had to walk real gingerly.

I had no money on me and I knew I definitely couldn't take a chance on calling or going back to Marissa's house. I figured that every cop in the city was working overtime looking for my black ass, so I had to be real careful about where I went and who I reached out to.

Marissa lived in an area known as Mt. Airy. And other than her, I didn't know too many people in Mt. Airy who would be cool enough to let me hide out at their crib. Plus, I knew the cops would have some type of financial reward for anyone who would rat me out and turn my black ass in, so I wasn't trying to hide out with just anybody.

The only person that I could think of who was *street* enough and cool enough to not rat on me and turn my ass in, was this cat name Grams. I had met Grams when I first came to Philly. I would buy some bags of weed from him and we would kick it with each other. He was from Philly all of his life, but he knew a whole lot of people from New York, so maybe that was why the two of us was cool wit' each other from the jump.

I had hung out at his crib a few times and I knew he lived not too far from Mt. Airy in a section called Glenside. Glenside was about three miles or so away from Mt. Airy and since I didn't know the Philly streets like I knew the New York streets, I had to take the only route to Glenside that I knew, which meant that I had to walk down Wadsworth Avenue.

Although it was a real late hour, I just knew in my heart that somebody on Wadsworth Avenue was gonna recognize me, or a cop on patrol was gonna spot me and bag my ass. The funny thing about being wanted by the police is that you really get paranoid and think the whole world knows you and is concerned with you. But as I walked, I had to remind myself that most people wouldn't be able to recognize me that easily.

My heart pounded as I walked toward Grams' crib in Glenside. I tried to walk as calmly and as coolly as I possibly could with a sack-load of shit in my pants, and I hoped like hell that Grams was home.

Finally, after about forty-five minutes of walking, I had reached Grams' crib. All of the lights were out inside his house, and I wondered what I should do. I mean, I didn't exactly know his living situation that good, and I didn't wanna be interrupting anything. But since I didn't have many options, I began ringing his doorbell.

I rang the doorbell for about five minutes and got no answer. Then I began knocking on the door. I didn't wanna knock too loudly, because I didn't want any of the neighbors to look out their windows and get suspicious about me. But finally, after about two more minutes, Grams came to the door.

"Yo, who da fuck is at my door at this time of night?" Grams growled with an obvious attitude.

"Grams, what up, baby pa? It's me, Promise."

"Who?"

"Promise, from New York! Yo, I'm in some shit! Open up the door."

Grams opened the door. He was real groggy and I could tell I had woke him up. He had on some slippers, boxer shorts, and a white wife-beater.

"Oh! What da fuck? It's you. What up, nigga?" Grams asked as he reached to give me a pound.

As I stuck out my hand, Grams let out a yell of disgust.

"Ohhhh shit! What the hell is that smell? Nigga, where you been at!? You smell like muthafuckin' shit! You drunk, nigga?"

"Nah, nah, I ain't drunk. Yo, it's a long story. I'll fill you in, but on the real, I need somewhere to stay tonight. I ain't got no cake on me or nothing."

"Where your girl at?" Grams asked, sounding like he didn't wanna take my smelly ass in.

"Honestly, I don't even know. A'ight, look. Grams, you like one of the only niggas that I vibe wit' out here in Philly. So I can be straight up wit' you and don't have to worry about you opening your mouth. You kna'imean? You a real nigga and real recognize real!"

"Fo' sho'!" Grams replied.

"A'ight, check it. I ain't never told nobody in Philly this, nobody except for Marissa. But before I came to Philly, I stayed in B-More for a minute, and that was because I was on the run and I'm still on the run. And shit just got a whole lot thicker."

"What's up, kid?"

"About a year ago when I was in New York doing my thing, I got into a situation and I bussed down a cop!"

"Get da fuck outta here? Did he die?"

"Hell yeah, he died!"

"Yeeeah! My muthafuckin' nigga Promise! Killing cops! My nigga!" Grams said as he reached out his hand to congratulate me.

Then he spoke up as if a revelation had hit him.

"Yo, somebody just shot like nine fuckin' cops in Mt. Airy! It was all over the news."

"Nine cops?" I asked.

"Yeah, and the nigga was on some ol' Larry Davis-type shit. He jumped out the window and everything and the cops didn't even catch his ass."

"Goddamn!" I said out loud. I became more frustrated because I knew I couldn't have shot no nine cops. Even when I overheard the cops talking while I was under the car, they said two cops had gotten hit. If it'd been nine cops, they would have known.

Some of those cops had to have been hit by bullets from other cops' guns. I wasn't sure how many rounds I had let off, but I didn't think it was no nine rounds. But truth be told, it didn't matter because if the cops were to catch me, they were gonna get me on all nine counts.

"So tell me, what's up, nigga?"

"Them cops that you talking about that got shot over in Mt. Airy, that was me who shot they ass."

"Get da fuck outta here! Say word?"

"Word is bond! I was chillin' at Marissa's crib and the cops came and raided the joint. Luckily, I got hip to what was about to go down. So I hid in a closet, and when them pigs opened the closet door, I was like *bla-dow bla-dow bla-dow*! I shot at them niggas and bolted from the closet and jumped out the window like fuckin' Rambo!"

"You for real, nigga?"

"Yeah, I'm for real! And then I hid out for damn near more than twenty-four hours underneath this abandoned car in some alley. And they couldn't find my ass. That's how I ended up like this, all smelly like shit! I was under that got-damn car for so long and the car was so low to the ground it was pushing down on my back. I had to piss and take a shit so I just did it right there on myself underneath the car while I was hiding out."

"Damn, Promise! You one grimey-ass nigga! So that's how y'all New York cats get down?"

"Yeah, kid," I said as I nodded my head. "I had to do what I had to do. And yo, the feds is after me for these banks that I robbed while I was in Virginia. The shit is just crazy!"

"Yo, stay right there. I'ma be right back," Grams said.

I stood there in front of his crib and I was desperately hoping that he would lookout for a nigga.

A smile lit up my face as Grams returned with a plastic garbage bag and some clothes in his hand.

"Yo, go on the side of the house, strip outta them clothes and throw those clothes away in that garbage can right there. Put them in this bag first. Here, this is some gear that you can rock. You can chill here and figure things out.

But after you throw those clothes away, come inside and take a shower, nigga! Yo' ass stink!"

I was so relieved to hear those words come out of Grams' mouth. And I did exactly as he instructed me to do.

One thing that I know is that a shower had never felt as good as that shower felt at Grams' house that night. As I showered and washed the dried-up feces and piss from my body, I thought about my daughter. I wondered about how she was living. Was she with some family that she didn't want to be with? Was she scared? Did she miss me? Did she think that I had abandoned her?

I got so vexed with frustration over not being in control of my life, and especially for having lost control of my daughter. Ashley was the most important thing in the world to me, and I had to figure out a way to get her back and then just bounce from all of this drama and nonsense. Maybe I could kidnap her and go to Mexico or something. I didn't know.

As I ended my shower I knew that I would see and be reunited with my daughter again. In fact, I felt so strong about it that in my mind, seeing my daughter again was a definite reality for me, not just a possibility. It was definitely going to happen!

And the other thing that was definitely gonna happen was that I was definitely gonna *see* Squeeze and Show. Yeah, I was gonna *see* them two clown-ass niggas!

FOUR

Grams had a cool one-bedroom apartment that he rented. And he let me sleep on the sofa bed that he had in his living room.

The first night I was there, I continued to fill him in on all of the details and criminal dealings I had been involved in. I told him about my daughter, and about Audrey, Pooh, Squeeze, and Show.

Grams couldn't believe that Squeeze wouldn't have welcomed me back with open arms, considering that we had a real history together. But at the same time he knew exactly how sheisty some dudes really were.

"See, one thing I learned about the street is that you learn real fast how to separate the real from the fake. And on the street, it's like the majority of niggas ain't really real," Grams said.

"Yeah, I know."

Grams added, "So yo, this is what I'm sayin'. If you telling me that they own Brooklyn Café, then them niggas gotta be holding some paper. And they got some other hustles going on? Yo, them niggas don't know me, so I ain't got no problem running up on them niggas and making them come up off they shit."

I smiled as I listened to Grams talk. Although he wasn't from New York, he had the spirit of a real street dude, and I liked and respected that. Listening to him talk reminded me a whole lot of the days I'd spent in the basement in Brooklyn, when we used to sit around and plot and scheme on how we was gonna get money.

I really had no choice but to trust Grams. But I knew that even trusting him was risky because of the fact that he could easily talk a good game and then turn around and rat me out just to collect on the hundred grand, or whatever the reward amount was that the police were offering for someone to turn my black criminal ass in.

If it turned out that Grams could be trusted, then I would respect him for as long as I lived. . He didn't even know me that well and yet he was willing to take me in, give me some of his gear to rock, feed me, and risk robbing Squeeze and Show rather than going after the easy reward money that the police were offering.

As Grams and I talked, he could sense how badly I wanted to get back at that nigga Squeeze for ratting me out to the police. But he had some real good advice that I heeded to.

"Promise, listen to me. You and I both know that Squeeze and Show are holding some real long money right now. You definitely need some dough, and hell, I need some money. Who da fuck doesn't need money? But you gotta be smart and move real slow."

"Fuck dat! I'm ready to move on them niggas right now! They had me under a car, laying in my own crap for more than twenty-four hours, like a fucking animal!"

"Promise, I know that. But trust me. I know how the streets work and how to operate in the game. And what you gotta do is just chill here at my crib, lay low for a few weeks. Give it about three weeks and let some of the heat die down. Don't even come outside or nothing. And then what you do is, you call Show just before you're ready to come out of hiding. But you don't get at him or Squeeze for dissin' you and rattin' on you. You don't even bring it up. You just play things cool, like everything is a'ight wit' you. You gotta do that just to feel them out and not let them suspect that you're about to hit they asses!"

"Grams, I feel you and I know where you coming from, but dog, I can't just sit here on this anger for three weeks!"

"Promise, trust me. You see how them terrorist cats did the United States on 9/11? Bin Laden and 'nem was patient for years! But when they hit us, everybody felt it! And that's how you gotta hit Squeeze and Show! Hit them niggas when they least expect it and make them muthafuckas respect yo ass!"

Grams was right. There was no sense in me striking too soon or reacting too emotionally. 'Cause all that would have done was got my ass locked up. I knew that Grams was really hot on this scheme for me to get back at Squeeze and Show simply because he was seeing a whole lot of dollar signs. But whatever his motivation was—even if it was truly about money—I was just glad I had him in my corner.

FIVE

The three weeks in Grams' crib felt more like three years. I couldn't remember the last time I had been in one spot for so long. I was alone in Grams' crib for the majority of the days I spent there. He would be out on the street hustlin' for most of the day and would only come back to his crib late at night to crash. The stay at his crib over the past few weeks had confirmed to me that I definitely didn't want any parts of the prison system. Not that his crib felt like being locked up. It was just the isolation that I couldn't take. I knew I would go absolutely crazy if my ass was caged up in some goddamn cell.

I was more than tired of eating chicken wings and French fries from the Chinese restaurant. I was tired of all of the trash television shows and tired of watching the news reports that focused on the nationwide manhunt for me. And I was tired of wearing Grams' gear.

On the twenty-first day of hiding out in Grams crib I decided to call Show and feel the nigga out. I called from Grams' phone and I made sure to block the number before I dialed. But each time I called Show's numbers, both his cell and his home number would ring out to voicemail.

So I decided to take a chance and unblock Grams' number before dialing Show. And the same thing happened each time: goddamn voicemail!

This went on for literally two days! For two days I got nothing but the nigga's voicemail. So then I decided to try something else to see if it would work. I decided to call this chick that lived in a section of Queens called Rochdale Village. Her name was Candy and she had been on my dick since high school.

Candy was the type of chick, who if she was feeling you, she would let you have uncommitted recreational sex (without foreplay). And she wouldn't trip about a nigga having a girl or not spending enough time with her and all of that. She would even spend money on a nigga and not expect nothing in return. Candy wasn't exactly a jump-off or anything like that. She was just mad cool. She looked a'ight and her body was a'ight. She had things going for herself. She had a good job with the Transit Authority, she had her own apartment, and the whole nine. But the bottom line was that she was feeling a nigga.

I didn't have Candy's cell phone number but I had her home phone number memorized and I immediately dialed her to see what was up.

The phone rang like six times and then her answering machine came on.

"Damn!" I said to myself. I knew that I had to leave a message but I just didn't feel too comfortable leaving her Grams' number as a callback number.

I began speaking to the answering machine, "Yo, Candy! What's up Ma Ma? This is Promise. I know that—"

"Hello," a voice on the other end said, while stopping the old-school answering machine.

"Candy?"

"Promise, I know this is not you calling me! AHHHH!!! Hey, what's up, Boo?" Candy was obviously glad to speak to me.

"Candy, I know that I ain't speak to you in a minute, and I ain't gonna even sit on this phone and front. But I'm calling you because I need a favor from you."

"OK, what's up?"

"I know you probably saw all of the shit on the news about how the cops is looking for me and all of that, right?"

"Yeah, I know all about that."

"Well, I've been laying low and I can't really tell you what's up just yet, but

I promise I'll let you know what's up."

"Promise, listen. You ain't got to explain nothing to me. How long have we known each other? Come on, now," Candy replied.

I laughed a little bit into the phone's receiver.

"So, what's up? You need some place to stay for a few days?"

I actually hadn't even considered staying with Candy but since she'd brought it up I decided to capitalize on the offer.

"Well, actually, if I could stay wit' you for a few days it would really help me out—"

Candy cut me off as she said, "Promise, it's done! You know I always got you. You remember which building I live in, right?"

"Yeah, I do. But I might not come through for another day or two. I'm not sure when."

"Well, I gotta work the next few days, so I'll be home every night this week. If you come through, just make sure that it's after eight at night."

"That's what's up!" I replied. Then I added, "Candy, you remember Show, right?"

"Of course!"

"A'ight listen, get a pen and take down his cell phone number. I want you to call him for me, but I need you to three-way him. And check it, I don't want you to let him know that I'm on the other end of the phone. OK?"

"OK," Candy replied, "What's the number?"

I proceeded to give Candy the number and then I instructed her that if Show asked her how she got his number, that she was to say that she had bumped into me on Flatbush Avenue a couple of weeks ago when I was leaving Brooklyn Café and that I had given her Show's number and told her that I would be staying at Show's crib. And the reason that she was calling was because she hadn't heard from me since that night.

"OK," Candy replied.

"Candy, are you sure you got what I said?" I asked.

"Yes, Promise!"

"OK, call him now, and make sure that your phone number ain't blocked when you call him. And just get into some small talk if you have to but make sure you don't tell him that I'm on the phone."

"OK, OK, now be quiet, it's ringing."

I put my phone on mute so that my voice wouldn't be heard.

Show's phone rang two times and the nigga picked right up.

Ain't that a bitch, I thought.

"Hello? Who this?" Show asked.

"What's up, Show? This is Candy."

"Candy who?"

"Come on now, Show! You know which Candy this is."

"Candy from Rochdale?"

"Yes."

"Oh, what's up, ma? I ain't speak to you in a minute. Where you been at? How did you get my number?"

"I got your number from Promise. He gave it to me the other night when he was leaving Brooklyn Café. He told me that he was gonna be staying with you and if I needed to reach him, that I should call you."

"Oh word? I don't know why da fuck he told you that! That nigga ain't staying wit' me. That nigga got too much heat surrounding his ass."

"But do you have a number where I can reach him or anything, 'cause I gave him my number and he ain't even call me or nothing."

"Nah I ain't got no numbers for him. But yo, fuck dat nigga. If you wanna hang out, you need to come to the spot, to Brooklyn Café. You know me and Squeeze own that spot now, right?"

"Yeah, I know. Me and my girls gonna come through and check it out. We might come through in a few weeks. It's still free for city workers to get in, right?"

"Yeah but you ain't gotta worry about that. Just call me when you wanna come and I'll put you on the guest list."

"A'ight, no doubt. Well, I gotta go. If you hear from Promise, tell him that I called for him."

"I doubt I'll speak to him, but if I hear from him I'll let him know."

With that, I hung up the phone and so did Show and Candy. And I immediately called Candy right back.

"Hello."

"Yeah, Candy. It's me, Promise."

"I didn't know y'all wasn't cool no more. What happened?"

"It's a long story. I'll explain it to you when I see you. But listen: if Show or anybody calls you or comes by your apartment, make sure that you tell them you haven't heard from me or seen me or anything. OK?"

"OK."

Before hanging up, I made sure that I took down Candy's cell phone number. After hanging up the phone with Candy, the first thing that I said to myself was, "Them niggas is on some bullshit!"

That three-way phone called had confirmed to me that Show and Squeeze both were acting in tandem and both were purposely dissin' my ass.

Show had picked up the phone right away when he saw a New York area code on his caller ID, but when I had been calling him from a Philly area code or from a blocked number, and even after leaving him messages telling him that I was gonna be calling him, he was nowhere to be found.

"Fuck that nigga!" I said to myself.

Later that night, when Grams came home, he relayed a message to me from Marissa. She basically just wanted to let me know that she was doing okay and that in case she and I didn't speak for a while, under the circumstances she completely understood. Marissa also told Grams to make sure that he told me that the cops had questioned her for hours but she hadn't given them any information.

Considering how a year ago I had wrecked Audrey's life, I was glad to hear that Marissa was doing okay. But I have to admit that I thought Grams had used bad judgment by even discussing me with Marissa. I wanted to press him on why he'd said anything at all to Marissa or how did Marissa know to ask him about me, but I decided not to mention it all. I still needed Grams' help and I didn't wanna piss the nigga off in any way.

It was a Thursday night and instinctively I knew that within the next twenty-four hours I had to get out of Grams' crib for good. Otherwise, I would be pressing my luck and really rolling the dice on my freedom.

So instead of questioning Grams on his decision to talk about me in front of Marissa, I decided to switch subjects and bring up what had transpired over the phone with Show.

"Yo, Grams. Tomorrow night, we gotta get to New York and see them niggas Squeeze and Show. Check this shit out: I tried to get in touch with Show, right? I call the nigga's cell and I called his crib. And both phones just kept going to voicemail. So check it, I call this chick from Queens that I'm cool wit', and I have her call Show from her home phone, while I was on three way—"

Grams, who was rolling up some weed, smiled and looked up at me and finished off my words. "And the nigga picked up, right?"

"Yeah, the nigga picked up 'cause he saw a New York area code on his caller ID. But I never said nothing. I stayed quiet and just let him and the chick kick it. And when the chick asked him about me, that bitch-ass nigga starts talking all kinds of underhanded shit! Talkin' about 'fuck dat nigga Promise!'"

Grams took a break from rolling the weed and added, "It's a'ight. You did the right thing. You let that nigga talk. Yo, I'm telling you, just let any nigga talk long enough and you'll know what he's really about."

Grams got up and walked to his closet and retrieved a brown paper bag. He reached inside the bag and pulled out a chrome .38 revolver.

"I know you ain't got no heat, so I got this for you from my man. I got my joint in the other room, so we'll both be strapped. We straight now."

I got up and gave Grams a pound.

"Yo, you said that Squeeze was rocking an iced-out Rolex, right?"

"Yeah."

"So, if worse come to worse, we at least leaving with that watch!"

"Grams, trust me, them niggas is holding cash. The club is a goddamn gold mine! They gotta have cash up in that club and we leaving wit' it, and with the watch and whatever else we want!"

By that time Grams had finished rolling the blunt. He sparked it and the two of us got high as we plotted exactly how we were gonna get Squeeze and Show.

We plotted for about an hour straight. All of our I's were dotted and all of our T's were crossed. The only thing that we had to do at that point was wait for Friday night to roll around.

SIX

I was more than ready to get up out of Grams' crib. It felt like I had been on house arrest or something. But thank God, Friday night had finally come. I was excited about getting back out into civilization, and I was even more excited about getting back to Brooklyn.

Grams had let me borrow another one of his outfits. It was a gray Sean John sweat suit that went well with my all-white Nike Airs. I hoped this would be the last outfit of his that I would have to borrow.

Anyway, it was a little after midnight when me and Grams piled into his black Yukon Denali and headed toward Brooklyn. We made a stop at the gas station and a stop at the McDonald's drive-thru window. From then on there wasn't too much talking as we listened to a G-Unit CD and continued to maneuver toward our destination.

About an hour or so into our drive, when we were about at exit 7 on the New Jersey Turnpike, I got the scare of my life. A New Jersey State Trooper had begun following us. Grams was driving and I had the front passenger seat reclined back as far as it would go.

"Muthafucka!" Grams shouted as he turned down the volume on the CD player.

"What's up?" I asked.

"A state trooper is tailing us."

My heart began pounding as I contemplated my options. I also began to wonder whether someone had spotted me. Maybe the girl in the drive-thru window at McDonald's had spotted me? I didn't know.

"You think he's gonna pull us over?" I nervously asked Grams.

"Hell, yeah! He wouldn't have followed us for this long if he wasn't gonna pull us over."

I really became nervous and contemplated having Grams slow down so that I could bolt from the car. I also thought about having Grams cause a realistic-looking accident just to create a real and major distraction.

"All your paperwork is straight, right?" I asked Grams.

"Yeah, I'm good."

We drove for about two minutes more and then the state trooper signaled for us to pull over.

Grams complied.

"Yo, just lay back in the seat and act like you sleeping," Grams instructed.

I did exactly as he told me.

Thirty seconds later the state trooper came to the window. From the sound of the voice, it sounded as if it was a female officer. A female officer was the last thing we needed. I say that because them women cops always seem like they got something to prove, like they gotta act extra tough and all that.

"How's it going?" the officer asked.

"Everything's good," Grams replied. He didn't sound nervous.

Even with my eyes closed, I could tell that the officer was shining her flashlight into the car. I tried my best to breathe very evenly, but I was scared like a bitch!

As a bunch of cars whizzed by in the background, it created a lot of noise and I could barely hear the officer's voice as she asked, "What's with your friend over there?"

Just chill, I told myself, *and keep your eyes closed.*

Grams responded perfectly. "Oh, he's sleeping. We ate some McDonald's and it messed his stomach up, so he's sleeping it off."

There were McDonald's bags in the front of the truck, so I thought that the officer might buy that line.

"Do you know why I pulled you over?"

"No, I don't," Grams replied with no attitude at all.

"Your windows. The tint is too dark."

"Oh, yeah? I'm sorry about that, officer."

"Let me see your license, registration, and insurance card," the cop said.

Grams complied with her wishes.

"You guys weren't drinking, were you?"

"Nah, we wasn't."

"Where are y'all headed to?" the officer asked.

"To Brooklyn."

"OK, I'm just gonna run your information and write you a ticket for the windows and then you can be on your way."

"OK, officer."

"There's no drugs or guns in the car, are there?"

"Nah, we not into any of that," Grams replied, sounding like a skilled actor.

The officer walked off.

"Promise, she's gone. But yo, you should sit up and act like you up. I think it would look more real when she comes back to the car."

I did exactly as Promise had suggested. I desperately wanted everything to go good because aside from being a wanted fugitive, we also had two guns in the car, duct tape, and a small amount of weed.

"Ah, shit!" Grams yelled.

"What happened?"

"Another state trooper is pulling over. Why the fuck do they need two cars?"

"That bitch made me! I think I should bounce into them woods over there."

"Nah, just chill and relax," Grams said, "They both coming to the car right now. The other cop is on your side of the car."

As the female officer approached the driver's side window, she ordered Grams to step out of the car.

"Is everything okay?" Grams asked. He now was sounding nervous.

"Oh, I see your friend is awake now. Just put your hands on the hood."

The other officer opened my door and told me to step out of the car and to also put my hands on the hood.

"I'm gonna ask you both this time. Are there any guns or drugs in the vehicle?"

"Nah," I said as Grams remained quiet and shook his head no.

Both officers patted us down and then the male officer looked under the front seats and inside the dashboard. But, thank God, he didn't look anywhere else.

"It looks good," the male officer told the female cop.

At that point the cop handed Grams his license and other paperwork and in an attempt to smooth things over, she explained to him that she would let him slide this time on the tinted windows but that he had to get it taken care of quickly.

"I'll make sure it's taken care of tomorrow, officer," Grams replied, sounding like a straight-up house nigger.

With that, the cops went back to their cars and pulled off.

"Holy shit!" I yelled. "Whewwwww!"

"Yo, Promise, word is bond! Nigga, you must have some kind of angel watching over yo' ass or something. I ain't never seen a nigga as lucky as yo' ass!" Grams said as he smiled with relief and pulled back onto the turnpike.

That traffic stop had thrown us way off schedule. We had wanted to get to the club at about 3 AM and scope things out, but now we probably wouldn't get there until around 3:30. But under the circumstances, we couldn't complain at all.

Finally, we did cross the Brooklyn Bridge and were rolling past Brooklyn

Café. There were people and cars everywhere.

"This spot is jumping!" Grams exclaimed.

"I told you!"

Grams and I cruised back and forth in front of the club. There was no place to park and we wanted to be in close proximity to the club so we could quickly bounce to the car when we were done.

It was now four in the morning and although there was a lot going on, you could tell that some people were also starting to leave the club.

"Yo, just park right here near this fire hydrant! We might get a ticket but whateva! We gotta hurry up!"

Grams did as I said. Then he climbed in the back of the truck and retrieved the guns and the duct tape. He handed me the chrome .38 and stuffed his gun in his waistband. He also managed to somehow bend the roll of duct tape so it fit into his back pocket. Then he pulled his shirt down to hide the bulges.

"You think that same bouncer's gonna be at the door tonight?" Grams asked.

"Yeah, he should be; but even if he ain't, I'll get one of them to get Show to let us in so we won't get frisked."

See, I knew now that it was a good thing that I had never tipped my hand to Show or Squeeze as far as being pissed off at them. 'Cause just like Marissa was telling me about the snake eyes, now it was my turn to perform and behave just like a snake in the grass, who out of nowhere just strikes out and attacks yo' ass!

As Grams and I walked across Flatbush Avenue with guns in our waistbands, he stated, "Promise, trust me. With a spot like this there has to be a safe, or some kind of cash box, or something! We leaving this spot with some cash tonight."

As we made it to the front of the club, I immediately recognized the bouncer and I took it upon myself to remove the rope and head toward the VIP entrance.

"Yo, my man what up? Is Show inside?" I asked the bouncer in an attempt to show him a little respect.

The bouncer looked at me and then he recognized who I was. He gave me a pound and was like, "Yeah, yeah he's in there. I don't know where he's at, but he's up in there somewhere."

"A'ight cool. Yo, he's wit' me," I said, referring to Grams.

The bouncer nodded his head. I was hoping that neither he, nor anyone else, would put two and two together and realize that I was the wanted cop killer. I was also desperately hoping that there were no undercovers staking the place out, looking for my ass.

As me and Grams made it inside, we decided to head to the strip club section of the club. Even though we had a mission to accomplish, I hadn't had any ass in three weeks so I at least wanted to look at something and rub up next to something thick, even if just for a minute.

"Son, this is what's up!" Grams stated as we walked around the joint looking at the numerous sexy strippers in their thongs.

We only stayed there for about five minutes and then we bounced. I began asking the different bartenders had they seen Squeeze, but none of them had. Then I asked one of the bouncers had they seen Show and he told me he thought Show was in his office.

"A'ight thanks," I shouted over the loud music.

So as to not seem suspicious, I didn't want to ask the bouncer where the office was, so I went back to the bar and I asked a different bartender if he could tell me how to get to Show's office.

Lloyd Banks' hit song "On Fire" was blasting throughout the club as I shouted over the music.

"Miss, excuse me. Show told me to meet him at his office tonight, and I just got here. Can you tell me how to get to his office?"

The shapely and sexy bartender yelled into my ear and she directed me to where I needed to go. I yelled into Grams' ear and told him that the office was upstairs, and that we could locate the steps that led to the office if we went back to the VIP entrance on the ground level where we had come in.

Grams and I both headed in that direction. Grams reminded me to just play everything cool.

"Yeah, when we get inside the office, just introduce me and act like everything is normal. We'll chill for a minute and then I'll give you a nod or something, or you can give me a cue and that's when we'll make our move. I'ma follow your lead, but don't worry about nothing 'cause I gotchu on this!"

We made it to the black metal spiral staircase that looked like it would lead to a private office. It definitely was not a staircase that the general public would use.

"This gotta lead to their office," I said to Grams, as he nodded for me to proceed up to the office.

When we reached the top of the staircase we knew that we had reached the jackpot. There was an office door which appeared to be locked with a "private" sign on it. The music from down in the club could still be heard, so we couldn't tell if someone was inside the office or not. With the loud music it would have been useless to knock on the door, and fortunately there was a buzzer-looking doorbell, which I didn't hesitate to ring.

I rang it twice and we got no answer.

"You think they're in there?" Grams asked.

"I don't know."

I rang the bell two more times and this time I laid on the bell for about thirty seconds.

Finally, the door was opened by a nice-looking dark-skinned chick who looked to be about nineteen or twenty years old. She was tall like a model and had this Naomi Campbell look to her.

"Can I help y'all?" she asked, with her titties practically fully exposed.

"Yeah, we looking for Show. Is he here?" I asked.

"Who are you?" the chick asked with all kind of neck-twisting attitude.

"Yo, tell Show that it's Promise."

The girl looked at me with all kinds of unnecessary drama, and then I heard Show yell and ask who was at the door.

The dark-skinned chick told him who I was and then on Show's approval, she let us in.

"Goddamn, nigga! It's like Fort Knox trying to get up in here!" I jokingly said to Show as I gave him a pound and a ghetto hug.

"What's the deal, kid?" Show asked. He came across like he was genuinely happy to see me. "What's really good?"

Squeeze, on the other hand, who was sitting behind a small desk on the other side of the office, didn't even say what's up, or anything like that. His first question was, "Yo, Promise, how da fuck you just bringing muthafuckas up in my office that I don't even know?"

I could tell that Squeeze was probably already pissed off about something.

"My bad. This is my nigga from Baltimore. He's good people. Squeeze, this is Kendu. Kendu, this is my mans and 'nem, Show and Squeeze." I said in order to protect Grams' true identity.

Everybody said what's up to each other while the sexy chocolate chick went over and sat on Squeeze's lap.

There was this awkward silence, and then Squeeze spoke up. He spoke with a toothpick sticking out from the side of his mouth.

"Yo, on da' real, I ain't tryin' to disrespect you, but Promise, you can't really stay up in here but a minute."

I looked at Squeeze and I couldn't believe that the he was still feelin' his self the way he was. I just looked at him and didn't respond. I could tell that my silence made him feel uncomfortable and he spoke up again real quick.

"I'm just saying, wit' yo' ass on *America's Most Wanted* and on CNN and all of that, I just don't need the heat from the feds, you kna'imean?"

I still didn't respond. There was more awkward silence in the soundproof office. The only thing we could hear was each other. We couldn't even hear the music from the club.

"Yeah nigga, what's up wit' that shit in Philly? I heard you bussed down like nine cops, and killed two of 'em," Show stated.

I remained quiet and didn't say a word. The room went back to being awkwardly silent. I simply looked around the office and quickly scoped out the whole layout. And at that point I nodded to Grams. That was my signal to him.

Breaking the awkward silence, I reached into my waistband and pulled out my gun. All the anger that had been built up inside me when I was underneath the abandoned car shitting and pissing on myself had suddenly returned.

Liked he'd promised he would do, Grams followed my lead and he also pulled out his burner. I had my gun pointed at Show and Grams had his joint pointed at Squeeze and his girl.

"You wanna know what was up wit' that shit? I'll tell you what's up wit' the cops in Philly! You know exactly what the shit was about 'cause you and his punk ass set me da fuck up! I know y'all ratted my ass out! I know it was y'all niggas. But payback's a bitch!" I said as I moved in closer toward Show.

"Money, don't even think about reaching for your joint!" Grams barked at Squeeze. "Me and my man got this."

Show stood up and demanded to know what was going on, while he stated emphatically that he and Show had not and would not have set me up.

"Show, sit yo' ass back down in that chair!" I ordered. "Y'all niggas knew that I was on the run for a whole year. When I show back up and find out how y'all are living, I thought it would be all love, like y'all would look out for your boy! But then y'all try to front on me! Come on, man! Can I live?" I shouted.

Then I continued ranting as Grams held everybody at bay.

"And why was I on the run? Huh, Squeeze? I was on the run 'cause *your* ass called me and told me we was rolling on Nine and his crew. I was laid up wit' my girl and I come up out of some warm pussy to help y'all niggas and then y'all front on me and try to play me. All I'm sayin' is, can I live? Can I eat?"

Squeeze attempted to interrupt me.

"Shut the fuck up, Squeeze! I'm talking now and I'm running this muthafucking show! This is my club now! What!" I boasted.

Squeeze didn't care what I had ordered him to do. He proceeded to swear and warn, "Promise, word is bond! You better kill me up in this piece tonight, 'cause I swear to God I'm a buss yo' ass when you stop buggin' off them drugs you was smoking!"

"Promise, you want me to handle this cat?" Grams asked with an attitude.

I was silent for a second. And then I spoke up.

"Nah, I see how this is gonna go down. Niggas still wanna play me for a sucker and disrespect my ass! You know what? Squeeze, and Show, both of y'all stand da fuck up and strip butt-ass naked, right now!"

"Promise, you really are trippin', for real!" Show stated.

"What?" I stated as I walked up to Show and slapped him upside the head with the butt of my gun. Show spun around and fell to the ground. Blood spilled out of his mouth.

"You thinking I'm bugging now? Huh, nigga? Take of your goddamn clothes right now! Or I'll murder yo' punk ass right here up in this club!"

Show and Squeeze still didn't budge. The sexy dark-skinned chick looked shook like crazy. She had amazingly lost that neck-twisting attitude and was acting completely humble.

"Grams, kill this nigga right here!" I ordered, and I was dead serious.

"Which one?" Grams asked. "This one?" he questioned as he sought confirmation and pointed his gun toward Show.

"A'ight! A'ight!" Show screamed as he began unbuckling his pants and removing his shoes. And before long he was standing butt-ass naked in his office.

"Squeeze, what the hell you waiting on?" I asked.

Squeeze shook his head as he began to unbutton his shirt and remove his clothes.

"Yo, word is bond!" Squeeze added as he continued to shake his head.

"What about her?" Grams asked.

"Don't worry about her ass just yet. Get them jewels and let's get this money first," I stated. "Show, where the cash at? And don't play me, you got thirty seconds or I'm blasting your ass."

"Look in my pants pocket," Show quickly responded. "Promise, you know if you needed some dough all you would've had to do is ask me."

I walked over to Show and kicked him in the ribs. "So why da hell you ain't pick up your goddamn phone, or return my phone calls?"

Show added, "'Cause, nigga, how da hell did I know if you was working with the feds or not? You disappear for a year and then you show back up and wanna get money? Shit don't work like that."

"Yeah I know, I know, I know. And that's why I'm getting my money the ski-mask way!" I stated.

Grams had collected Show and Squeeze's Rolex watches and their diamond-encrusted dog tags. And while he was getting the girl to take off her diamond earrings and remove her diamond ring, I shouted to Show, "You got fifteen more seconds. Where the hell is the money at?"

"I told you, it's in my pockets!"

Grams reached in their pants pockets and he pulled out a knot of money from each pair. Combined, it looked like it was about $5000.

"Show, you got five more seconds to show me all of the money!" I threatened.

"Where da safe at?" Grams growled, sounding like DMX.

"Two seconds," I warned, as I cocked the gun.

"One—"

"Just show it to 'em," Squeeze reluctantly stated from his face-down position.

"It's over there under the desk," Show gritted through his teeth.

Grams immediately scurried to Show's desk and located the safe, which was in the floor underneath a mat.

"What's the combination?" Grams asked, and Show yelled it out loud.

In no time Grams had the safe open and he let out a joyous scream. "Promise, this is better than raw sex over here!"

"A'ight, just load it wit' the jewels so we can be outta here."

Grams quickly gathered the loot and he also told me that he had snatched about a pound of weed.

When he was done he handed me the bag of cash, jewels, and weed, and he proceeded to duct tape the hands, feet, and mouths of Show and Squeeze.

"Yo, you wanna hit that?" I asked Grams, referring to the sexy chocolate chick.

Squeeze stared at me and he tried his best to yell through the duct tape that was around his mouth.

Although I was in the middle of a robbery, I was horny as hell and the icing on the cake in getting back at Squeeze would have been to hit his girl right there in front of his punk ass!

"Nah, Promise, that's whack. We got the dough. We ain't raping nobody! That's that punk shit," Grams stated.

"A'ight, just tape her hands, mouth, and feet and we're outta here."

With that order Grams bound the chick to a chair and the two of us calmly walked out the door and headed for Grams' truck.

As we walked out the door, I gave the unsuspecting bouncer a pound. And he told me to be careful 'cause Five-O was lurking everywhere.

I appreciated the tip as me and Grams jumped in the truck and were out. As I directed Grams toward Atlantic Avenue, I looked inside the bag of goods and couldn't believe how much cash was in the bag.

"Yo, there gotta be close to fifty thousand in that bag," Grams predicted.

"That's what's up!"

I showed Grams how to get to Rochdale Village in Queens. And as we got closer to Queens I used Grams' cell phone and called Candy. I knew that I would be waking her up but I knew that she would be cool about it.

"Yeah, I'm in Queens right now. I'll be there in like twenty minutes," I informed Candy.

SEVEN

Me and Grams pulled into the parking lot of a 24-hour Burger King and we divided up the spoils. We both took a little less than twenty-six thousand, and we each took a Rolex and a dog tag. I decided to swap the handgun that Grams had loaned me in exchange for letting him keep the weed that we had unexpectedly stumbled upon during the robbery.

"Yo, this was the biggest stick-up I ever did in my life!" Grams cheerfully exclaimed.

"Kid, this was my everyday a few years back," I boasted. "This is what I was born to do."

Rochdale was right down the block from the Burger King, so I had Grams drive down 137th Avenue and he dropped me off at Candy's building. And before we parted ways, I thanked Grams for looking out for me the way he had. He, on the other hand, was more than thankful for me having given him the opportunity to make so much loot during the stick-up.

"Yo, if you need me, dog, just holla at me and I got you," Grams assured me as he wrote down his home number and cell number on a piece of paper so that I would be sure to have it and wouldn't just be relying on my memory as I usually did.

"No doubt," I said as I gave him a pound.

Handing Grams one thousand dollars, I said to him, "Do me a favor. Make sure that Marissa gets this, and tell her it's from me."

Grams took the money and nodded his head. I instructed him on how to get to the Belt Parkway so that he could make his way to the Verrazano Bridge and onto the New Jersey Turnpike.

As Grams pulled off, he appropriately blasted Ja' Rule's song, "Clap Back."

I rang Candy's intercom and she immediately buzzed me into her building's lobby.

I rode the elevator up to her apartment and she was standing at her apartment door waiting for me. Although she looked as if she had just woken up, she was extremely excited to see me. She gave me the warmest hug and said that I looked as if I had gained some weight.

"You still look good, Promise."

"I try to maintain," I replied.

"Candy, you telling me *I* gained weight? Look at you, where the hell did you get that butt from? You ain't have that phatty a few years ago," I jokingly said as the two of us laughed.

Candy escorted me into her immaculate apartment, which had some bangin' shiny hardwood floors. Then she grabbed me by the hand and escorted me over to the couch. Wearing her pajama pants, slippers, and a T-shirt, Candy sat on her overstuffed leather couch and crossed her legs and looked at me.

"So, how have you *been,* Promise?" She stressed the word "been."

I didn't know exactly how to answer that question.

"How have I been?" I rhetorically asked.

"Well, how much time do you have and where do you want me to begin?" I asked.

The sun was up and it was still early so Candy went to the kitchen and began making breakfast.

"I got all day. Just talk to me," she encouraged.

I didn't mind talking to Candy, and in fact, it turned out to be somewhat therapeutic. I told her about Squeeze and Show and what was really up between me and them. She had already heard that Pooh had been killed and

I told her how and why he'd been killed. To my surprise, she told me that a different story had been circulating on the street about Pooh's killer. I had always thought it was Nine and his crew who had killed Pooh, but she said that everyone had heard that it was some Spanish kids that did it.

If Candy had heard that, then it was probably true. I mean, she had no reason to lie to me about it. But if it was true, that should have been the first thing that Show and his punk ass should have told me when I saw him that night with Marissa. If Candy knew what the streets was saying about who Pooh's real killer was, then him and Squeeze had to know what the deal was.

Whateva. I didn't even wanna think about that anymore.

So I continued to talk to Candy and I filled her in about the horrible way in which Ashley's mother had been killed. I filled her in on how I'd met Audrey and what had happened to her. I told her about all of the drama with the cops and the feds in terms of why they were after me. I told her about Marissa. I basically gave her a full rundown of what I had been through during the past year or so.

But as I began to talk to her about Ashley and as I expressed how much I missed her and was worried about her, tears began to well up in my eyes. I mean, I was too hood to just start bawlin' or to straight-up start crying in front of Candy, but she could easily see that talking about my daughter had caused me to get real emotional.

Candy came close to me and tried to comfort me, and she told me that everything would be all right.

"I hope so," I said. "I just wish that I knew where she was. That probably is eating at me more than anything. And the thing is, I can't just pick up the phone and start calling around searching for my daughter because I'll get locked up."

I didn't want any breakfast, so Candy came to the kitchen table and sat in front of me as we began eating what she had prepared. She asked me if there were any family members or anybody that I was close with that would be willing to help me out in terms of locating my daughter.

"Yeah, there's people like relatives and close friends that I could reach out to, but those are the exact same people that I can't have any contact with because the cops and the feds are watching my relatives and close friends so they can get a lead and catch me. You kna'imean? With me on the run, it's not like I can just pick up the phone and call whoever I want to, or just go by and visit whoever I want to."

"Well, I'll see what I can do for you. I mean, I know some people that work with me who might be able to help. There's this cool Italian dude at my job and I think his wife is a social worker, so maybe she might be able to get some info on your daughter."

"Candy, whatever you can do, I would really appreciate it. Matter of fact, if you can help me find out where Ashley is at, I'll hit you off with like two Gs. It'll be like a finder's fee," I said with a smile.

"Two thousand dollars? Promise, you ain't gotta do that!"

"I know I don't, but I want to."

So our conversation went back and forth for hours. And when we were done talking, Candy showed me around the apartment and explained to me where towels and soap were so that when I was ready, I could take a shower.

As I couldn't just leave her apartment and freely walk the streets, I couldn't take Candy up on her previous offer, which was to spend the entire Saturday with her. But I gave her fifteen-hundred dollars and told her to buy some food with that money. I also gave her my clothing measurements and instructed her to pick up some much-needed clothing for herself and for me.

Eventually I got tired, so before Candy went about her business for the day, she let me crash in her bedroom. She had a nice king-sized waterbed and one thing that I know for a fact is that sleeping on her bed was the best sleep I'd had in ages! It was so much better than the hard lumpy sofa bed that Grams had let me sleep on.

Chillin' at Candy's crib was real cool. And seeing her was even better. I really liked her vibe.

Later on that night, when Candy came back in and she was preparing to go to sleep, she started talking about all of this church and Bible talk. She also started telling me that I needed to pray and ask God to help me figure things out in my life.

I laughed as I said to Candy, "Yeah, right! God don't wanna hear from me. I already know that I'm going to hell, so it don't matter. Plus, I can't remember the last time that I prayed to God, and I ain't never read the Bible in my life!"

Even after saying what I had said, Candy didn't trip and she didn't get all pushy with the religious nonsense. But she did say that she was gonna show me something in the Bible that would shed some light on what I had been going through.

"When did you get all religious?" I asked.

"I'm not religious. I'm *spiritual*!" Candy replied. "And there is a big difference."

Trying to bring the conversation in another direction, I moved closer to Candy and said, "So why don't you and me let our spirits connect right now?"

"What you talkin' about?" she asked.

"I'm sayin'. . ."

"You sayin' what?" Candy asked with a smile.

"Why don't you let a nigga hit that?"

Candy fell out laughing.

"What?" I asked.

"Is that what it's gotten to now? That's how niggas ask for pussy?"

Then, in a playful attempt to mock my voice, Candy stated, "*Why don't you let a nigga hit that?*"

The two of us both started laughing at the funny situation.

I moved closer to her and I started kissing on her neck and I told her, "Come on, you know how I do . . ."

Candy was getting turned on and I could tell that she was gonna comply with my request and let me hit it. But out of nowhere she stopped and told me to hold up.

"I'ma give you some, but I just want you to see this first."

Candy left the room and I couldn't believe that the bitch came back with a Bible and flipped it open and started reading from Proverbs.

"Promise, this is from Proverbs chapter 1:10 -16

My son, if sinners entice you, do not give in to them.
If they say, "Come along with us; Let's lie in wait for someone's blood,
Let's waylay some harmless soul;
Let's swallow them alive, like the grave,
And whole, like those who go down to the pit;
We will get all sorts of valuable things
and fill our houses with plunder;
Throw in your lot with us,
and we will share a common purse" —
My son, do not go along with them,
Do not set foot on their paths;
or their feet rush into sin,
They are swift to shed blood."

"Do you understand what that's saying?" Candy asked.

"Yeah, actually I do. That's deep right there," I responded with full sincerity.

Candy added, "Promise, I am definitely not preaching to you, and I know that I have my own issues. But what I see as your problem is that you are associating with the wrong people. Squeeze called you that night to go after Nine and his people, and you listened to him, and now look. And I know how y'all used to stick people up and all of that. It's like when you're young and you don't know any better, that's one thing. But now, Promise, you can't look back at the past and try to change it because the past is the past. The only thing that you can do is focus on the future. And what I would say is just do you! Do you and stay away from the streets. Focus on finding your daughter and getting things straight legally. And I'm telling you, *start praying*! It works."

Candy reminded me so much of Audrey because she was really telling me what I needed to hear, and she was right.

"You right, Candy. And I'ma listen to you."

After I said that, there was this brief silence. Then Candy put the Bible away and came close to me and started kissing on *my* neck this time.

"*A nigga still wanna hit this*?" Candy asked in a joking way.

We both laughed, and then I replied, "Nah, you killed the mood with all of that seriousness and the Bible. But I needed to hear it, though."

Candy apologized for killing the mood. But the rest of the night wasn't a complete waste as the two of us just chilled in her room, watching rerun episodes of a *Sanford and Son* marathon on the TV Land channel.

EIGHT

Sunday afternoon rolled around.

Candy and I were in her living room, chillin', listening to the radio and drinking some rum and Coke. We had to turn down the volume on the music because it sounded like someone was at her door.

"You expecting somebody?" I asked as I immediately got nervous, thinking it was the cops. But I quickly realized that if the cops had had any inkling that I was in that apartment, there is no way that they would politely knock at the door and ask to come inside.

"Nah, I'm not expecting anyone."

"Yo, just to be safe, I'm gonna hide in your bathroom. I'll be behind the shower curtain," I informed Candy as I quickly scurried off.

Candy's bathroom was situated right near the living room, and the front door wasn't too far off from the bathroom.

I heard Candy ask who is was. And then I heard her unlocking the door.

"What's up, ma? We sorry to just be showing up unannounced but . . ."

From the sound of the voice it sounded like it was Show. And more than likely, Squeeze was with him.

"Damn!" I thought to myself. I knew that I had slipped up because I didn't have my gun on me. It was stashed deep in Candy's linen closet, along with the loot from the robbery.

"You heard from Promise?" Show asked.

There was a brief moment of silence.

"Squeeze, you gonna just come in my crib and not even speak? And I ain't seen you in I don't know how long?" Candy said in what sounded like her attempt to play things cool.

"My bad. Let me give you a hug," Squeeze stated. Then he added, "I'm just kinda heated right now, so you gotta forgive me."

"What's going on?" Candy asked.

"Just a whole lotta drama wit' Promise, that's all. You seen him, or heard from him?"

"Nah, actually, Show, I still haven't heard from him since that day I called *you* looking for him."

"You sure, Candy?" Show asked.

"Yeah, I'm sure."

There was some more silence.

"So what's up? You was just chillin' for the day?" Squeeze asked.

"Yup. Gotta get ready for work tomorrow."

There was some more silence as my heart still raced.

"Candy, was you by yourself all day today?" Show asked.

"Yeah, why?"

"I was just wondering why there was two drink glasses on your coffee table."

What da fuck? He think he a goddamn detective? I cursed and questioned inside my head.

"Oh, that's from yesterday," Candy lied . A horrible lie at that.

There was some more silence.

All of a sudden I heard Candy let out a scream. And I didn't know what the hell was going on.

"Candy! Don't lie to us!" Squeeze barked.

Candy didn't say anything.

"I'll choke the shit outta you if you lie to me!" Squeeze barked again.

I was ready to burst out of the bathroom and get the showdown started, but I nervously held my position.

"I'm not lying!" Candy said, followed by some coughing and gasping for air. She had probably just been freed from the grips of Squeeze's hand being around her neck.

"So if the drinks are from last night, why are there still ice cubes in them?"

"I don't know!" Candy screamed.

"Yo, Squeeze, didn't that nigga Promise have on a gray Sean John outfit at the club the other night?"

"Yeah," Squeeze responded.

My mind was racing because I knew that they were definitely on to me.

"Candy, whose Sean John jacket is that?" Show asked.

"Look! Y'all gotta go! Y'all can't be coming up in my crib like this!"

"Show, I'ma check the apartment for that nigga. I bet you his ass is up in here."

"No! You are not gonna just be walking through my apartment!" Candy yelled.

"Candy! Just chill and let us check the apartment!" Show screamed.

"No! Fuck that! I'm calling the cops!" Candy yelled back.

"You pick up that phone and I'll kill you!" Show said.

I was extremely heated and at the same time I was prepping myself for someone to come inside the bathroom so I could snuff 'em.

From the sounds of things, Squeeze was already rummaging through the one-bedroom apartment.

"You got anything?" Show yelled.

"Nah, the nigga ain't here!" Squeezed shouted back.

"I'ma check the kitchen," Show informed.

"Get the fuck outta my crib!" Candy yelled.

"A'ight, I'ma check the bathroom," Squeeze stated as they both totally ignored Candy.

I told myself to get ready.

Then I heard the sound of flesh slapping. It must have been Candy attacking one of them because the slapping sounds were followed by an outburst of female threats and curses.

I could tell that Squeeze had just entered the bathroom, so Candy must have been fighting and cursing with Show.

I was dead still and not even breathing.

"Get the fuck off me, bitch!" I heard Show yell. His yell was followed by a scream from Candy.

"Yo, Squeeze let's get up outta here!"

I heard the hinges on the bathroom door squeak . . .

Squeeze must have been checking for me behind the bathroom door. His next move had to be to check in the bathtub behind the shower curtain where I was hiding.

My heart pounded.

"I know that nigga was up in here!" Squeeze shouted as he sounded like he was shouting into my ear.

He had to be standing right next to the bathtub. I still was not breathing. But my fist was cocked and if the nigga pulled back that shower curtain, I was ready for whateva! Even if the nigga had a gun, I was ready to kill with my bare hands!

I wasn't gonna go out easy.

CAGNEY AND LACEY

BY

CRYSTAL LACEY WINSLOW

PROLOGUE

BROOKLYN, 1990

Cagney

"Yo, son, I'm out," I said to my homeboys just before I ran out the side door of my high school. It was only 9:30 in the morning and I'd just arrived. As I walked up the block I could hear footsteps slapping the cracked concrete, running toward me. I turned around to see Rick and Black. "Y'all niggas be bullshittin'."

"Nah, Cagney. My mom be beefin' when they send them letters home, talkin' 'bout I cut class," Black explained.

I sucked my teeth. "How old are you?"

"I'm seventeen, but that ain't got—"

"You damn near grown and you're worrying about your mom. You should have your mom in check by now," I scolded.

"Word," Rick chimed in.

I looked him up and down and shook my head. "Why you frontin' like you got shit on lock? I'm younger than both y'all niggas and I run shit in my crib," I boasted.

"Your mom is cool. But my Mom Dukes don't be havin' it," Black complained.

"Then *make* her have it!" I said and looked him dead in his eyes.

We ran around for hours, talking shit and ranking on each other, and somehow ended up at St. John's University. We snuck on campus and admired how clean the grounds were. I tried to holla at a few college girls, but they weren't having it.

"Hey, baby. What's up?" I said to a light-skinned chick with a big ass.

She stopped for a minute, thirsty to get attention. Then she looked at my sneakers—which were leaning to the side. And then at my gear—which was a little dated. She looked at me as if I were a parasite and said, "Boy, please . . . never that!"

"Never what, bitch?" I yelled, feeling disrespected.

She rolled her eyes and kept it moving.

After a few more minutes of goofing off, my stomach began to growl. I thought of a master plan.

"I'm hungry," I began.

"Me too," Rick agreed.

None of us had eaten all day. Truthfully, I hadn't eaten since yesterday afternoon. My mother hardly went food shopping because funds were low in my crib. My mother had seven children and I was the oldest at fifteen. Most nights, I didn't eat so my younger brothers and sisters could eat.

"Yo, I bet we can score some quick cash from one of these ball-playing mu'fuckers!" I said.

"How we gonna do that? We ain't got no burner," Black replied.

"Stupid! We don't need a burner for these corny niggas. If I even look at one of them too hard, I bet they'll be throwing their money at us."

I knew that although I was only fifteen, my looks were deceiving. I had been mistaken for an eighteen-year-old on numerous occasions. I stood six feet with broad shoulders. My body frame was naturally muscular from all the sports I played. I had large hands and feet with a deep baritone voice. My thick eyebrows were usually furled over in a menacing way, and my lips were usually twisted into a snarl.

For hours we lay in the cut like peroxide, waiting on our prey. A withering oak tree with overhanging branches shaded us from the hot summer sun. Finally, we saw a scrawny, clean-cut-looking guy with a heavy book bag, walking alone. I looked around and the grounds were almost empty. I told Rick and Black that it was going to be like taking candy from a baby. My agile body shadowed my would-be prey as I stiffly emerged out of the shrubs that littered the grounds.

"Just follow my lead and we'll be out in a New York minute," I said, displaying my humorous side. Rick and Black both laughed, even though they were afraid. Steadily I approached the stranger and bumped up against him to get his attention.

"My bad. Pardon me," I said.

As he began to walk away, I punched him in the back of his head—*BAM!*—which dropped him to his knees. Swiftly, I hit him with a mean left hook. His head snapped back and blood squirted from out of his mouth. I was sure I had bodied him. He keeled over and I pounced on him without provocation.

"Mu'fucker, give me your dough!" I demanded. My gruff voice was menacing and intimidating. My victim had curled in the fetal position, covering his head with his hands as best as he could. I looked over at Rick and Black and they were standing around nervously, waiting for me to hurry up.

"Give me your mu'fuckin' money," I repeated as he thrashed around on the ground like a mangy dog.

"I'm no American," he breathed. "I speak no English."

"What the fuck? You better give me your fuckin' paper before I blast your ass!" I warned and reached inside my sweatshirt for an imaginary gun.

"Don't kill me!" he begged. "Please, don't kill me!"

Impatiently, I waited for him to give me his money, but he refused. I dug my hands in his pockets, but they were empty. I snatched his book bag and tossed it to Black. As I got up, I was so frustrated with him for wasting my time that I kicked him in his groin. His face twisted up and distorted from pain as he screamed out in anguish.

"Bitch ass!" I yelled.

I watched him squirming like an animal, and for some inexplicable reason his actions fueled me. My thoughts were erratic and my adrenaline was amplified tenfold. I began to stomp his head into the ground repeatedly until his cranium cracked. Blood squirted and his neck lolled to the side. Finally, Rick pulled me off of him.

"Whatchu doin', man? You gonna get us locked up!"

I had gotten so caught up with rage that I lost sight of our purpose. I looked over and saw a few students and security guards running toward us.

We broke out.

That night we sat around smoking blunts laced with weed and crack cocaine and laughing about what had went down today. We scored twenty dollars from out of his book bag and dumped his books in a garbage can at the train station.

I went inside just before eleven o'clock and my mother was smoking her own blunt and drinking a tall can of St. Ides beer. I hated to see my mother smoking and drinking, but I knew that sometimes she needed to escape reality.

"Hey Ma," I said and kissed her on her cheek. She swatted me away as if I were an insect. None of my brothers and sisters were bathed or in bed. Their bodies were dirty and their stomachs were hungry. Immediately, I felt guilty for spending my part of the money on getting high when I knew I had mouths to feed. I promised that tomorrow I'd score some real cash and put some food on the table.

"Go take y'all asses to sleep," my voice bellowed after they began to irritate me. They were running around, yelling and screaming—blowing my high. I sat down on the sofa—which was where I slept—and started to doze off when something jolted me back up.

"This is Gilt McGronner, WLTV news, reporting on a tragic event that took place at one of the most prestigious colleges in Queens. A foreign exchange student was robbed and beaten to death on school grounds. Witnesses say that three young men entered the grounds and began taunting students. At some point they ran into Chiderjanran Muhammad, the son of Ali Muhammad, president of Saudi Arabia. Authorities say that when they found Chiderjanran, he was unconscious. A subsequent search revealed one thousand dollars in one-hundred-dollar bills in the victim's sock. Police aren't sure if he resisted the robbers or if he didn't have a chance to hand over his money. A tri-state manhunt is taking place for the perpetrators."

My heart dropped.

Damn, I thought. *That mu'fucker had one thousand dollars on him and didn't want to give the shit up. Well, ha ha! You can't spend that shit where you at!*

That morning I rushed to school so I could tell Rick and Black what I saw on the news. I knew that I was going to be the man at school. I was now a murderer. Whether it was intentional or not—I had done it. As I got closer to school, I peeped the detective car sitting in front. As I turned to do a 180, it was already too late. Two detectives were dead on me with their revolvers drawn. Turned out, Rick and Black both sang like canaries to their parents, who then called the authorities. In exchange for their testimony and cooperation, they both received probation. I was charged as an adult and found guilty of manslaughter. I was sentenced to fifteen years to life in prison. My mother never showed up once during my trial. My girl at the time, Maria, would skip school as often as she could to sit in on my trial. I didn't know it at the time, but the day of my sentencing would be the last time I'd ever see or speak to Maria.

I was handcuffed and carted away to Ossining State Correctional Facility, a prison in upstate New York. From that day on, I vowed revenge on my two former friends.

"Open your mouth . . . lift your tongue, grab your nuts, lift them up . . . bend over and spread your ass cheeks . . . cough . . ."

I entered the adult prison as a young punk. But I'd leave as a menace.

ONE

EAST LOS ANGELES, CALIFORNIA 1999

Lacey

I came in from *el barrio* to hear the mouth of *mi abuela,* my grandmother Carmen. My grandmother didn't know it, but I had joined a gang and we had just finished chasing a few rival gang members out of our territory. Guns were fired and one of my friends got slashed and I was covered in his blood. As I looked at my blood-soaked T-shirt, I was proud that I now belonged to a Mexican gang. I was following in the footsteps of my father, aunts, and most of my cousins.

"Lacey, go and give your *padre* a kiss on his cheek and tell him you'll see him lay-ter," my grandmother commanded. She was standing in the kitchen, smoking on a Newport Long cigarette with a filter. She had a massive amount of silvery-white hair that resembled a cotton field. Her pale skin was missing nourishment from the sun since she never went outdoors. She was my height, which was 5'1", and fragile. Since my grandmother was so petite, I usually took advantage of her and while my father was out gang-banging, I'd stress her nerves so bad that she chain-smoked. My grandmother was only forty-two years old, but she looked as if she were my *great* grandmother. She gave birth to my father when she was thirteen years old. My *padre* got my *madre* pregnant when he was seventeen.

"*¡Un momento!*" I yelled, shrugging my shoulders while pushing past her. I pushed so hard she lost her balance and fell up against the refrigerator.

Good for you, puta, I thought and ran into my bedroom and changed out of my bloody clothes. I had a slight bruise over my right eye and it had begun to swell.

"Relax, Homes, if you know what's good for you!" my grandmother screamed, causing a commotion. "Little *chivato!* Don't think I don't know about the clique she joined in *el barrio*."

My father came running into the kitchen to see what the fuss was about. He was wearing a silly tuxedo and his new wife was wearing a dumb *wedding* dress with cheap, white satin shoes. Her hair was done in soft curls and she had the stupidest grin on her face. A grin I wanted to slap straight.

"Hey Lay-cee, you givin' your *abuela* a hard time?" He smiled as his new wife joined us in the kitchen and wrapped her arms around his waist. She was a thin woman of average height with large feet and hands and a nappy Afro. They were on their way to El Segundo for their honeymoon.

Sharon was a bum. She'd met my father two months ago and they thought they were in love. For two adults, they were both idiots. I hated to call my father names because I loved him so much, but he let me down with this move. I used to idolize him, his handsome looks, and his strength. His *puta* wife's name should have been Midnight, she was so black. All you saw on her were her white pupils and teeth. She was always drunk and begging my father for money. The thought of her touching my father on his wedding night infuriated me more than my thirteen years could handle.

I looked my father's new bride up and down in her costume and dryly remarked, "You look so stupid. I thought *white* was for virgins!"

"Lay-cee," my father exclaimed, "You better watch it!"

"I don't want you to go!" I whined and punched my father in his chest. He didn't hesitate to haul off and back-slap me. I balled up my fist but instead of attacking him, I attacked his wife. She fought me back until my father was able to get her off of me. I thought my father would slit her throat for putting her hands on his little *chiquita*, but he did nothing.

Realizing that she had split my lip, busted my nose, and damaged my already swelling eye sent me into a fury. I ran and grabbed a knife from the kitchen and pointed it in her direction. I swung it a couple of times but missed. I was sweating and my breaths were short and rapid.

"Go ahead and do it, you little half-breed bitch!" Sharon challenged. "I'll whip your little ass in here."

As I gripped the knife, I wondered if I could take her. Then I remembered what my father told me on several occasions, "*Only attack your prey if the odds are in your favor. If not, chill out . . . live and take another day to strategize.*"

It wasn't over. I'd let her slide today. Tomorrow was a different story. When she saw me lower the knife this fueled her ego and she began to mouth off again.

"I'm the head nigga in charge! You think you're a man because you walk around here with boy clothes on. You dyke freak," Sharon ranted. "And when we get back, if I have to break your lesbian ass into pieces day and night until you respect me, then that's what I'm gonna do!"

Again, I looked to my father to intervene and defend me, but he said nothing. He just shrugged his shoulders as if he was helpless in the matter, but I knew differently. My father was the strongest man I knew. He had been gang-banging since he was twelve in *el barrio* and he had the scars to prove it. He had been shot six times, stabbed, and my own mother tried to poison him. So I couldn't understand why he let this woman get away with hitting on me!

Then my grandmother laughed a hideous cackle, as if she was amused.

"That's right," she chimed in. "She's the new woman around the house. Your no-good momma is dead."

All families have secrets. The secret in the Martinez family was that my father killed my mother and made it look like she was caught in the crossfire of two gangs feuding. Everyone said that he did this because she had cheated on him with his best friend, Chewy. He, too, was found dead. At that point, hate seeped into my body and grew. I knew I would do something I'd regret. Giving him one last chance, I begged, "*Papí*, please don't go! Pa-leeeezzzze—"

"Lay-cee, stop it! Stop whining like a li'l girl. I taught you to be strong. I taught you to be a soldier. I have a new lay-dee in my life, *Esse,* and you're gonna to have to get used to her-r-r," he said, dragging his words.

That night, the house was quiet. I called three of my closest gang members over to my house. My grandmother slept frightfully in her bed. You could hear her snoring, honking, and wheezing for blocks. She disgusted me. I crept ever so slowly into her bedroom and stood over her and just stared. I watched her chest heave up and down with her mouth gaping open. Drool began to cascade down her brittle skin and soak into her pillow. Long moments passed before she felt our presence and woke up. We looked eye to eye. Just as she opened her mouth to talk, her eyes realized something was up and exuded fear. Her eyes followed my arms as I swiftly brought them over my head. The shiny blade caught a stream of moonlight and illuminated off of her face. She let out a blood-curdling scream as I took all of my strength and plunged the knife deep inside her chest. Blood squirted past my head and hit the wall. As the knife entered her body I felt it cut through flesh, bone, and cartilage. Her body jerked once and both her hands went to try and pry the knife out. Her face twisted up and distorted into several frowns from the pain.

"KILL HER! KILL HER!" my friends chanted. "DIE, *PUTA*... DIE!"

"Laugh now, bitch!" I whispered in her old ear. My grandmother said nothing. She just kept releasing an agonizing moan and then a soft whimper.

"Homes, I bet you're wondering where the *woman* of the house is when you need her," I mocked her as I went into her nightstand and pulled out her pack of Newport cigarettes. I lit one and inhaled the smoke, as I'd done on many occasions. Then I passed it around. I sat patiently next to her on her bed, puffing on her cigarette, waiting for her to die. She just kept on gasping and wheezing and reaching her hands out for me to help her. Finally, after several minutes, enough was enough! I climbed onto the bed and straddled her. I took both hands and gripped the knife handle and leaned on top of the knife with all of my body weight. The knife sunk so deep that only the handle remained protruding from her chest. Her white bed sheets were soaked in blood, and so was I.

Once her body stopped squirming, I walked calmly to the telephone and dialed my father on his cell phone. I called three times before he finally decided to pick up. You could hear the grogginess in his voice.

"Momma?" he said.

"No, *padre*, your momma's dead!"

You could hear commotion in the background. The gang members were laughing and goofing off.

"Whatchu *vatos* doin'?" he panicked. "Lay-cee?"

Silence.

"LAY-CEE!"

"I guess the honeymoon's over, Homes!"

"No-o-o-o-o-o-o-o-o-o-o!"

TWO

OSSINING STATE CORRECTIONAL FACILITY, 2005

Cagney

The night before I was about to be released into the custody of the halfway house, I got called out of my cell by my counselor. I was hoping they weren't trying to pull no bullshit. I had served my fifteen years and was ready to get up outta there. While inside, I didn't have anyone to hold me down with visits and shit because I got locked up so young. I didn't have a girl, and my moms was too poor to support me in jail. So I had to do what I had to do. I extorted a few lame-ass niggas and soon I was able to send money orders home to help my mom out.

I had been in there for eleven years when I clinked up with this Brooklyn kid named Peanut. He was a cool dude that was in for a gun charge. Immediately I noticed how many chicks he had. They were constantly putting money in his commissary and coming to visit. In the two years we were locked down together, I don't think he had the same chick come visit him more than twice. He was the one who hooked me up with Kim. He was fucking with her friend, Latoya, and introduced us on the phone. Kim held me down for the rest of my bid and even gave me her address to do my parole at.

I walked into my counselor's office and he had a smirk on his face.

"Mr. Curtis, please, have a seat," he sternly said while looking down at my folder. I wanted to ask what was up but figured eventually he was gonna tell me. So I took a seat and remained silent. Finally he began to speak again.

"I have some bad news," he started off slowly. "Something's happened."

"Am I supposed to pry it out of you, or are you just gonna give it to me straight, no chaser?" I sarcastically replied.

"Your mother is dead. She killed herself. Is that straight enough?"

I said nothing. I couldn't let him see my pain. I knew that if I let an ounce of anger slip I might not be able to stop the flow. And that could jeopardize my freedom. I went back to my cell and got my man Peanut's cell phone. One of his chicks had snuck it inside the prison and one of the corrections officers had smuggled it into his cell for him. Nowadays, you can have anything while being locked down. Of course, for a few dollars.

I called my cousin, Rob.

"Yo," I said.

"What up, man?" he said and exhaled.

"Why didn't you come up here and tell me about my moms?"

"I didn't get a chance, man. And I didn't want to put something like that in a letter."

"When's the funeral?"

"Thursday."

"I'll be out at the halfway house. I'll see you there. One," I said and hung up. That night in my cell, I silently cried although I felt she was in a better place. She was miserable here on earth. All I thought about while being locked up was how I was gonna go home, make some quick paper, and take care of my family. I would never forgive myself for getting jammed up and leaving them alone.

When I got to the halfway and Thursday rolled around I couldn't summon enough courage to go and say goodbye to my mother. Something told me that if I didn't see it, then it didn't happen. In my mind, I wanted to remember her alive. I prayed a lot that day and asked God to forgive me. I didn't know if I even believed in God. I couldn't even remember the last time I called on Him. But I was a typical Negro: you always called on God when you've been brought to your knees. They say you will call on God either willingly or unwillingly, but you will lean on Him.

That Saturday after the funeral, I went by to see my brothers and sisters. I tapped lightly on the door until the second-oldest sibling came and answered. My sister Trina stood looking at me with accusatory eyes. When I tried to hug her, she pulled away. She kept her foot firmly in place, blocking me from entering the apartment.

"You're a day late," she said through clenched teeth.

Trina had grown up to be quite beautiful. She was around twenty-one years old now. Her eyes were distant and flat. She had French vanilla-colored skin with just a sprinkle of cinnamon. Her body was slender yet shapely.

"I just couldn't see Mommy in a pine box," I explained.

"You're a poor excuse for a son. And you're no brother of mine. Don't come around here anymore," she said and slammed the door in my face. I went to knock again but thought against it. She was angry now because she'd just lost our mother and she needed someone to blame. I'd give her time to grieve and then I'd come back.

The halfway was supposed to monitor you to make sure you're not out committing felonious crimes, but that was bullshit. All everyone did was plan capers and mastermind robberies while being locked down at the halfway. And on the weekend, you executed whatever crime you'd planned all week.

When I touched down, Kim had a couple of dollars waiting for me. She said she wanted to hold her man down. She was a cute girl, but I was looking for something different. Don't get me wrong, she was probably most men's dream. She had caramel-colored skin, long, light brown hair with blond highlights, full pink lips, small waist, wide hips and perky titties. She didn't have much ass but she was shapely. But my dream girl was someone somewhat exotic. I was looking for some different shit. Maybe a girl who spoke several languages.

Kim had a pretty decent crib on 126th Street in Harlem. The first day I came there, I took a look around. It was small and she kept it messy. She had dirty dishes piled up in the sink, and roaches infested her furniture. Shit like that I overlooked. I guess you could attribute that to my past living conditions.

The first time Kim and I fucked, I was disappointed. I was ready to get my fuck on since I hadn't had any pussy in years. And when I pulled it out she started panicking. She didn't say anything but I could see fear in her eyes. I tried as best as I could to hide my shit with my hands, but that shit wasn't gonna work. As I moved toward her I could visually see her trembling and tensing up.

Ignoring the signs, I began kissing her neck softly. I was pleased that she'd gotten dressed up for me really sexy. She had on a pink bra with black lace and the matching panties with the pussy cut out. A pair of thigh-high silk stockings held up by a garter belt hugged her thick thighs. Stilettos heels graced her small feet and when she walked, her ass spread open. Sexy!

I knew I had to pace myself or else I would cum too quickly. I inhaled her perfume and began to taste her skin. I licked and sucked her pink nipples and paused for a minute to admire her large areolas. Her breasts were perfect. I was about to make my way down and eat her pussy when she had to turn me off.

"Taste it . . . please," she moaned and I lost my appetite. I hate it when a female asked you to give her head. If I'ma do it—then it'll get done. Finally, I was ready to enter her. I positioned myself in between her legs and applied pressure. Her tight pussy resisted, and I could feel her body tensing up. I began kissing her to take her mind off the pain, but it didn't work. She began to dig her nails in my back as I maneuvered my dick farther into her wet pussy.

"Cagney, no . . . wait! Stop . . . it hurts," she said and tried to wiggle free.

"Baby, please . . . I gotchu. I won't hurt you, I promise."

I began to kiss her again. Long, sensual kisses. She exhaled and tried to relax, but when I tried to go deeper, she panicked.

"Cagney, it's too big," she complained.

When she saw me get frustrated and try to pull out, she changed her attitude and pulled me back in. She relaxed her legs, opened them wider, and allowed me to have sex with her.

Methodically, I pumped in and out as her wet pussy gripped my dick. We had sex in the frog position, doggy style, and then I let her ride me. Finally, I was ready to cum. I flipped her back into the missionary position and buried my face into her pillow as I released hot juices in her. We both lay there, breathing heavily, when I felt something wet slide down the side of my face. Too distracted to investigate, I tried to summon the strength to have sex again. Gently, I pulled out of Kim and was prepared to go again when I heard a soft whimper. I turned over and noticed she was crying.

"Baby, what's wrong?" I asked, although I really didn't care.

"My coochie hurts! Your penis is the size of my forearm. You're too much. It feels like you've ripped me open," she accused.

"So that means I can't get any more?" I joked.

"Are you serious?" Kim asked.

"Yeah," I said sternly but I was truly joking. I wanted to see where her head was at.

"Cagney, I know you have needs. And since I'm your girl then I guess I have to do it," she whined. "But please, be a little easier."

Damn, that was a little bit too easy.

"Ma, never fold so quickly! It shows a sign of weakness. And don't NO nigga want a weak-ass bitch!"

"What?"

"What I'm tryin' to say is, it's never any fun when it no longer is a challenge."

"But—"

"Kim, I'm done for tonight," I remarked dryly, rolled over, and went to sleep.

THREE

HARRISON HALL JUVENILE DETENTION CENTER

Lacey

I was locked up for three weeks when I received a kite from my cousin, Rica, saying that my father had put the barrel of his Colt .45 into his mouth and gave it a blowjob that blew his brains out. He couldn't accept what I had done to his *madre*. I received his letter that read:

> *Little Chiquita,*
>
> *I have failed you as a father. You have the strength of a bull, and up until now, I felt you followed in my footsteps. I should have never let anyone come between our love. I abandoned you and I will never forgive myself. You didn't kill your* abuela*; I did. And for that I will pay with my life. Stay strong in there and represent your gang to the fullest. You are a soldier! Make me proud.*
>
> *Love,*
>
> *Papí*

When I read his letter I wanted to cry, but I loved him too much to show such weakness. He was counting on me to be strong. So I took my anger out on my cellmates. For years I'd get into fights every day. One time, I broke a girl's nose because she didn't want to give me her pint of milk and chocolate chip cookies. When I was sixteen, I choked out another inmate and put her to sleep. We were watching an episode of *Cops* and I tried to emulate the police chokehold for fun. That incident landed me three years on parole when I get out.

The older I got, the more I adjusted and began to relax. I had already gained a notorious reputation that rang from jail to the streets. I was a legend in my hood, and they couldn't wait for me to come back and start gang-banging.

In my last year I began to change. I started attending the church in jail and started feeling remorse for what I had done to my grandmother. On my seventeenth birthday, I took my GED and passed, and even thought about getting a job and going to college when I got out.

On the morning of May 1, 2005, I was released from Harrison Hall Juvenile Detention Center in Santa Monica, California with $300 dollars in my pocket. As part of the conditions of my parole, I was released to the address of my aunt Rosario, Rica's mother. If I hadn't had an address, then I would have been put in the state's custody until I was twenty-one years old. At first, I thought it was odd that my aunt had offered her home to me. Then one day I got a kite from Rica that said her mother planned to kill me as soon as I got out, for killing my grandmother. The note also said that my aunt Rosario had also blamed me for my father's suicide.

My aunt had been gang-banging for over twenty years. She led a gang of women in *el barrio* in Compton. She was well-known for protecting her neighborhood and for having what many considered a black heart. Rica had sent pictures throughout the years of my family, and my aunt had changed drastically since her husband, Jorge, was gunned down by rival gang members.

My aunt Rosario was 100 percent Mexican with dark features. She had cut her thick, black hair into a crew cut; wore khaki pants, flannel shirts, and Converse sneakers; and had thirty-two tattoos. She had one that stood out on her arm, of Jesus crying with bloody tears looking toward the sky, with my *abuela*'s name and her date of death. On her other arm she'd gotten my face tattooed with a knife sticking out my skull. Rica said that once Aunt Rosario murdered me, she was going to have my date of death added to the tattoo.

I had two choices. I could come home and kill my aunt. If I did that, I would gain respect and take her place in *el barrio*. Of course, killing my aunt would have a domino effect. I would have to take out my cousin, Rica, as well. She had too much heart not to try to come after me to avenge her mother's death. Or, I could run as far away as I could. I had already decided that I wanted to leave gang-banging alone. I promised myself that I wouldn't kill another person, and I planned to keep that promise.

I was released at nine o'clock in the morning and had eight hours to go to my parole address and then report to my parole officer. I did neither. I went straight to Greyhound and copped a one-way ticket to New York City. I knew that a warrant would be issued for my arrest, but I didn't have a choice. If I went to my aunt's house, I'd be signing my death certificate. I climbed aboard the bus and prepared myself for a five-day ride to my future. As I rode the bus, I didn't know what tomorrow would bring. But I knew that I was never going back to jail.

I arrived at the Port Authority on 42nd Street to large buildings, busy streets, and loud noises. I had never been to New York, but while I was incarcerated, I'd read a lot about it. Since I'd been in, I heard a lot about New York starting to gang-bang as well with the Latin Kings, Bloods, and Crips. As much as I wanted a family, I vowed to never gang-bang again. I walked around aimlessly for hours and ended up in a place called the Bronx. Tired, hungry, and sweating freely from the summer heat, I leaned up against the wall of a local *bodega*. I realized that the faces had changed from 42nd Street, where the street was littered with elegant, conservative, upper–class white people. Around 125th Street, I saw mostly trendy, urban, Black people. And now I was on 135th Street and Riverside Drive. The area looked predominantly Spanish, and I decided that this was where I'd stay. I knew I could blend into society undetected.

I had approximately $220.00 left and needed to eat and find a place to live. I decided that before I spent another dollar on food, I needed to find a job. I went into the *bodega* and saw a young Spanish boy sweeping the floor and an elderly Spanish man behind the counter.

"Excuse, *Esse*," I said in my thick Mexican accent. "I'm looking for a job, Homes. Are you hiring? I work really hard."

He looked at me in my Dockers jeans, Chuck Taylor sneakers and flannel shirt and said, "*¿Habla español?*"

"*Sí.*"

"Where are you from?"

"East Los Angeles."

"Long way from home."

"Yeah, Homes."

"Can you wash hair?"

"I can do anything."

"Good. I don't need help in here," he said as I looked around and saw that most of the shelves were bare. "Walk down three blocks to a salon named Maria's. She's my sister. Tell her that Pedro sent you and that she should give you a job at the washbowl."

"*Gracias*! *Gracias*!" I said and shook his hand so vigorously that he had to pull it away. I ran the next three blocks with my knapsack firmly on my back, bobbing up and down, until I reached the salon. There was a pretty girl sitting at the front, painting her nails in a bright red nail polish. Her beauty made me feel self-conscious. I looked down at my boyish clothing and raggedy nails and promised that as soon as I saved some money I'd buy myself some nice things.

"*Hola,* is Maria here?" I asked.

"No. She not here."

"Do you know when she'll be back?"

"She no here!" she yelled and everyone stopped doing what they were doing and looked at me.

"Esse, you better watch your mouth!" Quickly all my positive thoughts about being reformed went out the window. I reached in my back pocket for a shank that I didn't have and then I remembered that I had left that life back in L.A. If this had been another place, another time, I would have broken her up into tiny pieces. Instead, I continued, "Her brother *Pedro* sent me here!"

She smiled and then I noticed that she discreetly placed an object back into her drawer, which appeared to be a gun. She walked from around her desk and embraced me.

"You're my brother's *amigo*?"

"*Sí*. He told me to come here for a job."

"Are you Dominican?" she asked.

"No. I'm Mexican," I stated proudly.

She took the smile off of her face and I understood. There has always been a rivalry going on in the Latin community. People born in Spain didn't like Puerto Ricans. Puerto Ricans didn't like Dominicans. People born in the Dominican Republic didn't like Mexicans. And Mexicans didn't like anyone. But overall, we stuck together.

"You talk funny. Where you from?"

"Los Angeles, Homes. I came here to look for a job. You know, legit."

"Follow me," she said and walked me to the back. "Do you know how to wash hair?"

"I can do anything," I eagerly said. This job was going to be easy.

"That's not what I asked," she said in English and then said in Spanish, "These Black girls come in here with their dirty hair that they wash once a week and complain if you don't scrub their scalps until you almost draw blood. You have to have strong fingers to work through their nappy hair."

I understood where she was coming from, but I felt uncomfortable at her remark. I didn't mention it, but my dead mother was Black and I'd hate for people to talk about her like that.

"I have strong fingers," I stated.

"Good. The last girl just quit. You can start tomorrow. We open every day. You can have one day off a week. Choose from Monday through Wednesday. You are not allowed Thursday through Sunday off. Those are our busiest days. If you miss work two days a month for any reason, you're fired. You make $3.00 an hour, plus tips."

"$3.00? Is that legal?" I interrupted.

"Look, take it or leave it. The only reason I'm hiring you is because you're my brother's friend. My shop brings in a lot of money. If you smile politely to these girls and wash their hair good, they will tip you nicely. You can make up to $100 on our busy days in tips. But the rule is, you can't speak English. You can only talk in Spanish. Make them believe that you don't speak English. Play dumb. Just smile when they ask you questions."

I left the beauty salon with a job and headed to 155th Street, where Maria told me that they rented furnished rooms. I walked up to a three-story building which had a sign in the window: FURNISHED ROOMS FOR RENT. I walked up the steps and rang a bell that read: SUPERINTENDENT.

An elderly Puerto Rican woman answered the door, but she didn't speak any English. Her frail body and massive amount of white hair reminded me of my grandmother. She showed me to a small room with a full-sized bed, closet, small color television, and dresser. It was the first room in the front of the house and a lot of sunlight came through. She mentioned that this room was $10 dollars cheaper than the other rooms because the tenants complained about the noise from the neighborhood kids and that she had another one available in the back of the house. That room was $160.00 dollars a week. I decided to keep this one. The bathroom was upstairs, which I'd have to share with three other tenants: two women and one man. The kitchen was down the hallway and we were expected to buy our own food. If I wanted use of the kitchen that would be another $25.00 a week, which would cover the gas bill. I decided to pass on the kitchen privileges for the moment. I only had $70.00

dollars left and needed to save as much money as possible. At that point, it was almost nine o'clock PM. and I was tired. I sat outside on the stoop, just watching life. I enjoyed watching the cars flying down the street. The kids playing tag and kick-the-can. I went inside, took a shower, and collapsed headfirst on my bed. Today was the first day of my new life.

FOUR

Lacey

Maria was right. I could make a lot of money in tips if I played the game. I smiled brightly, scrubbed hard, and said, "Me no speak English."

It was my first week of work and that Saturday I made $94.00 dollars in tips. I'd already made my rent for next week and had a few dollars to pay for kitchen privileges and to go food shopping. And the best thing about working in the shop was that we got to get our hair washed for free. The majority of the girls who worked for the shop were Dominican, with the exception of one lady, who was Puerto Rican. They all had relaxers in their hair to straighten it. Before I came there, I never used a relaxer. I had thick, wavy, heavy hair that hung down my back and touched my butt. I would put it into two braids. The third day I was there, Maria talked me into getting a relaxer to straighten out my waves. She had her best stylist do my hair. She cut the front in layers and left the back long. When she was finished, I looked in the mirror and didn't recognize myself.

"Now, if you can get some decent clothes, maybe you could get a boyfriend," Maria joked.

For a moment I felt uncomfortable. I hadn't thought about a boyfriend in years. When I got locked up, Carlito, my boyfriend, and I lost touch. Carlito took my virginity when I was twelve years old. It was part of my gang initiation, but we had stayed together until my arrest.

In the shop we were allowed five-minute breaks. I went outside and was burning up inside my flannel button-down shirt. I liked to wear it to hide my gang tattoos. I didn't want anyone meddling in my past or asking too many questions, so I wore long sleeves in the summer.

As I stood puffing on a Newport Long cigarette a police car pulled up. I could see that the officer was staring at me, which made me uncomfortable. Was he here to arrest me? How could he know so fast?

He approached slowly, all while staring directly in my eyes. I put my head down to avoid eye contact. When he got close he said, "Maria inside?"

Relieved, I said, "*Sí.*"

He walked inside and I peeked over my shoulder and saw him and Maria embrace. They talked for a minute and then I saw both of them look at me. Quickly I turned my head and felt their presence.

"Lacey, this is Hector. Our friendly neighborhood pig!" she joked.

I smiled politely and said, "*¡Me caigo del nido!,*" which means, "You don't say!"

Maria laughed. "Lacey, you can speak English. He's cool. Besides, Hector doesn't speak Spanish. What a disgrace."

"Hello," I said and looked up. He had pale skin, thin pink lips, a masculine body, and short, straight, black hair that was neatly cut and smoothed back with mousse.

"Is that a West Coast accent I detect?" Hector asked.

"Midwest," I lied.

"I thought you were—"

I interrupted Maria and said, "It was nice to meet you. My break's over."

For the following week, Hector would come in the shop, say hello to Maria and then come to the back and talk to me. Sometimes he would bring me juice from the store and then soon it turned to lunch. Maria would let me take longer breaks than the other girls so that Hector and I could talk. I could tell that she approved of us hooking up. I started to hunger for his presence. Every day around noon, I knew he'd be pulling up. And on my off days I'd sit in my room and wonder how it would feel to make love to him. Most times I couldn't believe that I was even thinking about a pig. Back in East Los Angeles, we hated cops. But I had to remind myself that I was a different person. I hated to think what would happen if he found out about my past and that I had a warrant for my arrest. That's why I was sure to tell him that my last name was Gonzales *instead* of Martinez.

Finally, after three weeks, he asked me out on a date. I was so happy and scared at the same time. I didn't have anything to wear. Maria told me not to worry. That morning she brought a bag full of outfits into the shop and when we closed, all the girls helped me pick out something to wear.

After trying on several outfits, I was down to the last one. It was a bright red ruffled dress that fit tight and zippered in the back. As soon as I walked out of the bathroom, everyone gasped.

"You look *bonita,*" Maria cried and everyone chimed in. "What size shoe do you wear?"

"I wear a size seven."

"Then these will fit," she said and pulled out a matching pair of red pumps. I looked at the heel and realized that I'd never worn heels.

"I can't walk in these," I nervously replied. "I've never worn heels."

For the next thirty minutes, I practiced walking. When I felt comfortable, Maria applied my makeup and I put on some red lipstick. I nervously waited for Hector to pick me up. He drove up in a red Camaro. He approached the shop with confidence.

Hector took me to a nice Caribbean restaurant on 137th Street. The whole night he told me how beautiful I looked. I blushed with every compliment. We drank wine and talked. He opened up about being the youngest of three siblings and having to live with an abusive father who was an alcoholic. I missed my father so much and wanted to tell Hector about my Papí, but

I knew I couldn't. I was going to make up lies about my past but decided against it. I thought it was best to remain silent and be a good listener.

"Are you okay?" he asked.

"Yeah, I'm fine. Why?"

"You seem to be daydreaming. Like you're caught up in a fairytale."

"Fairytale? Never. I don't believe in fairytales."

"Sure you do. Most women believe in fairytales," Hector replied.

"I'm not most women." I smiled.

The evening couldn't get any better. When he pulled in front of my building I said, "Do you want to come in?"

Hector leaned over, kissed my lips softly, and then said, "We have time for that. There's no rush."

I smiled sweetly and rushed inside. That night I had to dream about how he'd feel inside of me.

FIVE

Cagney

Kim and I had been fucking around heavy ever since I got out. The first couple of weeks I was home, I damn near fucked all of Harlem and half the Bronx. I had to catch up on the years that I was locked down. I hated to do Kim the way I was doing her because she was a good girl and maybe one day in the future, I'd regret not appreciating her. But for now, I didn't have any regrets. Kim was too nice. Too sweet. Too dependent. Too inexperienced. Too weak. I could go on for days. She wasn't a challenge. She wasn't wild and exotic. I knew what I was looking for, and when I found her—I was out.

Kim gave me two thousand dollars that she had saved from her tax return to get on my feet. I was supposed to buy some clothes to go on job interviews and start a small bank account. Instead, I ran through the money in one day. I went to Jimmy Jazz on 125th Street and bought Rocawear jeans, Lacoste shirts, white tees, fitted hats, and a few pairs of kicks. That day, while she was at work, I hooked up with a man from my past. I was walking past the Apollo Theater when I noticed what appeared to be Rick, sitting in the driver's seat of a blue Cadillac Escalade.

"Rick?" I asked as I approached. He had a few niggas standing around, kicking it.

"Who you be?" he sarcastically replied as he looked me up and down.

Immediately, my eyes hooded over and I bit my bottom lip.

"Don't front like you tough, you bitch-ass, snitch-ass nigga!" I yelled.

"Cagney?" Rick said as his eyes widened. "You home, nigga?"

He jumped out of his truck and came around to the street where I was standing.

"This my man I was telling y'all about. Remember, I told y'all that my man held me down and took the weight," he said. Both dudes looked at him and didn't have a clue what he was talking about.

Ignoring this silly nigga, I looked at his makeup. He was wearing an iced-out Jacob watch, new kicks, sharp gear, and he had a slight bulge in his pocket. He saw me scoping him out.

"You a'ight? You need anything?"

I was about to tell him to run his pockets but decided to think long term.

"C'mere, let me rap to you for a second," I said and put my arm tightly around his neck. "Pardon, me," I said to his two flunkies.

As we walked, I could tell Rick felt uneasy.

"You know Black got jammed up last year. He's doing a one to three," he stuttered.

"I didn't ask about Black."

"True, true."

"You seem like you're doing a'ight for yourself."

"I can't complain."

"You shouldn't. When I got sent up north, you was walkin' 'round in borrowed jeans and holes in your sneakers."

I could tell Rick felt even more uneasy and didn't know where the conversation was heading.

"So what do you want?"

"I want in."

"In where?"

"I want in whatever you're into. I need some money. My own paper, or else

I'm gonna have to start extorting niggas," I threatened. Rick's bitch ass knew he'd be first on my list.

"I hear that. Listen, me and a few cats," he said and began whispering, "we successfully pulled off a few jewelry heists."

"So that's where you gettin' paper? Knocking off jewelry stores?"

"There's a little more to it. We're famous! Have you heard of The Respectful Robbers?"

"Nah, man."

"Well, me and some other dudes are known to the media as The Respectful Robbers. We go in and make sure everyone is comfortable. Offer them water, say thank you. Yes sir, no sir. That kind of shit," Rick boasted.

"So when's the next jux?"

"Friday. If you want in, I'll have to ask the others."

"Ask the others? As in, give me permission to get down? What the fuck you mean?" I yelled.

"Listen, Cagney, calm down. You know I'ma vouch for you. But I have to clear it with my mans. I don't do this shit by myself. I'm the brains behind the organization."

"How many you got down?"

"Two more dudes. There's Reggie, he's the muscle and the triggerman. And then there's Larry. He's the lookout."

"Damn, do you really need three men to stick up a jewelry store?"

"It's usually a two- or three-man job. But it's *never* a four-man job."

"So whatchu sayin'?"

"What I just said." Rick tried to show some heart and put a little bass in his voice.

"Listen, I don't have time for this. We're cuttin' Reggie and Larry out of the next robbery."

"What? I can't do that, man."

"Look, I held you down for fifteen years while you sat out here, getting paid. You didn't even look out for my moms or send me a fuckin' money order. Nothing. As I see it, you got my mom's blood on your hands. You owe me. Either you gonna do this one stickup with me so that I can take care of my girl and get on my feet, or I'ma tap on your shoulder every chance I get. And that's not a threat."

I spoke sternly to Rick a little while longer and convinced him that it was more conducive to cut out Reggie and Larry than it would be to not let me in. He gave me his cell phone number and promised to get up with me tomorrow.

We met every day and went over the plan. Rick said he told Reggie and Larry that he needed longer to put the plan together and that they'd do the robbery next Wednesday.

On the morning of the robbery, Rick and I took the A train down into Brooklyn to Fulton Street. Toy cops patrolled the streets. I was supposed to be the muscle and lookout, while Rick would control the situation and take the cash and jewels.

When Rick pointed out the location, I knew that he had played me. There was no way there was any big money in there. I was sure that he felt I was a kibbles-and-bits-type dude. I decided not to check him now—but he'd pay for handling me this way.

It was 9:05 in the morning when we went at it. I caught the owner off guard and hit him with a swift left hook, then I backed him down with my gun. Rick shot me a dirty look. The rule was to never harm anyone.

"Fuck you, nigga. I'm runnin' this show!" I roared to Rick, sensing his anger. The store owner was startled at my outburst and tried to control the situation.

"You can take whatever you want. Just don't kill me," the store owner pleaded.

He was a fat, old walrus-looking man with a huge jowl and a large potbelly. His skin was pale white and a yarmulke was placed neatly on his balding head.

"Nobody's getting hurt. Just give us the cash and jewels and you won't get hurt. And don't try to be clever," Rick stated.

After I had secured the grounds and put the CLOSED sign back on the door, we started to load up our knapsacks. Just as I suspected, there were only gold nameplates, gold chains, and cheap rings. I knew expensive jewelry wouldn't be in such an impoverished neighborhood. When the owner gave us $900 in cash, I flipped.

"This all you got!" I said and let the butt of my gun smash into his right temple. He dropped to his knees and tried to cower in the corner. I let my Nike sneaker stomp his guts out. Finally, after the brutal beatdown, he showed us to a safe he had in the floor. When he opened it, I thought the whole room would freeze over because the jewelry was so icy. All you saw were large, clear, diamonds and yellow and red gold. Plus, there were a few stacks of money. Turns out, the stop in Brooklyn was his first stop. Then he'd head to 47th Street, known as The Diamond District, and dump all the expensive pieces. His last stop was the Bronx.

After we dumped the gold jewelry and reloaded our knapsacks with the diamonds and cash, the storeowner began pleading for his life.

"I don't want to die . . . please don't hurt me. Please, you don't have to do this," he begged as I ignored his pleas.

"Shut the fuck up!" Rick screamed. "Didn't I tell you that you weren't gonna get hurt! I don't talk just to be talk—"

Pop!Pop! The sound of my Beretta semi-automatic gun echoed.

I had turned around, placed the butt of my gun to the store owner's temple and pulled the trigger!

"No-o-o-o-o-o!" Rick yelled.

"Shut the fuck up!" I screamed and backed him down with my burner. "That mu'fucker had to go. He could have fingered us. And I ain't goin' back up north."

"Damn, yo," Rick said. He was visibly shaken. "This ain't how I do things."

"Well . . . shit changed." I grinned.

SIX

Lacey

The next couple of weeks, Hector and I were inseparable. I started dressing better by buying clothes that fit closer to my body. I picked out frilly dresses and shirts covered in lace. I no longer stood out like a sore thumb by wearing khakis and Chucks. I wanted to blend into the New York scene and look more like a girl. The only things that had a hint of my past were my tattoos and my accent. For now, I couldn't do anything about my accent, but I wanted to get my tattoos covered.

I had Wednesday off and went to a tattoo parlor in the village. I sat down and got my gang name covered up. I decided on two Asian symbols. One said PEACE. The other, LOVE. The tattoos looked so good I decided to get two more. I got my father's name on my shoulder and a strawberry tattoo placed on my upper thigh next to my pussy. I liked that one the most.

That night, Hector took me to the movies to see *Four Brothers,* starring Mark Wahlberg. This time, when he dropped me off, he asked if he could come inside. Gladly, I said yes. We walked into my small yet neat room and he sat down on my bed as I slipped off my shoes.

"Would you like anything to drink?" I asked.

"I'm not thirsty but I'm a bit hungry," Hector said.

I thought about what I had to eat inside and figured I could make him a turkey sandwich. "What would you like to eat?"

"You," he said and pulled me toward him.

I smiled.

Gently, he put his hand behind my neck and kissed me softly. His kisses slowly moved down to my neck and he began to gently suck my earlobe. I stood back and pulled off my shirt and waited for him to do the same. Following my lead, Hector pulled his shirt over his head and let it hit the ground. Then I pulled off my jeans and stood there in my bra and panties. He did the same and stood there in his boxers. Then I teased him by turning around before unclasping my bra. My large breasts fell into my hands and he walked up behind me. I could feel his hard dick pressing against my back. Slowly, Hector turned me around to face him. I was still modestly holding my breasts until he removed my hands. He bent down and began sucking on my nipples and my pussy began to throb. I wanted him to enter me so badly.

We made our way to my bed and I felt his heavy weight on top of me. Slowly he slid my panties off, parted my legs, and buried his head in my pussy. His wet tongue flickered rapidly, beating my clit as if to chastise me. Then he'd slow down and suck my clitoris while murmuring, "You taste so good."

I began to rock my hips back and forth, getting lost in the moment. I felt waves of pleasure cascading through my body and my legs began to uncontrollably tremble.

"Hector, please, enter me . . ." I begged.

He shook his head and began inserting his tongue deep into my cave. Hot juices seeped out and I moaned in pleasure. Finally, I was able to pull him up, but instead of letting him enter me, I turned him over to suck his dick.

I started off slowly by sucking the tip. When I had my rhythm right I began to lick his shaft. Up and down, slowly. Then Hector dug his hands in my massive mane of hair and began to guide me. I made sure his dick was wet and I engulfed it. My jaws caved in and out and he began to fuck my mouth.

"*Mamita* . . . don't stop. Make Daddy feel good . . ." Hector crooned.

"You like it?" I asked in between licks.

"I love it . . . Oo-o-o-oh, do that shit. I'm getting ready to cum," he moaned and tried to pull me up, but I refused. I kept sucking until his dick grew even larger in my mouth. When Hector gripped my hair even tighter, I knew he was about to explode. Hot juices seeped into my mouth and I sucked until I had him drained. Discreetly, I spit out his semen over the side of the bed and climbed on top of him.

"Lacey, that felt so good," Hector assured me.

"*Papí,* can't you get it up again? I want you to enter me."

He looked down at his limp penis and shook his head.

"I think he's done for the night."

Within seconds, Hector was sound asleep and I was wide awake from frustration. Reluctantly, I drifted off to sleep.

The next morning we awoke to his cell phone ringing incessantly. Finally, he answered it.

"Hello," his groggy voice answered.

I couldn't hear what was being said but I could hear a woman's voice. Hector's body language became distant and he pushed me off of his chest. After a few seconds of, "Yes . . . no . . . I'm on my way," he hung up and began getting dressed.

"Who was that?"

"My wife," he said while never giving me eye contact.

"Your what?"

Hector stopped dressing for a moment and held up his left hand, "My wife."

My heart dropped.

"I didn't know you were married," I said in a daze.

"Sure you did. I have this ring on my finger."

"But I didn't notice it. Why didn't you tell me?" I yelled.

"Look, I'll explain later. I'll pick you up from work," he said and tried to leave.

Immediately I jumped up and kicked Hector in his back as he was trying to exit. He fell forward and spun around quickly. I picked up the lone chair sitting in the corner and tried to bash him in his head, but he ducked and the chair hit the wall. He charged me and wrestled me to the bed and we began tussling. He smacked my face several times while pleading with me to stop. Suddenly, I realized that I couldn't win and gave up.

I burst into tears and was angered. I knew he had to be too good to be true. This is exactly why I never read fairytales as a kid. Love didn't exist.

SEVEN

Cagney

We went back to Rick's crib to split up the money and jewels. He had a nice apartment on 122nd Street in Harlem. When I walked in, I saw a brown leather sofa, 60-inch plasma television, and hardwood floors. I didn't go in the back to see his bedroom.

"You really doin' a'ight," I said.

"Yeaaah, man," Rick grinned. "Now that you got this score, you can do a'ight too."

"This one caper ain't gonna do it for me. I got bills. My girl been holdin' me down while I was locked up. I want to start pulling my weight."

"I hear that," he said as he counted the money. "So where you staying, anyway?"

"Not too far from here," I said evasively.

"Word? Where?" Rick probed.

"145th," I lied.

"My man live over there. What's the address? I may want to swing through," he continued.

"Man, I don't even know the address. I only know how to get there."

"True, true. Is it before or after the McDonald's on Broadway?"

"Damn, who you working for? Your snitch ass is asking too many questions."

"There you go," he said and was interrupted by his cell phone ringing. He picked up. "Hey Regina, I think you should come through. Yeah . . . yeah, and bring Daisy."

I couldn't hear what was being said on the other line, but I knew it was directed at me. I remembered that Rick said his man Reggie was the triggerman. I felt like if I didn't make a move, Rick and his crew would. I didn't doubt that Regina was Reggie and Daisy was his burner. I knew I had to remain cool and not let Rick know that I peeped his move. He was such an amateur and didn't know who the fuck he was fucking with. I knew I was going to put Rick to sleep but I figured we'd get more money together first.

"Who's that?" I casually asked.

"That's this bitch I'm fucking. I told her to bring her cousin. For you."

"That's what's up," I said. "I hope she's ready to get her fuck on."

"Oh, no doubt."

"So how much money we scored?"

"A little over thirty thousand. But the jewels is where we're gonna see our dough. We got about seven Rolexes, three Ulysses Nardins, nine Grimoldis . . . we got mad shit!"

I knew I didn't have much time to move. And I knew I needed to move in silence. "Put on some music before the bitches come through," I said.

"Go ahead," Rick said and pointed toward his CD player. I turned on the radio and must have given myself away by turning it up too loud because as I turned around, I felt the wind as a bullet zipped past my left ear. I dropped to the floor and reached for my .9 mm. This mu'fucker must've be crazy, trying to take me out! He had more heart than I'd given him. It was alarmingly clear that someone was going out in a body bag. The question was: Who?

Before Rick could get off the second round, I hit him in his left leg. When he succumbed and dropped to one knee, he started shooting randomly. Each bullet thundered loudly. That, coupled with the loud sounds on the stereo, was a dizzying combination. I was able to get a clear shot, which hit him in his chest. He fell backwards and reached for his chest, which was oozing in blood.

"I can't believe you killed me," Rick yelled. "How could you do this shit? I thought we were boys."

I leaned down to run his pockets and to remove his icy watch and chain. He had begun huffing and puffing, trying to stay conscious. Rick's eyes were darting around the room, as if searching for someone to come and rescue him. He drooled as his mouth involuntarily hung open.

I didn't say a word. I ran around as quickly as I could, gathering up all the money and jewels, and bounced. As I was coming down the steps, I could see two guys getting into the elevator. I didn't doubt that they were Reggie and Larry. I walked casually out of Rick's apartment building. Once outside, I hauled ass down the block. My legs quivered as they took flight down the narrow block. It had begun to rain as I sloshed through the puddles in an effort to get as far away as I could from the scene of the crime.

I went home and hid the money and jewelry inside the bottom of the closet in Kim's house. That shit was so dirty, I knew she'd never find it. One part of me wanted to give her back her $2000 that she'd given me. The other part wanted to save all the money I had. The better side of me decided to give her back her money. I didn't want any broad holding anything over my head. Besides, Kim was a good girl and she deserved better than me.

EIGHT

Lacey

For the next couple of days, Hector didn't come around, which only fueled my fire. Instead of him begging for forgiveness for deceiving me—he avoided me. On the fifth day he sent a bouquet of roses to my job. Everyone hovered around, smelling my roses, but it just wasn't enough. When he came by that evening, I knew I had to end it. I couldn't be second to his wife. But still, a part of me needed to hear his explanation.

"I always thought you knew," Hector said.

"How could I have known if you didn't tell me, *Esse*?"

"I'm sorry. It's my fault. I just assumed that someone around here would have told you. Everyone knows I'm married."

"That wasn't their place!" I yelled. "I thought we had something."

"We do. Listen, when I met you, my wife and I were going through problems. We had temporarily separated and then I swung by and saw you. I saw a beautiful girl with baggy boyish clothing, full lips, and sexy eyes, and I wanted to know her better. At that point, I didn't know if I was going back to my wife. Then she called and we decided to work on it for the kids."

"Kids?"

"Yes. We have two kids."

"Perfect little family," I remarked dryly.

"If we were perfect, I'd never have met you. Listen, Lacey, I care about you. And I wanted to know if you could handle this."

"Handle what?"

"You and me. Together."

"Why are you even married if you still want to fuck me?"

"I thought you didn't believe in fairytales."

"I don't!"

"Then you know that men have needs. My wife can't possibly satisfy all my needs."

"Maybe it's the other way around," I sarcastically replied. "You're twenty years old and can't get it up twice in one night!"

Hector put his head down. "That was a low blow. But I'll accept it for hurting you. Listen, if you ever need me, I'll always be here for you. I protect all my girls . . . just ask Maria."

"You and Maria . . ." My voice trailed off.

"I thought you knew that, too," he said.

I walked back into work, feeling betrayed. My next plan was to find employment somewhere else. I couldn't take watching Hector come around every day to talk to Maria. Several weeks later, I was still working there.

The summer heat baked the concrete and snatched my breath. I stood outside, smoking a cigarette, when a black Tahoe pulled in front. I watched as the passenger got out. She was a nice-looking Black girl with her hair pulled back tightly in a ponytail. She had an expensive bag draped over her arm, stiletto shoes, tight jeans, and a wife-beater shirt that exposed her small breasts. When HE got out of the car, my mouth hung open. He was tall with brown skin; broad, muscular shoulders; and tree-trunk legs. His eyes were small and slanted, and when he smiled at her, he had the sexiest smile.

He trailed behind the girl, and at first, I wasn't sure if they were related or if she was his girlfriend. Moments later my suspicions were put to rest when their lips smacked together and he reached deep into his pockets and peeled off a few twenties and handed them to her. As he passed by me our eyes met and I knew he was THE ONE. A chill ran down my spine and I shuddered. I followed them inside and watched the girl have a brief conversation with Maria until she was led to the washbowl. As the cute guy left he said, "Kim, hit me when you're done and I'll come back and pick you up."

"Okay," she crooned. "Cagney!"

"Yeah, baby," he replied.

"I love you," she gloated.

"I know."

I watched him carefully in a trancelike state until I heard, "See something you like?"

I turned around and it was Kim. I started to say something but Maria gave me a stern look. So I remained silent but thought, *I see something I want!*

So . . . his name is Cagney. Cagney and Lacey, I thought. *I like that.*

NINE

Cagney

I peeped shorty watching me every time I'd drop off Kim to get her hair washed. She'd come outside and stand in front and watch my movements. At first, I wasn't impressed by her. Every time she would come outside, she'd have on the same plain white T-shirt and cheap jeans. Her hair was always pulled back in a tight ponytail and she didn't wear any makeup. I didn't like women who wore makeup, but at least but on some lip gloss to entice me as a man. The one thing shorty had going for herself was her beauty. She had extremely long, silky black hair with a golden brown tan. Her eyebrows were naturally arched and she had dark, almost black, mysterious eyes. Her full, pouty, pink lips were shaped perfectly. But what stood out even more was her sexy shape. She had voluptuous breasts, an extra small waist, wide hips, a fat ass, and thick thighs that I could imagine being wrapped around my waist. One day I watched her watching me when the owner came outside and they began arguing about money. Right away I wanted to get to know the girl with the fiery temper.

TEN

Lacey

I wasn't used to being social in society and was a bit hesitant about making friends, considering my past. Each morning I'd go to work and then return immediately back home. After the recent breakup with Hector, the situation had me stressed. I went into work and was enjoying the slight summer breeze when Cagney appeared. He pulled up in front of Maria's, smoking on a cigarette while bopping his head to music coming from his car stereo. I noticed that Kim wasn't with him. We made eye contact and I quickly turned away. But I could still feel his eyes on me. Staring. After a few minutes he walked over.

Cagney

"What's good?" I asked. Shorty looked at least eighteen years old. My eyes immediately scanned her thick thighs, flat stomach, and large breasts. My dick immediately got hard. I had to stick my hand inside my jeans pocket to hold my dick down.

"Nothing," she replied.

"You new around here?"

"Yeah."

"Where you from. West side?" I asked hearing her accent.

"West side?" she said and frowned up her face.

"Yeah. The West Coast. You look and sound like a West Coast chick."

"*Hombre,* I ain't from the West Coast. And I'm not your chick. Chicken. Or chickenhead!" she said with a heavy accent.

"Oh, then you must be my bitch," I sarcastically replied. Then I said, "Nah, I'm just fuckin' with you."

She rolled her pretty eyes. "Bitches are tamed on leashes."

"I'd like to tame you in the bedroom," I said and smiled. Before she could lose her temper I said, "You asked for that one. What's your name?"

"Lacey."

"Lay . . . what?"

"LAY-CEE."

"That's different. My name's Cagney."

"The nerve of you!" Lacey laughed and I noticed she had the whitest teeth I'd ever seen.

"I know, right?" I said and put out my cigarette. "Come over here."

Lacey walked closer to me and I got a better look at her. For some reason you knew she was Spanish, but she also looked as if she had a hint of Asian in her from the shape of her face and nose.

"Do you think we could get up and go out?" I asked.

"Go out? Don't you have a girlfriend?" she replied.

I smiled brightly. She confirmed my suspicions.

"Let me handle that."

"You bet-ter. If you know what's good for her," she threatened.

"There you go, talkin' tough," I laughed. "Don't let your mouth get you into something you can't handle. You look like if someone blew on you, you'd fold."

Lacey gave me a look that said I really didn't know her. Ignoring that, I pursued. "So what's up? Can I take you out tonight?"

"Not tonight . . . maybe lay-ter."

"Later, huh? I see you want to play hard to get. I feel you. Just don't play too hard because you won't get got . . . at least not by me," I said, walking back to my jeep.

Before I sped off, I took another look at her and she gave me the finger. I burst out into laughter and drove off. This one had definitely gotten my attention.

ELEVEN

Lacey

When the handsome Cagney drove away, I couldn't get him off my mind. Immediately, I took a look at my clothing. Up until now I thought that I was dressing better. On one of my breaks, I decided to look through a few fashion magazines. I flipped through to get a better understanding of how women dress. While perusing each magazine, Maria told me that Pedro wanted to see me.

"But I'm working," I said, suddenly realizing that I needed to make even more money.

"It's okay. And it's important," she sternly replied.

Realizing that Pedro was the one who'd gotten me the job, I decided to see what he wanted. Today the sun wasn't as hot as it normally was this time of year. When I got to the store, Pedro was behind the counter and Carlos was cleaning up as usual. Pedro seemed really happy to see me.

"Hey, what'chu *vatos* doing?" I asked.

"Ah-h-h-h, Lacey. Come here," Pedro said and embraced me. "Follow me."

We walked in the back and Pedro began whispering.

"Lacey, you have earned my trust and I believe that you are loyal."

"Yes."

"How would you like to earn some money?"

"How much money and what do I have to do?"

Pedro then opened up a small safe hidden behind a shelf that held pasta and cans of soup. Inside the safe there were a few stacks of money and a block of cocaine.

"Do you know what this is?" he asked.

"What I look like?"

"Okay, okay, tough girl. All you have to do is take this package to an address and then receive a package. Bring it safely back to me and collect five hundred dollars."

"You're going to give me five hundred dollars for being a mailman?" I asked incredulously.

Pedro smiled. "If that's too much money, then I'll take some of it back."

"No! No! I'll do it. I need the money."

I left Pedro's bodega with the package inside my knapsack and headed to the address he gave me. I had to go to an apartment building on Riverside Drive. I knocked and was led in by a Colombian man who only said a few words to me. He had me wait by the door and went into a back room to check the product. I guess he was pleased because he gave me a package of what I suspected was money to take back to Pedro. Then he tried to usher me out.

"Wait. I'm not leaving until I count this money, Homes," I demanded.

"I cheat no one!" he yelled.

"Well, fuck you, *Esse*! This is business!" I dropped to my knees and began counting the money.

When I got back to Pedro's, he gave me an extra two hundred dollars. He said the man called him and told him what I'd done. For being smart and brave, Pedro said he had to reward me.

With my extra seven hundred dollars, I went shopping. I bought Express jeans, sexy halter tops from H&M, stilettos from Nine West, and lip gloss from M·A·C. I went home and tried on my clothes and loved the way my jeans hugged my ass. I never felt so feminine. I threw away my bright red lipstick and any clothing that was too Latin, like my frilly dresses with the pastel colors. And I also threw away any clothing that was too West Coast, like my khaki pants and Chucks.

I went to work with my new look and received some criticism from Maria.

"You look like a *moreno,*" she spat. This meant that I looked like a Black girl. I just smiled because I knew she was jealous. I looked good.

I waited for days for Cagney to come back and ask me again on a date. As one week turned into two, I fought hard not to give up hope. His girlfriend came in twice—without him. I didn't know if that was good or bad. Did he not drop her off because they had broken up? Or did he not drop her off because he was avoiding me?

TWELVE

Cagney

This morning I woke up in Kim's bed. Yesterday, I had successfully pulled off another jewelry store heist with the help of two new recruits, Ruddy and Maino. I met them at the halfway house and we vibed immediately. We all had something in common: We wouldn't hesitate to put a bullet in your head if you were standing in between us and our money or our freedom.

After I had my little run-in with the exotic Lacey, I pushed her to the back of my mind because I was on a paper chase. I kept meaning to go back and scoop her up, but things kept getting in my way. Since knocking off two more jewelry shops I had gotten my own crib on the low. I didn't even tell Kim about it. Rule number one when doing dirt: Never let anyone know where you rest your head.

I listened as Kim sang sweetly in the shower. Even though we'd had sex all night, I still wasn't satisfied. In bed, she wasn't fully letting go. I wanted her to be *nasty*. Suck my nuts and let me cum in her mouth. She was already a lady in public. Now I needed a freak in bed. When she emerged from the shower to my dismay, she was already dressed. I had anticipated her coming out with drops of water cascading down her shapely thighs. I'd hoped she'd sit down on the edge of the bed and let the towel fall loosely from around her breasts and hit the floor. Then, she'd knowingly rub baby oil into her glistening skin in circular motions. She'd rub her breasts . . . thighs . . . and then spread her legs and begin to massage her clit. After watching her put on a show, I'd have her . . . my way!

But once again, her lack of imagination had turned what could have been an exciting moment to a meaningless morning. Sourly, I kicked the covers off me and headed to take a shower. I looked at her and said nothing.

"Hey, you," Kim smiled sweetly. "I still have a few minutes before I have to go to work. Do you want me to make you breakfast?"

I didn't even look at her as I shook my head.

As I lathered my body I couldn't help but think about Lacey. The sexy girl who gave me the finger. Her massive amount of dark hair and features, sexy accent, and full pink lips had caught my interest. I decided that today would be the day I'd start the process of winning her heart. When I came out the shower to my surprise, Kim was still here. She was sitting on her bed with a sad, pathetic look on her face. I shot her a dirty look.

"Cagney, what's up?" she asked. "Did I do something?"

I looked at Kim in her Prada shoes and pocketbook, Tahari two-piece business skirt suit and diamond earrings (compliments of me) and knew I had to end it. I felt nothing for her. Not even lust. It didn't matter that she was attractive. Or that she was fashionably stylish. Or even that she was genuinely an intelligent girl. I knew that I was a *good* dude. And even though she was a *good* girl, I felt that we weren't *good* together. Once I realized that I didn't need Kim anymore, I felt relieved. She'd served her purpose. She'd gotten me through a tough time while I was locked down. She'd put a roof over my head when I needed it. She even comforted me after the death of my mother. But still, I had to do what was best for me. Some may say that I was being selfish. I'd say that I was indulging in my self-interest.

I thought quickly of what would be the best way to end this relationship. When I was younger, I'd fuck a girl and then not return her calls. Eventually, she'd get the hint. Now that I was a man, I realized that that was a coward's way of thinking. Kim deserved better.

"Kim, you know how I feel about you, but it's just not working out."

"What?" she said as her eyes popped open in surprise.

I shook my head and repeated, "It's just not going to work."

"Is there someone else?" Kim fearfully asked.

"No," I replied. Technically that wasn't a lie. Lacey and I hadn't hooked up yet.

"Then why?" she asked as her bottom lip began to tremble.

"You're a good girl—"

"Don't patronize me! I'm a *woman,* not a *girl*!"

I exhaled and said, "I don't want you to end up getting hurt. I'd rather leave you than to cheat on you."

"But you just said that there wasn't anybody else!" Kim yelled. Finally, she was displaying an edgier side.

"There isn't. But there will be . . . soon . . . because I'm not ready to be tied down. I think you deserve more than what I can give you. You're smart. Young. Independent. And you have a great sense of loyalty—"

Kim interrupted, "And somehow, all of that isn't enough."

"You're more than enough . . . for some other dude. I can't give you 100 percent as you deserve."

"Cagney, it can get better. I know you're the man for me. You and I together . . . we could be a power couple."

Kim was being more stubborn than I had anticipated. I tried to play the *"it's not you, it's me"* game but she wouldn't fall for it. So I had to switch lanes.

"Maybe you're not the woman for me. Your place is always disgusting. You party too much, runnin' 'round with your ghetto-ass girlfriends—"

"Ghetto?"

"Yeah, ghetto," I continued. "I can't stand that bitch Latoya!"

"You're making excuses!"

"See, there you go. I'm trying to tell you what it is and how I feel, and you don't want to listen. You're hardheaded. And most importantly, you can't satisfy me the way a man wants to be satisfied," I scolded.

At this point Kim was in tears. She wasn't sobbing uncontrollably, but tears were running down her cheeks and she'd begun sniffling.

"But I can work on all of this if you give me another chance."

"Nah, I only have one life to live and I can't waste it trying to fix something that I know won't work."

"Well, when did you have this revelation? Because it was a different story when I was making those visits to Ossining State Correctional Facility! Did you know it wouldn't work when I was running to cash my check to put half of it in your commissary? I gave you four fucking years of my life and you leave me within eight weeks of your release. I deserved better than this! In those four years, I didn't fuck anyone. I didn't date or even have a conversation with another man! I was loyal and this is how you repay me?"

"Kim, I don't have the energy to entertain this," I said dismissingly as I began to get dressed. She was trying to tug at my conscience. She wiped her tears as she saw me pack any articles that I had at her apartment.

"Aren't you going to work?" I asked, as I noticed she was already late. Kim just glared at me. I laughed and shook my head. This girl was crazy. As I laced up my Timberland boots she finally spoke.

"You ain't shit! Overnight, you've changed! I should spit in your trifling face. I hope that same bitch you're chasing fucking disses your ass. You think you're big shit because you're out stealing a couple of dollars. That shit ain't gonna last. When you get locked back up, don't come calling me," she threatened.

Instead of being angry with her for wishing bad luck on me I said, "May you find happiness. Someone to mend your heart that I've broken."

I knew Kim didn't mean what she'd said. I knew for a fact that women were emotional. Besides, I knew that I was about to live a love story. I felt that in my gut.

THIRTEEN

Cagney

After a few weeks of courting Lacey, things were about to be on and popping. I don't know why I was a little intimidated about having sex with Lacey. I definitely wanted to impress her while bringing her to feel a host of new sensations. I knew that if she allowed me in her bed, I was going to make love to her as I'd *never* made love to anyone.

When I arrived at her room, she wasn't dressed yet. Her silky hair was still wet, her clothes thrown on her bed, and she had a pink terrycloth robe hugging her vivacious curves. A few candles illuminated the room and she had Cuban music softly playing on an old CD player.

"Who's that?" I asked, referring to the woman's voice.

"Celia Cruz," she responded.

"Nice," I replied and looked at her shapely legs.

Quickly, Lacey grabbed her clothing from off her bed and said, "I'll just take a moment to get dressed. And then we can go."

My first inclination was to stop her from leaving the room. Gently, I put my hands around her waist and turned her to face me. She didn't say a word. Her dark eyes just stared provocatively into my eyes. Playfully, I pushed her up against the wall and began to lightly kiss her face. With each kiss I murmured, "Do you want me to stop?"

Effortlessly, Lacey took her hands and pushed me back. Ignoring her weak attempt, I began to lustfully suck her neck while stroking her ample breasts. Her breasts felt like soft marshmallows as my fingers maneuvered to arouse her. Her nipples popped out like a rosebud in spring. Soon we began to mutually touch and when she went to reach for my dick, I pulled back. I didn't want to frighten her off so I kneeled down, put her left leg on my shoulder and was face to face with her pussy. I opened her warm pussy and began to perform cunnilingus. My warm tongue flicked rapidly against her nether lips as her hips began to rock back and forth. As her pleasure intensified Lacey began to dig her fingers into my shoulder blade and murmur softly. Soon, I inserted my finger into her inflamed flesh and hot juices seeped out. Slowly I stood, picked up Lacey, and carried her to her bed as I would my wife on my wedding night.

I laid her down on her back. She looked passively up at me then provocatively spread her legs. I got an overwhelming feeling of dominance as I ripped off my clothes. Her eyes studied my every movement. When the boxers came off, I could tell she was shocked.

"Don't worry . . . I won't hurt you," I promised.

"I know, *papí*," she said in a baby-like voice.

I climbed on top of Lacey and positioned myself in the sixty-nine position. She didn't hesitate to perform fellatio. As she took me into her mouth she began to suck deeply on my shaft with expertise. Her long tongue licked up and down as if I was her favorite lollipop. Her petite hands guided my dick in and out of her slippery mouth and then she took the tip and began to tease me by gently nibbling, sucking and blowing until I was ready to climax. I pulled back slightly so that I could prolong my pleasure. I wasn't ready to cum.

As I continued to give her a clitoral massage Lacey begged me to enter her. I refused.

"I want you to cum in my mouth," I begged.

Lacey opened her legs wider, allowing me more access to her ripe pussy.

Then she began to sensuously stroke and lightly caress my ass. I tightened up as to not encourage her to try and stick her finger back there. Instead, she seductively began to hum on my scrotum. This action sent strong waves jolting through my body. Strong waves came cascading from my head to my toes and I climaxed into her warm mouth. As I exploded—so did Lacey. As we came together, I experienced an unusual closeness to her.

We both lay there, breathing heavily and sweating profusely. But I wasn't done. I wanted more. I needed to be inside of her. Now facing her, I could see she was a little surprised.

"You sure you can go again?" Lacey naughtily asked while licking her lips.

"The question is: Are you sure you can handle this?" I began stroking my big dick while towering over her.

"Bring it," she challenged and tossed her legs up over my shoulders. This was my favorite position because it allowed me open passageway to sink deep into her pussy. As I entered her I watched as my dick pushed through her stubborn walls. I loved watching my dick enter the pussy because it gave me visual pleasure. Her wet pussy began talking to me.

Swish . . . swish . . . swish . . .

"Baby, you feel so good," I whispered in her ear. I was still being easy on the pussy but wanted to go hard. I was enjoying what was bottomless coital infiltration and Lacey moaned her pleasure.

"*Yo te amo*," she sang.

"Say that shit," I said as my ass began to pump in and out at a faster rate. Soon, I had sunk as deep as my ten inches of dick allowed in her never-ending pussy. I switched positions and got on my knees and pumped rapidly. I spread Lacey's legs so wide, she had me amazed at the pliant positioning of her legs.

After we switched into numerous positions, I finally turned her around and began hitting it from the back. The angle of penetration and the small of her sexy back tantalized me until I couldn't hold my love much longer.

"I'm . . . getting . . . ready . . . to cum," I said through clenched teeth.

Lacey was unable to speak. She just shook her head rapidly and I felt her pussy contracting as her warm juices slid down my shaft. I wanted to cum with her and finally released into her. Once again, we both collapsed onto her bed, unable to move or speak.

At last I had found someone who could keep up with me . . . and I liked that a lot.

"You know we're making a love story," I said and kissed the side of her face.

"A love story? Like Bonnie and Clyde," Lacey replied as she looked over at my .9 mm automatic on her nightstand.

"Nah, like Romeo and Juliet."

She didn't reply. She just smiled and thought about my words and tried to make sense of them.

FOURTEEN

Lacey

"Baby, let's go to the Cherry Lounge and show off some of this new jewelry we got," Cagney said.

I shrugged my shoulders and said, "Whatever."

"A'ight. I'ma go and get me a shapeup. I might even go and cop me the Polo button-up from Macy's to wear with my True Religion jeans. What about you? Do you need anything?"

"Nah, *Esse*. I have more than I need. You've bought me so much shit I may never get a chance to wear it," I smiled.

"I like my lady to look sexy," Cagney said and slapped me on my ass. Quickly, I spun around and threw a right hook. He ducked and faked an uppercut to my chin. I pretended that he'd hit me and fell back on top of the bed. He dived on top of me and we began to passionately kiss. I felt his hard dick pressing up against my pelvis and I spread my legs.

"Ma-a-a-a-a," he moaned. "Not now . . . I gotta jet."

"Come on, *papí*," I breathed seductively in his ear. I was horny as hell since my period was only a few days away.

"Later," he said sternly and hopped off the bed. "It's going to be poppin' tonight at Cherry and I want us to be there. Wear something sexy and I'll be back around midnight."

"Wait!" I yelled.

"What?"

"We're up to three times. Are you in or out?"

"I'll call your three times and raise you one!" Cagney boasted.

"Bet!"

"Bet!" he countered.

That night, I'd decided to wear a basic black John Galliano dress with a V-neck collar. I wanted to showcase my cleavage. The back was cut low and stopped just above my ass. I decided to put on my Jimmy Choo stilettos and matching clutch bag. As for the jewelry, I went with the five-carat emerald-cut diamond earrings, pink Chopard watch with the dangling diamonds in the dial, and a platinum diamond cross.

As I waited impatiently for Cagney, I glanced in the mirror. I was amazed at the transformation I had gone through. Cagney said I was a diamond in the rough, and that all I needed was to be polished. All I knew is if I went back to *el barrio*, nobody would recognize me. I liked that thought. I liked it a lot.

Finally, Cagney beeped the horn. I peeped out the window just to be sure that it was him. I took another quick look in the mirror, grabbed my hot pink shirred mink jacket, and left.

When I got inside the car, I knew he was pleased. I looked at him for approval and he had the silliest grin on his face. Cagney wasn't big on dishing out compliments, but his eyes always displayed his feelings.

We got to the lounge in less than ten minutes. When we pulled up, there wasn't a line. Three bouncers stood outside guarding the doors, which were virtually empty.

"You sure it's supposed to be poppin'?" I asked.

"You know the party don't start until I roll up in there," Cagney bragged.

"*Papí,* pa-le-e-e-eze," I said and rolled my eyes.

Even though it was empty outside, inside the lounge was packed. I saw a few celebrities popping bottles of champagne with their entourages. A few guys gave Cagney a pound and he eased over to the bar with them, leaving me alone. Every now and then he'd glance over his shoulders to make sure that no one was speaking to me. Most guys in there knew I was his girl, but it didn't take long for a stranger to approach me.

"What you drinking tonight?" the stranger asked.

"Cristal," Cagney answered and pulled me by my hands toward the bar.

Cagney and his friends had all chipped in and bought a dozen of bottles of champagne. Around an hour later, I was having a really good time. The champagne had gone to my head and I kept giggling.

"What's so funny?" Cagney asked and kissed my lips.

"Nothing. I love you," I replied.

"Prove it," he challenged.

"I will . . . later," I sassily retorted.

"No, prove it now," he pressed.

"What do you want me to do?" I asked and licked my lips. I wanted so badly to leave and go home to fuck.

"Go bring me that pussy," Cagney said.

The champagne was really going to my head. I didn't think I'd heard him correctly so I said, "What?"

"Go get that pussy." He pointed toward a thin but shapely Black girl. She was on the dance floor, twirling her hips to Sean Paul's "I'm Still in Love With You." I watched as she wined her hips in a figure eight, dropped down to the floor, and grinded back up. She danced like she was fucking. I turned to Cagney and I could see he was turned on. I reached down and grabbed his dick and it was brick hard. I was furious.

"*Papí,* what the fuck is going on? How you gonna play me like that," I yelled.

"Come on, baby, you blowin' my high. I thought you said you loved me," Cagney said.

"You know I do," I replied as my eyes welled up with tears.

"All I want to do is have a little fun. That bitch over there been on my dick for years. Now, I could have fucked her behind your back, but you mean too much to me to lie to you. I want to have her."

"I'm not enough," I protested.

"Lacey, you're all I need. But sometimes I just wanna fuck. Let me fuck that bitch tonight and I'll make love to you."

Reluctantly, I stood up and walked hesitantly toward the girl.

"You can do it, ma," Cagney cheered.

I anticipated that this girl would shut me down immediately. I hoped she'd laugh in my face and tell me to beat it.

I tapped her on her shoulder and leaned in real close. "My name's Lacey."

She stared at me with a blank expression. I pointed toward the bar. "That guy over there is my boyfriend, Cagney. He was really hoping that you'd join us tonight . . . in our bed."

In my drunken haze, I could still see the gleam in her eyes when I made my announcement.

"I'm down for whatever," she stated. "By the way, my name's Peaches."

With that, we all left and headed back to my place. I wanted to object but I knew that Cagney didn't take *anyone* to his place. So instead of fuming, I took solace that Cagney didn't trust anyone enough to share where he laid his head—except me.

We all crept inside as best as we could, trying not to wake my neighbors. When I opened my door Peaches said, "This place is a dump."

"Shut up," Cagney said. He pulled her hair roughly and they began kissing. My stomach got queasy as I stood there, watching. I stared as his hands groped her breasts and moved down toward her ass. Peaches began tugging at his shirt before I took control and pushed her off of him.

"Strip naked," he told her and walked over and caressed my face. "Please do this for me, baby."

Cagney and I began kissing softly and he gently unzipped my dress. I stepped out of it and stood in front of him in my stilettos, bra, and panties. I looked over toward Peaches and she was completely naked. Her apricot-colored skin glistened in the moonlight that illuminated the room. Her body was tight. She had small breasts, shapely thighs, and a small, tight ass. I observed her closely because I wanted to be aware of what Cagney was seeing.

I decided that I wanted this to be over and stalling wasn't in my repertoire. I climbed on the bed and said, "Come here, *papí*."

Cagney and I started off kissing slowly and Peaches soon joined in. She began kissing his ears and licking his earlobes. We both caressed his chest and massaged his dick, which had become erect. I could feel that Peaches wanted to experience all that Cagney had to offer. He slipped on a condom before she climbed on his dick and began to ride him feverishly. Cagney pulled me up and said, "Sit on my face."

I climbed on top of his face and spread my legs wide. His long tongue slithered inside my pussy like a snake. I was now facing Peaches. As I fucked his face, Peaches rode his dick. When she leaned over and began to caress my breasts, I didn't stop her. The sensations began to become so overwhelming that I didn't stop her when she kissed me. It was different kissing a girl. Her lips were just as soft as mine.

As Cagney was about to climax he gently began to bite my clit, just the way he knew I liked it. This drove me crazy. My legs began trembling and hot waves gushed through my body. I began grinding my hips methodically until I reached my peak.

"I'm getting ready to cum," I yelled.

Cagney gripped my hips and I felt his body shudder. He pulled out of Peaches and we all switched positions. I laid flat on my back and spread my legs. Peaches leaned over and began to eat my pussy with her ass arched in the air. Again, Cagney wrapped up his dick before he entered her forcefully from the back and began ramming his dick in her ass.

She moaned in pleasure mixed with pain but she took all ten inches of his dick in her ass.

"How it feel?" Cagney asked.

"Do that shit, playah," Peaches said in between licking my pussy.

After I'd cum for the second time, I was ready for Cagney's dick. I pushed Peaches to the side and pulled Cagney on top of me. Gently, he eased his dick inside my deep cave.

"Your pussy is so tight," he crooned in my ear.

We started off slowly until our bodies were in sync. As his ass pumped in and out I wrapped my legs tightly around his trim waist. My fingernails gently dug into his masculine shoulders as he sank deeper and deeper inside of me. My pussy was so wet, it began to sing a love song. Tiny tears escaped my eyes as he nibbled on my shoulder blade. Peaches kept trying to get in but we wouldn't let her. Cagney was right. He did fuck Peaches. And he was definitely making love to me. We both came with such intensity we screamed out in ecstasy.

We lay there for long moments breathing heavily, unable to speak. Finally, Cagney said, "Three down, one more to go!"

This time we allowed Peaches to join back in. After we all fucked we were exhausted. I fell asleep wrapped tightly in Cagney's strong arms.

When I awoke the next morning, the last night's events haunted me. I looked over at Cagney and Peaches sleeping peacefully and got sick.

How could I? I thought.

I was disgusted. I went to take a shower to wash off my indiscretions. I stuck my head under the faucet and let the hot water cascade off my body. I grabbed the soap and began to scrub. I scrubbed my face, neck, stomach, legs, and pussy but still felt dirty.

I must have stayed in there for an hour. I walked back to my room with thoughts of kicking Peaches out. I opened the door and Cagney and Peaches were having "wake-up" sex without me.

I flipped.

FIFTEEN

Cagney

All I can remember is thinking that Lacey was coming to join us. I must have overlooked the rage in her eyes and stupidly thought it was lust. As Peaches rode on top, I was about to motion Lacey over when she balled up her fist and hit Peaches with a strong right hook to her left jaw. Peaches screamed in pain and instantly put her hands up in order to shield herself from further blows. I pushed Peaches off me and tried to control Lacey. That girl was stronger than I had expected. Her petite body frame had the strength of a bull as she went after Peaches relentlessly.

For long moments, I stood in shock. Lacey was handling Peaches like she was a dude. Instead of the traditional pulling of hair, biting, cursing, kicking and slapping that women usually do, Lacey was boxing her ass off. She was hitting Peaches with four- and five-piece combinations that I had not learned until I went to prison. Finally, I came to my senses and restrained Lacey before she killed Peaches in there.

Lacey was breathing heavily as she screamed, "Get the fuck out! You gonna go against me for that bitch!"

I looked at Peaches but she could barely see. Her eyes looked like two slits; they were almost swollen shut. Her nose was busted, lips split and she had large welts all over her body.

"I don't give a fuck about this bitch!" I yelled. "You gonna get us locked up with that dumb shit."

"Fuck you! You pussy eatin', little dick havin', broke-ass, punk-ass faggot!" Lacey yelled at me.

"What?" I asked. I was in shock that she would disrespect me in front of a stranger.

"You heard me, you broke bitch!"

"Bitch, suck my dick!" I replied.

Meanwhile, Peaches was getting dressed as quickly as she could.

"Your fucking mother is a bitch!" Lacey yelled back. As she said each word, she twirled her neck for emphasis.

When she disrespected my dead mother, I hauled off and slapped her. The instant I did it, I immediately regretted it. The look of hurt and pain on my baby's face hurt my heart more than I could have ever imagined. I realized that I'd never confided in her about my mother's suicide, so I'm sure she didn't realize how her remark would have affected me. I walked forward and tried to console her but she stepped back.

"Out," Lacey whispered. "Get out!"

I decided it was best that I leave. She needed time to cool off. A lot had gone on, and it was all my fault. As Peaches and I left, Lacey came to the window and yelled, "I thought this was supposed to be a love story!"

SIXTEEN

Lacey

After I beat the shit out of Peaches and kicked her and Cagney out, I called out sick from work. I knew I could never go into work and concentrate after everything that happened. I lay around in bed for two days, thinking. I took an introspective look at my life and concluded that everything I touched was destined to fail. On the third day since the incident, Cagney finally decided to come around. He banged on the door and then the window, calling my name, but I ignored him. I wasn't ready to see him. I started to realize that Cagney was controlling. And if it wasn't going his way—then he didn't give a fuck. I was in his good graces just as long as I kept my mouth shut and did everything he said. I was too strong to be bossed around by anyone. My father said I was a fighter!

Somewhere around the three o'clock hour, I got hungry. I had made my mind up that tomorrow I was rolling into work while I still had a job. Just as I opened the door there stood two men in plain clothes about to knock on the door.

"Hi," one man said while looking down at a composite picture. "You must be Lacey."

"I don't think so," I said and tried to push past them. At this point I realized that they were detectives. One of the two men grabbed me roughly by my arm and began to handcuff me as the other started reading me my Miranda rights. I tried to fight as best as I could, which only fueled the detective. He made sure he clasped the handcuffs so tight they almost cut off my blood circulation. Once inside the back of the police car, I tried complaining, but to no avail.

Back at the precinct, I sat biting my nails for hours. Nobody said anything to me. Then I was carted off to a room to stand in a lineup. After the drill, I was finally booked on assault charges. Peaches had picked me out of a lineup. As mad as the detectives thought I should have been, they couldn't help but notice that a calm came over me once I found out why I was being arrested. I thought they had found me and were going to extradite me back to Los Angeles. With this charge, I realized that I'd face a day in jail, see the judge and get released.

The next morning I was released. I went home to shower and went back to work. I told Maria that I had a summer stomach virus and that I didn't want to get everyone sick.

"I was worried about you," Maria said.

"I know, but I'm better now."

"You sure? You look a little funny." Maria scrunched up her face and tilted her head to one side as if she were trying to read my mind.

"I'm good. I'm *Mexicano*. I'm strong," I joked.

I half expected Cagney to show up and I actually wanted him to. I missed my man so much. Truthfully, he was all I had. My family back in L.A. wanted to see me *dead* and Cagney showed me what *life* was all about.

As the afternoon rolled around, Cagney hadn't shown up yet. I decided that if I didn't hear from him after work I'd call him and go over to his place. However, as I stood smoking a cigarette, Hector pulled up. He and I hadn't spoken in months. He jumped out of his squad car and was heading toward me. I tried to put out my cigarette and go back inside because I wasn't fucking with him. But he was on me too quickly.

"We need to talk," he sternly said.

"I don't have anything to say to you," I defiantly replied.

"This isn't about you and me, Lacey . . . Lacey Martinez!"

My heart dropped and my face distorted.

"Listen, I don't want an explanation. There's a warrant out for your arrest. Your fingerprints came back too late and the two detectives that arrested you are furious. They found out that you've violated your parole and want to send you back to finish out your three years of parole in California. If I were you, I wouldn't go back to your place."

"Hector, I . . . I . . . don't know what to say."

"Listen, it's just my way of saying sorry. Take care of yourself, Lacey. Don't bother telling Maria goodbye. I'll tell her for you. Now, get out of here."

Quickly, I kissed Hector on his cheek and hopped in a cab to Cagney's. When I got there his jeep was out front. I banged on the door forever until he finally came to the door. He'd been sleeping.

In silence I followed him inside his apartment. I could tell that he was pissed with me. He had a sour look on his face but I didn't have time to kiss his ass. So I got straight to the point.

"Cagney, I'm in big trouble."

"Where've you been?" he said as he tossed back a Corona beer.

"I was in jail!"

"What the fuck!"

"Yeah, Peaches had me locked up."

"I'ma beat that bitch's ass when I see her!" he yelled.

"Cagney, baby, it's bigger than Peaches. I have to confide in you," I said and broke down in tears. I was crying uncontrollably and could hardly get the words out. I think my outburst startled him and he came and embraced me.

"Sh-h-hhh. Don't cry, ma. I gotchu. Tell me your problems and I'll carry them on my shoulders. I'm a man," he assured me.

Instead of talking we started making love and then Cagney relaxed me by massaging my scalp. Finally, I was able to open up.

"When I was twelve years old, I joined a gang and started banging. There were two ways to get in. I could either get jumped in or sexed in. At the time, I had the biggest crush on the leader. He was eighteen years old and at the time I felt he was my world. I decided to get sexed in. He went first and took my virginity. Of course, the other six male members went right behind him. It's often frowned upon if you get sexed in, so once I was in the gang I needed to make an impression. I wanted to make a name for myself. I came from a family of bangers and my father was a legend in our community. Then he met this woman and I watched her control him. I was furious. On his wedding night I took my fury out on my grandmother. With my boyfriend and fellow gang members standing around watching, I took a steak knife and plunged it into my grandmother's heart. When I was arrested, I held my head high and didn't snitch. I wasn't a *rata*. My silence made my father proud. But he felt as if he had failed me and committed suicide.

"With my father dead, I didn't have his protection. And if I went back to my neighborhood, I'd be dead within a week."

"Dead?"

"Yes. Either my aunt would kill me for killing her mother, or my gang would box me out for wanting out. In jail, I vowed never to gang-bang again."

"Boxed out?"

"When you join a gang, you're in for life. If you want out, they put you in a pine box and shoot several rounds inside. You take the hits. If you survive, then you're out. If not . . ."

"Baby girl, why didn't you tell me this earlier?"

"I was afraid that I'd lose you."

"Lose me? How could you lose me? Didn't I tell you that I loved you?"

"Yes," I said as tears streamed down my cheeks.

"Do you love me?"

"Of course."

"Are you my soldier?"

"*Papí,* I'm your soldier."

"And I'm your soldier! I told you, what we're doing here is a love story!"

"Like Bonnie and Clyde."

"No. More like Romeo and Juliet," Cagney said and kissed my lips.

"Will you wait for me?" I asked, scared to hear his answer.

"Wait?"

"Yes. I'm thinking that I should turn myself in and do the three years. That way, the state won't be able to control me anymore. I can have my life back to do whatever I want and to live wherever I want."

"Baby girl, I'm not letting you turn yourself in. They gonna have to take you kicking and screaming. I can't live three years without you and so far away. The easiest way for me to get over a girl is to not have any contact with her. I can't chance falling out of love with you."

"So what can I do?"

"What can *we* do?"

I loved the fact that Cagney felt that we were in this together. But I was stumped in coming up with a solution. The only thing I could do was run.

"Cagney, the only thing we could do is avoid me being apprehended."

"I'm not gonna let them get you. This is just a fucked-up time for shit to hit the fan. My funds are practically nonexistent. And we need money so we could get up out of here. I'm thinking that we should go to Atlanta. Atlanta is the new New York."

"I've heard a lot about Atlanta."

"Then that's what it is. We're going. I just need one more jux before we jet. You know, start-up money. Atlanta is really cheap. But I can't do another jewelry store. They're hot right now. Anyway, they're at least a two-man job. You know Ruddy got knocked last week on a humble. And Maino is still in Miami with his chick."

"I could fill in for Ruddy," I desperately said. We needed that money so that we could move and start our lives over.

Cagney thought for a moment before saying, "Nah, ma. I know you get busy but I can't put you in jeopardy like that. I need something easier. Just a couple grand to get us out of here. Once we're in Atlanta, I have a few dogs I can hook up with to make us a living."

"Well, I may know someone who has that kind of money. Enough to get us out of here. And I wouldn't be in any danger."

"Word? Who?" he hungrily asked.

"His name is Pedro. He owns the *bodega* on 137th. I used to make a few dollars picking up packages—"

"What!" he exploded. "I know this punk-ass bitch wasn't using my girl as a mule!"

If I was more perceptive, I would have noticed that what I had just told him didn't sit well with Cagney. But naïvely I took it as my boyfriend pretending to be jealous.

After I filled Cagney in on all the details of how Pedro ran his operation, it didn't take him long to put a plan together, which we'd execute the next afternoon. He decided that we should pull off the robbery in broad daylight, at two o'clock in the afternoon, before the kids got out of school. Cagney figured that the later it got in the day, the more guarded people were. I hated to admit it but I was a little saddened that we were going to rob Pedro, since he'd been so good to me. But Cagney pointed out that Pedro didn't give a fuck about me. He had me dropping off kilos of coke, which could have had me serving more time in jail than I did for a murder. And comparing the type of money he'd make off of a kilo versus the amount of money I had been paid, I started to feel insulted.

Needless to say, I didn't get any sleep.

SEVENTEEN

Lacey

That morning I woke up feeling sick. I went in the bathroom and threw up my breakfast. I crawled back into bed and started having second thoughts. I needed Cagney to understand that no one was supposed to get hurt.

"What's the matter with you?" Cagney asked. He had gone out to run a few errands before we were to leave.

"Cagney, I don't know about—"

"Lacey, don't start. That's bad luck. Now, we're doing this for you. I need you to be willing to ride or die with me. Now, are you still down?"

Cagney's pep talk was exactly what I needed. I jumped out of bed, took a shower, and then we went over the plan. This time tomorrow we planned on being in Atlanta. Cagney had gone out and copped me a gun. It was a stainless steel .380.

"Can you use this?" he asked as he tossed it my way.

"I don't want to use it. But if I had to, trust me, I wouldn't hesitate to lay a man on his back!"

"That's what I'm talkin' 'bout!"

We arrived at Pedro's just before two o' clock. I had my hair pulled back in a tight ponytail. Cagney and I both had ski masks tucked safely in our jeans' pockets. But we agreed that I didn't need mine. Pedro would never rat me out to the police. He'd never go against the code. But if he ever found me—he'd kill me. We decided to park Cagney's truck back on 125th and took a cab to the *bodega*.

Cagney cased the *bodega* before he felt it was safe to go in. I told him that Pedro had a high school student come in the mornings to sweep up and stock before he went to school. And then he'd return after school and stay until sundown. During the day, Pedro was mostly alone except sometimes his brother would come to check on him. Cagney said that we didn't have more than five minutes in the store to get the money and drugs.

Calmly, I walked in, looking around. Thankfully, Pedro was alone listening to Celia Cruz on the radio. He smiled brightly when he saw me.

"Lacey, how are things? I haven't seen you in a while. Is my sister treating you good?"

"Things aren't good, Pedro," I said as I inched around the counter.

"I heard. You've been having man problems. You have Latin blood in your veins. You have no business with *el negro*. A gringo . . . maybe . . . if you like. But you need a good *chicano*," he lectured.

I looked over my shoulder and saw Cagney come in. He had his head hung low and the minute he slipped the ski mask over his head—it was on! I pulled out my .380 and said, "No, Homes. What I need is for you to come around from that counter and get me the money and the yayo. You have exactly *dos minutos*!"

I could tell that Pedro was in shock. He looked down at my gun and laughed his fears away.

"You're a disgrace," he said in Spanish and spit in my face. As the gooey liquid dripped down my cheek any regret or guilt I might have felt disappeared.

"Disrespect me again and I'll kill your sister!" I threatened.

Pedro began ranting in Spanish, which agitated Cagney. He came up and put the gun to Pedro's temple.

"Mu'fucker, you got ten seconds to get the money and the drugs before I blast your ass."

Reluctantly, Pedro led us to the back, where I'd gone on many occasions. He began to open the safe and handed over two stacks of bills. It had to be at least sixty thousand dollars. He didn't have any drugs in the safe at the moment. I assumed that he had another runner. All the while Pedro never took his eyes off of me. His eyes burned holes in my soul. He had the same look my grandmother had as I snatched her life. A look of hurt coupled with anger.

"Yeah, you had my girl fuckin' trafficking your drugs for $500 dollars a pop. Like she some cheap fuckin' laborer. You fuckin' hypocrite! Telling her to stay away from the black man. Her own fuckin' kind is who used her!"

Cagney then hit Pedro upside his head with the butt of his gun. Pedro's hand instinctually went up to block him from further blows but he didn't say a word, nor did he wince in pain. He was a strong, smart man. Pedro knew that if he didn't play hero, he'd live to fight another day. I knew Cagney and I had to get far away from here.

"Turn around and put your hands behind your back," Cagney demanded.

I then reached inside my knapsack and began to duct tape Pedro's arms behind his back and over his mouth. Cagney walked back out front and was now able to take off his ski mask. My hands trembled as I safely secured Pedro. I was working as fast as I could. However, just as Cagney was about to head out the front door, Hector walked in. Cagney froze. Hector looked at the empty counter and then at Cagney and pulled his weapon.

"Don't move! Put your hands where I can see them," Hector yelled.

Cagney began to put his hands up when I walked out.

"Hector?"

"Lacey," he said totally baffled. In that split second Cagney pulled out and discharged his weapon.

Pop! Pop!

The first bullet grazed the side of Hector's head and the second bullet hit him in his abdomen. Hector screamed in agony and dropped to one knee, discharging his weapon. The bullets randomly lodged in the walls. Within seconds Hector collapsed and doubled over. I ran to him immediately.

"Why did you shoot him!" I yelled.

"He recognized you," Cagney explained.

"So what!" I said through tears. "He would have let us go!"

"Are you crazy? He's a fuckin' pig!"

"He's my ex-boyfriend," I said and immediately regretted it. Cagney's eyes hooded over and darkened.

"Get the fuck up!" he yelled. "You sittin' here, cryin' over this mu'fucker!"

"We have to get him to the hospital!" I looked at Hector and I could tell he was losing consciousness. He was moaning in pain. I held his hand tightly and he squeezed my fingers, trying to fight for his life. I was sitting so close that I could smell his blood.

"He has a wife and kids. We can't let him die!"

"Lacey, I'm going to tell you this one last time. Get the fuck up and get it together. This mu'fucker could send me to the electric chair!"

When I continued to ignore Cagney, he walked over, leaned down and put a bullet in Hector's head at point-blank range. I watched in horror as Hector's head burst open. I was saturated in brain matter. Hector's gripped loosened on my hand and I realized he was dead. I looked up at Cagney and he had fury in his eyes. His small eyes were flickering back and forth rapidly and his small nostrils flared. There was a large vein pulsating from his temples and he was biting his bottom lip.

"Go in the back and kill your *amigo*!"

"What!" I said as my eyes widened in fear.

"I am facing the electric chair for killing a cop for you. If you love me—don't question me. We're in over our heads. And I need to be certain that if the heat comes knocking on our door, you won't be forced to snitch on me."

"I don't think I can do it," I cried.

"I thought you'd ride or die with me," Cagney asked.

I said nothing.

"I thought you said you'd ride or die with me!" he repeated in a desperate tone. "Isn't this a love story?"

"Like Bonnie and Clyde," I replied almost in a daze.

"Nah, like Romeo and Juliet," he replied.

Although, I told myself I'd never commit another murder, I really didn't have a choice. Pedro was the only thing in between us and our freedom. He could finger me for Hector's murder and it wouldn't be long before the cops connected me with Cagney. And I couldn't let my man go down for this.

I walked in the back and knew that Pedro's eyes would haunt me for the rest of my life. He knew that I would be sending him to his maker sooner than he'd planned on going. He began saying the Lords' Prayer in Spanish. Never did he beg for his life.

"Don't look at me," I yelled.

I couldn't face him. I moved cowardly and stood behind him, put the gun firmly to the back of his head and pulled the trigger.

EIGHTEEN

Lacey

We took longer in the bodega than expected. As we exited, Carlos was coming down the block. He noticed me and began to call my name.

"Lacey," he called. But I ignored him.

Stupid kid, I thought. He could have gotten himself killed. When he called my name again I felt Cagney pause for a moment. I knew he wanted to go back and finish off Carlos. But I pulled his hand and kept our backs to Carlos.

"He doesn't know for sure that it's me," I said convincingly. "Besides, we need to get as far away from here as possible."

We made it to Cagney's jeep. I desperately wanted to leave today.

"*Papí* lets go now. Let's just go. Leave everything behind."

"Lace, we have to go back to my crib. I mean, I don't want any furniture or clothes but I can't leave all that jewelry. We may need to sell it in the future."

"But we got so much money."

"I thought we'd get a couple of kilos as well, but we didn't. That means we need as many resources as possible. Being on the run is expensive. At first I thought we'd just be running from a couple of years in jail. Now were running for our lives. Lacey, I've been to jail. The real deal and I ain't going back to die in there."

I felt everything Cagney had to say. I didn't plan on going back to jail either, but I had an awful feeling. I think Cagney felt my anxiety and tried to make me feel better.

"Lacey, you're all I got. My family hates me. We gotta make it out of this. I want you to have my kids. I want you to be my wife," he said as he navigated his jeep through traffic, making sure he obeyed every traffic light.

Cagney parked his jeep a few blocks from his apartment and we walked swiftly to his building. Once inside I could feel a weight being lifted from off my shoulders. I went to take a shower while Cagney counted the money from the robbery. Each time the events would pop in my head, I'd force them out. I couldn't think about it at the moment. What was done was done.

When I emerged from the shower Cagney had all the money and his jewelry inside a black knapsack. He was on the phone with Maino, trying to sell his jeep for $5000 dollars cash. When he hung up he said Maino was with it and that he would send his little brother over with the money shortly.

"There was only forty grand in the bag," he sulked.

"Well, that's still forty grand more than what we had. You said it yourself that once we get to Atlanta, you'd be able to get your hands on more money."

"That was before I killed a cop. We gonna have to lay really low."

After Maino's little brother came and left we both decided to get some sleep. I clicked on the news to see if the robbery was on it. Cagney said that we'd leave early in the morning during rush hour and catch the Amtrak to Atlanta.

Just as I thought, the news reported the grisly double homicide that had taken place at Pedro's bodega. The sergeant was interviewed but he was tight-lipped about whether they had any suspects. But he promised that they'd apprehend the perpetrators and reminded the public that once in custody they'd seek the death penalty for killing a cop. Then the news had footage of Hector's wife and kids. She was crying and consoling her children. I couldn't watch anymore. I clicked off the television and climbed into bed. Cagney wrapped his strong arm around my waist and we both tossed and turned all night.

We got up early the next morning and again I clicked on the television.

"OH MY GOD!" I screamed. Our pictures were side by side on the news. Just as I screamed Cagney's phone began to ring off the hook. He didn't answer it. I could tell that he wanted to panic but he couldn't. He had to be strong or we'd both fall apart.

"Listen, this is a minor setback. We have to change plans. They're looking for a couple. I need you to go down the block and buy me a wig and some girly stuff. We're gonna make it out of here."

"Cagney, this is crazy. We're busted."

"Did the police kick in our door yet?" he yelled.

"No."

"Then don't give up on me. It ain't over until I say it's over!"

Cagney took me in the bathroom and cut off all my hair.

"When you go into the beauty supply shop, buy yourself a light brown, short wig. Don't get blond. Buy me a brown wig also. Nothing too flashy."

"What are you gonna wear? Do I have to buy you a dress and shoes?"

"Lacey, I wear a size eleven sneaker. I can't fit a pair of women shoes. Nah, I'ma shave my face and wear a sweat suit and sneakers like a dyke and you're my bitch. That's the best we can do."

I ran out and did as I was supposed to. At first I was leery going up in the store. But after a few moments, I realized that the Chinese storeowner didn't have a clue that I was a wanted felon. She barely looked at me or gave me eye contact. All she looked at was my money.

When I got back, Cagney was totally shaven. We both dressed in our disguises and left. We walked up the street together, trying to make it to the A train. Cagney said that once we were on the train, we should split up. As we walked up the street we both kept our heads low. We passed by a few block huggers when one of them started ranking.

"Damn, look at this fuckin' faggot," he said and pointed his finger in Cagney's face. Cagney remained silent as the group of guys burst into laughter. This fueled the guy and he kept on.

"This punk sissy mutherfucker is switching harder than my bitch!"

I looked over to Cagney and I could see his eyes hooding over. My stomach began to turn because I knew that whatever move Cagney made, I'd hold him down. As we walked, I could see the train just yards ahead. I silently prayed they'd let us make it there. I could smell the alcohol on their breath and weed on their clothing and it wasn't even nine o'clock in the morning. Soon they were all on our heels, calling us all types of sissies and dykes.

When one of them reached over and pulled off Cagney's wig, I knew it was going down! In what seemed like slow motion we both simultaneously swung around, side by side, while reaching for our burners. We both drew our guns with steady hands and aimed it at the young punk. Without hesitation we both pulled our triggers.

Pop. Pop. Pop. Pop. Pop. Pop. Pop. Pop. Pop.

We both poured lead into the young thug. His body lifted with each shot and we bodied him. Everyone scattered as his body hit the concrete. In the distance we could hear the sirens. I looked up and saw the flickering red and blue lights as a police car careened down the block. Immediately two police officers jumped out and gave chase. Cagney yelled, "Run!" to me and I took off down the block. I heard a few shots ring out but I just kept running. I could feel someone on my heels and as I turned around to fire, I was relieved to see Cagney. I began to slow down after a few blocks but he wouldn't let me. He grabbed my hand and wouldn't let me go. Finally, I was winded. When I fell to the ground, Cagney stopped.

"Cagney, run . . . I can't make it anymore."

"I'm not leaving you! Now get up!" he yelled. "Get the fuck up!"

I took a deep breath and we started off again. I followed Cagney into a building. We could still see that the police were hot on our trail. Cagney had dropped his knapsack with the money a few blocks back. We had nothing. When we got inside the building we ran up six flights of steps. It was only when we got to the roof of the building that I noticed Cagney had been shot. He was holding his side, where blood was leaking out, and I also noticed that he'd been shot in the leg. He was sweating profusely and we both knew that it would only be a matter of seconds before the cops busted onto the roof.

"Lacey, we only have a few moments. When they come in, I'm going to say that I forced you to do everything at gunpoint. You didn't a have a choice. I'll take the weight."

"Never! I can't let you do that. You said you were never going back!"

"I won't be there for long," he said and I knew exactly what he meant. He was ready to fall on his sword. Tears streamed down my cheeks and my lips began to quiver.

I grabbed Cagney's hand and walked us to the ledge of the roof.

"I thought this was a love story," I said while tears streamed down my cheeks.

"It is," he replied and knew what I wanted to do.

As the police kicked open the door to the roof, I held Cagney's hand tight, leaned over and gave him a kiss. We both took one last look over our shoulders at our past. I could faintly hear the police yelling, "FREEZE!"

We both turned around and decided our fate.

This was a love story. Just like Romeo and Juliet…

WALK WITH ME

BY

AL SAADIQ BANKS

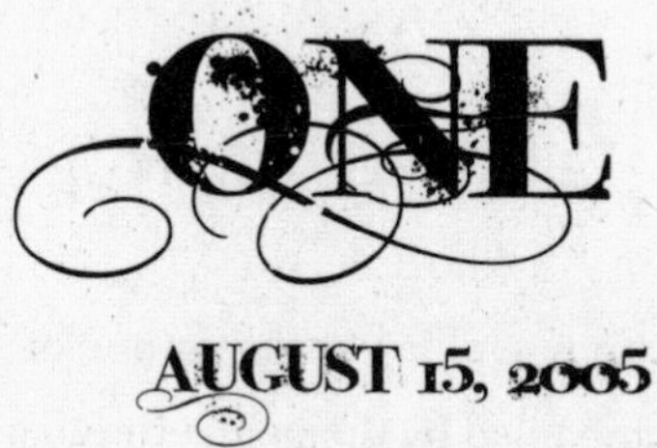

ONE

AUGUST 15, 2005

"Your Honor, this man is a menace to society, and I believe it would be a wise decision to remove him from the streets permanently before he does any further damage," the young, preppy-looking prosecutor says.

The judge looks the defendant directly in the eyes. His feelings of racism show all over his face. Anyone who is familiar with the federal judicial system knows that Judge O'Donovan hates not only black men, but also all minority men. Rumor has it that he's part of the KKK.

Judge O'Donovan's eyes are as cold as steel. His temples pulsate as he grits his teeth, causing his jawbone to flex. "Tyshon Walls, you stand before me being charged as a kingpin. You're being charged with drug trafficking, as well as weapons charges, along with the murders of two federal witnesses. How do you plead?"

Twenty-three-year-old Tyshon stands up slowly. His green state jumper hugs his upper body, exposing his overly muscular frame. His boulder-structured head sits in the center of his thick neck. His deeply receding hairline is a product of his stressful life. The shifting of his eyes makes him look sneaky and dangerous.

Tyshon stares right back into the judge's eyes without backing down. "Uhmm, uhmm," he clears his throat. "Your Honor," he says with a dry raspy voice, "they say you can never judge a man until you have walked a mile in his shoes." He stands there quietly for a matter of seconds before speaking. "Walk with me."

FEBRUARY 2005

It's midnight and the bone-chilling temperature of eighteen degrees is unbearable. The rain, accompanied by the below-freezing temperature, causes drops of hail to fall from the sky.

The sound of the golf-ball-sized rainfall splatters against the windshield of Freak's platinum-colored bi-turbo Porsche SUV. The squeaking of the windshield wipers and the sound of the heat blowing through the vents overpowers the faint tune of "Dreams," by rapper The Game that is coming through the speakers.

The driver and his two passengers all sit quietly as they vibe to the beat. The aroma of goodness trapped inside the vehicle is enough to get anyone high. The smoking of Purple Haze and sipping of 151 is how the three of them end all of their nights.

The smoke and liquor is the outlet they use to keep their sanity. Without it, their nerves would be shot. The hustle and bustle, along with all the other madness they're involved in, would drive the average man insane.

Freak and Jay sit up front, staring straight ahead like zombies. The swishing of the fast-paced wipers hypnotizes them. Tyshon sits in the back, holding his head down, just enjoying his high.

It's no coincidence that all three of them have the same thing on their mind at this actual moment. For the past year they all have been sharing the same fear, and that is the case they have pending.

The three co-defendants will begin trial first thing tomorrow morning. The results of the trial can change all their lives drastically. At the worst-case scenario, they can spend the next twenty years of their lives behind bars.

Freak cruises the block as he approaches Tyshon's house. He stops directly in front. It takes Tyshon approximately three minutes to gain his composure. He's so high that he's moving in slow motion. In fact, the whole scene seems to be playing in slow motion.

"Alright, y'all," Tyshon slurs, as if his tongue weighs a ton. He pushes the car door open and slowly extends his leg out. "I'll meet y'all at the courthouse," he says as he plants both feet onto the cement. The cold air smacks him in the face and snatches his breath away. "Be safe," he says as he slams the door.

"Miracle, later," Freak replies. "Miracle" is Tyshon's nickname.

Tyshon uses his forearm to shield his face from the hail that's making it extremely difficult for him to see ahead. Slowly he walks up the path that leads to his doorway. The wind creates a terrible resistance; yet and still, his body feels so light that Tyshon feels like he's floating instead of walking. His mind is playing tricks on him. It seems like the door is so far away, as if he'll never make it there. The closer he gets, the farther away it seems.

Freak pulls away slowly. The downpour of hail increases. That, coupled with the actual darkness of the block, makes it hard to see the road ahead of them. The wipers are no help at all. Neither is the euphoria of their high. Everything seems to be one big blur. Freak shines his high beams in order to get a better view.

They make it to the corner successfully. The red traffic light beams brightly, yet and still Freak manages not to see it. He just flows through the intersection carelessly.

As they ride up the block, Freak slows his pace without realizing it. His buzz is increasing. Enjoying the feeling and wanting to enhance it, he grabs hold of the bottle of 151 and quickly turns it up to his lips. He takes a huge gulp, attempting to drink his problems away.

As he passes the bottle over to Jay, the bright lights of the car behind them shine directly into their car, illuminating the interior, almost blinding them.

Freak continues to creep up the block. His mind is telling him to speed up, but the euphoria of his high is making him think that he has actually increased his speed.

The car behind them tails closely. Freak pays little attention to it until it swerves around him. The two cars ride side by side, just long enough for the other driver to accelerate and pass them. He now has them by a car's length.

Freak's high dampens his senses. His reaction time is so slow that he doesn't notice the car until it has passed him. Recklessly, the driver cuts directly in front of Freak. Freak slams on his brakes in the nick of time, just barely missing the back bumper of the black Chrysler 300 M.

Assuming that the driver is frustrated with his driving and decides to get in front, Freak just follows closely.

The brake lights of the Chrysler shine brightly through the pitch black tinted rear window, as the driver stops short in front of them without warning. Freak reacts many seconds too late. Before he knows it he has already crashed into the back of the vehicle.

Freak honks the horn like a maniac. "Stupid motherfucker," he slurs as he forces his driver's side door open. Jay is so high that he sits there, frozen stiff. He couldn't move if he wanted to.

The passenger's door of the Chrysler pops open, followed by the rear driver's side door. Finally the rear passenger's door opens up.

As Freak stands up, he tries to maintain his balance. His eyes are glued to the ground, trying to make sure that he doesn't miss a step. Feeling as if he has it all altogether, he finally looks up, only to be greeted by three men who are all approaching him rapidly. Despite the heavy wind, which is blowing in his face furiously, Freak still manages to see the reflection of the chrome handguns that two of the men grip tightly in their hands. Scared and surprised, Freak attempts to backpedal away from them. He tries to do so at a quick pace, but his legs don't seem to agree.

He locks eyes with the man who is farthest away from him. Even with the blurring of his vision he clearly recognizes the man. Freak doesn't know him personally, but they're not strangers to each other. They have been quiet rivals for the past few months. Freak controls the cocaine market on this side of town and his nemesis controls the market on the opposite side of town. They've never had open beef, but the tension has always been evident.

The men stand within ten feet of him. Without warning, the gunfire sounds off. *Boc, boc, boc!* The windshield shatters into tiny pieces. The gunman standing to Freak's right stands close to the passenger's side and fires three more times. *Boc, boc, boc!* The slugs rip through the passenger side window.

Freak truly thinks he's moving, but he's really standing motionless. He watches nervously as Jay's head crashes into the dashboard.

Boc, boc, boc! He hears again. The last shot ricochets off of the hood of the SUV and bounces onto the roof. Freak slowly drops to his knees, trying to protect himself. This is the biggest mistake of his life. Now the two gunmen are standing directly over him.

The shots begin ringing. The heavy downpour of rain muffles the noise of the shots. "Aghh!" Freak screams as the slugs rip through him from head to toe. His body bounces off of the asphalt as the bullets penetrate his flesh. They fire away until he shows no sign of life. In total they fire twenty-five shots.

"The city is mine!" the man in the background screams as he peeks around to make sure there are no witnesses. To his glory, there is not an onlooker in sight.

Seconds later, the three men jump back into the Chrysler and flee the scene quickly, leaving Freak and Jay lifeless.

TWO

SEVEN MONTHS PRIOR/AUGUST 2004

Freak and Jay sit in Freak's attorney's office. Freak's lawyer called an emergency meeting. There are three co-defendants, but only two are present. The third one was purposely not invited.

Freak, the head of the team, did what any boss would do. He paid for everyone's lawyer fees. Jay was arrested for sales to an undercover federal agent. The case consists of wire-tapped conversations, an abundance of cash, several weapons, and over five kilos of cocaine.

Jay always disregarded Freak's rule of never discussing business over the phone. He always felt that he was so slick and no one would ever catch on to what he was talking about. His negligence dragged Freak and Tyshon, a.k.a. Miracle, into a world of trouble.

"Hell no!" Freak shouts with fury in his voice. "I gave you a hundred and twenty-five motherfucking thousand! I ain't trying to do not one day in jail! You must be outta your fucking mind!"

"Calm down," the attorney begs.

"Fuck that! Calm down, my ass."

"Can you please just hear me out?" the attorney begs desperately. "There's only one option. I'm sure we can get around this," he claims.

"I don't give a fuck what you have to do, but you better do something!" Freak shouts angrily.

"Please listen?" he begs. "Michael," he says Freak's government name.

"Freak," he interrupts. "Never Michael; Freak."

"I'm sorry, Freak. You only have one prior conviction, and that's not even a drug charge. You, Jay, have no prior arrests. Tyshon, on the other hand, has an extensive rap sheet dating back to his younger years."

Freak, Jay, and Jay's attorney are all aware of where Freak's attorney is headed with the whole conversation. The lawyer hesitates before speaking again. "Listen," he says with his voice cracking nervously. He's petrified because he doesn't know how they'll react to what he's about to ask them to do. "Majority rules. We can pull this off if we just join forces. It all boils down to who flips first. Don't answer yet," he says. "Just think about it, first. Twenty years, or five years for conspiracy? Y'all make the choice."

"What are you saying?" Freak asks with a doubtful voice.

Jay's lawyer stands up. He decides to add his two cents. "He's saying, together we flip on Tyshon and we may walk."

"Man, hell no!" Freak shouts. "I ain't no fucking snitch! I don't get down like that," he says, feeling very disrespected.

"It's on you," Freak's lawyer says. "Freak, I've been through this situation many times before," he claims. "As we speak, Tyshon's lawyer is probably talking him into snitching on you. The feds have probably propositioned him already. He's spent over half of his life in jail already. Do you think that he wants to spend the rest of his life there?" he asks, trying to make them see his point. "Also, they know that he's the smallest man on the totem pole. After they brainwash him by telling him how greedy you are and how you're only concerned with yourself, then they'll show him how small his cut of the pie was and how you always got the bigger slice. Trust me; after that, Tyshon will tell everything that he knows. I say, we beat him to the punch."

Freak and Jay sit quietly as their attorneys stand there as a team. Jay's attorney just nods his head, agreeing with everything that Freak's lawyer is saying.

The attorney's statements spark Freak's curiosity. "How do you know that he hasn't already flipped?" Freak asks.

"Trust me, he hasn't flipped yet, but they have him weakened."

Something tells Freak that his lawyer is just talking. "How the fuck do you know?" he asks angrily.

"Listen, me and one of the feds are this close," the attorney says as he raises his right hand high in the air, crossing his fingers. "We golf together every Sunday. He tells me everything. Give me the word, I call him and we put it all in motion. It's your call."

Jay already has his mind made up. He's ready to do whatever it takes to get himself out of this situation. Freak, on the other hand, is unsure. His pride won't let him give in that easily.

Freak tosses the idea around in his head for a few minutes. Finally, he gives the attorney the OK.

Twenty minutes later, three federal agents enter the office. The seven men make their way to the federal headquarters, where both Freak and Jay give their statements as to how Tyshon was the head of the organization and how they moved at his command. To ignorant ears, all the lies sound so true.

As they were fabricating their stories, they both felt like shit, but that didn't stop them from flipping the script. "Every man for himself" are the words they constantly tell themselves as they commit the cowardly act they both have looked down on for their entire lives. They both dread the day when they have to sit on that bench and testify like Sammy the Bull.

THREE

FOUR MONTHS PRIOR/MAY 2004

Freak cruises cautiously up the suburban block in the rented Chevy Impala. He slows up as he reaches the middle of the block. He quickly combs the area very attentively before turning into the paved garage.

He parks the car and snatches the key out of the ignition. "Come on!" he instructs. Jay and Miracle hop out of the vehicle and follow him up the steps closely. He leads them directly into the apartment.

Once they're inside, Miracle is shocked at the emptiness. It looks nothing like he expected. Judging by the exterior of the house, he expected it to be laid out lavishly.

The living room only consists of a mix-and-match leather sofa and love seat, a small coffee table, and a tiny 27-inch television sitting on top of a raggedy oak wall unit.

Miracle stands in the center of the room as Jay paces throughout the apartment comfortably while talking on his cellular phone. Miracle has never been in the apartment before, but it's obvious that Jay has because he seems to know his way around.

The sound of Freak's urine splattering into the toilet echoes throughout the hollow apartment. As Miracle stands there, he can't help but wonder what Freak was in such a big rush to bring them here for. He can't begin to imagine what it's all about but he knows it has to be something good, because he has never seen Freak this hyped in all the time that he's known him.

Finally, the moment of truth arrives. Freak steps through the corridor cockily. He always has a certain swagger to his walk, but at this moment he's really extra with it. "Follow me," he mumbles as he passes Miracle. "Jay, hang up that fucking phone! Tell that bitch you'll call her back," he snaps. Jay does as he's told. He then follows suit as Freak leads them into the kitchen.

He stops short directly in front of the stainless steel, double-doored refrigerator. He places one hand on each door handle and grasps them tightly. "Listen niggas, all our prayers have been answered. We no longer have any worries. I told y'all to sit tight. Big Bro had a plan, right?" he questions. "Didn't I?" he asks arrogantly. "Miracle, when we were down Northern State, what did I tell you?"

The anxiety is killing the both of them. His long speech is making them more anxious by the second. "We're about to take over the world," Tyshon whispers in a low, mob boss-type voice.

"They done fucked up! They done fucked around and gave me the motherfucking catalog, now I'ma show these motherfuckers how to ball!" Freak says as he snatches the doors of the refrigerator open.

To Miracle's surprise he doesn't see a bit of food. The only thing in his eyesight are racks full of brick-shaped boxes.

"What the ... ?" Jay asks with a surprised tone, while Miracle stands there, still unclear of what's going on.

Freak snatches two of the bricks from the rack and hands one to each one of them. "Bust them motherfuckers open."

Jay snatches the steak knife from the sink and cuts through the casing, while Miracle struggles to get his open. Not only is this the first kilo he's ever opened, it's also the first kilo he's ever seen in real life.

Jay's eyes light up. "Damn! This is definitely that shit," he whispers as he examines the work thoroughly.

Still struggling to open his, Miracle decides to give up to save himself from any further embarrassment. He doesn't want to look like a rookie to them. He places the brick on the counter and continues to watch Jay.

"Didn't I tell y'all?" Freak asks. "Didn't I tell y'all?" he repeats, while gloating. "I told y'all all I needed was an inch and I was gon' take a motherfucking mile," he brags. "Niggas fucked up when they let me meet Poppy. All I needed was to be introduced. I knew I could take it from there. I'm a bad motherfucker," he sings. "I walked in there with nothing and I walked out with the key to the city," he laughs.

"What the fuck did you tell him?" Jay asks.

"I told him who the fuck I am, and what the fuck I'm about," Freak replies sarcastically. "I told him if he got the work, I could move the work. Then I made him think it was a privilege to fuck with me. I acted like it wasn't no biggie for me. Like I wasn't impressed with him at all. I laid it on the table like, listen, this is what I do; either we can do it together, or I'll just keep fucking with the cats I'm fucking with. I bluffed the hell outta that motherfucker." He laughs. "I gave him a million reasons why he should fuck with me. He bit, of course. Fifty motherfucking keys," Freak mumbles under his breath. "It is not a fucking game! Dig the twist, niggas, everybody in the land is at Michael Jordan (23). We at Allan Houston (20), all day," he says. "Them cross-town niggas ain't gotta chance. We're about to put them straight outta business, ya hear me?" he asks with his eyes stretched wide open. "The city is ours, no bullshit. Now listen, the nigga gambled with us, big time. I don't want to let him down. I don't want him down my back calling me every hour and shit. If we take too long, he may not fuck with me like that again. I don't want him to think that we can't handle that many joints. Y'all know how the saying goes: 'You never get a second chance to make a first impression.' I told him we would finish these in no more than two weeks," Freak informs. "But on some real shit, I really want to shake these motherfuckers in one week. That shouldn't be a problem, being that we're $3 cheaper than them dudes. All the clientele in the town will be coming our way, feel me?"

Miracle and Jay just stand there, absorbing it all in, thinking of all the money they're about to make.

Miracle was released seven months before Freak. In just one short month, Freak has already hit the jackpot by winning over the connect. He promised Miracle that he would make it happen once Miracle got home, and that he did. At that time, Miracle had a slight disbelief in him, but now he's a believer.

"Man we gon' have to pull the guns out," Freak says. "Them cross-town niggas gon' be coming for our heads after we put the town on freeze," he laughs. "The city is about to be ours!"

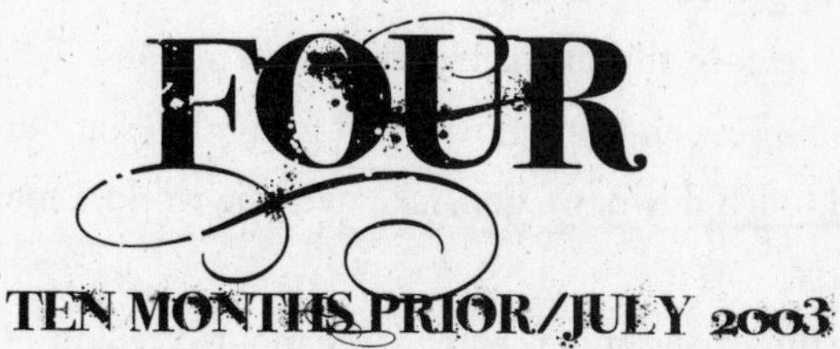

FOUR

TEN MONTHS PRIOR/JULY 2003

Miracle lays on the top bunk of the prison cell inside Northern State Prison, where he's been housed for the past eighteen months. The clutter of the tiny prison cell makes him feel trapped, but over the years he has gotten accustomed to it.

In a few short hours this entire experience will just be a memory for Miracle because tomorrow he'll be released, bright and early in the morning.

"Listen, just go out there and do whatever you have to do to maintain," Freak says from the bottom bunk where he lays face up, staring at the fuzzy cotton that hangs from the raggedy mattress. "Don't go getting in no petty-ass trouble, though. I need you out there. When I hit the bricks, it's going down. I got big, big plans," he claims. "My man Jay, you gon' love the shit outta him. I can't wait until y'all meet. He's just like us," he says. "Jay told me it's a lot of money on the street right now. He's doing his thing on a small level right now, but when I get out there, I'ma turn it up. He got a solid connect and a little team out there. The only thing is, he's on some small-time block shit. You see, Jay my man, and he a good dude and all, but he don't see the big picture," Freak informs Miracle. "He cool with getting that little bit of street paper. I ain't trying to go back to that shit. I caught my case fucking with that petty-ass street corner, nickel-and-dime shit. I ain't hustling backwards. This time I gotta do it big or I ain't gon' do it at all. You smell me?"

"Absolutely," Miracle agrees.

Freak and Miracle have been bunkies for the past thirteen months. They hit it off instantly from the very first day they met. It was thug love at first sight.

Freak got shipped to Northern State an entire year before Miracle. Freak is due to hit the streets in approximately six to eight months.

"Don't go out there and get knocked off for no bullshit," Freak warns. "I'm short. When I touch down, we gon' take over the world. I mean that shit," he says aggressively.

Miracle lay still, staring at the center of the molded ceiling. He's clueless as to what he's going to do when he hits the streets. He just hopes that he can hold it down until Freak gets home. Then hopefully, he can get in where he fits in, following Freak's lead.

A part of him has faith in Freak, but the other part believes that Freak is just blowing smoke like the rest of the inmates who just talk a good one.

Miracle really hopes that he will finally be a part of the winning team. If anyone in the world deserves a turn, it definitely has to be Miracle.

He just lay there envisioning how lovely things will be when Freak gets home. That is if, things go the way that Freak says they will. He lay there, allowing his imagination to run wild until he finally falls asleep.

FIVE

EIGHTEEN MONTHS PRIOR JANUARY 2002

Miracle stands in the front of the crowded courtroom. He stands there humbly as the judge speaks. "I hereby sentence you to eighteen months," he says coldly.

As the gravel bangs against the mahogany desk, Miracle replays the incident that led to this charge.

The small crowd of hoods huddles together in a closely-knit circle. The man standing in the center shakes the dice inside of his loosely cupped fist. "This money, right here!" he shouts before blowing inside his fist.

Whoop! Whoop! Police sirens sound off before the roller gets a chance to throw the dice. Everyone's attention switches to the police car that has pulled up directly behind them.

"Everyone against the car," the driver shouts as both police officers exit the vehicle. "I gave y'all a warning, but y'all didn't take heed. I came through here over an hour ago and asked y'all to give me my corner," he says. "And y'all still standing here. So, everybody against the car. I hope y'all got ID. Whoever ain't got ID is going down to the precinct for a record check."

The words "*record check*" make them all nervous. None of them can actually stand a record check in their real names. They're all either ex-cons or fugitives.

The driver radios in for back-up units before beginning his search. Two more police cruisers reach the scene in a matter of seconds. "Check the area," the first officer instructs the other officers as he and his partner begin frisking the row of men who now stand lined up around the vehicle.

Worry is evident on all of their faces as they watch the cops search the area high and low, like hungry bloodhounds. They try and stand there nonchalantly, acting as if they don't have anything to worry about, but their eyes tell the truth. They're scared shitless. There is no telling what these experienced cops will find. It shouldn't take much expertise because in all actuality, there are enough drugs hidden in this area to send all of these guys away for several years. The area is filled with so many illegal elements that the average dummy could luck up and find something.

The men get more and more nervous as they watch the police search spots in which they have never thought of stashing drugs. Some of the officers walk almost six blocks, searching. The fact that they've walked down to other drug dealer's territories looking for drugs makes the collection of men even more frightened. Now they're really sure the police will find something.

After frisking all of them and finding them to be clean, the officers take it to the next level. "What's your name?" the cop asks the first male in line. "You got ID?" he asks without giving the man a chance to answer the first question. The young man quickly calls out a name and the officer repeats it to the dispatcher on the walkie-talkie. The dispatcher starts the statewide record check on him. The officer goes down the line, asking their names one by one, and calling them into the dispatcher.

Finally, the officer makes his way to the last young man in line, who happens to be Miracle. "You got ID?" the officer questions.

"Yes, sir," Miracle replies respectfully. He doesn't want or need any trouble with them. Miracle digs deep into his back pocket and locates his prison ID. He hopes that they'll be lenient on him being that he's the only one who has identification.

The officer smiles at the sight of the ID. "How long have you been home?" he questions.

"Two weeks," Miracle answers shamefully.

"Two weeks?" the cop replies hastily. "And you back at it already? You don't learn, huh? How long were you away?"

"Only eleven months," Miracle mumbles.

"Only eleven months?" the cop teases. "That wasn't enough for you? What did you need, eleven years, maybe?" he asks sarcastically.

"No, sir," Miracle replies while lowering his head in shame.

The policeman calls his name into the walkie-talkie and awaits all their responses. "Watch them," he instructs his partner as he glances at the ground, walking away in search of anything illegal.

Everyone is so busy watching that particular officer that they don't even notice the short cocky white officer walking confidently through the alley of two abandoned buildings. In his hands, he holds several years of heartache for someone. "Got 'em!" he yells as he holds both hands high in the air. In one hand, he has a plastic Ziploc bag full of little crack vials. In the other hand, he holds a handgun. He has a paper towel wrapped around the rubber-gripped handle. He stands there, awaiting praise. The other policemen gloat as they watch all of the men's hearts drop to their drawers with fear.

The static of the walkie-talkie sounds off. The dispatcher is calling in with the results of her record checks. The cop walks away in secrecy. After obtaining the information that he needs, he walks close to the group of nervous males. "Whose shit is this?" he asks.

No one replies. They just stand there, staring at the ground as if he hadn't said a word.

The officer becomes furious. "Oh, nobody don't hear me, huh? Whose shit is this?" he repeats. He stares coldly into their eyes one by one. The heat that comes from his eyes burns their souls. He walks down the row until he stands face-to-face with Miracle. He quickly snatches him by the arm and escorts him to the rear of the police car. Miracle doesn't put up the slightest bit of resistance, totally submitting.

By now, all the police officers have the group of young men surrounded. "Yo, put them in the car with y'all," he says. "He's riding with us," the officer says, referring to Miracle.

Wrong place at the wrong time, Miracle thinks to himself. What a fine time he chose to stop and watch a dice game. The officer shoves him inside the vehicle and slams the door behind him.

At this moment all the males are sealed inside the police cruisers that are lined up behind the first police car.

The cop sits laid back in the driver's seat. He slides the middle partition open so Miracle can hear him speak. "Listen, I'm only asking you one time," he warns, while looking straight ahead. "Don't fucking lie to me," he says aggressively. He hesitates before speaking again. "Is that your shit?"

"No," Miracle interrupts before the officer can barely finish his question.

The officer turns around slowly and looks directly into Miracle's eyes. "Well, whose is it then?"

"I don't know, sir. I just stopped here ten minutes ago," Miracle claims.

"Well, you shouldn't have stopped," he says sarcastically. "You should have kept it moving. I just record checked you. Your record is fucked up," he reminds Miracle, as if he doesn't already know this. "Either you tell me whose shit that is, or you wear it. It's up to you," he states bluntly. "With your criminal history, it will definitely stick. You do know that, right?"

Miracle's heart fills with fear. He truly realizes that the case will surely stick, even though he's completely innocent to the entire matter. He's positive that no judge in the world will find him innocent to any crime with a record like his.

He knows that he has to try and say something to the officer to change his mind. But what, he asks himself. Miracle thinks quickly. "Sir, I really don't know whose it is," he admits. "Honestly, I just stopped here," he says, hoping that he sounded convincing enough.

"Tell me, who's the man?" the officer mumbles, while staring straight ahead out of the window.

"I don't know," Miracle replies quickly.

"You mean to tell me, you are out here every day and you don't know who the man is?" the cop asks with evidence of disbelief in his voice.

"I'm not out here every day," Miracle says as politely as he can. "I only been home for two weeks."

"You have two choices," the officer states bluntly. "Tell me who's the man, or tell me whose shit it is."

What a choice, Miracle says to himself. He's not enthused by either one. "Please, listen, sir," he pleads. "I was on my way to the store. I don't know anything."

"So, you don't know nobody out here," the cop asks while pursing his lips, as if he doesn't believe a word of Miracle's story.

"Yeah. I grew up with them," Miracle shamefully admits. After saying it, he realizes how much of a mistake he's made. He's sure the officer will continue to try and get him to talk. He's dug himself into a ditch. Now he has to dig himself out. "I'm clean, officer. I been staying out of trouble since I been home. I ain't been doing nothing," he states in a high-pitched voice. "That's on everything," Miracle cries. His eyes show pure sincerity, yet the officer still refuses to believe him.

"Wow, you've been clean for two whole weeks," the officer clowns. "Listen, do you really expect me to believe that you don't know anything? I ain't buying that shit," he says. "You got five seconds to tell me who that shit belongs to. Starting now: one," he proceeds to count. "Two . . ."

"Sir, I swear, I don't know."

"Three . . . four . . ."

"Honestly," Miracle cries.

"Five . . . it's yours!" the officer shouts. He rolls down the passenger side window. "Yo," he calls out to his partner. "Bust the doors and let them out," he instructs. "It's his shit. He's wearing it!" he says as he points to the back seat where Miracle is sitting.

Miracle can't believe his ears. "Officer, please," he begs, before the officer slams the partition in his face, muffling his voice. He feels so hopeless right now. He closes his eyes and slouches deep into the seat. Wrong place at the wrong time, he repeats to himself over and over all the way to the precinct.

MONTHS PRIOR/JULY 2000

Miracle sits in the dayroom of Bordentown Correctional Facility. He has two months in on his eleven-month jail sentence.

As he's sitting there watching television, an old Tupac video comes on. Just hearing Tupac's voice takes him back to the street. Hearing the tune makes Miracle think back to a girl he met right before he got locked up. He wonders how things would have turned out for him if he hadn't been arrested.

Miracle sits low in the passenger seat of the two-door Jaguar XK8, just enjoying the tune of Tupac's "Picture Me Rolling" ripping through the speakers.

The car is beautiful. The snow-white interior screams out from the deep midnight blue body. The white leather convertible top accents the vehicle tremendously.

Miracle's homeboy, Yah-Yah, cruises through the neighborhood, flossing as if the vehicle is his. "Picture me rolling," they both sing along with Pac.

Just riding in the vehicle is like a dream come true for the both of them. Right now, they feel like two big-time drug dealers. Neither of them has ever imagined riding in a car with this much prestige, not even in their wildest dreams. It's amazing what a few bottles of crack can do for you.

Yesterday, one of their most loyal customers came through. The Caucasian man visits the block so regularly that they can damn near set their clocks to him. On a good day, he comes through every hour on the hour. He's almost like part of the family. They even have a nickname for him. They call him White Bread.

Normally the white boy has a wallet full of money, but yesterday was different. This particular day, shockingly, he didn't have a single quarter in his pocket. He begged for credit for almost two hours before they propositioned him. As bad as he was fiending, there was no way in the world that he could refuse their offer. He gave them the car keys with no hesitation. In return, they gave him forty five-dollar bottles of cocaine. He rented them the brand new car for the week, for only a lousy $200.

Miracle and Yah-Yah agreed that they would alternate use of the vehicle. Tonight happens to be Miracle's night. He already has his entire night planned out.

A few days ago, Miracle met his dream girl. Tonight they will be sharing their first date. He can't wait to see the look on her face when she walks out of her house and sees him riding like this. He's guaranteed that she'll be highly impressed when she sets her eyes on this beauty. This vehicle is just the bait that he needs to spend tonight partaking in hours of sweaty sex.

Yah-Yah pulls in front of the corner *bodega* and double parks in the middle of the street. "I'm out," he says sadly while opening the door. "Hit me up later. I'll be around," he mumbles with a saddened look on his face. He hates to get out of the car. In just one day, he has already gotten attached to the vehicle. Suddenly reality sets in. He goes from being a drug kingpin back to the regular petty nickel-and-dime hustler that he really is, in just a matter of a few seconds.

"I'm about to go scoop Shorty," Miracle says, referring to his date. "I'll bring her back through so you can peep her," he says as he kicks his leg over the seat and slides over the console into the driver's seat.

Once Yah-Yah is out of the car, Miracle plants himself into the butter-soft seat and makes the adjustments to fit to his liking. He leans real low, barely able to see over the dashboard. With his left hand held high on top of the steering wheel, he steers up the block coasting five miles an hour, emulating a pimp in a Cadillac.

HOURS LATER

Miracle exits the parking lot of the movie theatre in East Newark. His date is going lovely. The car made an even bigger impression on her than he expected. She was all over him throughout the entire movie. He wasn't able to watch a complete scene. All he can remember is her tongue lodged into his mouth and his hands everywhere. There isn't one place that she didn't allow him to explore on her body. From the looks of things, he assumes that neither one of them will be getting a wink of sleep tonight.

Miracle switches the CD. His date relaxes herself to the tune of D'Angelo's "Lady." She hits the electric switch on the side of the seat and the chair automatically drops back slowly.

With the convertible top peeled back, a tremendous breeze flows through the vehicle. The wind flows freely through her hair. She closes her eyes tightly and bops her head to the beat. Miracle strokes her long, silky hair vigorously as he cruises up Raymond Boulevard.

Fifteen minutes later, Miracle coasts up 7th Street. It's all eyes on him as he crosses the intersection. He puts his camera face on, displaying a look of pure arrogance, as his boys gawk at the beautiful supermodel of a passenger who sits beside him.

Miracle double-parks in the middle of the street and hops out. He blushes goofily as he walks toward the small group of boys that is gathered around the phone booth in front of the small *bodega*. He slaps their hands one by one. The looks on their faces tell him that they're highly impressed with his date. That alone makes him blush even more.

"Goddamn," Yah-Yah mumbles, barely moving his lips just in case the girl is peeking at them. At this moment, she's just laid back in the seat, eyes closed, pretending to be asleep. "Where the fuck you find that one?" he asks while staring directly into the car. "I know she got a friend. Bring me in," he begs. "Where she from?"

"Ah, ah," Miracle teases. "You asking for too much info," he clowns as he fires a few playful punches at Yah-Yah's chest. "I'm out, y'all. If y'all looking for me, I'm at the Holiday Inn," he whispers cockily as he backpedals away from them.

He hops into the car, slams the gear into the drive position, and peels off, loudly screeching away. He honks the horn three times before flying up the block.

His date opens her eyes and admires him sneakily. Coincidentally, he turns toward her. They lock eyes briefly before her bashfulness kicks in, making her close her eyes with shame. The sight of her laying back with her eyes closed and her juicy, full, cherry lipstick-plastered lips slightly parted, gives Miracle an instant erection. He wonders if her lips are for show, or if she really knows what to do with them. He hopes that she won't let such a beautiful set go to waste.

The car screams as Miracle zips through the block recklessly. He slams on the brakes just short of the stop sign. As he inches into the intersection, he looks both ways to make sure it's clear. To his left he spots a police car approaching. He sits still as the cruiser passes right in front of him. As soon as the cop car has cleared his path, Miracle coasts through the intersection carefully.

As he reaches the middle of the next block, his attention is directed to the bright flashing lights that appear in his rearview mirror. He slows down in order to let them pass by him.

Because he's focusing on his rearview mirror, he doesn't notice the flashing lights that are coming right before him. Finally he looks ahead and spots two more cars coming at him. A third car follows shortly.

The sight of the police frightens Miracle even though he knows he hasn't done anything wrong. His past of mistaken convictions has instilled fear of the law in him, even when he's innocent.

The noise of the sirens makes Miracle's date sit up attentively.

Miracle's heart begins to pump extremely hard. His passenger can sense his nervousness, causing her to become nervous as well.

Miracle looks up ahead and notices that a police car with flashing lights is stretched across the intersection, acting as a roadblock.

He nervously approaches the intersection, where two policemen standing one on each side greet him. They both have their guns drawn and aimed directly at him.

Confusion sets in. *What the fuck is going on?* Miracle asks himself, as he looks around baffled. To his surprise, he's surrounded by over twenty police officers.

In a matter of seconds, they rush in for the attack, dragging him out of the car like an animal. They slam him onto the ground abusively. Before he knows it, Miracle's hands are cuffed behind his back while he's sitting in the back seat of the police car. Everything is happening so fast that he doesn't have time to analyze the situation.

From the police car, Miracle watches his date standing by the car, crying like a newborn baby. He can clearly hear her pleading to the cops how she just met him. She also explains to them all the details of their first and obviously their last date.

Minutes later, a Caucasian couple arrives at the scene in a Ford pick-up truck. As the couple jump out of the truck, Miracle feels a slight sense of hope when he realizes that the man is White Bread, the actual owner of the vehicle. He's sure the man can save him.

The white male walks around nonchalantly as the female paces around, ranting and raving like a maniac.

Miracle can't understand what is actually going on. He looks at White Bread with hope of catching his attention. He figures maybe the man will explain to the police what exactly is going on.

The man purposely avoids eye contact with Miracle until the police officer escorts the couple to the rear of the police car, where Miracle is sitting.

The officer snatches the door open. "Is that him?" he asks.

Him who? Miracle asks himself. He wonders what all this is about.

The Caucasian man looks in Miracle's direction but not once even makes an attempt to look Miracle in the eyes. Without saying a word, he nods his head.

"White Bread, what's happening," Miracle asks before the officer slams the door in his face. The officer immediately begins writing in his pad. Miracle assumes he must be filling out a police report but for what, he doesn't have the slightest clue.

After a ten-minute conversation with the couple, the officer hops into the cruiser and exits the scene, leaving the couple standing in front of their vehicle.

"Officer," Miracle calls out from the backseat. As they're riding up the block, Miracle looks to his right. There he sees his date walking up the block with her head hanging low. As they pass, she just so happens to look in his direction. They lock eyes briefly before she shakes her head with disgust. "Officer," he repeats. The driver ignores him as if he hasn't said a word. "Officer, what's going on?" he asks desperately.

The officer continues to drive, staring straight ahead.

"What a fucking date," Miracle mumbles under his breath.

SEVEN

FOUR HOURS EARLIER

A hundred miles away, a middle-aged white couple is having the biggest argument in their entire ten-year marriage.

"Greg, this is it. I can't take it anymore. I've dealt with this as long as I possibly could," Megan claims. "I've stood right by your side through over twenty rehabilitation programs. The bills are piled up so high that I don't know where to start. We are dead broke," she states. "I've exhausted every dollar that I had in the credit union. You chose a fine time to lose your job. What is the matter with you?" she asks desperately. "You should have taken your sorry ass to work, but no. You want to stay home, smoking cocaine all day and night. You blew a $150,000-a-year job. In ten years you've gone from a well-respected architect to a cocaine addict. Look at you, you're a mess," she says. "You are not the man I married. You are now a complete loser, with a capital L."

Her words are tearing Greg apart. Each tear she drops breaks his heart, piece by piece. He realizes that everything she's saying is true. He can't do anything but stand there with shame while Megan belittles him. This isn't their first time going through this. They've been down this road a few times already, yet he can't seem to stay away from the cocaine. She has threatened to leave him so many times, but the love for the cocaine seems to override the love for his wife.

"I don't know what to do. I called your boss and begged him for your job, again. As much as he wants to help you, he said it's out of his hands. I didn't have a clue that you were absent from work for three weeks straight!" Megan claims. "We've lost everything. Everything! Ten years of marriage and everything we have accumulated, you destroyed. This house is the last thing we have and we won't have this if we don't come up with six months' worth of mortgage and the back taxes!" she yells. "What the hell are we going to do? I can't borrow the money from my mom. I'm too embarrassed. I deserve better!"

The look in Megan's eyes changes from sadness to fury as she thinks back to all the hurt he's caused her. She doesn't know what has come over her. She unconsciously looks to her left and grabs the first thing in sight. She grabs the beautiful handcrafted vase by the neck and flings it furiously. "You sorry piece of shit!" she screams at the top of her lungs.

Greg ducks his head low in the nick of time as the vase crashes into the wall behind him and shatters into tiny pieces.

Megan doesn't stop there. Missing him only infuriates her more. She snatches the huge glass lamp from the end table and makes her way toward him.

"Megan, please," Greg pleads for his life. "Please?" He realizes that she's totally fed up with him. He's never seen her perform like this. She has never even raised her voice at him. He continues to back away from her. "Please, stop, Megan," he begs.

Megan's mind snaps back. She stops dead in her tracks. She slams the lamp to the hardwood floor violently. Glass disperses everywhere. "Get out," she cries as she buries her face into the palms of her hands. "Get out!" she yells hysterically. "Give me the car keys and get the hell out!"

Greg stands there foolishly as she demands the car keys that he doesn't even have in his possession. "Megan," he whispers.

"Megan, my ass!" she interrupts. "Just go!" she shouts. "Give me the keys and go," she snaps while holding her hand out, palm up. His stalling is pissing her off even more. "Now!"

"Megan, listen . . . the car . . ." Greg fumbles.

"The car what, Greg? Where's my car?"

He lowers his head with shame.

"Greg, where is my car?

Greg stands there foolishly without responding.

"Where's my freaking car? Did you crash it?" Megan asks. She's getting more and more excited by the second. A burst of strength comes from deep within her. She lifts the glass coffee table up high in the air and charges Greg like a raging bull. "Where's my car?" she asks as she approaches him quickly.

"Megan, Megan, somebody stole it," he lies just as she gets within arm's reach of him.

Her eyes stretch wide open. She halts, "From where?"

Greg stands there without replying.

"Where were you?" she asks.

He stands there quietly, trying to get his lies together.

"Greg, don't lie to me. Were you in Newark?"

Greg hates to lie to her but he has to. If he tells Megan that he rented her Jaguar to some drug dealers in exchange for cocaine, their marriage will be history. He's sure that she will never forgive him for that. He can hear it in her voice. She can't take it anymore. This is the last straw.

"Were you in Newark?" Megan repeats.

Finally, Greg answers. "Yes," he mumbles while staring at the floor. "I jumped out and one of the little thugs jumped in and took off," he lies.

Megan drops the table onto the floor and begins sobbing away. Greg stands there, full of shame, as he watches his addiction tear his home apart.

Greg hates to lie on the boys, but his marriage is first and foremost.

EIGHT

YEARS PRIOR/OCTOBER 1998

Miracle sits on his rock-hard cot in Jamesburg Correctional Facility, where he's been incarcerated for quite some time now. He's been here for close to sixty months so far. Almost five years down, and two more to go.

At the tender age of sixteen years, he's already spent seven years of his young life in jail.

As Miracle sits on the edge of the bed, he stares at an old yellow-stained newspaper clipping that he holds in his hand. Just reading the article brings tears to his eyes. He stares at the headline, which reads, "ENTIRE FAMILY TRAPPED IN DEADLY FIRE."

While sitting there, his mind takes him back to a little over five years ago.

Miracle's body trembles as he stands in Juvenile Court in front of the Honorable Judge Stone.

He stands next to his social worker, almost glued to her side. He's not the only defendant. Standing beside them are five of his friends along with their parents, mainly their moms. Miracle is the only child here with no parental representation.

Also in the courtroom are members of the fire victim's family. They have been crying ever since they entered the courtroom.

Finally the moment of truth has arrived. The sound of the gravel rips through all of their souls. “Ladies and gentlemen!” the judge shouts with a sympathetic face. “This has to be one of the hardest decisions that I have ever had to make, as long as I’ve been on the bench. In twenty years, I have never encountered a situation this heart-wrenching. And I truly wish I didn’t have to make the decision today. I retire next month,” he informs. “And God knows I wish I could have retired without judging this case. As bad as I hate to do this, I have no other choice.”

All the parents’ hearts drop to their knees. Hearing the judge’s statements assures them that they aren’t about to hear good news. A few of the women have already started crying before hearing his decision.

“I sure hope I’m making the right decision,” the judge mumbles. “I hereby sentence all six of these defendants to juvenile life, which is seven years. Court adjourned!” he yells before banging the gravel. He stands up quickly with his eyes full of tears. He exits the courtroom with his head hanging, hoping that he’s made the right decision.

NINE

APRIL 1994

A tapping on the door interrupts Miracle's classroom. "Aw, man," Miracle sighs under his breath as Mrs. Hernandez slides her chair back and stands up. The peep show is now over. Miracle has been secretly peeking underneath Mrs. Hernandez's desk for the past hour.

His eyes have been glued to her lace-trimmed pink satin panties. He hasn't heard a word that she's said. He swears that she knows that he's watching and is doing it purposely.

"Excuse me, class," Mrs. Hernandez says as she switches her way sexily to the door. Her tight mini-skirt grips her plump rear like a glove. All the male students love being in Mrs. Hernandez's sixth-grade class. The swaying of her hips hypnotizes the young boys. They all have a secret crush on her, but no one in the classroom has a bigger crush on her than Miracle. Miracle had the audacity to write her a love letter. She saved him the embarrassment by confronting him secretly, telling him that he's way too young for her and how they could never be. She let him down very easy. Still, to this day, in his mind he really believes that she's his girl. Some days he can't get a bit of work in, because of his daydreaming about him and Mrs. Hernandez.

Mrs. Hernandez is a fine young Latino woman. She's straight out of college just a few short months ago. The twenty-four-year-old sexy bombshell dresses more like a barmaid than a teacher. She wears the skimpiest outfits. She not only has the male students wrapped around her finger, she has the principal and the rest of the faculty mesmerized as well. In the few months that she's been here, she already learned to control every man in the building as if they're puppets, and she's the puppet master.

Miracle has to be the luckiest student of them all because he sits directly in front of her. He can tell you what color panties she wears on any given day. That is, if she has any on at all. Some days Miracle is blessed with the opportunity of watching her curly bush for six glorious hours. On those days he almost begs for detention.

All the students watch anxiously to find out who is knocking on the door, but instead of someone coming in, Mrs. Hernandez steps out.

Once she steps out of the room, the students lose their minds. The yelling and screaming starts up instantly. Spitballs get shot from straws all across the room, while other students jump on top of their desks and dance away as if they're auditioning for a music video.

The sound of the door opening makes everything come to a halt. They all get back to their seats and sit there with the most innocent-looking faces you could imagine. Miracle crouches down in his seat real low, preparing for Mrs. Hernandez's peep show.

Everyone's attention is directed to the door as Mrs. Hernandez enters the room, accompanied by two white men who are dressed in suits and ties. Miracle's foster mother and father sadly lag way behind.

Fear fills Miracle's body as soon as he sees his foster parents' faces. Fury is evident. He knows that he must be in deep trouble.

Both of the white men's faces are blank, while Mrs. Hernandez's face shows sympathy. She shakes her head before saying a word. Miracle happens to be one of her best students. Not only is he the most helpful of her students, he's also the most intelligent and most obedient child in the classroom. "Tyshon Walls," she calls out while lowering her eyes to the floor. "Clear your desk, and step to the front of the classroom," she instructs.

All the children watch attentively as Miracle does as he's told. As he's leaving, they all wonder why he's being taken out of the classroom.

DAYS PRIOR

Frustrated but determined, eleven-year-old Miracle makes his one hundredth attempt to complete his back semi-flip. For the life of him, he can't seem to successfully complete it.

His best friend, Junior has tried coaching him step by step, but for some reason Miracle can't seem to grasp it. Junior has taught all the neighborhood boys to flip. Everyone, except Miracle, caught the hang of it almost instantly.

Miracle uses all the strength in his little bony legs as he bounces on the stack of old raggedy mattresses. Each time that he lands, the smell of old urine fills his nostrils, but that doesn't stop him. He just has to get this back semi down pat.

All of his friends have deserted him. They got so bored watching him try the same flip over and over. They've dispersed into the yard next door; leaving Miracle all alone in the yard of the abandoned four-story building. The surrounding area is so cluttered with junk that it resembles a junkyard.

As he's concentrating, the smell of fire fills the air, but Miracle doesn't pay any attention to it. Flipping is the only thing that's on his mind. He continues to bounce up and down on the mattresses.

Here I go, he says to himself, trying to psyche himself up. "Come on, Miracle, you can do it," he says aloud. He bends his knees slightly, digging deep, trying to get a good strong bounce. He bounces once, then twice. He lands on the tips of his toes, and as his body is emerging into the air, he allows himself to float freely. Totally disgusted, he finds himself lying flat on his back once again.

While he's lying there, all five of his friends zoom past him at top speed, running out of the backyard. "Miracle, come on!" they all yell simultaneously.

He jumps up and quickly joins them in flight, without even knowing why he's running. He's clueless to the matter, but he's sure whatever it is, it must be serious because his friends are running faster and harder than they have ever run before. From the looks of it, they appear to be running for their lives.

By now, thick clouds of dark smoke hover in the sky. Miracle gags as the smoke fills his lungs. As the young boys run up the block, the nosey neighbors watch them, wondering what they have done.

The smell of fire and the loud noise of the many fire trucks attracts everyone to their porches. In a matter of seconds, everyone figures that the boys must have started the fire.

ELEVEN

TWO YEARS PRIOR/MAY 1991

In the Essex County Youth house, nine-year-old Tyshon "Miracle" Walls sits in the center of the room bashfully. His body trembles due to nervousness.

He didn't volunteer to stand here. His social worker forced him to do so. He has to complete this program in order to be released. It's all part of their Sharing is Caring program.

Miracle has to stand in front of the group next. He truly despises that. His traumatic past caused him to be an introvert. He has always had difficulty with talking about his problems. He always felt that opening up would not help at all. It only exposes his problems to everyone.

Fifteen other young boys occupy the room, Miracle being the youngest of all of them. In fact, he's the youngest child in the entire youth house. He's been here for four months already.

As young Tyshon sits there, he stares straight ahead, trying to focus on the young male who is sharing the details of his life and commenting on how much the Sharing is Caring program has helped him.

While listening to the teenager's story, Miracle's mind takes him back to the day that led him to this youth house.

Miracle walks into the dark backyard, following behind a small group of teenagers. They walk all the way to the back until they reach a raggedy little shack. They step through the tiny entrance, totally disregarding the wafer board sign that reads NO GIRLS ALLOWED written with silver spray paint. The leader has made a special exception tonight. For once, he's allowing a girl to come into the clubhouse.

This isn't just any girl. Her name is Melissa Johnson.

She's been living on the block for years. She's all the boys' dream girl. At the age of twelve, Melissa has a better body than most grown women. Melissa is the fastest girl in the entire neighborhood. All the neighborhood parents try their hardest to keep their children away from her. She supposedly lost her virginity almost two years ago. Rumor has it that she's already had sex with a few grown men.

Boys her age can only dream about her because she doesn't have the slightest interest in any of them. She constantly reminds them that she only deals with boys fifteen years old or older. Last week, Melissa allowed the clubhouse leader, fifteen-year-old Snake, the privilege of having sex with her. That act made her an official Queen of Hearts.

This raggedy shack is actually the boys' clubhouse. Miracle is honored to be their newest member. At age eight, he's proud to be the youngest member ever accepted. He's been a member for a few weeks now. He had to go through hell just to be here. It's still not official yet; he still has to pass a few more tests. He only passed Phase One so far, which consisted of him getting beat down by the other members. They beat him terribly, but his desire to join the club made him bear all the pain they put him through.

While Miracle feels his way through the dark shack, a light from a candle shines dimly. A musty mildew aroma fills the air instantly as he plops onto the old sofa.

As soon as they all sit down, the king of the clubhouse, Snake, pulls a pint of Mad Dog 20/20 from a wrinkled brown paper bag. He cracks the top and takes a huge swig before passing the bottle over to the next member in line, which happens to be Melissa. She doesn't hesitate to turn the bottle up. She takes two swigs before passing it to the next member.

As the bottle is being passed around Miracle sits there nervously. He dreads the fact that his turn is approaching quickly. He's never had liquor before. Just the thought of it makes his heart pound rapidly.

In no time at all, it's his turn. "Here," the boy says as he hands over the bottle.

Miracle slowly reaches for it. Instead of turning it up quickly like the rest of the members, he holds it momentarily while trying to figure a way out of drinking it. He really doesn't want to drink it but he's afraid to admit that to them. He's sure they'll kick him out of the club for that.

A million excuses run through his head, but none of them are good enough to blurt out. "Drink that shit, li'l nigga," Snake yells aggressively.

Miracle does as he's told. He turns the bottle up to his lips and holds his breath before throwing the liquor into his mouth. He swallows it quickly. The disgusting taste lingers on as it trickles down his throat. Finally, it's over, he says to himself as he passes the bottle back to Snake. The thick coating of alcohol that blankets his tongue almost turns his stomach.

Miracle studies the looks on all of the members' faces as he sits there awaiting the results. He doesn't have the slightest idea of what to expect.

Everyone takes another swig and it's his turn all over again. This time he turns the bottle up a little quicker.

Ten minutes and five turns later, Miracle reaches for the bottle once again. With no hesitation, he slams the liquor down his throat. His taste buds must have gotten accustomed to the taste because this time, he barely tasted the liquor.

Suddenly, he gets the urge to urinate. Miracle stands up while simultaneously passing the bottle over to Snake. Once he's standing solid on both feet, a strange rush shoots up to his head, almost knocking him off balance. The strange feeling frightens him terribly.

All of a sudden the room begins spinning right before his eyes. Miracle has to grab hold of the back of the sofa just to keep his balance. He tries to take a step, but instead he stumbles. The sound of everyone's laughter echoes. He looks over to his right. The room now appears to be filled with twelve occupants. He's baffled. He could have sworn that only four other people were in the room just a few short moments ago.

"You all right, li'l nigga?" the three Snakes ask.

Miracle nods his head as he tries to focus on the middle Snake. He looks over to three Melissa's, who happen to be taking another gulp.

Miracle takes another step and falls face first onto the wafer-board floor. He looks up helplessly, hoping that Snake will help him to his feet, but instead Snake just laughs demonically. Miracle struggles desperately. He's only been lying there for a few seconds but his intoxication makes it feel like hours.

Finally, he manages to make it onto one knee. As he props himself, his stomach muscles begin tightening up and his mouth stretches wide open simultaneously. This exact motion repeats itself four times before he throws his guts up. "Aghh," he gags. The process repeats itself once again. "Aghh," he grunts again. He peeks to his right. The room is spinning in slow motion.

"Ha, ha, ha," they all laugh simultaneously.

"Aghh," Miracle throws up once again. The force knocks him off his one knee. He lands face first into the puddle of guts and Mad Dog. This only makes the teenagers laugh even more. Scared and in pain, Miracle begins to cry like the baby that he is. Not able to move at all, he just lays there.

Minutes later, the sound of heavy breathing and moaning sounds off. The cry of pain catches Miracle's attention. Miracle manages to lift his head out of the puddle long enough to look to the sofa. What he sees shocks him. Melissa lies sprawled across the sofa butt naked, with her legs spread wide open, while Snake stands in between them pounding away.

Suddenly her cries turn into screams of torture as Snake digs into her furiously.

"No!" Melissa cries as he slams her face first onto the sofa. Snake mashes her face onto the cushions of the sofa, almost suffocating her. Another member runs over to her and grabs her from behind. Melissa's screams become louder and louder as Snake rams her from behind.

Miracle can't believe what is happening. He thinks he knows what's happening, but he doesn't know if the liquor is playing tricks with his eyes.

After the three boys have their full turn with Melissa, they all back away. She then clumsily collects her clothes and dresses herself while sobbing. The three of them watch with huge smiles on their faces as she staggers out of the clubhouse, feeling distraught and violated.

TWELVE

TWO YEARS PRIOR/JUNE 1989

Seven-year-old Miracle crawls around the living room of fifty-four-year-old Great Grandma Loraine's house. He's been living here with her ever since the tragic death of his grandmother Charlene. The horrifying event has had a terrible effect on him. He still hasn't slept one full night since that awful day.

At the innocent age of seven, little Tyshon has had a series of traumatic events that may affect him for life. Several psychiatrists have already treated him without any success.

"Vroom, vroom," he yells as he drags his racecar across the thick, plush carpet.

The ringing of the doorbell startles him, causing him to run directly to the door. He snatches it open quickly, without even asking who it is that is standing behind the door. Before he can get the door open fully, two gun-toting bandits force their way inside, almost knocking him to the floor.

"Miracle, who is it?" Great Grandma Loraine asks as she makes her way into the living room.

Tyshon stands there, frozen stiff. He's so frightened that he can't find the words to reply.

"Oww!" Loraine screams as she spots the gunmen. The first gunman pushes Miracle to the floor as the other one runs directly to Loraine. He grabs her by her arm and pulls her close to him. She almost faints as he presses the barrel of the gun against her temple.

"Where is Wise?" he asks.

"W-Wise?" she stutters with a confused tone.

"Yeah, Wise. Walter," he revises.

Walter is Loraine's only son and Miracle's great uncle. Walter has been getting into trouble ever since he was a juvenile. He always stays in the mix of something. Loraine can't imagine what kind of trouble he's gotten himself into now. Whatever it is, he has really outdone himself this time. Never before has she been affected by any of his mischievous deeds.

"I have not seen him in weeks," she manages to blurt out in a trembling voice.

"Ma'am, I'm not bullshittin'," the gunman says sternly. "Where is he?"

Miracle looks closely at both of their faces. Neither of them looks familiar to him.

"I swear I have not seen him in weeks." Right now Loraine is more scared than she's ever been in her life and it's evident. As she is a religious person, swearing and lying are two things that she never does.

"I swear, I haven't seen him in weeks," she lies again in order to save herself and her only son.

"Listen, tell me where the fuck he is," the gunman snaps. "I know you know where he's hiding." He's getting more and more furious by the second, and Loraine can sense it.

Loraine wasn't aware that Walter was in hiding, but now that the truth is out, she realizes the gunman must have a point. Common sense should have told her that something wasn't right. Walter hasn't been home in days and when he does come, he just pops in and out. That's very unlike him. "I have not seen him and I don't know where he is," she replies with a frightened tone.

"Listen, bitch," the gunman snaps. "Tell me right the fuck now!"

Loraine has never been so disrespected in her life. The word *bitch* has never been used when referring to her. Instead of getting excited, she just sits back and hopes that he'll simmer down.

"Your son ran up in my house, tied me up, and robbed me right in front of my fucking family," the gunman informs her.

This news really disturbs Loraine, although it doesn't shock her the least bit. Her body trembles as she looks into the man's eyes. She really can't believe that this is happening. "I have not seen him," she repeats.

"You better tell me where the fuck he's at," the gunman whispers, with his mouth closed, gritting down on his teeth.

The way his temples are pulsating lets Loraine know that he's getting angrier. "Listen, I don't—" she manages to say before he interrupts.

"Fuck that!" He reaches down to grab hold of little Miracle. The gunman snatches him onto his feet by his puny little arm. Once he has him on his two feet, he shoves Miracle onto Loraine's lap. Finally, he grabs hold of the phone. "You gon' call his ass, right now!" he shouts as he mashes the phone receiver against her ear. He aims the barrel of the gun at Miracle's forehead. "Dial the number or I'ma blow his fucking brains out."

Loraine looks down into Miracle's beady little eyes. Tears of fear are trickling down his face but he isn't making the slightest whisper of a noise. She asks herself what she should do. What is happening? She can't sit there and watch them kill her great grandbaby. She'll never be able to live with herself after witnessing that act. *God, please help us,* she begs silently. *Please don't let them hurt my grandbaby,* she pleads.

The gunman cocks the hammer of the revolver to let Loraine know that he means business. Hearing the click helps her to make up her mind. She quickly grabs hold of the phone and dials the number nervously.

The man watches closely, paying attention to every number that she's dialing. "No funny business, or little man is history," he threatens.

After she's done dialing, the gunman leans his head close to hers so that he can hear clearly. The phone begins to ring.

"Ma, what's up?" asks the voice on the other end.

The gunman snatches the phone from her hand. "Wise, what's up, nigga?" he shouts into the phone. "Where you been? I've been looking all over for you," he says in a calm but aggressive voice. "I couldn't find you nowhere, so I decided to pop in on Moms and see if she knew your whereabouts."

Wise doesn't have a clue as to who this could be. The voice doesn't sound familiar at all. He's baffled because no one calling him "Wise" should be in his momma's house without him being there. "Who is this?" he asks curiously.

"I asked you not to disrespect me in front of my family, right? I asked you!" the gunman yells as he replays the scene in his mind. Fury sets in his eyes. "In front of my fucking family! You put the gun to my newborn son's head. You thought I wouldn't find out who you were, huh? Guess what? I found out! It's a small world. Money talks," he shouts as the tears drop from his eyes. Being disrespected in front of his family was a total violation. He dreamed of the day that he could get even with the violator.

Loraine is scared out of her mind. Miracle can't get any more scared than he already is. He's wet his pants twice already.

Walter never thought that this day would ever come. He never thought that particular robbery would catch up with him.

"Wise, it's Judgment Day," the gunman mumbles. "You threatened to kill my seed. My motherfucking seed," he repeats. "You fucked up, though. You shoulda killed me," he whispers. "But you didn't, and now I got Mom Dukes. I hope that $20,000 can buy you a new mother."

Boom! The bullet crashes into Loraine's forehead. Splashes of blood splatter onto Miracle's face. Loraine's lifeless body collapses onto the carpet face first, dragging Miracle with her.

Miracle lays there in total shock as the gunmen run out of the house, leaving Great Grandma Loraine lying there in a puddle of blood, as dead as she can be.

THIRTEEN

MAY 12, 1987

At the young age of thirty-seven, Charlene is already the grandmother of five-year-old Tyshon "Miracle" Walls. Miracle is Charlene's pride and joy. He means the world to her; not only because she's her only grandson, but because he's the last memory she has of her daughter, Nakia.

Miracle's the spitting image of his mother. His jet-black hair, pearly white teeth, and caramel complexion makes him look identical to her. He also carries himself just like she used to. From the way he walks down to the way he talks. Each and every time Charlene looks at her grandson, she envisions her daughter in his place.

He's too young to understand how much of a miracle that it is for him to be here. In fact, he doesn't even know the situation. Charlene dreads the day that she has to explain to Miracle what happened to his mother. She'll just have to deal with that day when it comes. For now, she's the only mom he knows.

"Miracle," Charlene calls out.

"Yes," he replies politely.

"Are you ready for your surprise?"

"Yes, what is it?" he asks innocently.

Today is his birthday and she has a special surprise for him. Today she's taking him to his favorite place in the entire world.

"I'm not telling you," Charlene replies in a teasing manner. "Wait until we get there." She grabs her car keys and heads toward the door. Miracle races right behind her. He's filled with so much anxiety. He quickly passes her and waits for her at the back door of her candy apple red Mercedes Benz 190E. Charlene is the first and only person in the neighborhood to own this particular car, thanks to her husband, Tyshon.

Nakia always said that she was going to name her first child after her father, even though he stopped communicating with her once he found out that she was pregnant.

This car is the only thing that the feds allowed her to keep. It was in Charlene's mother's name. That's the reason that they couldn't confiscate it, like they did everything else.

A little over a year ago, Big Tyshon was nabbed in a federal drug sting, which landed him life in prison on kingpin charges.

Charlene seats Miracle in the rear seat before hopping into the driver's seat. Before pulling off, she blasts the tunes of En Vogue and they both sing along loudly as they cruise up Central Avenue.

This is a game they play whenever they're riding. They take turns alternating verses of each song that plays on the radio.

As they merge onto Parkway South, Miracle assumes that he knows exactly where they're going. "Ooh, Grandma!" he shouts with joy. "I know what the surprise is!"

"What?" Charlene asks with a big, beautiful smile on her face.

"Chuck E. Cheese!" he shouts cheerfully.

"How did you know?" she asks, sounding sort of disappointed.

"'Cause, that's why," Miracle replies. "You have to take this way," he says as he points up ahead of the road.

Charlene tunes him out as her favorite song begins to play. She blasts the volume and sings along. She waves her free hand in the air from side to side, performing like she's in a concert. "When I . . . had youuuuu," she sings, "I treated you badddddd . . . and wrong, my dear."

Miracle cuts her off just before she could start the next verse. "Hold on to your love . . . you got to hold onnnnnnn."

They quickly approach 18th Avenue's underpass, just before Irvington, New Jersey. Just as they come within two feet of the underpass, *boom!* The windshield caves in and shatters into tiny little pieces. Charlene loses control and the car begins to swerve. The car smacks into the divider in the middle of the highway, tossing little Miracle into the front passenger seat. His body slams hard into the dashboard. The impact was so hard that the hood of the car is pressed flat as a board. *Beeeeeep!* The horn sounds off continuously.

Miracle looks up to see what could have happened. To his surprise, he sees three young kids running across the bridge. He then looks down and notices a red brick lying on the middle console. He assumes they must have thrown the brick over onto the parkway.

Miracle looks over to his left. He screams at the top of his lungs as his eyes focus on the second worse sight that he has ever seen. "Grandma!"

His grandmother's face is smashed into the steering wheel, with blood pouring from her skull. He's so distraught that he doesn't know anything else to do but scream. The entire incident reminds him of a scary movie.

Miracle buries his face deep into the palms of his hands, trying to erase the vision. He slowly opens his eyes with hope that this is only a nightmare. He loses it when he realizes that she's still there and this is a reality. "Aghhh!" he cries.

What a birthday present.

FOURTEEN

MAY 12, 1982

"Doctor, do something!"

Everyone begins scrambling around foolishly. None of them have ever been in a situation like this. Medical school forewarned them of this type of procedure, but they all hoped that they would never have to witness it themselves.

"Doctor, what's going on?"

"Nurse, get Dr. Patel! Hurry!"

The nurse takes off quickly. The doctor places the oxygen mask over the patient's face. He desperately awaits a response.

"Doctor, help her please!" the mother cries as she watches her fourteen-year-old daughter lie stretched out across the delivery table, with her eyes rolling back into her head. "Doc, please save my baby?" the girl begs desperately.

At the age of thirteen, Nakia was pregnant. She kept her stomach concealed underneath oversized T-shirts until she was almost seven months pregnant. Her ignorance kept her from obtaining any prenatal care. By the time Nakia's mother found out, it was already way too late to get an abortion. The last two months of Nakia's pregnancy was hell on young Nakia. She lay in her room, sick and bedridden. In no way was she physically or mentally ready for pregnancy.

Another doctor comes running into the room as the obstetrician and the nurse scramble around with confusion. "Ma'am, I'm sorry but you have to exit the room," the doctor says as he politely shoves Charlene out of the room.

She tries to resist but he applies his strength to force her out of the room. Just before he slams the door in her face she cries, "Please save my baby!"

The door sounds off like the sound of someone beating a drum as Charlene tries to kick the door off of the hinges. "Let me the fuck in!" she screams.

Twenty minutes later, the door finally opens and Charlene runs in without hesitation. The doctors and the nurses crowd around the bed, making it extremely difficult for her to see her daughter. Their long, saddened faces frighten her.

Suddenly she gains a slight bit of hope as she peers at the back of the room where a young nurse stands, holding a baby wrapped up in a sky blue blanket. Charlene quickly switches her attention over to the bed. She peers over the doctor's shoulders. She truly hopes that her eyes are deceiving her. "No!" she cries as her eyes settle on the sheet which is covering her daughter from head to toe. "No," she cries again. "You motherfuckers killed my baby," she cries as she jumps on the doctor and commences to beat him brutally.

It takes ten security guards to drag Charlene off of the doctor. She cries loud and hard as they restrain her. "God, why did you take my baby?" She falls to her knees while looking up to the sky. "Why did you take my baby?" she cries.

FIFTEEN

AUGUST 15, 2005

Tyshon "Miracle" Walls struggles to fight the tears back. He's not alone, though. Many of the spectators that occupy the room are crying as well. After hearing his story, they can't help but feel sympathy for him.

Miracle looks over to his attorney, who gives him the head nod, gesturing for him to take a seat. Miracle sits down slowly. As his body is descending, he lowers his head and focuses on his lap.

Right now, Miracle feels 200 pounds lighter. He no longer feels the burden that has weighed him down his entire life. For many years, doctors and friends told him that he needed to open up and tell people what was on his mind. They told him he would feel much better once he did so. For the life of him, he couldn't seem to do it. If he had known that he could enjoy the feeling of freedom that he now feels, he would have forced himself to do it a long time ago.

Once he's seated, he exhales, "Aghh." He then looks up at the judge, who is sitting there with his chin resting in the palm of his right hand. The blank look on his face confuses Miracle.

Clap, clap, clap. The loud sound of the judge's clapping echoes throughout the courtroom. "Encore!" he says sarcastically. His cheeks are as red as fire. "Mr. Walls, you asked me to walk with you and indeed, that I have done. I've been walking with you for the past hour. My feet are sore," he says sarcastically. "And so are my ears. Sore from the trash that you just filtered through them," he snarls.

"I thought I had heard it all before but you, Mr. Walls, have taken this thing to the next level. I have to commend you on your creativity," he says sarcastically. "How long did it take you to come up with those excuses for all of your negative behavior? From what you're telling me, you have to be the unluckiest man in the world. Unbelievable! I would hate to ever meet a man who has really lived the life that you claimed to have had. Charge after charge and you're not guilty of one, huh? That, coupled with the tragic deaths of your mother and your grandmothers, would probably make the average judge melt," he says. "But me, I'm not the average judge. I'm a different kind of judge. I have a keen eye for bullshit," he says while staring coldly into Miracle's eyes. "And you, my dear son, are a bullshitter. Pardon my French," he says as he looks around at the people in the courtroom.

By now Miracle already knows how the story is about to play out. This has been his life for as long as he could remember it.

Why would it change now? he asks himself.

It's just as he figured, no one would ever believe that this is actually the story of his life.

"I find you guilty of drug trafficking, as well as the murder of the two witnesses whom you claimed were close friends of yours."

Miracle thinks back to the two informants that the judge is referring to. Miracle befriended and loved both Freak and Jay. He never imagined that they would cross him and dump all the weight on him. At first, he couldn't understand why he was being convicted of murdering the key witnesses. Halfway through his pre-trial, the backstabbing matter revealed itself, catching him by total surprise. Still, to this day, he doesn't have a clue as to who could have murdered them.

"Good story," the judge commends. "You'll have plenty time to come up with more entertaining stories," he says sarcastically. "Maybe you can become one of those infamous urban gangster book authors? I hereby sentence you to double life."

All the spectators are shocked at the judge's verdict. They all sit with their mouths stretched wide open in awe.

"Court adjourned!" Judge O'Donovan screams as he bangs the gravel. "Bailiff, remove that menace from my courtroom!" he yells while standing up from the bench. "Good day, folks."

Miracle stands up and places his hands behind his back submissively as the bailiff cuffs him. Together, they stroll the aisle slowly. The spectators look in his eyes as he passes. Expecting to see some type of pity in his face, they're all shocked. He looks straight ahead coldly.

As he approaches the door, he takes one look back. As he watches the spectators sob away, one tear manages to sneak from the corner of his eye. He quickly sings a verse from his favorite song, by rapper Jäy-Z. "I can't see it coming down my eyes, so I gotta make the song cry," he sings under his breath as the single tear freezes in the middle of his cheek.

He refuses to allow anyone to see him cry. Although he's totally innocent, he has to play the cards that life has dealt him.

The End

KEEPIN' IT GANGSTA

BY

J.M. BENJAMIN

ONE

"I'm standing outside the New Jersey State Prison in Trenton, New Jersey, live, awaiting the final fate of death row inmate Derrick 'The Dicer' Jordan. This is a day when some may say justice is about to be served, while others would disagree and proclaim this day to be a tragedy. This is based on whether or not you agree or oppose with the decision made by the Essex County Supreme Court nearly seven years ago, when they sentenced 'The Dicer' to death. He was tried and convicted for the gruesome murder and decapitation of police officer Robert Smith and at 9:45 PM, only two hours from now, the long-awaited chapter will be brought to an end. Derrick Jordan's violent past finally caught up with him. He was the alleged leader of a notorious drug gang which operated around the Prince Street Housing Projects in Newark, New Jersey and was believed to have been responsible for numerous murders over the years. This is Dan Howard, bringing you live coverage for Channel 7 *Eyewitness News*. Stayed tuned as the hour of closure to this heinous crime winds down."

"Are you sure you're going to be okay, Ms. Jordan?" Gino Carvelli, Derrick's attorney, asked Derrick's mother as they pulled in front of the body-infested prison.

"Um-hmm," she replied with a nod of her head as she wiped the remaining tears of the floodgate, compliments of Gino's handkerchief, with shaky hands.

Just moments ago, Althea Jordan was an emotional wreck and did not think she would be able to carry out her son's request. Her heart felt as if a pair of vise grips was clamped onto it, and slowly but surely, they were tightening. Literally, she was physically, mentally, and emotionally exhausted, not to mention spiritually as well. The past few years of battling with her son's situation had taken a toll on her, turning her salt-and-pepper hair into a full set of sterling silver, making her appear far beyond her fifty years of age. She could not believe how rapidly seven years had flown by. To her, it seemed like yesterday that Derrick had been arrested and charged with the death of a policeman. But now here it was, her firstborn and only son was about to have his life taken away from him at the young age of thirty-two.

As she glanced out the one-way, 5 percent tinted windows of the Mercedes limo, Althea couldn't help but to notice the many different signs that were being held high in the air by the numerous spectators and protesters.

Two in particular caught her eye: AN EYE FOR AN EYE, one read, while the other read, ONLY GOD CAN JUDGE.

Being a God-fearing Christian woman, Althea understood the quotes from the signs more than anyone knew she did. A tear managed to fall from her eye over the first one, as she smiled at the latter.

"Okay, when we get out, I want you to stay close to me. Don't stop for anything and don't answer any questions. I'm going to get you inside safe and sound," Gino assured her.

"Thanks, Gino. For everything."

"I wish I could say you're welcome, but I can't because I didn't do anything. I would like to have done more, but your son made it very difficult for me to do my job, Ms. Jordan. I hope you can understand that."

"I do understand that. At least you tried your best, and for that I thank you," Althea replied, flashing him a warm smile.

Gino returned the smile. "OK, here we go."

"You raised a cop killer!"

"Your son's an animal!"

"He's a monster!" These were some of the words Althea heard from the crowd as she and Gino exited the limo just before the media recognized and rushed them.

"Mr. Carvelli! Mr. Carvelli! Have you spoken with Mr. Jordan?

"No comment."

"Ms. Jordan, how do you feel about the judge's final decision?"

"Mr. Carvelli, why didn't you appeal?"

"No comment," Gino replied again as he and Althea Jordan were bombarded by the media.

As instructed, Althea stayed close to her son's attorney and refused to answer any questions concerning Derrick. It saddened her that the media would attempt to make a spectacle out of the death of her son, but she was determined to not be intimidated by the gang of reporters that hovered around them like vultures. She could now see the entrance of the maximum-security state prison ahead as Gino Carvelli navigated her through the crowd. She also couldn't help but to hear the continuous chants and heckles from the emotional crowd about her son being a vicious killer. For a minute it felt as if her legs would give way from under her just before she reached the entrance, from all the mayhem. But the words from one of the reporters miraculously caused her to regain and fortify all of her strength and life back into her body, when the slim Caucasian woman repeated her question.

"Do you believe your son is innocent, Ms. Jordan?"

That question made Althea stop in her tracks and spin around to face the woman.

"No comment!" Gino interjected, answering for his client's mother.

"It's all right, Gino. I want to answer."

Hearing Althea's words caused the entire crowd to go silent in anticipation. Everyone was curious to hear what the mother of the convicted cop killer, who was about to be executed, had to say. At minimum, there were at least twenty microphones shoved rudely in front of Althea's face as the reporters waited anxiously for the next words to come out of her mouth.

"To answer your question: yes, I do believe that my son was innocent, and still believe he is despite what the court system says. And regardless of what you people think, my son is not an animal, he is a human being. You are the ANIMALS," she spat in a hysterical manner.

"Well, why did he plead guilty then, Ms. Jordan?" one of the reporters shouted. Gino made an attempt to interject by coming to Althea's rescue, sensing her breakdown, but Althea waved him off as she forced herself to regain her composure. She wanted to address the reporter.

For a brief moment Althea paused; she wanted so badly to answer the question truthfully, but she knew that it was not her place. She had given her word to her son that she would not intervene in his wishes. Vowing to respect them, she instead said what she thought to be appropriate.

"Honestly, I cannot answer that. That is something that only my son and God can answer."

With that being said, Althea Jordan turned her back to the crowd and buried her face in Gino's embrace, leaving both the media and pedestrians unsatisfied and in a frenzy as she stepped through the prison door.

TWO

Derrick lay like a statue in the gray-walled six-by-nine-foot single cell's bunk with his hands behind his head, staring up at nothing in particular. One would have assumed that Derrick's attention was focused on something interesting on the ceiling, but that couldn't be farther from the truth. For his thoughts were somewhere else.

"Jordan, how are you feeling?" asked the death row housing officer.

"Why?" asked Derrick nonchalantly.

His response did not come as a surprise to the officer. He had been the assigned officer for the death row inmate for close to ten years and remembered when Derrick Jordan had first come in. From day one, Officer Salvado recalled the inmate everyone referred to as 'The Dicer' coming in with a gangsta attitude. Salvado figured that, like so many inmates before Derrick, humility would eventually overcome the tougher-than-nails man. He would have bet money that Derrick would follow suit, but it would have been money lost. Just as the day that he first set foot on the tier, nearly seven years earlier, Derrick 'The Dicer' Jordan had always KEPT IT GANGSTA!

"That's what I respect about you, Jordan," Salvado admitted. "All these years you've stayed one way. You never switched up. I used to think that you were overrated and that all the stories about you were just hype, but you finally convinced me that you are indeed a coldhearted and ruthless individual. I don't know what you've been through that got you like that, but I feel sorry for you, young blood."

Derrick froze the officer with a murderous look, but as usual he kept the composure in the tone of his voice when he spoke. "You right, you don't know what the fuck I been through. You don't know nothin' about me, and you definitely don't know 'me', so don't be feelin' sorry for me!"

"Whatever you say," the bewildered officer replied. "Anyway, I came down here to see if you had a special meal request, since this is your last one and all," the officer added as he changed the subject.

Without breaking his stare, Derrick looked directly into the officer's eyes and his stone face and death mask caused the turnkey to look away.

If there was ever any doubt in his mind about Derrick before, there was none now. Judging by the other's pitch-black pupils that made him cower in fear, Salvado had to turn away. He was absolutely convinced that Derrick was indeed a true killer.

Derrick's next response confirmed that fact. "The only request I got us that you hurry up and get this shit over with. Other than that, I don't want to eat jack!"

Salvado walked off without looking back at Derrick. "Suit yourself," he said while he was still in earshot distance.

Glad to be rid of the nosey officer, Derrick laid back on the cell bunk that had been his bed for the past six and a half years. Judgment Day had finally come knocking on his door and, like his condemners who wanted him dead, he was eager to open that door and embrace what lay ahead. Deep down inside, he had always imagined his life ending in some unordinary manner. It wasn't hard for Derrick to deal with that because he was far from an ordinary person and he never lived an ordinary life. Yet, he wasn't the least bit bitter about the path he willingly chose to travel down to obtain his infamy. Throughout his life he bore many titles for many different reasons, but he never complained. Due to his malicious antics while growing up, Derrick had been deemed a hoodlum, a thug, and at times thought to have been the devil in the flesh, but the one that outweighed them all was the one deeming him a "menace to society." And the embodiment of that now had him paying the ultimate price for his actions, which, sadly, was his life.

With that playing heavy on his mental, Derrick placed his hands back behind his head again and began reminiscing back to when it all began . . . .

THREE

"Ay, bus boy, bring us another large pizza and pitcher of Coke. Hurry up!" Big Mike barked at the skinny Italian worker behind the counter.

Derrick had just walked through the local pizzeria hangout door unnoticed when he heard Big Mike order the additional food. Big Mike was the bully at his school and Derrick hated him with a passion.

Big Mike was exceptionally big in every sense of the word. Although he was only a sixth grader, the bully stood a soaring 5'8" and weighed in at 180 pounds. His hands were as large as a gorilla's and his feet were the size of a professional basketball player's.

Everyone at school was scared to death of him; that is, everyone except Derrick. And that was the reason Derrick was at the pizzeria. Just the day before, Big Mike and a bunch of his flunkies confronted Derrick after school.

"Ay, Derrick, I heard you was talking shit about me and stuff, sayin' you can kick my ass. Whassup wit' dat?"

Derrick would've replied right back at Big Mike because he knew the bully was trying to provoke him, but he thought twice about it because he was outnumbered six to one. Instead, he stepped around one of Big Mike's gophers and just kept on walking.

That was when he felt it.

"Punk!" Big Mike shouted before poppin' Derrick in the back of the head.

That caused Derrick to freeze in his tracks. Everybody fell silent as all the kids waited to see Derrick's reaction to the violation. But Derrick just sighed loudly and continued to walk away.

With his young heart getting bigger and feeling very victorious, Big Mike laughed and everyone joined him.

"Yeah, I told you he ain't shit. He ain't nothin' but a bitch-ass sissy," Derrick heard the bully say as everyone else continued to laugh. It was the same laughter that taunted Derrick in his sleep and made him toss and turn all night long. It was the same laughter that caused him to play hooky from school the next day and show up at the pizza shop.

Big Mike had just bit into another slice of pizza after telling a dirty joke. His table full of friends was in an uproar. The joke had been so hilarious that Big Mike was trying to prevent himself from choking as his eyes welled up with tears of humor. Those same tears stopped him from noticing the wide-eyed expressions of his crew's faces as they suddenly became silent.

The only thing Big Mike did hear was the deadly whisper when Derrick spoke into his ear.

"Laugh at this, chump!" was what Big Mike heard right before he felt the sharp pain in the middle of his back from the six-inch blade of the steak knife Derrick plunged into it.

Derrick served ninety days in the juvenile detention center for that cold-blooded incident. He was only ten years old then. Afterward, both the younger and older kids gave him his props as being an up-and-coming gangsta.

But Derrick didn't want their props or respect—he wanted them to fear him! And he went about establishing and cultivating that fear every chance he got. From that day forward he became a marble-hearted individual who fought, stabbed, and shot his way through whoever stood in his way.

Coming from a fatherless home with a hardworking mother who couldn't control him, Derrick had an abundance of time to terrorize the streets after dropping out of school. When Althea found out about his extracurricular activities in the streets after he quit going to school, she was furious and gave him an ultimatum. She told him to clean up his act or get out of her house. But Derrick chose to do wrong and left her home to be on his own, setting the stage to be raised in the streets.

Later on in life, Derrick learned the hard way that the mean streets of Jersey didn't give a fuck about him or anybody else, so he became one with the streets and chose not to give a fuck about anybody, either. He understood that weakness was a trait that was frowned upon out there and vowed to live every day of his young life without that characteristic. On the streets, the weak got beat while the strong moved right along. He became the latter, roaming the grimy, snake-infested ghetto with the intent of perfecting the art of maneuvering within it with complete immunity.

Throughout his young life of terror, Derrick tried his hand at various things. In an attempt to stick up a neighborhood butcher shop at age fourteen, Derrick made his first major mistake, one that would play a significant role in years to come. He underestimated the elderly Hispanic shop owner's swiftness. Before Derrick had a chance to react or realize that he was not dealing with any ordinary vic, the Hispanic man known as Vito already had his double-barrel shotgun drawn and raised in Derrick's direction. Not even the least bit afraid, and thinking that he was juvenile hall-bound for sure once again, Derrick was already contemplating his next move, being as though he'd allowed the butcherman to get the drop on him. This was not the first time he'd had a weapon drawn on him and knew it wouldn't be the last. His only concern was coming out on top despite the predicament. That is why he'd made up his mind to take his chances and go all out in a blaze by shooting his way out of the store, rather than returning back to what he'd considered to be a living hell. Derrick despised jail, or any confinement for that matter, and vowed to stay out despite of his way of life.

Derrick stood in the center of the store, aiming his stolen .38 revolver at the gray-haired man with his fingers steady on the trigger. It was as if he were in the midst of a Mexican standoff, while the twin barrels of the shotgun lined up with his head. Mind already made, Derrick was ready to spring into action, but just as his fingers were about to comply with the decision his mind had made, he noticed the butcherman lowering his weapon. Unbeknownst to Derrick at the time, the butcherman had already known of him and his reputation. Although he didn't condone what Derrick was into, Vito respected and admired the young kid with a big heart. Derrick reminded him of himself when he, in fact, was an up-and-coming young gangsta, indulging in the same type of behavior as a youth as Derrick. That is, until someone had given him a chance. And because Vito took a liking to Derrick, he wanted to extend the same courtesy.

"*Oye, momento*. I'm going to put my piece down," Vito said, laying the double barrel on the counter top. "Now you can still do what you came to, or you can earn it like a man."

Completely thrown by the Hispanic man's words, Derrick was reluctant.

"What the fuck you talkin' 'bout?" he spit, gripping the revolver's handle even tighter.

Unfazed by Derrick's attempt to intimidate him, Vito continued. "How would you like to earn what you intended to take?"

That comment drew a laugh out of Derrick. He knew this had to be some type of joke. He had never worked an honest day's work in his entire life and found humor in the gesture. He was a natural-born hustler, not to mention a gangsta at heart, and every dollar he ever possessed was not in the least bit easy to come by. Thinking this was a tactic the elderly man used as a means to get him to let his guard down, Derrick placed his other a hand on the .38's handle and stood firm.

"Yo, you think I'm new to this, *papi*? I'm true to this. Now give that paper up 'fore I put one in you," Derrick commanded.

"Well, then that's what you're going to have to do then my friend," Vito replied calmly. "You're going to have to kill me if you want to take what I earned." He locked eyes with Derrick.

Something in the manner in which Vito stared at him caused Derrick to gain instant respect for the older man. He had never met anyone who stood up for themselves in the midst of a life-threatening situation or didn't fear him, especially while he had a gun pointed at them. It was that day that Derrick learned the true definition of a gangsta, and his decision at that time would play a major part in his future as he befriended and frequented the butcher's shop after the encounter.

A year later, Derrick teamed up with two of his local hood crimeys and played a little snatch–and-grab from the A&P supermarket. They narrowly escaped after an off-duty cop, who happened to see what they were up to, began chasing them. Derrick barely got away by dipping into a back yard, only to be attacked and bitten by a German shepherd.

Once linking back up with his two crimeys, Derrick was the butt end of their jokes when he told them the story about the dog. He found no humor in their jokes.

The next day, after getting off work, Derrick hooked back up with his same two crimeys from the A&P snatch-and-grab, though this time they just did some hanging out.

"Whatchu got in the bag, yo?" one of them asked Derrick.

"I cut up some meat at the shop. Y'all hungry?"

"Hell yeah," the other yelled. "Let's fry that shit up at my crib."

"Word, but, yo, let's spark some weed, knock off a forty right quick, and go to the crib and eat," one of the two suggested.

"I'm wit' that," Derrick agreed.

"Sounds like a plan to me," the other crimey said in favor.

Moments after blazing the smoke and finishing off the brew, the crimeys were hungrier than a hostage. Derrick wasn't because he had chowed down before meeting up with them.

"Yo, that shit look kinda funny," one crimey complained when Derrick unwrapped the meat and threw it into the frying pan.

The starving one of the pair piped, "I don't give a fuck what it looks like, I got the munchies like a muthfucka, kid. Feels like I can eat a mu'fuckin' horse right about now."

Derrick handed a plate of the cooked meat to each of the crimeys and watched as they wolfed it down.

"Damn! Yo, Dee, this is a'ight, here."

"No doubt, you cooked the hell outta this. What is it, some kinda expensive steak or something? This taste like some exotic shit."

"Nah, kid, nothing like that," Derrick smiled slyly. "It's that fuckin' mutt that bit me in the ass yesterday," he continued as he began a chilling laugh. "I hope you niggas enjoyed it, 'cause I diced the mutt up especially for you two clown mu'fuckas!"

As he watched, the two surprised young felons began simultaneously spitting out and vomiting up the offensive dog meat, and in Derrick's mind feeding the two cooked-up dog meat was only a small price to pay for clowning him, compared to what he was really capable of.

From that day forward, Derrick was officially viewed as someone who was not to be messed with or made fun of. The dog meat incident earned him the nickname "Dicer" as word spread. It was the same street moniker that would perfectly describe him to a tee as years progressed, as he repped it to its fullest.

Derrick snapped out of his trance upon hearing the housing officer's keys tapping on the cell bars.

"I know you said you didn't want anything to eat, but the guys downstairs sent you up a nice T-bone steak, nicely diced," Salvado added. "No pun intended." He tried his hardest not to laugh at his own humor.

"Get the fuck away from my cell," Derrick coolly stated without even looking up at the man.

"Suit yourself." Salvado's words fell on deaf ears because Derrick's mind was already somewhere else.

FOUR

"Damn! Shorty thick to def!" one of Derrick's henchmen shouted above the roaring music.

"Word, son, she definitely got a phatty," agreed another member of the crew.

They were all watching a strikingly bodacious sista with a skintight catsuit on. It fit so tightly it appeared as if someone had painted it on her. She was dancing not too far from their table to Lil' Kim's throwback track from her *Hardcore* album. In the dimly-lit club, at first glance it looked like shorty was dancing with no clothes on at all. Her apple bottom and hips swayed in rhythm to the beat, her moves flawless, as she dropped it like it was hot and imitated the infamous booty bounce that the video chicks are well known for. Only the way shorty was doing it, you would've sworn she created the dance herself. She had all the men in the club, from the ol' heads to the young hustlers, mesmerized by her moves. The young hustlers eyed her more hungrily, figuring that with the right amount of game and the right amount of cash, there was strong possibility one of them could have shorty up in a hotel room at the end of the night, performing a private version of her dance.

But that was only half of the show. When the short and equally thick red-boned cutie who had been sitting next to Derrick stood up, shit really became super freaky. Wearing a tight white wife beater that did nothing to hide the firmness of her breasts and the hardness of her nipples, the T-shirt was torn low enough to see her diamond-pierced navel. She sported a pair of booty cutters that would make any man, and even some women, drunk with lust. It wasn't until she unexpectedly got up and moved to join her girlfriend that she received the attention that her body commanded.

Without hesitation, the two began an exotic dance that had both their bodies entwined, tangled, and twisted like two snakes in a snake pit. Pandemonium broke out as these two fine female specimens became totally engulfed in their erotic dance, prompting Derrick's entourage to dig into their pockets and begin tossing money at the women like they were tossing confetti, all the while cheering the females on. The ladies themselves needed no cheering on and were seemingly oblivious to the rants and raves going on all around them; they were enjoying their performance and would have performed their dance for free, with or without a crowd. The money being thrown at them was only an added bonus for the pair.

To make sure everybody got what they were paying for, the red-bone, as if on cue, began to gently guide her partner to the floor of the stage. She slowly lay her down and climbed on top of her before the two started a passionate rhythmic grind, like two lovers in heat. Derrick's team went wild, every dick in the house had to be stiff and ready to explode with the scene that was unfolding in front of them. Even Derrick, emotionless as he most often was, was caught up in the frenzied atmosphere. Suddenly the red-bone, who had been seated right there next to him minutes ago, pulled a Madonna and Britney Spears re-enactment by placing her tongue in the other girl's mouth and they kissed. The whole place went bananas.

In a quick instance Derrick had his attention to the freak show ripped away when his top lieutenant interrupted.

"Yo, Dee, that nigga Robert just stepped up in here, kid. I think we should bounce out the back before we bump heads wit' that chump, feel me?"

"Nah, we good. Fuck that clown," Derrick replied offhandedly. He was reluctant to let his rival's appearance break up this whole party atmosphere he was enjoying. He couldn't recall too many times when he actually did something that he enjoyed, other than . . . well that's a whole different thing, he laughed to himself.

Damn, he thought. Here it was, he and his own were finally out having a decent time in one of the hottest spots in town, minding their own business, relaxing after a profitable day on the block, grindin'; and now he would have to bring this night to an end 'cause this clown-ass nigga Robert decided to show up.

"A'ight yo, that's enough," Derrick said to the girls in an attempt to cease the sex-driven dance show they were performing. However, the women were so caught up in the rapture that they ignored Derrick's command, and that caught his vein. No matter the gender, race, or age, Derrick was not used to anyone not adhering to his orders.

"Yo, you hear what the fuck I said?" he repeated angrily, hopping up out of his seat with his Sean John jeans already unzipped and his manhood in hand.

Hearing the thunder in his voice caused his entourage to pause, some moving out of Derrick's path as he commenced to do the unthinkable.

"Freak-ass bitches!" Derrick barked as he pulled an R. Kelly on the two women, hosing them down with urine as if he were a certified fireman.

The women, having been caught off guard, both screamed obscenities as Derrick continued to spray them with his piss water, paying their cries no mind.

"Ya hot asses needed to be cooled off," he said as he shook the remainder of the liquid from his Johnson at the women, then zipped his pants. From his pocket he pulled out a monstrous bankroll and peeled off five one-hundred-dollar bills and began plucking them at the two girls, whose faces were both filled with rage. They had never been so humiliated in their lives, but despite the degradation and embarrassment that they just had to endure, the women both scrambled to retrieve the now urine-stained money and hurried to get away from the man they had often heard to be a psychotic. Although they were indeed attracted to bad boys, this was above and beyond and they wanted no parts of the man now.

"You sick motherfucka!" one of the females yelled as she and her girlfriend stormed out of the VIP section.

"Go tell ya momma," Derrick retorted sarcastically.

By now Derrick's whole team were bellied over in stitches from laughter by their boss's performance. This was not the first time they had observed the man disrespect a woman, or anyone for that matter, in such a way. Without having to say it, they all felt that new episode was running neck-and-neck for first place with the time Derrick had made a clique of annoying gold diggers drink a mixed bottle of Cristal and piss. Pistal, he'd called it.

As the commotion began to die down, one of Derrick's lieutenants leaned over and whispered in his ear.

When Derrick ever so slightly turned his head in the direction his lieutenant, he saw his longtime enemy making a beeline straight for his VIP table. Never the one to be intimidated, Derrick shifted from party mode into street seriousness as he prepared for his adversary.

"Officer Smith, to what do I owe this pleasure?" Derrick asked coolly, deep down inside mocking the man's presence by deliberately addressing him with a lower rank.

Robert Smith was a first-grade detective out of the Fourth Precinct on 17th Avenue that covered the Prince Street and Hayes Homes area, along with the other equally notorious drug and murder-infested neighborhoods that were nearby. It was no coincidence that he was assigned to this area; it was partly promotional and partly emotional. Like Derrick, Robert was also from this neck of the woods and he did everything he could possibly do for his neighborhood when he joined the force and was assigned to the area.

Though he was a couple years older than Derrick, Robert had watched closely as the young hood steadily climbed up the criminal ladder until he finally reached the top-dog positions. During that time, Smith was also climbing a ladder, studying to become a law enforcement officer, becoming one and ascending within the ranks of the department so he could put away villains such as Derrick, whom he had grown to hate with an unhealthy passion. Robert had a borderline obsession with seeing Derrick's demise.

It seemed like all of his life he had been hearing stories and urban legends about this young, supposedly ruthless kid everyone referred to as The Dicer. He made a solemn vow to be the one to put an end to The Dicer's reign of terror and the iron-fisted grip that he held over the community. Bringing down Derrick "The Dicer" Jordan was Detective Robert Smith's personal crusade; his calling, he liked to think of it as.

"Get the fuck up," growled Robert just as three of his colleagues, who were there to back him up, pushed through the crowd and took up positions by his side. Their guns were drawn to dramatize that they meant business.

The freak show was officially over, the party atmosphere ruined. Derrick smiled, keeping his composure.

"This better be good, off-is-sir Smith," Derrick said, purposely mangling the word *officer*. "'Cause you know my lawyers eat play cops like you for breakfast."

"We'll see about that when I get you down town, Killa!" Robert shot back putting a heavy emphasis on the word *Killa*.

It was as if he and Derrick were in the gym sparring together and Robert just knew he had landed a good blow. Or so he wanted to imagine.

Derrick, not even fazed by Robert's words, burst out laughing. "You gotta be kidding me."

His whole response, his invincible demeanor, made Robert furious and he was seething with anger, just to the point of exploding. He looked Derrick threateningly and said, "You can either come the easy way or the hard way."

As if he were moving in slow motion and with a deadly grin on his face, Derrick began to rise from his seat, all the while his cold eyes locked on Robert.

"Yo, y'all niggas chill," he said, never breaking his stare with Smith, "I'll be back before y'all can pop the next bottle. Then we gonna see what them shorties really working wit.'"

That quick quip caused his whole team to laugh out loud, and as Robert and his entourage escorted Derrick out the club, you could hear calls from his crew in the background. "Them niggas ain't got nothing on you, Dee. Keep ya head up, yo! I'ma call the lawyer . . ."

After having Derrick waiting in an empty room for nearly two hours without seeing or speaking to anyone, Robert barged into the tiny interrogation room like a lion about to pounce on his prey. His dark face was devoid of all expression except hate. It was written on his face like a giant Guess Jeans billboard high upon a tall building somewhere. This was a day he had imagined in his mind for a long, long time: having the infamous Dicer somewhere alone. Instead of questioning him, Robert's version of the meeting always ended grislier, with him putting two in Derrick's head. Such was the case that day, though he wanted to bring Derrick down within the confines of the law. Today, having brought Derrick in, Robert thought he scored a victory.

"Looks like we finally nailed your punk ass this time, *Killa*!" Again, Smith put extra emphasis on the word *Killa*, only this time he let it marinate in the air before letting another word come out of his mouth.

Derrick beat him to the punch. "Charge me then, bitch. If not, get the fuck outta my face." He calmly inspected his fingernails out of sheer boredom.

"I think I just might do that. Yeah, I think that's what I'll do," Robert said in a failed attempt to sound like he was in control. Again he repeated with a sneer, "Yeah, I think that's what I'll do."

"Yo, you mean to tell me you brought me all the way down here for some *bullshit*?" Now Derrick was the one putting emphasis on his last word, clearly becoming agitated as he questioned Robert's intent.

"Nah, I brought your slimy ass down here because of those three mutilated bodies we found in Westside Park earlier this week. You are The Dicer, am I right?" This was Robert's way of having a little fun at Derrick's expense. "And these particular murders fit the M.O. of The Dicer, and again, you are one Derrick 'The Dicer' Jordan." At this point Robert picked up a pencil off the desk and pretended it was a knife. He began to imitate dicing motions like a chef would do if he were dicing up carrots for a stew. He looked at Derrick and ended by saying, "I figured there was a connection."

Robert had a satisfied grin on his face as he repeated the little dicing demonstration in his head. He was absolutely enjoying himself.

"After all that, all you can say is, 'you figured there's a connection?' Puh-leez," Derrick spat. "You hafta come better than that, my man."

"Better than that? Better than what?" Robert's words danced out his mouth. "Oh, you best believe I have better than that."

"If you say so."

"No, I *know* so, you sick asshole."

"Smith, you just talking outta the side of your neck," Derrick added with a grin as he leaned back in his chair.

"Yeah, well, see how much shit I'm talking when they throw the book at your ass. I got a witness that is gonna burn you good on them three bodies you carved up. You goin' away for a looooong time on this one, Killa." Robert stared at Derrick, looking for any break in his reaction.

Derrick liked playing mind games, so he felt comfortable going tit-for-tat with Robert. He leisurely glanced at his diamond-encrusted Rolex, and then looked back at the detective. "A witness, you say? If you ask me, bringing me down here was nothing but a big ol' waste of my time. Who you think you bluffin' with that 'I got a witness' bullshit? Chump!" Now Derrick was the sparring partner landing the good blows.

Something about Derrick's last statement, and moreover, the way he said what he said, caused Robert's antennas to shoot straight up. The attentive detective also saw the smug look on Derrick's face, and that's when Robert became a little concerned. Worried really. He tried hard to not show any signs of panic when a thought overtook him. His face flush from thinking about the unthinkable, he pulled out his cell phone and walked to a corner of the room, out of earshot of Derrick.

After a few minutes of hushed conversation, Robert clicked the phone off, angrily shoved it back in his pocket, and stared blankly into space. He did not want to believe he'd heard what he just heard.

When he finally faced Derrick, Robert's face was three shades darker with fury. It took all of his strength not to end Derrick's life the way he always dreamt he would. He could always say he killed Derrick in self-defense. Who would ever question that? They'd probably give me a promotion, Robert thought. But then that would make him just as much as an animal as Derrick, his rational self spoke. But he was still mad and when he spoke, all the venom, the hate, and the years of planning Derrick's downfall spilled over.

"You sonofabitch! You fuckin' low-life sonofabitch!" Robert screamed and in one swift movement, rushed toward Derrick. He grabbed him out the chair and pinned him to the table. "You no good sonofabitch!"

Thinking it best, Derrick just dummied up and allowed the detective to get whatever was in his system out as long as he didn't feel like he was in imminent danger because if he were, he would have stopped Robert cold.

Derrick stared at Robert with a smirk. "What's ya problem, man?"

The smirk just made Robert more upset. He still had Derrick pinned to the table and as he leaned his face into Derrick's he spoke so low, he almost whispered his words. "The witness was killed an hour ago and I'm willing to bet that some way, somehow, you were behind it. So hear this and hear this good, tough guy: I'm going to get you and I'm going to get you good, so help me God!"

At that point Derrick shrugged loose of the detective's grip and firmly pushed him away. Robert, emotionally drained, was in no condition to put up much of fight anyway so he just stood there, watching Derrick fix his clothes.

Derrick still smirked when he said, "Damn, man. One minute you telling me you got this witness; next minute you telling me you don't have this witness. Make up your mind, 'cause you confusing the hell outta me." Derrick almost wanted to laugh. "Maybe instead of manhandling me, you should be out there looking for a new witness, off-is-sir."

This sparring match was over, and Derrick knew he had landed the blow that ended it, even before he and Robert got into the ring. All that was left to do now was to revel in his victory.

Robert couldn't believe the cockiness of the thug. He decided to switch tactics in one last attempt to get under Derrick's skin. In the boxing ring, it would be something akin to throwing a low blow, a cheap shot

"When I bring you down, and trust me, I will bring you down; I wonder how your mother and your sister are gonna feel when your ass is sitting in jail for the rest of your LIFE. Huh, wise guy? Tell me, how you think they gonna feel?"

The low blow thrown, instantly Derrick's facial expression went from calm to deadly. Cop or no cop, now Derrick was the aggressor. He was the lion and Robert the prey. Derrick clenched his teeth and moved within striking distance of the detective.

Robert's only thought now was, maybe the low blow wasn't such a good idea.

"Bitch! Don't you EVER speak about my family! If you ever let my family come out your mouth again—" Derrick stopped short. "Matter of fact, if you ain't chargin' me wit' shit, let me the fuck up outta here. You can't hold me, nigga! Either that, or I need to make my one phone call."

The little hairs on the back on Robert's neck stood at attention when he heard Derrick's outburst. He wasn't a fool; he knew Derrick was a stone-cold killer and known to be a little crazy, so when Derrick cut himself off in mid-sentence, Robert knew he'd pushed too far. Trying not to provoke him any further, knowing it wasn't the time or the place, Robert instead did the only thing he could do under the circumstances.

"Get the fuck outta here!" Robert spat with extra venom in his voice.

He purposely made like he was adjusting the gun on his waist, just in case Derrick's rage became uncontrollable.

Without saying another word Derrick got his feet, walked straight out the door, and left.

The detective seethed as he watched the known killer, the animal he had sworn to bring down, saunter out the door.

FIVE

BAM! BAM! BAM! was the sound of the rapid knocks from Derrick's knuckles as he pounded on the door. *BAM! BAM! BAM!*

"Who is it?" a female's voice yelled from the opposite side of the door.

"It's me, open the door."

"Derrick, what are you doin,' banging on my door in the middle of the night like you crazy, boy?" Tonya asked in a half-sleepy tone.

Instead of answering, Derrick pushed his way inside the apartment.

"Boy, you done bumped your head, bustin' in here like this. Remember, this is my place. You don't pay no bills in here," Tonya screamed as she closed the door behind him.

"Look, Tee," Derrick started with a highly vexed attitude. "I don't want you fuckin' wit' that nigga no more. I'm telling you."

"Derrick, you don't tell me what to do."

"You better leave that nigga alone before I—"

"Before you do what, Derrick? Huh? Before you do what?" Tonya interrupted with a sneer planted on her pretty face, hands on her shapely hips. "You not my father and sure as hell ain't my man, so don't be comin' in here, givin' orders like you run me. Maybe people in them streets is scared of you, but I'm not, and I don't have to listen to you."

"Look, sis, you don't understand. Why you keep messin' with this dude, when you know he only fuckin' wit' you to get at me? How you gonna be wit' that police-ass nigga that's trying to put your own brother up under the jail?

Huh? That shit don't make no sense, my sister involved with po-po like that." Derrick tried to talk some reason into his sister but instead, she just laughed at him.

"So what if he's a cop? He's still a decent guy, and he treats me good. And, IT'S HIS JOB TO LOCK UP CRIMINALS!"

When Derrick left the precinct and headed to his sister's house, he did not expect things to go the way they were going, but he wasn't surprised. It wasn't the first time Tonya had defended his nemesis in the midst of heated discussion. Feeling somewhat defeated, he shook his head in dismay as he sat down on the couch and continued to plead with her. He calmed down and used a much more reasonable tone when he spoke to her this time.

"Sis, why you always pickin' these mutt-ass niggas over me and Ma? Dick get you that fucked up, you gotta go against the grain like this? I know you looking for love, but you been looking in all the wrong places. First it was that clown-ass nigga Barry you up and left Mommy's crib to be with. Talking that you-in-love shit; but when the chump house got raided and he left ya ass in jail, who you call? Ma. Then that lame-ass nigga Anthony knocked you up, broke ya nose, then say the baby wasn't his, plus gave ya ass gonorrhea. Who you call? Me. And then how you repay me? By fuckin' a dude you knew I was beefing with, and let the nigga get you on tape! I almost went to jail behind that shit, trying to protect ya name, and now you wanna fuck with a pig that's trying to put me away. Come on, yo! You think that mu'fucka don't know he can get to me through you? That faggot-ass nigga playing you, Tee, and I'm just trying to get you to see that." Derrick hoped his words hit home. However, he might as well have been talking to a brick wall.

"First of all, who I choose to bring into my bed has never been any business of yours. You and Mommy could have easily told me 'no' when I came to y'all. But don't try to throw Ma up in this. If anybody hurt her more, it's you. And she still favors your sorry ass over me, but I don't bitch. I'm just glad that everything you've done already hasn't come back to haunt us, and you should be glad, too.

"You need to grow the fuck up, Derrick, and leave them streets alone before somebody—"

"Somebody what? Huh?" Derrick reflexively barked, cutting his sister off in mid-sentence. He jumped up and grabbed her by the throat, lifting Tonya's 120-pound frame violently with one hand. He could feel the muscles in his grip tightening around his sister's neck as she gasped for air, and knew by her facial expression that he was cutting off her circulation. But still, his grip remained. "You think I'm afraid to fuckin' die? I don't give a fuck about that shit, but I'm not gonna let you or no mu'fuckin' body else put me in the ground before my time, you hear me?" He shook her nearly limp body again, as if it would make her answer any quicker.

"Dee, I can't breathe," Tonya managed to murmur. Seeing his sister's face now appearing somewhat ghostly, Derrick released his death hold with a powerful jerk, causing Tonya to fall back onto the sofa. Tears stormed out of Tonya's eyes as she tried to regain her breath, but her throat was as dry as sandpaper. Unable to formulate enough saliva to swallow, Tonya got up off the couch and scurried to the kitchen. Derrick watched stone-faced as Tonya stuck her head under the sink to drink from the tap.

At that specific moment, conflicting emotions of love and hatred toward his little sister battled for supremacy within his blackened heart. There was no question that he had love for her, but it was times like these that he needed her backing him up unconditionally just because he was her brother. Because she wouldn't, it took everything inside him not to choke the life out of her naïve body.

"Fuck it!" Derrick growled impatiently as he headed for the door. "Do you, then! I see I'm wastin' my time wit' your stupid ass."

"I hate you!" Tonya screamed at his retreating back, now catching her breath. He slammed the door shut, nearly knocking it off the hinges as he exited her apartment in a volcanic rage.

Derrick jumped into his black-on-black Navigator and peeled off. He drove aimlessly through the darkened city streets, deep in his own thoughts, reflecting back to the time when he first heard about his sister dealing with the detective.

"Ayo, son, let me holla at you for a minute," Derrick's main man, Kas, said as he rolled up on him.

"What's good, fam?"

"Yo, not for nothing kid, but yo, I was at the multiplex wit' this freak from Sue's Rendezvous, and I saw your sister Tonya wit that lame-ass nigga Rob."

"Rob?" Derrick asked, the name not immediately registering in his head.

"Yeah, that pig-ass nigga Smith."

"What?" Derrick snapped.

"Word, son. I figured you ain't know. That's why I slipped it to you on the low. You know I had to pull my man up."

"Yo, good lookin' out. That's peace," Derrick responded with death on his mind.

After that conversation, Derrick flew in a blind rage. He heatedly jumped in his Legend Coupe and headed straight downtown. Though he had no reason to doubt his man Kas, deep down inside he was hoping that what Kas had told him was some sort of mistake.

Reaching his destination, Derrick brought the Coupe to a neck-snapping halt. He double-parked and hopped out of the whip, determined to get to the bottom of the bullshit he just heard. Somebody had some explaining to do.

As soon as he entered the building, he came face-to-face with the object of his rage.

"Yo, mu'fucka, stay the fuck away from my sister!"

Detective Robert Smith had a grin of sarcasm plastered all over his face. He knew it was only a matter of time before Derrick found out about the relationship he had with his sister. He knew they were bound to have a confrontation about it sooner or later, but he didn't think the thug had the balls to do it in a precinct full of cops. Still, Robert wasn't the least bit worried. The rest of the other police officers stood about in disbelief and silence, as if Derrick had just busted in with C-4 taped to his chest. Robert was the only one who wasn't fazed by Derrick's actions.

"Let her tell me that herself," Robert retorted.

"What? You think this shit is a game, nigga? Yo that's my WORD, if I EVER see you near her, OR hear about you being near her again, I'ma push ya mu'fuckin' wig back!" Derrick threatened just before he spun around and pushed his way out the door.

As he was leaving the police station Derrick realized that he was dirty, remembering that he still had his .40 caliber tucked in his waist. With that in mind he hurried down the stairs, bolted out the precinct doors, jumped back in his car, and sped off. Only the white-hot anger of hearing that his sister was seeing a sworn enemy, who was also a cop, could make him run up in a police station strapped.

"Bobby, you want me to go after his ass? You know we can book him for threatening an officer," one of his colleagues offered.

"Nah, let him go. His time is short and I'll eventually get him myself."

As Derrick sped away, he knew he had crossed the line by throwing a death threat in front of dozens of witnesses, especially when those witnesses were cops. But the damage was already done, he told himself as he drove to confront his sister.

Since that day, Derrick had been patiently waiting for the time when he could cash in on the threat that he'd promised Detective Smith.

Althea Jordan followed Gino as they made their way to the front row of the viewing room. She could literally feel the numerous piercing eyes on her as she found her seat, and could hear the many whispers and murmurs as she sat. She didn't have to actually hear what they were saying. She already knew. Gino placed his hand on top of hers and gave Althea a pat of reassurance. He admired the woman's bravery. He himself did not think he would have had the same amount of courage, had it been his own son.

"How are you holding up?" Gino asked.

"I'm fine," Althea replied, despite how she was truly feeling inside. She stared at the execution chamber through the bulletproof window. It was hard for Althea to accept the fact that just mere moments from now, her son would be led out and placed in the chamber, where he would be relieved of his soul and sent to his intended resting place, whether Heaven or Hell. No mother would ever want for her child to taste the fires below, but Althea knew that her son had made his bed a long time ago of his own accord, and he willingly chose to lay in it without any qualms. Her only hope was that God would have mercy on him. Tears of sorrow at the thought began to invade Althea's eyes, but she strongly managed to fight them off once again, just as she had before. She'd told herself a million times she couldn't help but to feel somewhat responsible for her son's predicament. After all, she was his mother. Now, telling herself for the millionth and one time that she had no say so whatsoever in her son's decision-making, Althea couldn't help but to reflect on the past.

It had been an extremely bloody night for Derrick. Because of his position and legendary reputation, he'd committed a gruesome act like he'd done so many times before in the past. Once again, he had to prove that he was not to be fucked with by killing in the most horrendous way possible. Now that the death was over with, all he wanted was to jump in the shower and take a long hot one to rinse the filth and dried blood off his weary body.

With that in mind, Derrick went into the bathroom to peel out of the blood-soiled clothes so he could dispose of them.

With that task completed, he entered into the shower. Standing directly under the piping hot water, he watched as the combination of dirt and blood melted off him as it flowed down the shower drain. Looking at it, he couldn't help but to think about how many times he had found himself in the same situation. As the spray from the shower came down on his head like a waterfall, Derrick closed his tired eyes. Instantly the images and faces of the numerous bodies of the people he had murdered over the years paraded around in his tortured mind. There had been too many to count, and he had forgotten most of their names. Sometimes, he even forgot why they had to die. Some were personal, while others were simply business.

There was only one particular incident when Derrick had come remotely close to feeling any remorse for his actions. Back when he was climbing up the criminal ladder, at age nineteen, he stumbled across what he was convinced was a profitable move. He had watched, stalked, and followed a young drug dealer who was making major paper in a town called Plainfield, which was also in Jersey, until he found out where the kid laid his head. After determining the best time to commit the home invasion, Derrick ran up in the young dealer's house. Unfortunately for his teenaged girlfriend and infant child, the young and apparently stupid dealer underestimated Derrick's tolerance level and played Russian roulette with their lives.

At times like this, Derrick could still envision the young girl, who couldn't have been any older than seventeen, lying across the king-sized bed with her six-month-old son cradled in her arms. Her brain matter was plastered across the headboard and bedroom wall; the little boy's, all over her face. For the cowardly route the young drug dealer had taken, Derrick hacked his head off and buried it in Orange Park. Till this day, he doubted the decapitated head had ever been found. Though it was his first time ever killing a female or child, he had eventually come to terms with what he had done.

After what seemed to be hours in the soothing shower, Derrick stepped out feeling refreshed and renewed. Upon entering his bedroom he noticed the red light flashing on his answering machine and immediately became alarmed. Anyone wanting to contact him did so by calling his cell phone because no one, outside of his mother and sister, had his home number. Therefore, it could only be one of the two loved ones, and they would reach out to him only in an extreme emergency. Knowing that, he hesitantly hit the PLAY button on the machine.

"It's me, honey," he heard his mother say in a voice full of tears. "I know you're probably not home . . . but I couldn't remember your cell phone number," the woman who gave birth to him said before struggling to continue. "Um, I hope you get this message real soon 'cause I need to see you right away. It's—it's important. Please . . . come as fast as you can." Her sniffles were cut off when she hung up.

Hearing the distress in his mother's voice triggered something inside

Derrick. Not since he was a child, when he witnessed her in an abusive relationship with his no-good bastard of a father, had he heard her sound so nervous and afraid. He couldn't figure out why his mother was so upset. Whatever it was didn't matter, because he was about to find out for himself.

Just like Superman, in a blink of an eye he was out of his towel and dressed in his triple black creeping attire of a black hoodie, black jeans and black Timberlands. Now moving faster than a speeding bullet, Derrick was out the door in a flash.

"Jordan!" Salvado yelled for the second time as he broke Derrick's train of thought.

"What?" Derrick barked back, agitated at being disturbed.

"Here, put these on," the guard said as he handed Derrick a pile of neatly folded clothes. "It's almost show time and Chaplain Johnson's here to talk to you, too."

"About what?"

"Come on, man. At least have some respect for the Father. I saw your mother on the news earlier; isn't she a religious woman?" Salvado didn't realize he had struck a nerve.

"Yo, don't ever mention my mother again, YOU HEAR ME?" Derrick spat as he came out of his usually calm character.

"Okay man, calm down. I apologize," Salvado pleaded, bitching up, not wanting to piss off a soon-to-be dead man.

"At least give the chaplain a minute."

"Whatever, yo."

"He's all yours, Father," Salvado added before leaving to give them privacy.

"God bless you, my son."

Derrick dismissed the holy man's comment.

Unnerved by Derrick's demeanor, the chaplain's eyes opened wide in amazement. He had heard how difficult a person Derrick was to deal with, but he hadn't expected this. Being a man of the cloth, it was his teaching and responsibility to find the good in each individual, but something about Derrick left a bad taste in his mouth.

The chaplain fought the chills that ran through his body and continued after he cleared his throat. "Derrick, I'm here because God sent me. He sent me to offer you the opportunity to confess and wash away your sins. All you have to do is accept the Lord and Savior Jesus Christ into your life and into your heart, so that you may enter into the Kingdom of Paradise."

"Ha!" Derrick spat, unmoved by the chaplain's speech.

All his life people had tried to instill some kind of religion in him. In his younger years people tried to convert him into a Jehovah's Witness, a Muslim, and a Christian, but he never grasped the concept of believing in the unseen. He considered himself to be an atheist. Derrick's motto was that if there was a God, then why would He allow Derrick and his family to go through the constant struggles in life? This is why Derrick had given up all hope and abandoned the whole God theory. He was convinced that if God did exist, he didn't pay any visits to the hood.

"Confess my sins? To who, old man? I have no sins to confess to anybody. And I damn sure don't have any remorse. Listen, Chap, take it how you wanna take it, but I don't believe in what you believe in. In fact, the only thing I do believe in is myself. And let me tell you something else: I don't believe that there's enough room for me in the place you call Paradise. Fo' real, fo' real, I don't even believe that they can handle me in Hell, either." Derrick laughed. "'Cause that's exactly where I'm headed. A one-way trip straight downtown." Derrick smiled as he pointed toward the floor, then spit out into the hall, barely missing the chaplain's shoe. Had the clergyman not moved, the glob of mucous would have landed on him. After being at a loss for words for a few seconds, the chaplain finally managed to get a couple out of his mouth. "My son, you are a lost soul. I will pray for you and ask God to have mercy on your soul."

"Save your prayers for somebody who really deserves them, old man," Derrick told the chaplain as he began to change into the execution attire. "I'm not the one! Now get the fuck out my face."

Wide-eyed, and without another word, the chaplain walked off with his head bowed and his Bible in hand.

Buttoning up the dress shirt his mother had brought him, Derrick's mind again began to wander to an earlier time.

"Don't worry, everything is going to be all right," were the last words Derrick had said to his mother as he assured her with his famous wink. He then pulled off, leaving her standing on the front porch.

She still had tears in her eyes as she tightly wrapped her arms around herself.

After Derrick dressed in the black and gray G-Unit ensemble and black, low-cut Timberland Chukka boots, he stood, rather than sat, by the metal bars to await his fate. Judgment Day had finally come and he was all too prepared. He had no remorse for what had been done, nor was he bitter behind the outcome. Unlike others, he had lived his life like a gangsta and intended to go out like one. He had done what he wanted, how he wanted, and when he wanted in life with no regards for anyone. Now, it was all over and he was content. As he stood with his hands clasped in front of him, waiting, Derrick once again went into a trance . . . .

SEVEN

"License, registration and insurance," the highway patrol officer requested as he stood by the driver's side window.

Derrick had been so preoccupied with reaching his destination that he hadn't even noticed the state trooper behind him. He didn't realize he was being flagged down until he saw the flashing lights of a police car in his rearview mirror. The possibility that he was speeding never entered his mind, but he may have unconsciously lead-footed on the pedal just a little bit.

"No problem, officer," he said as he reached into the glove compartment.

Derrick wasn't the least bit worried despite how he was traveling because he knew all his paperwork was in order and legit. He retrieved the registration and insurance and confidently handed them over to the officer.

"License."

"Oh yeah, pardon me," Derrick responded as he went into his back pocket for his wallet, only to come up empty-handed. *What the fuck,* he thought as he patted himself down in all the places his wallet could possibly be.

"Sir, is there a problem?"

"Nah, no problem at all. It's just that I think I left my wallet and license at home," Derrick replied. "But I know my license number by heart," he added, hoping that would be acceptable.

Derrick couldn't have picked a more fucked-up time to get pulled over. Interstate 78 was the wrong place to be driving late at night, Black and without proper ID.

Judging by the dubious look on the young white trooper's face, Derrick knew what was coming next. He contemplated his next move. There was no way he was going to let it play out in the direction it was going, especially with the chrome Desert Eagle tucked in the waist of his belt.

"Sir, I'm going to need you to step out of the vehicle for me, please," the officer commanded with his hand on the butt of his gun.

"Come on, man, cut me a break. My name is Derrick Jordan, social security Number is 222-66-8880. My license number is 000272H1705, the same name that is on the registration and insurance. I know it's too late for you to wanna be doin' some paperwork. You probably got a nice little wife and kid waiting for you when your shift is over. We both just want to go home," Derrick said in his most persuasive voice. He hoped the trooper would let him go on his way.

Suspicious of Derrick's motives, the young officer drew his weapon and repeated his request, only this time it was more of a command. "Sir! Please STEP OUT OF THE VEHICLE, slowly," he said with authority while his gun was pointed at Derrick's chest.

"Shit," Derrick mumbled under his breath.

He knew the state trooper had the drop on him and any chance of him finessing his way out of this situation was dead. Even if he made it to the hammer in his waist, more than likely he'd be dead before he could get a shot off. His only other option, other than complying with the trooper's orders, was to try and make a mad dash for it. What had started off as a routine traffic stop had rapidly spun out of control, leaving Derrick desperately searching for an out. He had come across enough police to smell when one of them had an itchy trigger finger, and this young officer's body language said he was just waiting for the opportunity to blow away a Black man. Derrick didn't move; he sat there like a stone statue, contemplating a way out of this dilemma. His thoughts were interrupted...

"Mr. Jordan," the officer said sternly. "This is your LAST warning! GET

OUT OF THE CAR, NOW AND KEEP YOUR HANDS WHERE I CAN SEE 'EM," the trooper barked in a voice that relayed his heightened sense of the imminent danger he might be facing.

As Derrick's mind ran on fast-forward, speeding through all possible exits to this situation, with time running out, he looked up at the rearview mirror and saw what he dreaded most.

Two more police cars, their lights flashing in the darkness, zoomed down on him.

"I'm not going to tell you again. STEP OUT OF THE CAR!" the trooper said with confidence as backup arrived.

At that very moment Derrick knew the outcome of his fate.

EIGHT

"Jordan, I need you to go to the back of your cell. Drop to your knees and face the wall," instructed the death row housing officer.

He was accompanied by three other officers, all of whom were to be the overseers of the execution.

As told, Derrick assumed the position.

"Open Cell 28, D-Block."

Stepping inside the cell, one officer immediately handcuffed Derrick and placed shackles around his ankles, while the other officers stood guard. This was one of the tensest moments in the death sentence routine, because no one knew what to expect when the time came for a convicted death row inmate to make that walk toward death's door, not even the convicted himself. The guards had seen some of the most cold-hearted killers break down at this precise moment, and eventually had to be carried kicking and screaming to meet their Maker.

The prison sent its burliest guards to deal with the condemned escort trip. Whether the inmate was 200 pounds or 90 pounds soakin' wet, a dying man could suddenly become Hercules when faced with his inevitable fate.

As twisted as it may seem, the guards often set up a gambling pool close to an inmate's execution date. Bets were made on who would get a last minute reprieve; who would beg for forgiveness; who would be exonerated; and as the date got closer and closer, who would ultimately break down.

Derrick gave the officers no problem. He had visualized this day, this routine, this moment in his mind many times, and if anybody bet that Derrick "The Dicer" Jordan was going to go out like a sucker, they made a fool's bet.

"Okay, now I'm going to help you up," the officer said after making sure Derrick was properly restrained. "Ready?" He waited for some type of response as a cue to help. Instead, Derrick lifted himself up on his own.

"Whoa! Take it easy, Jordan," said the officer, alarmed by Derrick's sudden reaction.

Instantly the other guards got on the offensive, thinking there was about to be a problem. This was the last thing they wanted.

Seeing their nervousness caused Derrick to laugh to himself while still keeping a stone face. *Fuckin' cowards,* he thought.

"C'mon," Derrick told them. "Let's get this shit over wit'."

The officers all sighed in relief.

"Everything's cool," the senior guard assured the others. "Let's move."

As they escorted him out of the cell, Derrick could see the jailhouse mirrors sticking out on both sides and all the way down the tier of inmate cells. These inmates were the same people he had been on death row with for the past six and a half years of his life. Some of them had been on the tier double, even triple, the number of years he had been there. Some of them had committed some of the world's most vicious and treacherous crimes. Society deemed that these same vile men should not continue to exist in this lifetime. It was amongst this small percentage of hard-bitten sadistic criminals that Derrick found himself. Society's worst of the worst.

It started with a single tapping sound that broke through the silence. *Tap*!

Then one tapping filled the air. *Tap! Tap! Tap! Tap!* in rapid succession.

Clink! Clink! Clink! Clink! was the sound that joined the tapping.

Ting! Ting! Ting! Ting! Ting! Ting!

All three sounds electrified the air, the tapping, the clinking, and the tinkering. *Tap! Tap! Tap! Clink! Clink! Clink! Ting! Ting! Ting!*

Those were the sounds that rang out in Derrick's ears as he slowly shuffled down the middle of the tier. The sounds were made out of respect by the other condemned inmates on the death row cell block whenever one of their own walked that last walk, down what they called The Hard-Knock Trail. The sound itself was the inmates banging objects against their cell doors, toilet bowls, windows or other places in their cell while grappling ahead as Derrick continued the lonely walk down the desolate corridor that was reserved solely for the doomed and the damned.

Solemn faces and blank eyes peered at him as he passed the cells of his death row comrades. No one spoke. That was the code of The Row. The constant *Tap! Tap! Tap! Clink! Clink! Clink! Ting! Ting! Ting!* spoke volumes.

On the walk off the death row cellblock, the guards never rushed a man to his death. That's why they always came and got the inmate well ahead of schedule, leaving enough time for any problems they might encounter.

Though Derrick walked slowly, it was only the result of his legs being shackled. He kept a steady pace, far from dragging his feet. He was going to meet death like he lived life. As a gangsta!

With an officer in front, two by Derrick's side and one in the back, they reached the door that lead off the death row cellblock. Even as the door behind them slammed shut, Derrick could still hear the respectful noises: *Tap! Tap! Tap! Tap! Clink! Clink! Clink! Clink! Ting! Ting! Ting! Ting!* Through it all, he continued to keep his composure.

That is, until he saw his only lifeline.

Althea's heart nearly stopped at the sight of her son. She had been sitting there for the past two hours, waiting to see her baby arrive. If it had been left up to her, she wouldn't have been in attendance, but Derrick's dying wish was to have her present when the Angel of Death came for him.

He had written in a letter that he wanted Althea to be the last beautiful thing he saw on earth before his soul left his flesh. And, just like his other wish, she honored and respected what Derrick asked of her.

Althea tried her best not to burst into tears about the promise she made to her only son, but seeing him now and knowing what was about to take place and why, made it extremely difficult not to. Painfully succeeding in holding back the floodgate of tears, Althea managed a smile as she and her beloved son made eye contact.

What was once an ice-cold stare melted into a warm look the moment Derrick laid eyes on the smile that was on his mother's face. She was the only one who caught the change in expression; after all, he was still her baby and she knew him all too well.

SQUE-E-E-AK! was the sound the legendary death chamber's massive metal door made when it was opened. As he scanned the audience of viewers, Derrick was not the least bit surprised to not see his sister among the crowd of spectators. He thought maybe she would have come just to spite him after she had received his invitation letter, to make sure he was finally put where she'd always thought he belonged. As the guards struggled with the door to the chambers, Derrick reflected back to the letter he had sent Tonya in attempt to make amends and clear the air between them the best he knew how. He had wondered whether his demeanor was too gangsta for his sister, even on paper.

Yo Tee,

I'm not into all the formalities that mu'fuckas may start a letter off with. You know who I am and how I am and vice versa.

The reason for this kite is to basically address some unresolved issues that the two of us have had in the past before I breathe my last breath.

Cutting straight to the chase, it's no secret that from the time you were able to determine right from wrong, good from evil, and the difference between love and hate, you never particularly cared for me, and I've never faulted you for that. Shit, if I wasn't me, I would hate my ass too 'cause I'm a fucked-up individual, but I don't have to tell you that. I know growing up you've always resented me for not being there the way you needed your big brother to be, but if you think about it, I was there for you at times when you really needed me, and even when you didn't want me to be, which were the times when I did what was best for you. Like the first time I put my hands on you when you was thirteen. When I caught that nigga fuckin' you in Mommy's house, I slapped you and fucked that nigga up. Not out of anger, but out of hurt and guilt, because I know you didn't know any better and in some way I'm to blame 'cause I should've been there to protect you from shit like that. For days I couldn't get that fuckin' picture out of my head, how this eighteen-year-old nigga got my little sister's legs up in the air with his dick up in her. Just so you know, I made sure that dickless nigga never fucked nobody else's little sister no more! No need to thank me.

I knew from that day, though, you officially started hating me, harboring hatred in your heart, and that's what drove you to start doing all the dumb shit you were doing with all those niggas, and over the years you got a lot of mu'fuckas hurt.

Even with that pig, Robert. Later on I got the real scoop on how you were the one who actually pushed up on him. Had I known that the day I choked you up, I probably would've snapped your fuckin' neck. So consider yourself lucky, as they say, and just know that that nigga ended up like he did on the strength of you. After all, ya know ya Big Bro gonna always keep it gangsta!

P.S. My expiration date is September 11th (yeah, ain't that a bitch) at 9:45 AM. It would be nice to see your face one last time before I depart. If I do, I know I don't have to tell you not to shed any tears!

Just before he stepped into the cast-iron execution chamber, Derrick took one last glance at his mother and gave her his famous wink.

Right then and there, Althea knew that her son was all right in spite of what was about to happen. Still, her heart couldn't help but skip a beat when she saw the guards strapping Derrick to the hospital-style gurney.

Derrick lay motionless as he was secured to the apparatus that would administer the lethal injection into his vein. He could hear sounds coming from out the guards' mouths but couldn't exactly make out what they were saying. Not that he really cared. He was too busy deep in thought as his mind took him back to his last taste of freedom.

"Sarge! Come take a look at this," yelled the young white officer from the back of the car.

Meanwhile, Derrick lay face flat on the hood of the Acura. His hands were cuffed behind his back and he was surrounded by four young redneck highway patrolmen. The white officer who pulled him over had already found and confiscated the chrome hammer he had tucked under his shirt. Now, as he heard the despair in the other officer's voice as he shouted from the trunk of his Derrick's whip, Derrick knew what caused the officer's tone. He lifted his head up just a little bit to see what was going on back there, and what he saw confirmed what he believed; but when he heard the yells he knew it was official.

"Holy fuck! Jesus Christ!" the sergeant exclaimed as he covered his nose when his officer popped the trunk of the Legend.

When the officer urgently called him to the rear of the car, the sergeant walked back there and didn't know what to expect. As soon as he reached the trunk, the officer directed his attention to the puddle of blood under the vehicle. He immediately ordered the officer to open the trunk. When he did, the stench coming from within it caused the sergeant to yell out the way he did. The young officer's reaction was worse as he bellied over and nearly vomited out his guts.

"Secure the detainee!" the sergeant shouted to the rest of his colleagues, who were still standing around the front of the car.

Hearing the strain in their superior's voice caused the entire team to draw their weapons.

"What's going on back there, Sarge?" one of the troopers yelled as he trained his weapon at Derrick's head.

"Ivanko, get back here," the sergeant called out.

The young rookie sprinted the few yards to the back of the car and as soon as he reached the side, the foul aroma instantly penetrated his nostrils, stopping him dead in his tracks. Like his fellow officer, he too fell to his knees and threw up all over the asphalt road.

"What the fuck?" he screamed through the coughs that rocked his body.

"Here, put some of this under your nose," instructed the sergeant as he handed the rookie a jar of Vick's VapoRub, which masked all kinds of awful smells.

The sergeant gave the officers a moment to get themselves together. He understood what they were experiencing; he had been buckled to his knees once or twice in his career, too.

"You guys all right?" the sergeant asked his men. "Pull yourselves together. Ivanko, I need you to put on some gloves and open up one of them bags," he added, making reference to the three black garage bags piled up in the trunk and the source of the gut-turning stench.

For a minute the rookie looked at the sergeant as if he had lost his mind. But realizing he was the low man on the totem pole, the one with the least amount of seniority, he understood why he was appointed the dirty work. It was either do as he was told or find another job.

With that in mind, he reluctantly pulled out his latex gloves and proceeded to follow orders.

"Motherfucker!" he yelled as he stumbled back, nearly losing his balance.

"Ivanko, what is it?" the sergeant asked.

Ivanko was shocked speechless. He couldn't talk if he wanted to. His eyes and his mouth couldn't comprehend or explain the sight before them. So the sergeant, getting no response from Ivanko, moved in closer to look for himself.

"JEEESUS!" was what came out the sergeant's mouth.

Oddly, the sergeant had been hoping the contents of the bags would be some kind of illegal game, like deer or brown bear, though he was doubtful that Derrick had been out hunting with the Desert Eagle they found tucked under his waistband. But now there was no mistaking the horrible smell, and what he saw confirmed what the sergeant had suspected all along.

In the opened bag were the remains of a human head, with the wide-open eyes full of horror. The terrified look on the severed head made the sergeant shiver. After all the years he had on the job dealing with dead and sometimes decomposing bodies, this was the first time he had come across a decapitated one. He had seen his share of brutal slayings but even for a veteran like himself, his eyes told him this had to be one of the worst ones yet.

He was positive that after tonight, he would be having nightmares about the grisly find. He was equally sure that the John Doe who had been dismembered had died a most horrible and agonizing death.

Unbeknownst to the sergeant, the face that would forever haunt his memories was one of his fellow brethren in law enforcement. A fellow officer of the law.

The only thing that Derrick had to be thankful for that night was that only he knew who the diced up body belonged to at the time. There was no doubt in his mind that had the Ku Klux Klan-like officers known the body parts were that of a murdered cop, there would have surely been a lynching party on the side of the highway, and Derrick would have been the guest of honor.

Like the rest of the world, who was captivated by this atrocious crime, the officers wouldn't learn the identity of the mutilated corpse until the forensic DNA tests were done. By which time Derrick had been transferred to a more secure facility in Essex County, out of the reach of any rogue police seeking retribution for this monstrous act.

And it was there where Derrick's fate was handed down to him...

"Derrick Jordan, I sentence you to death by lethal injection! May God have mercy on your soul!"

Derrick remembered hearing those words from the judge nearly seven years ago, and hearing them again brought him out of his trance and placed him back into the present. "... sentence you to death by lethal injection! May God have mercy on your soul!"

Only this time it was the warden reading the final order of death by the Essex County Supreme Court. Now the time had come for Derrick to die. "Mr. Derrick Jordan, is there anything you would like to say before you are put to your death?" At that question, one of the most frightening and psychotic smiles ever known to mankind spread across Derrick's face.

"Yeah, FTW," he replied coldly.

Unaware of what the initials meant, everyone looked at each other in a state of confusion, including Derrick's attorney; but when Gino Carvelli glanced over at Althea Jordan, and saw that she was fighting back tears, there was no doubt in his mind that she knew what the letters represented.

After waiting a few seconds for Derrick to elaborate, the executioner proceeded.

Derrick's eyes remained glued to the ceiling at nothing in particular, which is why he never noticed the needle that pierced his left arm. Instantly he felt the fluids enter into his veins, and he attempted to resist its effects as he wondered how long he could actually last. He had told himself that when it happened, he would boldly stare Death directly in the face. And that was exactly what he did.

The onlookers, both those who were actually inside the chamber with him and those who were seated outside of it, watched in awe or contempt at Derrick's approaching death.

At least all but one did. Althea couldn't bear the sight as her son danced with the Grim Reaper. It took all of her willpower not to jump up and try to save his life. Just before she turned her head away and buried her face into Gino's shoulder, she saw that Derrick's death had suddenly turned into a violent wrestling match.

It had been a hell of a fight, but Derrick "The Dicer" Jordan had finally lost. As the poison took effect, his body began to shake violently and just as quickly, his body went limp like a rag doll.

Throughout the entire ordeal, his eyes remained open. A prison doctor closed them after officially announcing that Derrick Jordan had expired. He then pulled a sheet over his now-lifeless body.

The audience who had been watching the execution started to rise and exit the chamber's room, one by one. They were all silent, caught up in their own thoughts about what they had just witnessed.

"Let's go Althea. It's over. He's in a better place now," Gino stated reassuringly while gently helping her up from her seat.

At his first attempt, Althea didn't budge. It seemed as if the life zapped right out of her, along with her son's.

"Althea, come on, sweetheart; it's over," Gino repeated. "There's nothing we can do for him now."

After those softly spoken words, Gino finally got Althea to stand. He wrapped his arms around her and gave her a comforting hug.

"It was his decision," he whispered to her before he escorted her out of the place of her son's recent death.

NINE

"Ms. Jordan, do you have anything you want to say to the public?" one of the reporters waiting outside was the first to ask. "Ms. Jordan, what do the letters 'FTW' mean to you?"

Althea wondered how long it would take before one of the reporters asked her that. It was the one thing her son had allowed her to answer on his behalf once he had been executed. Stepping up to the microphone she boldly stated, "Fuck the world!"

Pandemonium breaking out would be an understatement to Althea Jordan's response. Once again, she was bombarded with a million and one questions, but she turned to Gino.

"Please, Ms. Jordan has just been through a lot. Let her be," replied Gino, pushing his way through the crowd toward the waiting limousine. Althea still hadn't uttered a single word.

His law firm's chauffeur was there with the door open when Gino and Althea reached the car.

"Gino, do you mind if I ride alone? I need some time to myself," Althea said in a hoarse voice once they were inside the safety of the Benz limo.

"Not at all. Take as much time as you need. Mike?" Gino called out as he tapped on the limo's window that separated them from the driver.

"Sir?"

"Drive Ms. Jordan wherever she wants, no matter how long it takes."

"Yes, sir."

“Thanks Gino. You’re an angel.”

“I wish. You just call me when you get in. No matter the time. Okay?”

“I will.”

Althea kissed the lawyer on the cheek just before he exited the Mercedes. The limo then pulled away from the prison with no intended destination in mind.

After taking in a much needed deep breath, Althea exhaled a huge sigh. As promised, she sat through the misfortune of her son’s death and shed not one single tear drop. But now, as she was chauffeured about in the limo, an uncontrollable river of tears rolled down her eyes and stained her sad face.

How could I have let this happen? Althea thought. As she searched for answers in her mind, angrily she began to place the blame on who she felt deserved it. Althea pleaded with her daughter on numerous occasions to cut ties with Robert after she spotted him with a local girl from the neighborhood, but Tonya would not take heed or believe her mother. She was naïve like that. She was so naïve that she chose loyalty to the dead police officer over the loyalty to her family, which is why she declined Derrick’s invitation to attend his execution. Sadly, Tonya honestly believed that her brother had intentionally and deliberately murdered her boyfriend just to spite her and deprive her of happiness, the one thing she longed for.

If only she knew, thought Althea.

Regret suddenly replaced the thoughts she was having about her daughter. For the umpteenth time Althea reflected back to the past and wished she had never made that fatal phone call to her son nearly seven years ago.

Althea knew that the phone call to her son would eat at her for the rest of her life. She would always tell herself that maybe if she hadn’t made the call, her son would still be here today.

Maybe.

EPILOGUE

"Ma, what's wrong?" Derrick asked, out of breath, as he burst through the door of his mother's house.

He spotted her standing shakily at the kitchen door. So affixed on his mother's ashen face was Derrick that he hadn't noticed the obvious.

As he moved closer to his mother, his eyes left her tear-streaked face for an instant, and it was in that Derrick noticed the obvious. His eyes only told him what he was seeing; his mother would tell him what had happened.

Before he could even begin asking his mother questions, she started to babble. Although Althea was somewhat incoherent as she spoke through her sobs, Derrick was able to piece together a little about what had taken place.

More concerned for his mother than the actual situation, Derrick embraced his mother and tried to calm her sown. "Calm down, Ma," he said. "I'm here." He let her cry in his embrace.

"I . . . I called him over here," Althea sputtered with a wild look of despair on her face. "He… he hit Tonya . . . and I only wanted to talk to him," she continued as Derrick comforted her.

She coughed a few times and Derrick gently guided her to a wooden stool where Althea slumped down with her head in her hands.

It wasn't until Derrick brought her a glass of water and some tissues to wipe her eyes that she was able to continue.

"I told him, don't be puttin' his hands on my daughter, but . . . but he only laughed at me. Said Tonya was his now. Said that he was gonna put you away forever." His mother started crying again.

Derrick knelt beside his mother and took her hands gently in his. "It's okay, Ma. Ma, don't cry. It's going to be all right." Derrick tried his best to reassure her, wanting to know what happened next, but prodding slowly. "Tell me what happened next," he said softly.

"I don't quite remember. I was chopping up some vegetables for dinner when he came in. When he started talking . . . I remember thinking about my babies, and how this man was trying to destroy my family. I blacked out after that. I . . . I don't remember stabbing him, Derrick," Althea said, surprised at her own action.

Now after his mother told him the story that his eyes had already seen, Derrick stood up and walked around the kitchen table to get a full view of the corpse lying face down in a pool of blood.

Daaaamn, Derrick thought as he took in the scene. His mother had sunk the butcher knife into Detective Robert Smith's back, all the way up to the handle. Just to confirm the obvious, Derrick squatted down and placed his hands to the side of the cop's neck to feel for a pulse. No sign of life.

Looking at the dead detective, Derrick felt a little cheated. He wished he had been there to see the cause of so much of his troubles take his last breath. On that thought, he straightened up and went back to comfort his wreck of a mother.

"Ma, listen to me," he said as he lifted her chin so he could look directly into her eyes. "I'm going take care of this. I'ma make all this right. Don't worry, I got this."

"But . . . but he's dead," Althea told him, pointing in the direction of the detective's still body on her kitchen floor for emphasis.

"Don't worry about that. I'll take care of everything. You just go in your bedroom and get yourself together while I clean this mess up. But before you do that, you have to listen to me, okay? Ma, look, you have to promise me one thing. I mean, *really* promise me," Derrick said in a voice that only a son trying to protect his mother could muster. "You have to promise me this, that's all I ask."

"What, Derrick?"

"That you won't ever talk about what happened here tonight. To no one. I mean, not even Tonya. That bastard Robert was never here," he coached his mother while trying to stoke a little of the anger that drove her to stab him in the first place and ease her conscience. "You don't know nothin' about nothin' if anybody was to ever ask you. All right, Ma?"

His mother shook her head forcefully from side to side. "I can't do that, Derrick. We should call the police . . . because I killed him."

"Nah, Ma, that's the last thing we gonna do. That's not gonna work," he said almost pleadingly. Searching his brain for something to tell her that would make her understand, suddenly it hit him. He decided to appeal to the strong maternal instincts he knew existed inside of her.

"If you go to jail, who's gonna look out for Tonya? You know it can't be me, 'cause I'll be dead or locked up sooner or later behind runnin' them streets. Plus, you know she doesn't even talk to me. So, it has to be you!"

Althea was about to protest, but Derrick cut her off.

"There's no time for this, Ma. You just have to promise me so I can hurry up and fix this before someone comes."

His mother closed her eyes, as if wishing this whole scene would disappear. When she opened them, she looked her son in the eyes and nodded. "I promise," she said in a voice that was weak and drained.

"Good. Now go in your bedroom and get yourself together," Derrick instructed again. "I'll be finished up in here in a minute."

As if she were the child and he was the parent, his mother obediently rose from the stool to do what her son said.

When she left, Derrick started doing what he did best. This sort of work was nothing to him; only thing he felt strange about was doing it in his mother's house. First things first: he found some old plastic shower curtains and an old blanket. He laid the shower curtains down first, next to the body, and placed the blanket on top of the curtains. Then he rolled the body of the dead cop onto the makeshift body bag and wrapped it up nice and neat. Peering out of the window cautiously to make sure the coast was clear, he carried the body out of the house and placed it in the trunk of his car. He then hurriedly went back inside the house to clean the blood off the kitchen floor, erasing any evidence of foul play ever taking place in that house.

Derrick had just placed the rags and mop head he'd used to wipe up the blood in a garbage bag, when his mother walked back into the kitchen. He took her by the arm and walked he though the living room toward the front door. Neither of them spoke as they made it to the front door, a mother and son arm in arm, their secret locked away forever.

"Remember," Derrick said, trying to lighten his mother's load. "You promised." He smiled warmly, as if she promised to take him to a ball game or something. "Don't worry, everything is going to be all right," he assured her with his signature wink just before kissing her on the forehead.

Derrick hugged his mother one last time, darted down the porch steps, jumped in his car, and pulled off.

The moonlit streets were abandoned in the wee hours of the night as Derrick pulled the car around back of the butcher shop that he inherited when Vito, old Spanish man, passed away. Just hours ago he had left the establishment after putting in work on some fool who chose Derrick's spot to rob. He was in the process of washing the dead kid's blood off of his own body when he received the phone call from his mother. Now he was back in his workshop again, only this time it was for a different cause.

Over the years, much flesh and bones had graced the presence of Derrick's machinery, and in his own psychotic mind he believed that they all deserved it. This time was different; this would be the first time that Derrick would dice up and dispose of a body that he didn't kill himself. This milestone didn't really bother him as much as the fact that it was his mother who took out his archenemy. *Smith deserved what he got,* Derrick thought, *and deserves what he's 'bout to get.*

Everybody in the streets knew that fuckin' with a man's mother was the ultimate violation, punishable by death. So, whichever way to look at things, Detective Robert Smith would have been a dead man walking anyway, Derrick's mind told him.

For as long as Derrick could remember, his mother had tried her best to protect and convert him, but his own rebellious ways caused Derrick to take the route he chose for himself. No matter how he turned out, Derrick knew that his mother always loved him and was there for him unconditionally. And with all the heartache that he caused her over the years, she never once turned her back on him. Now it was his turn to be there for her. No price was too high to pay to protect his mother.

Regardless of the circumstances that put Derrick in possession of the dead cop's corpse, he wasn't about to let his mother go down for murder if he could help it, no matter who she killed. One thing Derrick was grateful for was having the necessary skills and experience to handle the task at hand for his mother. There was no way he would allow this little misfortune—Derrick erased the thought of it being a crime 'cause he would never accept the notion of his mother being a criminal—to be traced back to his mother in any kind of way. The thought of her spending one single day in a jail cell, let alone a lifetime, left a bitter taste in Derrick's mouth. That's why he placed the burden of making sure she would never see the inside of a prison, on his shoulders.

After dragging Detective Smith's body across the sawdust-covered floor, he picked it up and dropped it on a cutting table like one would do a large slab of meat. Derrick went to work. He meticulously went about cutting up the body, sawing the head off last. He found a little humor in the expression on the face of the dead detective; the sheer shock and horror that was frozen on it made Derrick chuckle.

"Ma Dukes punished your bitch ass," Derrick laughed aloud to himself.

The detective must have been shocked when he realized that Althea had pushed that butcher knife in his back, and the horror must have came when he realized the knife was buried deep inside him and he was on his way to the crossroads.

After Derrick finished dismembering the body, his rubber gloves and smock were splattered with blood. Satisfied with his work, Derrick took a few minutes to stretch before continuing with the ritual of bagging the body parts. He retrieved three separate trash bags and began to fill them in a way that they would almost weigh the same, again saving the head for the last.

Loading the bags into the trunk of his whip, Derrick decided to come back later and clean up the mess he made. His sole intent now was to get the chopped-up pieces of the cop to his regular burial spot before the sun rose. He knew that it was just a matter of time before someone realized that Smith was missing. And when that happened, Derrick wanted to be clean because there was no doubt that the finger would be pointed at him. For the first time since that day, this was the only time Derrick ever regretted threatening Robert in the precinct full of witnesses. The news about Robert messing with his sister made Derrick react on impulse, and he figured that now, that act would make him the most likely candidate for causing Smith's disappearance.

Derrick never noticed the patrol car in his rearview mirror until it was too late, because his mind was elsewhere. Contemplating on whether to stop and pull over or run and gun it out, Derrick knew the final outcome wouldn't be good. So, rather than having his life end on the highway and risk something about Robert's death being traced back to his mother, he opted to pull over.

He had some hope that in choosing to pull over, and the fact that all his credentials were in order, he'd be allowed to go on his way with a minor traffic citation at the least.

In the event that the mangled body was found in the trunk, Derrick knew what the consequences would be and he accepted that fate to protect and secure the safety of his mother, the woman who brought him into this world. He would sacrifice everything he had, everything he was, to shield his mother from harm. She killed to protect her family and he would go head to head with the devil himself to protect her.

When the events unfolded during what turned out to be a not-so-routine traffic stop, Derrick never once gave his decision to be apprehended a second thought. Not during the stop, not after the discovery of the body, and not during the trial. Not after being sentenced to death, not even when he was being strapped to the prison's death bed. Walking into that cold dreary execution chamber and spotting the one person in attendance that made his decision worth it, made Derrick feel that his short and treacherous life had some kind of meaning; and if giving his life to protect his mother was part of that meaning, then he would bum rush Hell's door for all the devious things he did do, yelling, "Fuck the world, this one is for my moms . . . I'M KEEPIN' IT GANGSTA!"

Tonya Jordan switched off her television as she dried her eyes. She did not expect to react the way she had, but when she heard the announcement of her brother's demise and saw her mother looking emotionally drained up on the podium she began to weep uncontrollably. When she first received the invitation letter from her older brother she cursed him for the mockery. All her life she had blamed Derrick and built up hatred toward him for not being there for her as a child, when she felt she needed him the most. Never having a father figure to love, Tonya ultimately turned to Derrick seeking fatherly love, but just as their own father had done, Derrick had abandoned her. When she grew older and discovered her sexuality, Tonya did all she could spite her brother, leading to her searching for love in all the wrong places, which is why when she'd read Derrick's letter it cut her deeply. It was the same letter that she'd read over and over until she'd finally figured out her brother's mindset. She now knew that it was never Derrick's intentions to hurt her, but in his own irrational way, protect her. Tears began to spill out of her eyes again. She wanted so badly to tell her brother that she know understood that he was just "keepin' it gangsta," but knew it was too late.

Melodrama Publishing Order Form

WWW.MELODRAMAPUBLISHING.COM

Title	ISBN	QTY	PRICE	TOTAL
Myra	1-934157-20-1		$15.00	$
Menace	1-934157-16-3		$15.00	$
Cartier Cartel	1-934157-18-X		$15.00	$
10 Crack Commandments	1-934157-21-X		$15.00	$
Jealousy: The Complete Saga	1-934157-13-9		$15.00	$
Wifey	0-971702-18-7		$15.00	$
I'm Still Wifey	0-971702-15-2		$15.00	$
Life After Wifey	1-934157-04-X		$15.00	$
Still Wifey Material	1-934157-10-4		$15.00	$
Eva: First Lady of Sin	1-934157-01-5		$15.00	$
Eva 2: First Lady of Sin	1-934157-11-2		$15.00	$
Den of Sin	1-934157-08-2		$15.00	$
Shot Glass Diva	1-934157-14-7		$15.00	$
Dirty Little Angel	1-934157-19-8		$15.00	$
Histress	1-934157-03-1		$15.00	$
In My Hood	0-971702-19-5		$15.00	$
In My Hood 2	1-934157-06-6		$15.00	$
A Deal With Death	1-934157-12-0		$15.00	$
Tale of a Train Wreck Lifestyle	1-934157-15-5		$15.00	$
A Sticky Situation	1-934157-09-0		$15.00	$
Jealousy	1-934157-07-4		$15.00	$
Life, Love & Loneliness	0-971702-10-1		$15.00	$
The Criss Cross	0-971702-12-8		$15.00	$

(GO TO THE NEXT PAGE)

MELODRAMA PUBLISHING ORDER FORM
(CONTINUED)

Title/Author	ISBN	QTY	PRICE	TOTAL
Stripped	1-934157-00-7		$15.00	$
The Candy Shop	1-934157-02-3		$15.00	$
Sex, Sin & Brooklyn	0-971702-16-0		$15.00	$
Up, Close & Personal	0-971702-11-X		$9.95	$
				$
			Subtotal	
			Shipping**	
			Tax*	
	Total			

Instructions:

*NY residents please add $1.79 Tax per book.

**Shipping costs: $3.00 first book, any additional books please add $1.00 per book.

Incarcerated readers receive a 25% discount. Please pay $11.25 per book and apply the same shipping terms as stated above.

Mail to:

MELODRAMA PUBLISHING

P.O. BOX 522

BELLPORT, NY 11713

Cartier Timmons and Monya White were born to teenage mothers who were also best friends. At 15, Cartier formed her own crew aptly named the Cartier Cartel. The main and only vision of the crew; Cartier, Monya, Bam, Lil Mama, and Shanine was to do petty crimes in order to wear the flyest gear. While Monya loves boys, clothes, and money (in that order), Cartier is tired of the petty boosting to keep a few dollars in her pockets. Always wise beyond her years, Cartier observes how the corner boys hustle drugs and figures her crew could do the same. Cartier realizes too late that her and her crew are in more trouble than they can handle. Once a rival drug-hustler gets murdered, Cartier's Cartel will need to make a life-altering decision.

Release Date: April 2009